THE ADVENTURES OF

MAQROLL

ALSO BY ALVARO MUTIS

MAQROLL

Alvaro Mutis

THE ADVENTURES OF
MAQROLL
FOUR NOVELLAS

Amirbar

＊

The Tramp Steamer's Last Port of Call

＊

Abdul Bashur, Dreamer of Ships

＊

Triptych on Sea and Land

TRANSLATED FROM THE SPANISH BY
Edith Grossman

HarperCollins*Publishers*

FIRST EDITION

Designed by Alma Hochhauser Orenstein

Library of Congress Cataloging-in-Publication Data

Mutis, Alvaro.
    [Novellas. English. Selections]
    The Adventures of Maqroll : four novellas / Alvaro Mutis ; translated from the Spanish by Edith Grossman. — 1st ed.
      p. cm.
    Contents: Amirbar — The tramp steamer's last port of call — Abdul Bashur, dreamer of ships — Triptych on sea and land.
    ISBN 0-06-017004-2
    I. Grossman, Edith, 1936– . II. Title.
PQ8180.23.U8A24   1995
863—dc20   94-42341

95 96 97 98 99 ❖/HC 10 9 8 7 6 5 4 3 2 1

Contents

Amirbar   1

The Tramp Steamer's Last Port of Call   93

Abdul Bashur, Dreamer of Ships   153

Triptych on Sea and Land   257

Amirbar

To the memory of my grandfather
Jerónimo Jaramillo Uribe,
who once prospected for gold along the Coello River
in El Tolima

La vie n'est qu'une succession de défaites. Il y a de belles façades—il en a de pires. Mais derrière les belles, presque autant que derrière les pires, la défaite, toujours la défaite et encore la défaite—ce qui n'empêche pas de chanter victoire, car au fond l'homme n'est réellement vaincu que par la mort—mais encore, uniquement parce qu'elle lui ôte tout moyen de proclamer contre l'évidence qu'il ne l'est pas. Alors, il s'est fait même un allié de la mort et il compte beaucoup sur elle pour lui donner toute la gloire que lui a refusé la vie.

Pierre Reverdy, Le livre de mon bord

. . . because women in the mines seem to be the work of the devil and because it has been proven that there is no profit in having them work there. On the contrary, the jealousy and violence which occur on their account are a great danger to everyone.

Shamuel de Córcega, A True History of
the Mines Where the Jews Toiled to
No Avail in the Mountains of Axartel

*(Sóller, Mallorca: Imprenta Capmany,
1776)*

I spent the strangest days of my life in Amirbar. In Amirbar
I left shreds of my soul and most of the energy that fired
my youth. Perhaps I came down from there more serene, I don't
know, but I was everlastingly weary too. What happened to me
since then has been a matter of simply surviving each day's difficulties. Trivialities. Not even the ocean could give back to me
my vocation for dreaming with my eyes open; I used that up in
Amirbar and received nothing in return."

I was bemused by Maqroll the Gaviero's words. He had never
been a man given to confidences of this kind. On the contrary,
he always had favored the direct narration of his wanderings,
drawing no conclusions and deriving no moral, and this evocation of his days in Amirbar awakened unusual curiosity in me.
Debilitated and exhausted by the long treatment he had been
obliged to undergo in order to control the malaria that was
killing him, the Gaviero had allowed these words to escape, creating an opening that revealed a hidden world of defeats over
which he normally exercised inflexible vigilance. We were sitting
in the sun on the patio of my brother Leopoldo's house in
Northridge, in the San Fernando Valley, at the height of the
transparent, interminable California summer. His words obviously signaled a desire to open the floodgates of memories that
for some reason he had jealously guarded until now. In the
course of our friendship, he had often enjoyed narrating episodes
of his life, but he had never mentioned Amirbar, and at the time
I did not know what the name referred to.

In the weeks that followed, as he regained enough strength to
travel to the Peruvian coast, he told us about his experiences as
a gold prospector in the cordillera, and the wreckage of his glori-
ous plans in the intricate galleries of Amirbar. But before transcribing his story for my readers, I should describe the circum-

stances of our meeting on this occasion. They are so characteristic of Maqroll's nature and destiny that I could not possibly omit them. The detour is not very long, and as I said, I believe it is well worth taking for a greater appreciation of what follows.

* * *

The first thing I asked myself on my way to him was how the Gaviero had ended up in a ruinous motel along the gloomiest, most impersonal stretch of La Brea Boulevard. I was in Los Angeles on business and spent most of each day at the Burbank studios. One night, when I went to pick up my mail at the reception desk of the Château Marmont Hotel, where I always stayed when I was in the city to work, I was handed a brief message written on grease-stained paper with no letterhead: "I'm at 1644 La Brea. Come as soon as you can. I need you. Maqroll." At first I did not even recognize the rather shaky signature. I went up to my room to drop off some papers, and left immediately to see my friend. He was not in the habit of sending urgent messages, and the trembling letters of his name indicated a state of health worse than precarious. The address he had given me was a sordid motel with a narrow driveway that extended past a row of rooms with numbers painted on the doors in a violent lemon yellow. Three or four cars were parked in front of units that had lights at the windows. The Gaviero had forgotten to tell me his room number, or perhaps he wanted me to speak first to the porter who sat inside a narrow cubicle at the beginning of the driveway. I knocked at the glass, and a large man with uncombed hair came out, wearing a dark-brown polo shirt and Bermuda shorts that cut into his middle below a prominent, beer drinker's belly. He spoke rudimentary English with a heavy Arabic accent. A deep scar on his face started in the center of his forehead, crossed his nose, and ended in the middle of his chin. I mentioned my friend's name, and instead of telling me his room number he asked me into the cramped, evil-smelling place that he called his office. He came directly to the point without even introducing himself. "I been waiting for you. He said you knew each other many years. I know him a long time too, and I owe him favors. But the owner here's a Jew he don't forgive nothing and don't want to hear excuses. Our friend owes for three weeks and Michaelis comes tonight to collect. It's good if you give me the money he owes. In his condition I don't want to throw him out on the street. Ninety-five

*dollars altogether." His words were not so much brusque as con-
cerned. Clearly he had his back to the wall. I gave him the
money, and as he was handing me the receipt, his wife came in,
a tall woman who must have been very beautiful at one time
but whose extreme thinness and gaunt face gave her a spectral
appearance. She too spoke with a heavy Middle Eastern accent.
She greeted me with an awkward smile and then, in a French
somewhat more fluent and comprehensible than the porter's
English, said she was very glad I had come. My friend urgently
needed help and someone to stay with him. I left them and
went to the Gaviero's room. It was next to the porter's office but
for some odd reason had the number 9.*

*The door was not locked. I walked in after I had knocked
and a faint voice answered, "Come in, come in, it's open."
Maqroll the Gaviero lay in a bed with faded pink sheets on
which perspiration had left wide, dark stains. He was trembling
violently. The expression in his wild-looking, brilliant eyes was
agonized and desperate. Several weeks' growth of heavy graying
beard added to the impression of fatal abandonment. The
decor—faded reproductions of female nudes and, facing the bed,
the inevitable mirror over a bureau adorned with dusty pink
ruffles—made the Gaviero's presence in the room seem both
pathetic and grotesque. He indicated with his hand that I
should sit in the only armchair, covered in a greasy, flowered cre-
tonne of indeterminate color. I moved it to the head of the bed,
sat down, and waited for the attack of fever, which prevented his
speaking clearly, to abate somewhat. He took a bottle of pills
from the night table and tossed two of them in his mouth, swallowing them with a little water, which he poured with great difficulty from a pitcher that stood on the same table. His hands
were shaking so much that half the water spilled on the sheets. I
tried to help him but he refused, the shadow of a smile on his
lips. His teeth chattered when he attempted to speak. We waited
in silence for the medicine to take effect. At least a quarter of an
hour went by, and then the trembling gradually lessened. When
he could talk, his voice sounded firmer than it had at first.*

*"It's very powerful medicine, and it leaves me almost more
stupefied than the fever," he explained. "That's why I don't
take it as often as I should. I was on my way from Vancouver
and decided to spend a couple of days here before continuing
south. I wanted to see Yosip and persuade him to come in with
me on a business deal I'm going to try in Peru." Before I could*

ask who Yosip was, the Gaviero continued, "Yosip is the manager of the motel. We were together on a few Mediterranean
ventures I've already told you about. He was born in Iraq, but
his parents were Georgian. He's been everything from a mercenary in Indochina to a pimp in Marseilles. A rough character,
but he's an honorable man and a good friend. I guess he hit you
for the money I owe. He had no choice. But you can trust him,
and have good times with him. One drink loosens his tongue,
and then there's no end to the stories he tells. Anyway, I had an
attack of malaria, and it's kept me in bed for a month and a
half. I always carry medicine with me to control the symptoms,
but this time I was careless, so here I am. I caught the fever in
Rangoon, so long ago now that sometimes I think it happened
to somebody else. In Rangoon, in the teak trade with some
English partners who were crookeder than a phony dervish. All
that hard work, and I didn't make a cent. What I did get was
this fever and some memorable erotic theories from a widow who
owned a run-down factory that made incense for religious ceremonies in Kuala Lumpur. I'll tell you about it one day. It's
worth hearing. A doctor in Belfast prescribed these quinine pills.
They're effective, but they give me a splitting headache and constant nausea. I've outmaneuvered the fever with the pills, but
this time the fever won."

I suggested that before anything else we ought to call a doctor. The fever had so weakened him that organs like his heart
and liver might be affected too. He did not receive the idea
with much enthusiasm, saying he had no trust in doctors
because they complicated everything. I insisted, and we decided
I would bring one with me the next day, an idea he agreed to
very reluctantly. We talked awhile longer about old memories
and mutual friends. When I wanted to give him some money
for his immediate expenses, he said, "No, don't leave anything
with me. Give it to Jalina, Yosip's wife. She brings me food
and anything else I need. If you leave it here, somebody will
steal it. Night and day there's an unending parade of whores
and faggots, and since I have to leave the door open—when
the attacks come I can't bear to be closed in—they just come
and walk away with everything they can carry. I've lost my
clothes, my shoes, my papers, but Yosip and Jalina have my
passport and the money for my passage to Matarani. It's safe
with them. Some women who've stayed with me have taken
things as payment for their services; the rest is carried away by

the shadows I see whirling around me when the fever comes."

I tried to reassure him, saying that from now on I'd make certain no one else would rob him. But the most important thing was to have a doctor's diagnosis that would let us know how he was and what had to be done to get him out of this situation. He thanked me with a smile that tried for warmth although his lips had begun to tremble again. It was after midnight when I left him, half asleep and drenched in sweat that was soaking the sheets. Yosip and his wife were eating supper in the office, and I told them I would be back the next day with a doctor. I gave them the telephone number of the hotel in case they needed me, and a few dollars to cover any expenses. They said the Gaviero was eating very little and refused to even taste many of the dishes Jalina prepared for him. There was a tone of affection and loyalty when they mentioned Maqroll, especially on the part of the woman, who called him by an indecipherable diminutive. It sounded like "ruminchi," but I did not want to ask her about it. I thought that would be like intruding on an intimate landscape where I did not belong.

At the studios the next day they gave me the number of a physician on call during filming. I telephoned him, and he turned out to be Uruguayan. His voice had a serene authority, which made me feel very confident. We agreed that he would come to my hotel that evening and we would go to see the Gaviero together. We met in the lobby at six sharp, when he was about to call my room and I had come down to wait for him. He was a man of average height, with a smiling face and expressive eyes almost hidden by heavy deep-black eyebrows and an equally black thick mustache that made him look like the bandit in an operetta. We left for La Brea, and on the way I gave him some background on the Gaviero. I spoke of our long friendship, his nomadic life, and some of his most eccentric character traits. The doctor remarked that for some years now tropical fevers had been fairly simple to cure, but when patients are careless and stop treatment on the assumption that they are free of the disease, it becomes chronic and can damage the spleen and liver and even cause serious cardiac lesions. We drove into the motel, and he could not hide a look of surprise although I had warned him about how my friend was living. Yosip and Jalina came out to meet us, and the couple's appearance surprised the doctor even more. He made no comment, and we walked to the room where Maqroll lay sleeping, convulsing lightly and gasping *for breath. He opened his eyes and greeted us with an absent air.*

He submitted to the examination with a resigned patience that was not typical of him. He listened to the recommendations regarding his treatment, and his smile was courteous yet skeptical. According to the doctor, the new drugs would help him in short order. He would, however, have to be in a hospital to guarantee regular, controlled medication, which would be impossible in the motel. The bouts of fever left him unconscious or drowsy for long periods, and he would not take the medicines at the prescribed times. The Gaviero agreed to everything, offering no objections except an economic one: he had no money and did not see how he could go into a hospital under those circumstances. I said I would take care of it and we could settle accounts later. He shrugged and thanked me, staring into a distance that was no less intense and painful for being hypothetical. I drove the doctor back to the hotel, where he had left his car. As we rode along the interminable dullness of Santa Monica Boulevard, the Uruguayan maintained a silence that attempted to be discreet but revealed his difficulty in reconciling my position, with its managerial responsibilities in South America, and my friendship with someone so alien to the world of large Hollywood movie studios. Finally, and with some help from me, he steeled himself and asked where I had met so curious a character, with a name whose nationality was impossible to identify. I replied that we had met during one of my routine trips through the Antilles on an Esso tanker, in the days when I worked for that company. Maqroll was chief stoker, and our friendship was born during one of his breaks, when I saw him engrossed in an erudite volume on the Wars of the Spanish Succession. We began talking, since that subject interests me as well, and we agreed on the indisputable right of Louis XIV to claim for his grandson the throne left empty by the House of Austria. We saw each other again on subsequent voyages, and then, as often as our successive changes of occupation would allow, it became our habit to meet in the most out-of-the-way places in the world. "I never would have thought him a man concerned with intellectual matters," observed the doctor with a certain professional caution. "I wouldn't describe him that way," I answered. "The mere word intellectual would be a major trauma for the Gaviero. He's a man with deep and very sincere interests and a very personal fondness for the past, and these are paired with a good knowledge of literature that he acquired at the periphery of

the world where so-called intellectuals tend to live." The doctor
did not seem very convinced; he had not yet recovered from
meeting someone like Maqroll. I regaled him with condensed,
superficial versions of certain episodes in the life of my friend,
which did nothing to restore his peace of mind. When we
reached the hotel, he gave me the address of the hospital where
the Gaviero was to be admitted, and said goodbye with some
reserve.

The following day I rode in the ambulance to pick up
Maqroll. He could barely stand. Yosip and his wife asked me
anguished questions about what would happen to their friend.
They displayed an affectionate concern for him that was revealed
in their awkward queries and uneasy, hesitant objections.
Maqroll reassured them, saying it was not their fault he had to
leave, but since he was obliged to follow a very strict regimen, it
was absolutely necessary for him to be hospitalized. I gave them
the address of the hospital, so they could visit him. When the
stretcher was lifted into the ambulance, Jalina clutched at my
arm in sudden distress and repeated several times, "S'il s'agit
de le soigner, ça va. Mais vous êtes responsable si ça ne
marche pas. C'est un ami comme il n'y en a pas
d'autres." I did what I could to reassure her and reaffirmed that
I was as old and good a friend as they, that there was nothing to
be afraid of, that everything would be fine and we would see
each other in the hospital. Two large tears ran down her face,
which still preserved the dimensions and presence of a Mediterranean haughtiness. Yosip observed the scene with the feline
serenity that mercenaries acquire through long companionship
with pain and death. As we drove up La Brea in the direction
of the freeway to the San Fernando Valley, where the hospital
was located, the ambulance siren cut a path through traffic.
Maqroll looked at me with a mixture of amusement and surprise. He remarked that his friends from the motel had seen him
survive so many extraordinary transformations that the idea
they had formed of him did not exclude a certain suspicion of
immortality. Seeing him leave in an ambulance for the hospital
was an exceedingly harsh blow to that image of him, which
must have been necessary to their survival. "We often serve as a
guarantee against death, and what we really do is take her with
us, always one step behind, though we pretend to ignore her," he
said, returning to one of his most deep-rooted obsessions.

The treatment Maqroll received in the hospital, which had a

*biblical name and strict Quaker rules and regulations, quickly
began to produce results. The attacks of fever became less frequent, and the Gaviero soon left the wheelchair to walk slowly
along the paths of an aseptic garden where the flowers and the
orange trees, with their fruit of an improbable yellow color,
seemed to be made of plastic. I usually visited him at the end of
the day, when my work at the studios was finished, and on Saturday and Sunday afternoons. Occasionally I saw the porter
and his wife. Their suspicions of me had given way to a rather
brusque cordiality, which I found moving. The Gaviero's recovery
had reassured them, as had certain information he must have
given them about our relationship.*

*One Saturday I visited him in the morning and discovered
that he had put his few belongings into the kind of small bag
given away by airlines, which looked as if it had been subjected
to journeys much more arduous than those normally made in
planes. Maqroll was waiting for me in a chair, and everything
about him revealed an impatience and uneasiness that were out
of character. Before I could ask what was going on, the Gaviero
gave a hurried explanation. "Very early this morning the doctor
called and authorized my discharge. Yesterday we had a long
talk, and he agreed that the dismal, impersonal hospital atmosphere was doing me more harm than the fever. You know these
institutions have never been my favorite places. Not even when I
worked in them as a caretaker, at the Hospital de la Bahía or
the Hospital de los Soberbios.* I could never shake the feeling
that they're the antechambers of death, even when they're as
lavish as a luxury hotel, like this one. So I'm leaving. You said
you'd come today, and here I am, ready to go back to the motel
or anyplace else where there are no doctors or nurses." Maqroll's
decision to leave the hospital did not surprise me. I had noticed
his rejection of the ambience, his desire to get away from it as
soon as he was partially recovered. Still, just to be sure, I
decided to speak to the doctor and learn what he thought in
more detail. I telephoned him from the room, and in fact he said
that he believed my friend could leave but it was advisable for
him to rest somewhere homelike and quiet, someplace very different from the motel, where we had rescued him just in time. I
told this to the Gaviero and suggested he spend a few days at
my brother's house, in the privileged climate of the San Fer-*

Reseña de los hospitales de ultramar (Poems) (Bogotá: Procultura, 1986), pp. 79, 88.

nando Valley, *not far from Northridge University and its exten-*
sive orange groves and white, silent buildings. He agreed, some-
what reluctantly. He did not want to be a bother in someone
else's house, his presence would disturb their routine, and further-
more he did not even know them. I reassured him, explaining
that they would be delighted to welcome him into their home,
that they had no children and were accustomed to being with
friends whose lives were as unusual and eventful as his own.

Life in the house in Northridge soon followed a pattern of
open informality. The Gaviero was charmed by my brother,
with whom he had long discussions regarding different kinds
of whiskey and the advantages of the dark ones over the light,
which they considered fit only for hypocrites who don't know
how to enjoy a good Scotch and want people to think they dilute
their whiskey with water. My brother's wife, Fanny, attempted to
balance these deliberations with wonderful dishes from her reper-
toire, including an outstanding chicken in mushroom sauce and a
tongue with capers that Maqroll praised with sincere enthusiasm.
I visited them on the days I had free, after I had finished at the
studios, and of course on weekends, which I spent in their com-
pany. Maqroll was recovering before our very eyes, and he began
to speak more frequently of his plans to work a quarry on the
Peruvian coast. The nomadic fever was burning in him again.

One day, as we were enjoying chicken prepared over the grill
on the patio at the foot of the pool, along with a young Beaujolais
I happened to have found at a liquor store in Burbank, my sister-
in-law asked Maqroll how a seaman like him could possibly be
interested in something as landbound as a quarry. Who had
pointed him toward an undertaking that could in no way be rec-
onciled with his former life and adventures? Some very difficult
days might be waiting for him there, she added. The Gaviero was
silent for a long time. I was accustomed to these absences of his,
but my brother and his wife were still amazed at how my friend
could lose himself in the intricate web of his past, his dark famil-
iarity with the demons locked away in the most secret corners of
his being. At last Maqroll looked at us as if he were returning
from an inconceivable journey, and made the remark about the
strange days he had spent in Amirbar. As I said before, I had
never heard him mention that name. I did not know what it
meant and did not think it was related to any of the stories he
had told me in the course of our long friendship. "What is Amir-
bar? What does the word mean?" my brother Leopoldo asked, not

*knowing that when Maqroll replied he would disclose a tor-
mented portion of his memories that had been hidden until then.
The Gaviero was in no mood to expound on the subject that day.
He would only say, his gaze still clouded with longing and
despair, "Amirbar was the name of the Minister of the Fleet in
the kingdom of Georgia. I suppose it comes from the Arabic Al
Emir Bahr. Another day I'll tell you what happened to me there,
and in other places like it, when I was trapped in the devastating
madness that people so casually call gold fever."*

*Like everything that had to do with him, the narration of his
past depended on a complex alchemy of humors, climates, and
correspondences, and only when it had been fully achieved
would the floodgates of his memory open, launching him into
long recollections that did not take into account either time or
the disposition of his listeners. But it is also true that the experience brought to his listeners a kind of enchantment that dissolved the daily routine of their lives.*

*On a Sunday afternoon, one of those days when the Califor-
nia summer seems eternal, as if it had settled forever into a
burning serenity that makes us suspect we are witnessing a
supernatural phenomenon, I proposed that we try an old-fashioned: I had been experimenting with the recipe and had almost
absolute confidence in the results. It was a question of substitut-
ing authentic island rum for bourbon and adding a little port to
the mixture. Everyone agreed, although I did notice a fleeting
expression of uncertainty on the Gaviero's face. This was nothing new, for in many of our encounters Maqroll, who was
always orthodox with regard to alcohol, never quite approved of
my heretical mania for modifying consecrated recipes. The drink
was a success. The light was turning soft and velvety, and a
timid breeze began to dislodge the Libyan desert heat that had
prevailed all day. It was almost eight o'clock, but there was still
plenty of light. We were talking about port cities, and Maqroll
had just told us of his encounter with a Portuguese coast guard
cutter that tried to stop him outside Oporto. He was carrying
contraband, of course, and his associate Abdul Bashur waited for
him in port with all the uneasiness that one would expect. He
had gotten away at the last minute by faking a crucial mechanical failure. When he finished his story, my friend fell into one of
his wells of silence as he tasted my recipe with a vague, approving smile. Suddenly he looked at us as if seeing us for the first
time, and began:*

Well, about the gold mines. It isn't something that can be told quickly. It's like a slow poison engulfing us—we don't realize it's there until it's too late. Like a secretive drug, or those women we don't even notice initially, and then they turn our lives into an inescapable hell. I first heard about gold mines from my dear friend Abdul Bashur, may the gods keep him. He proposed going to a piece of land his family owned in the mountains of Lebanon, where they apparently had found traces of gold. At that time we were involved in a rug-smuggling business. We sold them in Switzerland to a group of interior decorators and made a very good profit. Our friend Ilona acted as our intermediary with the Swiss, and we took care of transporting and buying the merchandise. Not easy work. Bashur's proposal regarding mines was tabled, and I didn't think about it again. Years later I was in Vancouver, trying desperately to get out and waiting for my friend the painter Obregón, who had promised to help me. I spent my time in taverns and bars along the waterfront, looking for someone with whom I could talk a little about the sea and share the most tolerable of the Canadian whiskeys. I met an old prospector who had traveled every corner of the globe searching for the lode that would make his fortune. As a way to continue the conversation, I mentioned what Bashur had said years earlier. "No," he replied, "there's nothing in Lebanon and never has been. They circulate those legends to intimidate the Druze, who are the lords and masters of the mountains; the stories are an excuse for getting them out of the places where they graze their flocks. It's very complicated. But no, there's nothing. The place where it's still fairly easy to find gold is along the spurs of the Andes. You look for abandoned mines and try to get them to produce again." Then he launched into a lengthy discourse about government permits, rights to mineral exploitation, and, finally, the almost palpable current possibilities for finding gold there. I wasn't aware yet of the almost bottomless capacity for dreaming of these men, hopeless victims of a consuming desire that corrodes them and makes them see illusions as concrete realities. I left Vancouver for Baja California, where I carried cargo along the coast of the Gulf of Cortés in a freighter that I came to own in partnership with two obscure Croatian characters who left me practically destitute. Then I recalled what the Canadian prospector had said, and I decided to use the little money I still had to search for abandoned mines along the central spur of the three mountain chains where the Andes die on the shores of the Caribbean.

I traveled downriver to the center of the country and began visiting the villages along the spurs of the cordillera where the mining tradition was still alive. To become familiar with the atmosphere of the mines, I took a job as watchman at one of the abandoned shafts on the banks of the Cocora River.* I've already told about the visions, terrors, and disillusionments I experienced there. Perhaps fantasy predominates in that story, probably because it was my first contact with an alien world so different from the sea, the ships, the ports I had known all my life. When I left Cocora I was ready to undertake the thorough exploration of a gold mine on my own and register it in my name. I searched for a few months and finally came to a small settlement called San Miguel, where there was still talk of a gold mine whose first galleries had been excavated by a group of Germans. The name attracted my attention: it was called The Hummer. Apparently the men from Hamburg discovered several outcroppings of a lode that initially seemed very promising. Then they lost hope of locating it again and abandoned the site, leaving behind useless tools and machinery. Years later some Englishmen, who were associated with local ranchers, made another attempt to work the mine. They had more luck than the Germans, and it seems they found significant quantities of gold. Then one of the many civil wars endemic to the region broke out, and the owners, engineers, and laborers were all shot in one of the shafts, on the pretext that they were hiding weapons in the mine for the insurgency. One gallery was dynamited to get rid of the bodies, and The Hummer became a place that spawned ghost stories. Occasionally someone would climb up there with plans to dig deep in the mine, but he'd soon

* "The Snow of the Admiral," *Maqroll* (New York: HarperCollins, 1992).

be back in town, telling horrifying tales that were surely the product of a desire to hide his failure.

In San Miguel there was a café run by a man who also rented rooms on the second floor to transients: cattlemen who wanted to buy pastureland, tax collectors, snake charmers who sold miraculous cures and on Sundays would wrap an enormous semi-anesthetized snake around their necks and climb on a box to tell the tale of their travels and consequent discovery of the medicine that cured every ailment. The café, like all the others in the region, was staffed by opulent women in short, tight dresses that showed off their thighs. It seemed curious to me that only men went into the café. A few wives or girlfriends would wait in the street for hours to take their men home when the aguardiente had left them totally besotted. I had traveled the three hundred kilometers between the provincial capital and San Miguel in a *chiva,* a kind of truck that carries both passengers and freight, and had established a cordial relationship with the driver, Tomasito. He was one of those men who combine the good-humored, open character of people from the hotlands with a notable, and infallible, natural intelligence. He introduced me to the owner of the café, giving me the highest recommendation. During our trip he spoke about The Hummer and the legends that had grown up around it. When I asked him if he thought gold could still be found there, he answered, "As for the finding, sure you can find it. The rough part is the looking, and for that you need a very cool head, because any man who looks for gold always ends up half crazy. That's the problem." Later I would remember Tomasito's words and be able to gauge all the truth they contained. I rented a room that overlooked the village square. I had to become accustomed as quickly as possible to the noise from the café. Until very late at night there were loud voices and the sound of dishes being washed and glasses clattering against the enameled metal tables. A phonograph tirelessly ground out three or four records, always the same ones, but the songs lamenting betrayal by a woman or her unexpected departure could hardly be heard over the din. I spent a good deal of time sitting at a table in the rear, where at regular intervals I was served a thin beer with a slightly medicinal taste, which was advertised along the roads and in the cities and whose Teutonic name promised something better. This was where I learned the rest of the story of The Hummer and its tales of ghosts and visitations. I also created certain ties with some of the waitresses, who would sit with me when it wasn't too busy and tell me about their lives and ask for advice on their love affairs and troubles. In all of them there were unexpected reserves of innocence that had no connection to their short, tight skirts, gaudy makeup, or the way they moved among the tables, swaying their hips, displaying their cleavage, and always provoking lecherous comments from the drunken patrons, so far from their houses hidden in the dense fog of the cordillera. They were not women who gave themselves easily. To achieve that, a man had to carry on a long, convincing courtship, which was accepted by the women with peasant skepticism and the sharp guile of those who have already had to elude the perils of a life on the edge of conventionality. Yet they still respected that conventionality and dreamed of returning to it and finding stability, their greatest aspiration. The first time I invited a waitress to come to my room, her reply was not angry, but it was categorical. "Look, honey, I'm no whore and I don't ever intend to be one. I work here because I have to support my kid. His daddy was a lieutenant in the Rurals. Poor guy, the CFA killed him before we could get married. Maybe it never would've happened, but he promised. You look like a nice man, and they say you've been around. Let me give you some advice: If you really want to be with one of us, you have to spend some time on it. That's the only way, and even then I can't make any promises. Want another beer?" Her admonition was so direct and clear that for the sake of continuing the conversation I ordered one, although each time I finished a bottle of the insipid brew I promised myself it would be my last. We talked quite a while, and she turned out to be a source of valuable information. Her parents lived near the shafts of The Hummer, and she knew the place very well. She was a tall woman, with slender, sinewy arms and legs, small, firm breasts, and the narrow hips and prominent buttocks of an adolescent. Her face was thin, and her elongated chin and fleshy lower lip made her look vaguely like a Spanish *infanta,* an impression that vanished immediately in the intense expressiveness of her dark, tobacco-colored eyes and the heavy black brows that almost merged with her wild, curly hair and left little room for a slightly receding forehead. Her disquieting appearance belied a cheerful character and lively sense of humor, which had been tempered by her knowledge of men, acquired more in her work as a waitress than in bed. Our friendship solidified, and neither of us thought of changing it into something else. Often, when she saw me absorbed in reading the books on mineralogy I had brought with me, or one of the other books I always carry, she would sit at my table until a customer called.

I had stopped in Guadeloupe on the way to my adventure as a miner, and in a secondhand bookstore in Pointe-à-Pitre I paid very little money for some books I thought might be useful: *Géologie Moderne*, by Poivre d'Antheil, *Minéralogie Appliquée*, by Benoit-Testut, and *L'Or, le Cuivre, l'Argent, le Manganese*, a huge, tattered volume from the late eighteenth century, written by one Lorenzo Spataro and filled with good sense and rational, practical observations. To relieve the dryness of this reading, I had with me a book that gave me inordinate pleasure. Émile Gabory's *Les Guerres de Vendée* has a wealth of documentation and a clear intelligence in describing people and events, which are rare in works of overwhelming scholarly weight. It led me through the labyrinths of history with a lighthearted amiability more appropriate to the narration of gallant adventures. I've always been fascinated by the saga of the Vendée, the response of Western Europe's most lucid, exquisite period to a brutal, blood-soaked carnival that produced all the mean-spirited gloom of the nineteenth century. My friend Dora Estela, better known as "the Governor," reproached me. "You read too damn much. You'll go blind. Books aren't good for much except confusing people." It was simple enough to tell her what the treatises on mining were good for, but as for the other volume, I had to be content with a vague allusion that left her extremely dissatisfied. "If all that happened already and everybody's dead and buried, what's the use of digging up the graves? You should worry more about the living; maybe then you'll get somewhere." I pointed out that the living are often deader than the characters in books, and I was so convinced of this fact that I couldn't even listen carefully to other people anymore, because I was afraid I'd wake them. "Well, you're right about that. The dumb things people do sometimes wear you out more than trying to hear what the dead are saying." That was the Governor; an extraordinary woman. If I had listened to her, what bitter times I could have avoided.

One day when I began to ask her for more precise details about the mine, she said, "Look, the best thing is to go up there and see for yourself. I can't tell what you need to know. Come to think of it, I have a brother who lives near my parents and works as a guide for the gringos who climb up there once in a while to explore the galleries. He stays with them for weeks at a time, until they get tired and leave. Eulogio's coming next week with some livestock to sell in the capital. I'll introduce you and ask him to go up with you. He doesn't talk much, because he got a scare when he was a kid, but he has a lot of experience and everybody knows he's honest. Don't worry if he doesn't answer you sometimes. He will sooner or later. You have to be patient with him." I had, in fact, been thinking about going to see the mine. The manuals, written with the clarity and rigor of every textbook published in France, had given me enough background to examine the site and draw conclusions about its possible exploitation. Dora Estela's offer solidified my plans, because the help of a local guide would make my task much easier. We agreed that she would let me know when her brother arrived and put me in touch with him right away. I tried to imagine what the Governor's brother looked like. If he resembled her, he probably had the face of a highwayman—enough to put fear in the stoutest heart.

* * *

Night had fallen without our realizing it. The sky still held the kind of diffused light seen in summer over the Indian Ocean. The breeze that had brought us relief at the start of the Gaviero's tale withdrew, and the heat returned, accompanied by the kind of magnificent stillness that precedes certain rituals. I asked if anyone wanted another of my old-fashioneds made with port, and the refusal was both courteous and unanimous. Maqroll expressed his desire to stay with straight bourbon, and Leopoldo and Fanny moved to cold white wine. I followed the Gaviero's example, and then we were ready to listen to more of his story.

* * *

Until that moment, my interest in gold mines had been purely speculative. I mean, they interested me as a way to explore a world I did not know, the sort of challenge that allows me to go on living and not look for false escapes. The sea has always offered me this, often with devastating generosity. That is why, when I'm on land, I suffer a kind of restlessness, a frustrating sense of limitation verging on asphyxia. It disappears, though, as soon as I walk up the gangplank of the ship that will take me on one of those extraordinary voyages where life lies in wait like a hungry she-wolf. When I was young, I signed on in Cardiff as the lookout on an Irish whaler whose crew had fallen sick with food poisoning. The lesson of the sea, the long hours I spent perched at the top of the mainsail, staring at the horizon, all of it was a plenitude so intense and complete that nothing afterward has given me the same sensation of limitless freedom and absolute possibility. But some of it always returns whenever I'm on a ship, even if I'm down in the grease and infernal heat of the engine room. You must be wondering what appealed to me in mines so far from the sea. Well, it's very simple: It was a final attempt to find on land even a tiny portion of what I always receive from the ocean. I know now it was futile, that I was wasting my time, but I didn't know it then. Worse luck for me. Don't think I'm glorifying the sailor's life. Work on a ship can be a crushing trial; in fact, it almost always is. Even when it's the kind of job I did for Wito on the *Hansa Stern,** when I was keeping the ship's books, the sea doesn't allow an easy life. I thought my time had come when hurricanes in the Gulf of Mexico made the cargo shift and Wito was lost in the silence of his premonitions. . . . Well, we'd better get back to The Hummer, because if I lose the thread, who knows where I'll end up.

Dora Estela's brother came to San Miguel with the cattle he was going to load onto two trucks that had been waiting for him since the previous day. He rented the room next to mine and was in there with his sister for quite a while. I heard the sound of voices arguing violently, followed by sustained weeping I thought would never end. I went down to the café to wait for him. I did not want to be an involuntary witness to their family dramas. An hour later they walked in and came directly to my table. Dora Estela's eyes were puffy, and tears had smeared her mascara, leaving dark shadows on her cheeks that made her look older. Still, she appeared calm, as if she had resolved something that had been tormenting her for a long time. Contrary to my conjectures, her brother did not resemble her at all. He was a young man of medium height, with certain European features that looked Asturian. His slow movements revealed exceptional physical strength. An air of kindness, or perhaps affability, did not quite match the superb muscular energy that suddenly seemed useless, and alien to his character. We greeted each other, and his handshake transmitted a spontaneous cordiality that turned into incomprehensible mumbling when he attempted to express the feeling in words. The Governor told him what I wanted in a way that indicated they had already discussed the matter. I was con-

*"Ilona Comes with the Rain," *Maqroll* (New York: HarperCollins, 1992).

cerned that this had been the reason for their argument, but as if she had read my mind, she quickly reassured me. "Eulogio mixes up what I do with how I dress. He's always trying to talk me into leaving and going back home. No matter how hard I try, I can't make him see that I'm in less danger of living a bad life here. Up there, every peon thinks he has the right to a roll in the hay, like he owned me. I always think my brother finally gets it, and it's always the same story whenever he comes back. Well, let's talk about the mine. Tell the gentleman," she said, addressing Eulogio, "what you can do for him, if you really want to do it. I already told you he's a good man and you can trust him." He sat looking at me, and I sensed his effort to put his words in order, but when he began to speak he was fluent and clear. "The mine's got gold, Señor," he said, "that's for sure, though the folks who come here to try and open it again want results right away. But that can't be, because the Rurals blew up part of the mine, right where the lode's buried. You need patience. I don't know much about mines, but I've been there with some men who looked like experts. I heard them say you got to check for outcroppings in every gallery still standing. I'm happy to go with you. I just got to load these cattle and settle some things with the drivers and send a telegram to the city and let them know the shipment's on its way, and then we can go up. It'll take me a day and a half, maybe two. So you decide." I said it was no problem, that I was ready to leave whenever he was free. I mentioned his salary, and he did not reply. "Don't worry about that, Señor," said his sister, who had long practice filling in the spaces left by Eulogio. "He'll do it because he knows you and I are friends and that's enough for him." I said that under no circumstances did I want to hire him without paying the wages he deserved. I didn't think it was right. I also intended to employ him for as long as I needed him, and that's something that has a price. "Excuse me," interjected Eulogio, whose expression had not changed during his long silence, "but let's wait until you see the mine and make an estimate of the time and work, and then we'll talk. I also think we should decide on my pay, but it's better to do that later. When you're up there you'll know why I'm saying this."

Eulogio's prudence in formulating his responsibilities was not very reassuring. The damn mine probably had plenty of nasty surprises in store. Dora Estela began to wipe her face and repair her makeup, and was about to say something, when a customer called to her from another table. While she was gone I made plans with

Eulogio to leave in two days' time. I asked what I should bring, and he answered that for now I ought to leave my gear with the café owner. I could trust him. "Take what you got on and two changes. You can come back for the rest later. If you decide to do it, you have to buy tools and apply for a government permit to work the mine. Don't ask for it yet. It's pretty complicated, and we don't know if it's worth it." I asked if it was dangerous to get a permit, and he reassured me. "Nobody cares about that around here," he observed. "They wiped out the CFA, but other groups turn up all the time, and that's what they're really interested in." I asked what the famous CFA was. I had heard it mentioned before. After a long pause that I thought would end in total silence, he replied in an exasperated tone. "Ah, listen, Chief, they're all crazy. CFA means Companies for Federal Action. A bunch of desperadoes. I don't think they even know what they want. They destroy everything, they fight the army until they get killed, they slaughter cattle and people for no good reason, and then they disappear into the mountains. Nobody knows who gives them money or weapons. It looks like the army wiped them out, at least around here, but before you know it there'll be others. It's like a plague. We've had it for more than thirty years, and there's no end in sight. Well, anyway, it's all arranged. I'll take care of the livestock as fast as I can, and we'll meet here." He stood and shook my hand with the same cordial energy he had shown before, as if he was not accustomed to expressing his feelings in words and used gestures instead. When Eulogio walked past his sister, who was at the bar waiting for a customer's order, he placed his arm around her shoulder and kissed her cheek, as though she were a little girl he was bound to protect. She smiled at him with an expression in which traces of her weeping could still be seen. Without really knowing why, I was deeply moved by the scene. I could feel inside myself the struggle these two waged against a hostile world where cruelty and savagery seemed to be their daily bread. Dora Estela came to talk to me. She stood, leaning her hand on the table that displayed the garish colors of an advertisement for the famous beer we were obliged to drink. "How'd you like him?" she asked with great interest. "Very much," I answered. "He's honest, and he knows The Hummer and its history. I can really use him, and I'm very happy to have his help. You two don't look alike. No one would think you're brother and sister." She smiled without managing to lift her Basque smuggler's frown even a little. "Yes," she said. "He's the good-looking one in the family. He favors my mother, and she claims her family's Spanish. Her last name is Almeiro, and nobody else around here is called that. I take after my father. What can you do?" I said I didn't think she had been the loser when looks were given out, and she shrugged as she returned to the bar, showing off in her walk the well-delineated firmness of her gymnast's buttocks.

We left at dawn, when the sun had barely made its presence known in a thin, orange-colored strip that threw the silhouette of the mountains into relief. You've probably felt the same vague uneasiness when you set out for unfamiliar places at that hour. There's something unsettling about the milky darkness of dawn in the tropics. The world and its objects and creatures lack a definite profile, a tangible presence, and seem to appear with an invocatory purpose more appropriate to the sleep that has not yet left us completely. Eulogio's painful silences made no small contribution to this strange sensation. He had lent me a gentle mare, while he rode a horse worn out by its many trips along the steep trails of the cordillera. Until quite late in the morning, in fact, we struggled up a path that must have turned into a raging torrent during the rainy season. The large rocks covering the ground made the trek significantly more difficult. But toward noon, when I thought we would continue all the way up to the barrens—they were visible now, with their tatters of fog moving among the bristling upland vegetation—we began to descend in a zigzag pattern through terrain that was even more rugged and more difficult for the animals. I asked my guide why people talked about going up to the mine, when we were actually descending into a ravine, the bottom of which was hidden by vegetation and thick fog. "Because in the beginning you go up for so many hours that people got used to saying it. The mine's really at the bottom of this gully. Not too far away we have some coffee planted along the stream. We take the cattle up to pasture on the Acure Flats." We continued our descent almost until nightfall, which comes early and abruptly in these places. When we reached the stream at the bottom of the canyon, we followed its course, making our way through dense growth where humid heat was saturated with heavy vegetal aromas that evoked what the sixth day of creation must have been like. From time to time clouds of bluish fireflies approached and then disappeared behind us in the lianas and parasitic plants hanging from the great trees. Crickets and frogs kept up their insistent, exasperating pattern of signals as if announcing our presence to someone hiding at the bottom of the ravine. Finally, when it was very late—our route through the labyrinth of forest had been barely marked by a narrow path that was difficult to follow in the dark—we reached a clearing where the current became a still water and we could hear the hoarse bubbling of its repose. A cabin, its roof partially caved in, stood on the shore. It had been invaded by vines with deep-blue flowers, which covered the structure and produced an effect, even more eloquent in the moonlight, of something created with a taste that bordered on vulgarity. "We'll stay here, Chief," said Eulogio. "The mine's back there, at the foot of the canyon wall. We'll see it tomorrow. Now we have to rest." We had brought a Coleman lamp, and Eulogio lit it so we could go into the cabin. We spread the saddle blankets on the floor to use as beds. I wrapped myself in a small blanket I always carry with me, a memory of the time I lived in Alaska. Eulogio went out to unharness the horses and bring water to make coffee. In the midst of the devastation caused by the invading forest, the cabin still had the remains of a stove and a few hooks nailed into the dangerously tilting walls. I was half asleep when Eulogio came over with the coffee. Without waking completely, I drank the intensely aromatic, thick brew, which instantly produced a sense of well-being. He said something about eating, but I was already sinking into the deep, deleterious sleep caused by exhaustion.

A vast, deafening clamor suddenly woke me. I thought I had slept late, but dawn was just breaking and all the forest birds had launched in unison into a disorderly, frenetic chorus. Eulogio was already up, preparing breakfast with the unhurried movements of an officiating priest. He had placed slices of corn bread to toast on a round sheet of tin that he said he had found under the embers of the previous night's fire. We washed our faces in the stream, whose clear, icy waters seemed Virgilian and classical. "Okay, let's go see this thing," said Eulogio. "We'll take the lantern so we won't have trouble going in. You take this in case some animal's living inside," and he handed me a machete similar to the one he was carrying. He held the unlit lantern in his other hand. We left the clearing and went into the forest, heading for the wall of the gorge, which rose majestically until it was lost in a sky filled with low, ragged clouds. When we reached the foot of the wall, we saw a platform made of logs held in place by large stones—a kind of terrace to three mine entrances that were somewhat higher than the normal height of a person. Everything had an abandoned look, enough to discourage the most enthusiastic visitor hoping to start up these ruined works again; the wind blew through the structure with a disconsolate, childlike sob. "We have to begin with the tunnel on the left. It connects with the other two farther inside, but those entrances are full of deep holes and it's hard to get through," Eulogio explained as he lit the lantern and turned the air screw to get the brightest light from the little hood of ashy silk.

I don't suffer from claustrophobia, and I've lived for months in the hold of a ship, but enclosed spaces always make me think of catacombs, of burial rites, of a return to the unknown that crushes my spirit and undermines my overworked reserves of curiosity and daring. The first thing I noticed were the interior dimensions of the extensive gallery we were walking through. "For now we'll just look over the galleries; later I'll show you particular places where maybe you'll find something interesting. Don't worry about the water dripping from the walls and roof. The real problem is when it disappears all of a sudden and the air starts to dry out. That won't happen here." And in this way he introduced me to the place he knew so well that I felt a growing confidence in the work I proposed to do in The Hummer. I had been intrigued by the name, but now that I heard the persistent moan of the wind in the dark labyrinth of underground corridors, it seemed not only appropriate and accurate but even obvious and not very original. I mentioned this to Eulogio, who told me that in every mine the wind blowing through the galleries produces a sound peculiar to the place, which miners can distinguish, and often interpret in their own way.

After several turns to the right and left, we saw a light that grew larger as we approached. It was the main entrance. When we had almost reached it, Eulogio stopped and pointed to a passage on the right that must have been another gallery but was sealed off by a haphazard pile of rocks. "I think this is where they buried the English and the laborers and the women who worked with them," he said. "It's the only gallery that goes underground for many meters; they dug it to follow a vein that was supposed to be very rich. Who knows if it's true. People made up a lot of crap about what happened, and by now nobody knows the real story. At the district headquarters, they burned all the files and reports about the killing. So many years ago, and the soldierboys still don't want anybody talking about it. I'm telling you because if you go to the provincial capital and apply for mining permits, they'll try to get you to talk so they can find out what you know. They shot foreigners, and that made a lot of scandal, and people talked more than usual. You just ask for your papers and act like you don't know anything. They're real bastards. You'll see."

As I learned more about the history of The Hummer, I swung back and forth between a justifiable discouragement and the hope, not always as palpable, that everything would work out. The odd thing is that I experienced this as something transitory and circumstantial, and my interest was not driven by the internal mechanism that normally impels me into these ventures. You surely know about my search for the sawmills on the Xurandó, about the brothel in Panama City, and my senseless voyages around the Mediterranean and the Caribbean in undertakings that were not always protected by the law. Each time, I threw myself into the game with all my heart, lived it as if it were the great adventure of my life. But this was different. At least in the beginning. Later on, my relationship to the mine changed radically, and I'll tell you how because it was so unlike my earlier ventures. But perhaps you're tired and would like to continue this another day.

* * *

We said it really wasn't very late, that we were listening to him with growing interest. The bottle of bourbon was empty. I brought another, along with more ice, and we asked the Gaviero to continue his story. On summer nights in California, time stretches like an elastic, compliant material, perfect for hearing the confidences of someone who had a store of tales that could lead us from one marvel to another until dawn.

* * *

Waking in the cabin never again had that element of shock. On the contrary, the astonishing noise made by the birds was a kind of hymn of gladness to the wonders of the morning, which filled me with joy. I began to feel as if they were singing directly to me, encouraging me to explore the dark underground world of the mine. As I expected, Eulogio proved so indispensable and useful a guide and adviser that I became convinced I would not have even gotten inside The Hummer without his help. Our work in the days following our arrival enabled me to determine with some precision, subject to later testing, the sites where it was worth verifying the presence of a gold-bearing seam. We marked them with stones, but in a way that would be meaningless to anyone else entering the galleries. "Nobody comes here anymore," commented Eulogio, "but it's better if we're the only ones who can read the markers. You never know. Each stone should be exactly three meters north of the place that interests us. It's a trick I learned from some English who were here years ago and never came back." We placed the markers as he suggested, and after spending a week at the mine we returned to San Miguel to buy the tools we needed: Rock samples had to be removed and subjected to very simple chemical tests that we would perform on-site to avoid attracting attention. On the way, at the spot where the steep ascending path ended, Eulogio said goodbye. He had to go back to his ranch to pay the hands and brand some cattle. He lent me the mare and suggested I let her graze in the lot behind the café. The Governor's brother had a natural rectitude, a calm, thoughtful way of doing things and expressing his opinions, which seemed unusual in someone who could barely read and write and had spent his life enduring the brutalizing fatigue of farm labor. Another quality I learned to value was his positive, concrete way of judging everything connected to the exploration and exploitation of the mine, an attitude that helped to moderate the impulsiveness and wild speculations awakened in me by the first results of our prospecting. As I came to know Eulogio better, I could detect some of these same qualities in his sister, although they were less apparent in Dora Estela because her peculiar sense of ironic humor was tinged with a very feminine desire to emphasize the weaknesses of her interlocutor, especially if he was a man. Since then, I've moved through many landscapes entirely unlike the cordillera, and I've known people of many different conditions and races, but I've never forgotten the brother and sister who offered me solid help and friendship, and at the same time taught me a lesson of surprising maturity and independence of character, virtues that are not precisely typical of the people who live in these regions. You know what I'm referring to.

Dora Estela was waiting for me in the café, curious to hear about my trip to The Hummer and what I thought of her brother. I told her everything in detail, and she was pleased by my opinion of Eulogio. Again she remarked on the difficulty he had in speaking, and when I said it was more a matter of thinking before he spoke instead of the reverse, which is the custom in those countries, she was very happy. The café was unusually busy during this time. I sat at my usual table starting early in the morning, since my room provided no escape from the noise, which was just as intense upstairs. There were new waitresses, from a distant province, whose dark, tobacco-colored skin and ample hips announced the African blood of people from the coast. They spoke in loud voices and swallowed their consonants, especially *s* and *rr*. Their easygoing tone, their eagerness to talk to everybody in a loud voice amid outbursts of often gratuitous laughter and exclamations like sudden explosions of a gaiety more learned than natural, completely changed the ambience of the café. The records were not played anymore: The newcomers always sang as they walked to the tables to wait on the patrons. Dora Estela reacted to the new atmosphere with signs of displeasure that combined a certain fear of competition and the reserved, constrained character of people from the cordillera. I've noticed this same distance, which often turns into open rejection, in many other places in the world. It's so evident in Asia, for example, that when you have to deal with people there, it's very important to try to learn ahead of time where they come from.

The Governor showed me the shop where I could buy the tools for taking rock samples, and the pharmacy where the chemicals for testing them were sold or could be ordered from the capital. When everything was ready, I sent a message to Eulogio, confirming that I would be at the mine on the day we had agreed upon. This time the trek seemed shorter and easier. When I reached the clearing in the forest, I felt a sense of relief and again had the impression I was entering a place with classical resonances. When I thought about it that night, I realized it reminded me of those peaceful still waters where Don Quixote conversed with Sancho and evoked the golden age of a legendary past. Eulogio arrived soon after I did, leading a mule that carried enough supplies for a prolonged stay at the mine. When I mentioned paying for these provisions, he replied, "I marked it all down. When we decide on my salary we can add it up and have just one bill. It's better this way." Again I found my guide's good judgment, as well as the equitable, thoughtful way in which he placed a value on his work and services, very appealing. Since it was growing dark, we left our explorations for the following day and sat in the grass to eat the dried meat with fried yucca and the slices of roasted plantain that Eulogio had brought from the ranch. He told me his wife prepared the food. That was how I learned he was married. I asked about his family, and he said he had two young children, one ten years old and the other five. He had met his wife when he was in the army and serving in a southern province. She was very young, and he said she was incurably shy because of her accent, which the people of San Miguel found hilarious. Eulogio's pauses before speaking decreased as we came to know each other better, and eventually our talk took on an almost natural fluidity. Unlike his sister, Eulogio was completely lacking in the ironic humor that made Dora Estela a conversationalist with whom no precaution was ever enough. His seriousness, however, did not prevent him from often expressing appropriately caustic opinions about people.

When night had fallen, the murmur of the river and the imposing silence of the forest brought back the Cervantine image I mentioned before. It was a curious impression at the entrance to a mine that seemed to hide more than one tragedy and not a few mysteries, which surrounded it in an aura of gloomy desolation.

The samples we obtained the next day were examined in the light and gave little indication of a rich vein. According to both my companion and my books, there was no point in testing them. Since our previous visit to the mine, a fixed idea had been growing in me with increasing insistence. I wanted to knock down the wall of stone blocking the gallery that apparently contained the remains of the murdered workers and search there for possible outcroppings. To my surprise, when I told Eulogio of my idea, he did not oppose it in principle. His arguments were of a more practical nature: It would not be easy for only two people to remove the wall. I suggested that we try, and as I expected, the work was not especially difficult. It took us two days to clear the entrance, and we entered the shaft with the help of the Coleman. We spent many hours examining the corridors that branched off in greater profusion than in the other galleries. We found a good deal of abandoned machinery, eaten away by rust and almost impossible to identify. There was absolutely no trace of human remains. The next day we explored the site again and found no signs that the earth had been disturbed, or any indication of an explosion. On the contrary, the gallery seemed better preserved than the others, the walls had firmer supports, the ground was more carefully leveled, and the steps leading belowground were neatly finished. We were about to leave, when Eulogio discovered markers like the ones we had left in the other galleries. We stopped to examine them and found that they did in fact indicate places that hid something of interest. By a process of elimination, simple to follow because of the circumscribed area in which the markers were located, it was easy enough to determine where they were pointing. We spent the next day on this task, and the Governor's brother again showed his ability to move through an abstract, complex world similar to the one mastered by chess players, to my endless amazement, perhaps because I am absolutely deficient in that kind of talent. It did not take us long to locate the sites, and after some superficial scraping we discovered outcroppings of the supposed lode, which looked like the ones we had found in other parts of the mine. Still, we took samples and went out to examine them. They were calcareous rock with no trace of the elements that indicate the presence of ore. Eulogio was disconcerted. "Something's very strange here, Chief, because it's no fairy tale that people were shot by the Rurals. Nobody makes up a story like that. A cousin of mine and his wife—she was our relative too—were killed in the massacre, and their three little children came to live with my parents. I think they're buried here and this gallery was sealed off to hide it. I always heard they were buried where the lode is. People make up lots of things about mines, but I always heard the same story and nobody ever doubted it or said it wasn't true. What we found isn't worth anything. The same stuff the gringos dug up, and the other people I came here with. Either we find those dead folks or we leave here empty-handed just like everybody else. You'll see." I didn't know how to respond to my guide's reasoning. But his incontrovertible logic hid a conclusion that made me feel understandably discouraged and uneasy: I had come to The Hummer not to look for corpses but to find gold. Lurking behind this matter were the kinds of complications I had already encountered in my voyage up the Xurandó, and I had absolutely no desire to go through anything like that again. You know very well [*Maqroll was addressing me now*] that the military and I don't get along very well, we don't speak the same language, and I'm always the one whose life is in danger. As far as they're concerned, civilians are what engineers call a negligible quantity. "Let's not sit here with our arms folded. What should we do?" I challenged Eulogio, more to shake him out of the lethargy caused by our failure than to find an immediate solution. He fell into one of his full-stop silences and kept pounding the rock as if he could find in it the answer we needed. After a long while he raised his head, and looking at the bottom of the transparent still water, he began to speak. "We have to stay here. What we've done the others did too, but we have to find a way to see if there really is a lode or not.

Forget about the dead. That's another story. We're not sure they're with the lode. People must've made up that crap. I can't explain, but something's telling me we should go on, we should stay. You're not like the others I've been here with. It's like you come from farther away and have seen more complicated things. I don't know, it's different. Well, there's something, I don't know." He disappeared again into the silence that was his refuge and did not speak for the rest of the day.

My companion's words held a conviction he could not fully express. It had to do with me, something he saw in me that afforded him a vague certainty, almost a premonition, and moved him to insist on our continuing the search. I resolved to do as he said and wait to see what would happen. We spent the next few days reinforcing gallery walls, widening some of the interconnecting corridors, and trying to repair the holes in the floor of the center and left-hand entrances, which had filled with water, making passage extremely difficult. Some were more than a meter deep, and it took us a long time to haul the earth we needed. I think this is an opportune moment to tell you that I've never been especially interested in the supernatural or in run-of-the-mill mysteries or esoteric doctrines. It seems to me that what we carry inside us, what seems so familiar and ordinary, presents enough problems, enough vast, indecipherable spaces, without inventing others. Until now, in my case at least, God has chosen the simplest, clearest ways to manifest his presence. The fact that we sometimes don't know how to see them is another matter. I don't think about it very much; it hasn't been of particular concern to me. The life we have to face each day demands all my attention and doesn't leave me much time for higher speculations. What happened at The Hummer belongs to the world of rigorous logic. The unsettling part might be that Eulogio, awestruck and filled with premonitions, foresaw it.

The rains arrived without warning, and in just a few hours what had been an idyllic pool in an eclogue by Garcilaso became a torrent of mud carrying ruined trees, animals with their mouths brutally agape and almost all their skin torn off against the rocks, sections of buildings, and even parrots in cages, shrieking in terror. We took refuge in the mine, bringing in our gear and the three animals we had with us. With planks from the cabin we built a roof to keep us dry and waited for the storm to pass. "There are four or five downpours like this," Eulogio explained. "Then it just rains a little in the afternoon and everything goes back to normal." On the first night I barely closed my eyes, but succeeding nights proved not only that it was easy to sleep in the mine but that sleeping in total darkness was very soothing. We turned off the lantern early to save fuel, which was why I gave up reading at night. Once, when I stretched out my arm to extinguish the Coleman, I felt everything moving around me. At first I thought our precarious wooden framework had given way, but a muffled roar belowground, followed by a second tremor, indicated another cause. "It's a quake," Eulogio said calmly. "Don't move. Nothing'll happen. This thing won't fall in, don't worry. It happens a lot. It's almost over now." The earth moved two more times, with greater force than before. Eulogio was right. The planks of our roof and the vault of the gallery were not affected. A moment later we heard a baffling noise that we thought was a slide in the gorge. It sounded as if a gigantic foot had stepped into a pit of thick mud or wet clay and then suddenly slipped. We turned off the lantern and went to sleep, if not exactly tranquil at least certain that our gallery had withstood the earthquake and not been damaged, which was saying a great deal. The next morning Eulogio woke me, gently shaking my shoulder. He was dressed and carrying the lantern. "Come, I'll show you something interesting," he said in a voice that was calm although it betrayed some disquiet. I dressed quickly and followed him to the central gallery, where we had been filling in potholes. When we reached it, he held the lantern in front of him while he kept me back with his other arm. The ground had caved in, uncovering steps that led to a shaft from which there rose a dense odor, a smell of fresh mud, something that recalled dirty clothes or the sweat of spent horses after a race. We walked down the steps and found ourselves in a circular space—a shape entirely foreign to the usual excavations in mines. It was a ceremonial space, an extraordinary catacomb with no practical purpose. Eulogio brought the light close to the walls, revealing human skeletons in improbable positions. Ocher-colored rags, impossible to identify, hung from the bones. It was easy to distinguish the women because of the shreds of skirt clinging to their legs. Skeletons of children lay at the feet of the women. We found human remains along the entire length of the wall. A few of the skulls had pith helmets and probably belonged to the British engineers who operated the mine. Above us, the sobbing of the wind seemed to continue the frozen screams of the skulls, whose jaws hung open in grotesque, heartrending grimaces. I've had many encounters with death, and it holds no mystery for me. It's the end of the story, that's all. I've never liked speculating about it; I don't think there's really much to say. But the theatrical placement of these people, of the most diverse ages and conditions, was like a sinister joke, a gratuitous, sadistic taunt that both enraged me and filled me with pity. We left that place, not saying anything, and took refuge in the cabin, close to the river, which had recovered its original shape although the water was still opaque and rust-colored. We stayed there a long time in silence. On Eulogio's mouth there was the hint of a nervous grin that looked like a smile and really expressed something quite different. I don't think my face looked very natural either, because Eulogio glanced at me from time to time with surprise and bewilderment. "What animals, my God, what animals," he said after a protracted silence. "Those people didn't do anything, damn it. The bastards!" I walked over to him and put my hand on his shoulder, but I couldn't utter a word. To myself I said with a dull fury that I didn't know where to direct: "Now you'll find gold. It's right there, watched over by the bones of innocents. Don't you get the message?" Eulogio continued talking as he stared at the water, tears running down his cheeks. "Mr. Jack must be there, nice old man with his white mustache and his nose all red with drink. Start first thing on Saturday and go on a two-day bender. Drank nonstop from a bottle he always had with him. Swam here buck naked in the afternoon and invited the women to join him. Had kids all over the place. And Mr. Lindsey, the Jamaican foreman, pitch black, a mouth full of gold teeth, scare the kids with them when they were bad. Rough and strict, but always took care of his people. All the others. God! How could they kill them like that? No way to live here anymore. They'll kill us all because nobody moves, nobody does anything. They're crazy, and so are we." For a long time he continued his confused lament, the exclamations, the memories of those who had once been his friends and relatives and now lay in the astonished circle of their meaningless grave.

In the afternoon, the rain returned, insistent, unending. A light, warm rain that barely reached the ground but created a boiler room atmosphere, punishing the nerves and depressing the spirit. We took shelter in the gallery and heated some coffee. By now Eulogio was calm but submerged in a bruised, defeated melancholy as he began to examine our situation. We clearly had to leave as soon as possible. Working the vein that might be in the circular chamber was unthinkable. We mustn't mention finding the victims to anyone. Let somebody else discover them someday, or let them be buried again by the water that had reached the steps: made of pounded dirt and held together with boards, the water was washing them away. If they asked in San Miguel why we came back so soon, the answer was that we hadn't found anything and were going to try our luck someplace else. We had to take everything with us. We couldn't leave any trace, any object, any sign that we had been there. If they asked about the quake, we had to say we had hardly felt it. We had slept in the cabin, and the water made so much noise we couldn't hear anything else. He went on to speculate at length about how the military behaved in situations like this, and I could only agree with him. And so the next day we packed up our gear and went back to San Miguel. On the way, Eulogio told me about other sites in the area where miners had dug for gold. Some seemed to hold good possibilities for making a find. He mentioned places and locations along the river. They obviously meant nothing to me but did indicate that it would be worth my while to try them before deciding to leave the region altogether. I had confidence in Eulogio. He was not a person who would create vain hopes in an attempt to console me for the abrupt end to my efforts at The Hummer of dismal memory. I returned to the room above the café and sat again at my usual table. Dora Estela asked about our explorations, and I responded with the answers her brother and I had agreed upon. I had a feeling he had told her everything, but I preferred not to go too deeply into the matter. The owner also came to my table and asked if I needed the money he had kept for me in a safe built under the bar. I said I had enough with me for the next few days, until I left with Eulogio to look for another mine. The situation was beginning to take on characteristics that were so familiar, and fit so well into the design of my bad luck and drifting, that I felt I was in my element, which immediately afforded me the serenity of resigned forbearance. I had spent only a small portion of my money, and I could try one or two more explorations before having to resort to extraordinary measures. Dora Estela introduced me to a friend who agreed to spend a few nights with me if I wrote letters for her in English to a man she had met in the capital, a Swedish engineer who had come to install flour mills. In his letters, he spoke of marriage with the ineffable candor that only Scandinavians can preserve amid the Lutheran wiles of their pitiless business dealings. She was a short, plump blonde with smooth white skin and a sunny disposition that helped one to forgive a limited intelligence, which often verged on simple-mindedness. In bed this deficiency was made up for by an abandon that always gave the impression she was experiencing passion for the first time. Her name was Margot, which did not suit her at all. Perhaps that was why it had become Mago, which didn't suit her either.

I had made some friends in the café, especially among the *chiva* drivers. Tomasito, who had brought me to San Miguel and with whom I maintained a warm friendship, introduced them to me when they stopped in. Each truck had a name that reflected the driver's personality, except in the case of Tomasito, whose *chiva* was called "Maciste." When I asked him why he had chosen that name, he said his father used to describe anyone who was very powerful as being stronger than Maciste. Tomasito didn't know Maciste was a famous hero in a silent movie about Nero's Rome. He wasn't at all happy when I informed him of this fact. He preferred the vague image that reminded him of his father. I don't remember if I told you that in the famous *chivas,* just behind the driver, there were three or four rows of benches consisting of simple wooden boards with no backs. There was ample space in the rear for freight. The *chivas* were vehicles of proven endurance, which the drivers modified according to spontaneous mechanical inspirations that would have amazed the engineers and designers in Detroit. In fact, for many long years these trucks drove up and down the serpentine roads of the cordillera and showed no real signs of wear. Talking with the drivers, who were tough, strong men with nomadic spirits, was sheer pleasure for me. Each trip they made held some surprise, some episode or accident that tested their inventiveness and endurance. They had a girlfriend in every tavern along the highway, from the burning heat and wild vegetation of the lowlands to the ragged clouds and icy winds that enveloped the mountaintops, with their stunted plants and the brilliant, unsettling flowers of their tormented trees. The drivers left a record of their passing in devastating passions, tragedies of violent jealousy, and children named for improbable tango singers. I can still remember all their names—my unforgettable companions during long days of alcohol and reminiscences—and their heroic *chivas:* Demetrio, the owner of "Let Others Cry"; Marcos, who drove "I'll Leave Him Here for You to Raise"; Saturio and his "Andean Hurricane"; Esteban, the owner of "Garbo Remembers Me," and so many others who used their trucks to advertise a character trait that was either secret or too well known. When I talked to them about my plans to be a miner, they tried to dissuade me with the same arguments I secretly made to myself: It was work for gringos with the souls of moles, and in the end gold was good only for fattening the government, dressing up whores, and making bar owners rich. "It's okay for somebody who stays in one place, has roots like a banana tree, and dies not knowing what life is all about," Saturio told me. He was an immense man of Indian and black ancestry, who joked a good deal and liked to fight and had killed a jealous husband who was waiting for him one day at the door of a tavern in the middle of the barrens. Saturio picked him up and threw him into a ravine. The body was never found because the river was in flood. When I told them about my life as a sailor, they would look at me, intrigued, and interrupt to point out a resemblance, a coincidence, something that reminded them of their own lives as errant truckdrivers with no home port. Dora Estela was not very fond of my friends, whom she considered untrustworthy, not because they were dishonest but because they never settled down anywhere and left nothing good behind them. Always the same longing for respectability and permanence, preserved by these women despite the arduous trials of their apparently directionless lives.

One day Eulogio appeared with encouraging news: He had reliable information about an abandoned mine not far from the spot where his family owned a small coffee grove on the banks of the stream. He had been to see me several times, whenever he came to town with livestock or produce. On each occasion he mentioned what he had learned about mines and likely sites in the area, but he did not think any of them was sure enough to risk expenditures of labor or money. But this one seemed to promise more solid, concrete results. He asked me to visit the place with him to explore the possibilities. I had begun to feel a desire to return to the world of the mines. Life in San Miguel was taking on a certain repetitive rhythm that I found tedious despite the drivers, who in any event tended to be away for long periods of time. A few days earlier Margot had received a letter and a plane ticket to Stockholm from her Swedish suitor. Surprisingly, she showed no great enthusiasm and seemed to view this radical change in her life with serious misgivings. One morning Tomasito drove her to the provincial capital, where she would take a plane to Miami and from there continue on to the Swedish capital. She cried constantly, while an innocent smile played over her lips as if she were begging forgiveness for her

tears. I knew I wouldn't mourn her absence, although the spontaneous flowering of repeated ecstasies inaugurated each night in
bed did have something memorable about them. I was alone
again, and I spent hours immersed in the complex and impas-
sioned factions of the Breton royalists and their fierce battles
against the Blues. The dense historical material in Gabory's
exhaustive book kept me two centuries away from the din of
glasses, voices, curses, and laughter that held sway in the café.
From time to time Dora Estela would sit beside me, making no
comment, or giving my arm a friendly squeeze and saying,
"Damn, you got a lot of patience to read such tiny print. You'll
go blind. I'm telling you. Coming!" And she would leave to wait
on a customer or do her accounts with the owner, who, from his
position behind the bar, watched over the dense human tide
surging through this establishment where he was the unappealable authority.

Eulogio and I left a few days later with the same animals, tools,
and equipment we had taken to The Hummer. During the first
part of the journey he barely opened his mouth. We were making
the same ascent as before. But at the top we took a trail along a
ridge that sloped very gradually toward the river and seemed to
end far beyond the pastoral still water of bitter memory. As we
moved along the rocky path with its occasional rough steps to
mark the descent, Eulogio began to describe our destination.
"This was a king's road. They say it goes all the way to the ocean.
I don't believe it. But you can travel for days, even weeks, going
up or coming down, and the design is so perfect that it's all
exactly like what you see now. We'll stay on it until tomorrow
afternoon, then we take a branch road down to the river; there
it's not just a stream anymore, and we have to use Blackbird
Bridge to get across. They call it that because it's a covered bridge
and lots of blackbirds nest under the tin roof. Don't worry, we
won't be sleeping outdoors. We're going to the house of some
relatives of mine; they raise potatoes and barley in the flats at the
end of this ridge. The next day we travel till about noon, about
half a day, and come right to the mine entrance. It doesn't have a
name. The family that owned the land around here opened the
mine about fifty years ago. When the old people died, the children divided the land and sold a lot of it to local people. They
lived in the capital and weren't interested in traveling to places so
far away. Then their children sold off the rest, and now there's
only small farms like ours and the one where we sleep tonight,

and they hardly produce enough to eat and buy seed. The mine's on land that belonged to a daughter of the first owners. People say she was very beautiful. She never got married and finally went to live outside the country. The story is she liked women and came here with a young couple. The husband was an engineer, and he began studying the only gallery that had been excavated. One day they found him dead on the riverbank. They said he and his horse went over the edge when they were crossing the gully where the mine is, but they never did find the horse, and some people came out from the capital to bury him in San Miguel. By that time the two women had gone away, and nobody ever heard about the owner again. My father tells these stories, and he heard them from his father, and he saw it all. He was the one who found the body, half eaten by buzzards and its neck broken." I interrupted to ask if every mine in the area necessarily had a sinister history. I was utterly amazed when he answered with the greatest naturalness, "Yes, Señor, every mine has its dead. That's the way it is. An Indian who lived around here and told fortunes used to say there's no gold without a corpse, no woman without a secret. But getting back to our business, I can tell you nobody's tried to explore this mine since. It's not easy to get to. The entrance is in the wall of a cliff that goes straight down to the river, and you can only get to it by a path that's almost too narrow for the animals. You have to lead them by the reins and be very careful. The wind blows through the opening, and the noise it makes doesn't ever stop. My father says the vein is good, but nobody's tried to work it because for that you need money, and I already told you that around here we're all poor as hell." I asked him who owned the land where the mine was located, and he said there was no owner: The land apparently belonged to the government, because at one time they were going to build a railroad up there.

We followed the king's road over well-laid flagstones and centuries-old traces of horseshoes, which made it seem venerable and as old as Numantia. With equally noble sonority, the stones amplified the sound of our animals' hooves. The landscape was incredibly beautiful. Small meadows lay on each side of the ridge, ending in apparently impenetrable forests or precipices from which there rose the clamor of water plunging headlong down the slope of a rocky riverbed watched over by the solemn flight of hawks. The square fields laid out on the gently rolling surface of the narrow plain had a quality of austere frugality, of self-sacrificing productive labor, which was solemnly underscored by tin-roofed structures, and houses whose covered galleries were gaily decorated with geraniums, and corrals, and bluish smoke rising from the kitchens. "Good land," I thought. "Tragic mining legends have no place here; they don't harmonize with the idyllic order of these fields." As if he could read my thoughts, Eulogio remarked, "A lot of armed men from every faction come through here. They murder, they destroy everything, and then they leave. We stay, I don't know why exactly. We were born here and we'll be buried here. But sometimes I think this land is so good it makes certain people angry. They don't want it, they got no use for it, but they don't want it to be here. Bad people, always bad people. You can't ever talk to them. They shoot, they burn, and they leave. All of them. They're all the same. Things are quiet now. Who knows how long it'll last." The afternoon was waning, creating the translucent atmosphere that seems to invoke an ephemeral instant of eternity in the midst of every object's new-born presence. It was growing dark when we reached the house where we would sleep. The owners had gone down to the river to pick the ripe coffee berries. We were greeted by Doña Claudia, an older woman who had known Eulogio since he was a boy and made constant jokes about the difficulty he had in expressing himself. He accepted her teasing good-naturedly and laughed with her, alluding in turn to a supposed boyfriend who still asked for her in San Miguel. Doña Claudia prepared a generous supper for us, which was in no way easy to digest. Barley soup with fatback, a dish of creamed potatoes, rice with kernels of young corn, and a slab of dried meat pickled in chili peppers. Large cups of coffee were waiting for us on the gallery, where we could sit and watch night advance with the urgency of an obligation always met by powers that do not take us into account. As we drank the steaming coffee—the aroma immediately reminded me of the motley cafés in Alexandria—Doña Claudia, who remained standing, began to question Eulogio. She asked first about his wife and children and then about his land and the livestock he was raising on the flatlands at the foot of the great barrens. Eulogio responded to everything in stony monosyllables. I was taken aback. With me his speech was more fluent and almost never faltered. It was clear that when he talked to someone who had known him since he was a boy, the speech problems of his childhood returned. "And now where are you two heading?" she asked, looking at us with lively curiosity. "The mine in the cliff.

To see what's there." Doña Claudia shook her head in a gesture of amiable reproach and observed, "Well, Eulogio, you're hopeless. I don't know where you get these crazy ideas about mines. There's never any gold, and the damn mines don't bring anything but bad luck and ruin. Did you tell the gentleman what they say about that place?" Eulogio couldn't say a word, and I answered quickly, "Yes, Señora, he told me everything. All about the pretty owner who liked women and the death of the engineer. Is that what you're referring to?" She nodded. "I've had plenty of situations like that in my life, Señora. It doesn't worry me. I'm a sailor by trade, and I can tell you that each ship has its story too. What matters is whether we can find the lode, and if it has gold." Doña Claudia continued shaking her head to indicate how hopeless we were, and asked if we wanted more coffee. We declined, and she said good night and left. Eulogio and I stayed awhile longer, and then the fatigue of our journey drove us to the hammocks hanging in a room with a high cedar ceiling that smelled vaguely of the Orient and cathedrals. I thought of the Mexhuar in the Alhambra and the tombs of King Fernando and King Alfonso in the Cathedral of Seville. In one of those caprices of memory whose secret it is better not to question, I dreamed all night about Abdul Bashur, my dear companion in so many mad ventures, killed in the wreck of an Avro that exploded as it landed on the runway at Funchal. "More friends are waiting for me on the other side than I have here," I thought while I attempted to fall asleep again amid the dizzying procession of images and evocations parading across my mind.

We left the next day at first light. Doña Claudia saw us off with a substantial breakfast and repeated warnings to be careful on the narrow trail that crossed the ravine. We followed the king's road for some time, and when it began an abrupt descent to the plain, which was visible in the distance, we took an offshoot and soon reached the edge of a vertical wall that dropped straight down to the banks of the river, a torrent of water roaring and bellowing like a caged animal. In the middle of the precipice was a path carved out of the rock and so narrow it produced an alarming sense of vertigo. We dismounted and led the animals single file. The saddlebags, loaded with tools and provisions, banged into the rock wall, and every step the animals took dislodged stones that rolled down into the abyss with a menacing clatter. Turning back was unthinkable. We could only move forward, more and more slowly and cautiously. After at least an hour on the path, which left us disheartened and inconceivably weary, we came to a small ledge that went into the rock and led to a circular space; at the far end, the water of a brook fell from the top of the canyon with a sound that shattered an ambience of strange ceremonial seclusion. The grotto had a floor of fine white sand, and enough room for the horses and several people. The water did not splash against the rock but fell in a stream that took on a peculiar metallic gleam in the midday sun, which had just penetrated the area. The entrance to the mine was in the left-hand wall, almost hidden by pale-green ferns that stood out against the shadowy background. No breeze moved them, and it seemed almost as if they had been painted onto a piece of disquieting scenery. We spread the saddle blankets on the sand and lay down to rest. My legs were stiff and painfully cramped from the tension of each step I had taken along the brink of the precipice, and my close watch over the animals. We said nothing for a long time. I asked myself why in hell I had risked so much, only to end up in a grotto that produced a chilling sense of nameless rituals, of secret propitiatory sacrifices. I stared at the entrance to the mine. The feeling of absurdity and intolerable foolishness grew until it stripped away all my illusions, all my interest in penetrating a world that offered nothing but confirmation of my oldest presentiments and most ancient terrors, held in check by a nomadic calling and my steadfast refusal to settle anywhere for long. The water flowed gently through the center of the white sand floor and then ran out of the grotto and fell into the gorge, hugging the walls, silent except for the sound of its quiet motion, which helped to create the otherworldly atmosphere of the place. We slept until just before dawn. Curiously, the air was not exceptionally humid despite the presence of the waterfall and stream. Perhaps the high rock walls retained the considerable heat of the day. We were awakened by the strident chorus of a flock of parrots that nested on the upper edge of the grotto.

*   *   *

Maqroll was silent for a moment and then said he would leave the story of the new mine for another time. It was so different from his experience at The Hummer that he did not think it should be told at the same sitting. We went to bed, curious to learn what had happened to our friend in a place as filled with foreboding as the one he had just described. In the days that followed, I accompanied the Gaviero to the hospital for various *tests. We would know the results in a week. Yosip and his wife visited us from time to time and were extremely gratified to see Maqroll making so palpable a recovery. Once, when Jalina and I were alone on the patio, she expressed her gratitude for what I had done to assist their friend.* "He saved us several times from very serious situations," *she said.* "He's very noble, but it isn't easy to help him or return all his kindness. The last time we worked together was on a ship that carried pilgrims from the Adriatic and Cyprus to Mecca. He was bos'n and part owner of the ship. It was registered to Abdul Bashur, a great friend of his who died. Another unusual man, but much harder and more practical than Maqroll. Yosip made a mistake in assigning the bunks, and a gang of Albanians tried to kill him. Just then Maqroll came down to the hold. He always carried a revolver, and he fired it into the air. The Albanians let my husband go, and when it looked as if they were going to attack Maqroll, he said something in their language that made them pull back, all the fight gone out of them."* I had heard such stories about the Gaviero before, yet he never gave the impression of being a man inclined to fighting or imposing his will on anyone. Evidently he would for those he cared about, but not for himself—then his irremediable fatalism made him indifferent to other people's excesses. From the moment I saw Jalina in the office of the La Brea motel, I had been struck by her profound, unconditional, almost savage affection for him. Again, this was not the first time I had met a woman with an almost doglike loyalty to Maqroll.

When we went to learn the results of the tests, the doctor told us the Gaviero was out of danger. The threat of organ damage as a result of the fever was disappearing. In a few weeks he would be totally recovered. When we left the hospital, Maqroll was holding the test results in his hand. He shrugged without saying a word, tore up the papers one by one, and threw the pieces into a trash can at the entrance. I wanted to stop him but held back, thinking it would be an intrusion on the privacy he guarded so jealously. We returned to Northridge and did not speak of the matter again. We were all waiting for the Gaviero to continue the story of the mine, but no one dared ask him to. Maqroll was always extremely careful about choosing the right moment, the most favorable atmosphere for his tales, and you had to wait for those times to appear spontaneously or risk his being silent forever. The occasion arose one night when we went *outside to watch a meteor shower that filled the sky with a heart-stopping radiance. We were sitting at one end of the pool. I brought out cold beers, which we all needed to help alleviate the heat that had settled over the valley. Maqroll observed that the most impressive meteor shower he ever saw was from the deck of a ship waiting to enter the port of Al-Hudaydah, on the Red Sea. "For more than an hour the stars fell, one after the other. There was something melancholy and fatalistic in the calamity of worlds turning to dust at immeasurable distances from our petty lives, so anonymous, so full of vanity." The tone of his voice seemed to promise a return to the account of his mining days, and after a short silence, he went on with the story as if the interruption a few nights earlier had never taken place.*

*   *   *

Speaking of the Red Sea, I remember now that I never finished telling you what happened to me at the mine in the grotto. The two things are connected. You'll see why later. The shrieking parrots woke us the next morning, and we prepared coffee on a small alcohol stove that Doña Claudia had lent to Eulogio. Revived by a drink that my companion made even stronger than his compatriots did, we pushed through the ferns and began to explore the interior of the mine. We lit the Coleman and had taken only a few steps, when a sizable flock of terrified bats swooped past our heads and flew out of the grotto. An intense odor of excrement signaled the presence of animals inside the mine. We soon grew accustomed to the smell and continued farther into the gallery, where we saw a good amount of machinery, rusted beyond all recognition, and heaps of ruined tools. We began a slow, patient examination of the walls and ground, and in a few hours came upon a vein worth careful inspection. It extended some twenty meters along the intersection of the wall with the gallery floor, then abruptly ran upward until it disappeared into the roof. We had no tools with us, since we had intended only to look over the interior and determine the number of galleries. We returned to the sand that was our home and lay down. Crouching for so long in the tunnels had given me an almost intolerable backache, but I stretched out on the ground for a while and the pain disappeared. We had something to eat, drank another cup of steaming coffee, and went into the mine again, this time with the tools we would need and a second Coleman, to facilitate our taking samples. We brought these back a few hours later, but by then it was growing too dark to do the tests. "You know, Chief," said Eulogio, "this vein looks really good. Something makes me think we're in for a surprise. Hell, it's about time. After all that climbing and scratching, it's only fair we get lucky." I said he was right but I couldn't tell much about what the vein promised because I didn't know anything about that. We'd see tomorrow. We went out to the edge of the ravine to feel the breeze and forget the dense, sacristy-like atmosphere in the grotto.

The next day we tested the samples, and they turned out positive, as Eulogio had predicted. But they had to undergo a more detailed laboratory assay in the provincial capital, and if our analysis was confirmed, the mine needed to be registered with the government so that we could work it in our name. Eulogio offered to take care of these procedures with a power of attorney that I would draw up for him. "Looking the way you do, Chief, and with that passport you use to wander all around the world, you'll excuse me for saying so, but you're not the right man to deal with those people. The mine'll be in both our names, and you'll be the main partner, no doubt about that. But if you go they sure won't give you a permit, and on top of that they'll probably throw you out of the country. They're real bastards and don't trust anybody. I know what I'm talking about. They think everything's the guerrillas, and you never know what they'll do." His words were more than persuasive, and I agreed to his plan. We packed our gear, covered the mine entrance with the ferns we had displaced when we went in, and prepared to leave the next morning at first light. The warm sand under the saddle blankets formed a comfortable bed that adjusted gently to my body, and I enjoyed a wonderful, undisturbed sleep. Yet shortly before dawn I was awakened by a strange sound, as if someone far away were repeating the same word over and over again. I could not decipher what was being said until I realized the sound was caused by the wind that entered the grotto, moved along the walls, and left through the opening at the top. As it blew past the mine entrance, it produced the modulation of a word murmured very quietly at an indeterminate distance. I went back to sleep until I was awakened again, this time by the sounds of the animals as Eulogio saddled them. I washed my face in the stream. The water had a slight iron taste that reminded me of the curative thermal waters at a spa. I mentioned this to Eulogio, and he said it was because the land was very rich in minerals, which appeared to confirm his hunch about the lode we had discovered. Going back along the precipice seemed easier, although the roar of the torrential river produced the same vague, uncontrollable terror. We followed the king's road along the ridge until we reached the house that belonged to Eulogio's relatives. Doña Claudia came out to greet us with a cordiality that revealed her sense of relief at seeing us safe and sound. We ate and went to bed. Before falling asleep, the word I had heard at the mine passed through my mind, and now I could make it out with absolute clarity. It was Amirbar. Eulogio was still awake, and I told him what I had discovered. He thought for a moment and said, "Yes, that's it, more or less. But it doesn't mean anything, does it?" I replied that in Georgia it meant General of the Fleet. It came from the Arabic Al Emir Bahr, which translates as Chief of the Sea and is the origin of the word *almirante,* or admiral. A sound came from his throat, a mixture of disbelief and compassion. From then on we called the mine Amirbar. I lay awake for a long time, thinking about the enigmas posed by what we call chance, although it is no such thing; just the opposite, it is a specific order that remains hidden and shows itself only occasionally in a sign like this, which had left me feeling a dark uneasiness whose origin I could not determine.

I was back in the room above the entrance to the café, its balcony overlooking the square. Eulogio had left on the first truck heading for the capital, and I remained behind to wait for the outcome of his negotiations. A strange fever began to take hold of me, coming in waves during the day and staying at night to fill my dreams with a mad procession of recurrent, obsessive images. The poisonous delirium of the mines was manifesting its first symptoms. The other evening I said that this kind of possession isn't easy to define, for it works deep inside us and has nothing to do with the concrete desire to find great treasure. That isn't the principal motive behind it, but something more profound and confused. Gold is involved only as something we tear out of the earth, something the earth guards jealously and gives up only after an arduous struggle in which we risk our lives. It's as if we were going to hold in our hands, at least once, a tiny, cursed piece of eternity. This obsession is not comparable to the power a specific drug may have, or the fascination that gambling can hold for us. In some ways it resembles both of these, but the origins lie in deeper layers of our being, a secret ancestral source that must go back to the time we lived in caves and first discovered fire. Our life changes completely, or rather the codes we've established for living change instantly. They leave us to face their destiny elsewhere. People with whom we once had a clear, solid relationship are enveloped in the strange aura emanating from this uncontrollable, devastating fever. Even old habits that have merged with our very lives—in my case it was reading—take on another dimension. The wars of the Vendée, the nocturnal ambushes, Charette and the Marquise de la Rochejaquelein, the Blues and the Convention, Bonaparte and Cadoudal, the whole intoxicating saga that came to nothing, that not even the princes who were the reason for so many sacrifices ever recognized or appreciated—all of it appeared in an odd light, and in my mind the reasons for so much heroism faded to something unpredictable and absurd. Gradually I came to realize that I lived only in the mine, where the walls seep moisture from another world, where the deceptive gleam of the most worthless fragment of mica could carry me to the heights of delirium. Dora Estela immediately sensed the symptoms of the change in my spirit and said, point-blank, "Oh, honey, you got mine sickness. I hope you can beat it, otherwise it'll destroy you. This is just the beginning, but if it gets the upper hand you'll wind up buried in the mine shafts like a mole and they'll have to pull you out. You stay close to Eulogio, because he's pretty simpleminded and that protects him. Don't go in that cave alone, because the earth will swallow you up." Her predictions were not very reassuring. She spoke with so much conviction and such sincere distress that she succeeded in alarming me. I began to long for her brother's return. I wanted someone with me who was safe from the spell of the gold, someone whose innocence made him immune to the harmful effects of a disease that threatened to destroy the integrity of my being and the fragile safety net of my reasons for living.

Eulogio brought news that might have pushed me even deeper into the menacing whirlpool. The vein contained a significant amount of ore, and a permit had been granted to Maqroll, called the Gaviero, carrying a Cypriot passport, and to Eulogio Ventura, a native of San Miguel. The mine had been registered under the name of Amirbar. The die was cast. I told my partner about the symptoms of the affliction that had begun to torment me. I did it as directly and as simply as possible, and he understood the problem immediately. "Look, Chief," he said, "the mine's so hard-hearted she'll cure you. It's so much work to get any gold out that in the end you'll be sorry you ever started. This fever's very bad when you're lucky right away, but then it becomes easier to take. Don't think about it. The trouble is you were here alone all this time; that's what hurt you. My sister's no help. She hates the mines and is really scared of them. She got that from my mother who always says mines are the devil's work, that the devil's the only one who lives underground, right in the middle of hell. Let's just get to work and not think about it anymore. It all began when you started hearing funny words when the wind blew through the grotto. Amirbar! How the hell'd you ever come up with something crazy like that? I don't care if you are a sailor. You just tell yourself the ocean doesn't matter up here." As I had hoped, and as Dora Estela had said, Eulogio had the strange ability to pull me out of the whirling delirium that was beginning to swallow me, and bring me back to a more tolerable reality. I mentioned before that his was the power of the innocent. The Russians know a good deal about this. They view the innocent as privileged beings and think their voices must be heeded by the rest of us, who live in a confusion of ambition and avarice.

We arranged to leave early the next day. Eulogio left to take care of some matters concerning his ranch and to buy supplies, and I stayed at the café, trying to lose myself in the vicissitudes of Count d'Artois in Brittany and his undistinguished role in the action at the Vendée. Once, when she wasn't busy, the Governor came to my table, looked straight at me with the intensity of a pythoness, and said bluntly, "What you need now is to spend the night with a good woman. That'll scare away the ghosts of the mine, and you'll feel better. When we close tonight I'll come up to your room and keep you company, okay?" Her offer, made in so unexpected a way, surprised me, but I knew she was probably right. I said I'd be delighted to wait for her but that she had to be careful because her brother slept in the next room. She replied that Eulogio would be at his girlfriend's house, where he often stayed when he spent the night in San Miguel. It was past midnight when she came to my room. She undressed with a few swift, sure movements and slipped into bed with the agility of an affectionate cat. Her temperament was unusually responsive to pleasure, and her caresses had an almost curative intention: She clearly wanted them to remain etched in my memory and exercise their beneficial effect during my troubled nights at the mine. Her long, firm, peasant legs, more slender than they seemed when she moved among the tables in the café, encircled my body with movements adapted to the rhythm of a pleasure that was postponed with Alexandrian wisdom. What I received from Dora Estela that night helped me to withstand trials that could have shattered me. We barely slept, and daybreak found us in an embrace that was both a farewell and a final immersion in pleasure, an attempt to defeat the silent, erosive labor of forgetting. This was how the Governor joined the ranks of the women to whom I owe a sense of solidarity and the consoling certainty that I have a place in the memories of those who gave me the only real reason to go on living: the dazzling testimony of our senses in communion with the order of the world.

Our return to the mine had the quality of an enthusiastic start to promising work. My obsession had calmed down, just as Dora Estela said it would, shrinking to an expectation that did not go beyond the limits of the normal and the tolerable. But still, deep inside me, the germ of a disorder I had learned to fear like few other things in life was silently stirring. Our first job was to channel the stream so that the running water would wash the rock after it had been crushed in a rudimentary mill that Eulogio had bought from the family of a miner who had died years ago in a truck accident on the highway. We set up the mill and channeled the stream with the greatest patience and care so that both would operate with a minimum of interruptions. Within a week we were washing the first rock crushed in the mill. The results were better than expected. One afternoon we stood looking at the small heap of gold dust and tiny nuggets shining in the sunlight with a brilliance that kept us in hypnotized silence. Suddenly I was assailed by doubts: It was nothing but pyrite. When I asked Eulogio, he looked at me indulgently and said, "But, no, Chief, that was the first thing they tested for in the samples. If it was pyrite we would've known it then. It's gold, Chief, it's gold, and first-rate stuff." We did not have the same gratifying results every day, and we began to weigh the gold once a week, which helped avoid the brief, daily disappointments that threatened to rouse the specter of the sickness I had experienced in San Miguel. When we had enough gold to warrant a trip to the capital to sell it, Eulogio assumed the responsibility for traveling there, first taking precautions that I thought exaggerated. Then he told me about a miner—a well-known draftsman and a very talented political cartoonist—who had been killed in an ambush because he was supposedly carrying gold, although on that occasion he had almost nothing with him. The crime went unpunished, and his death was mourned by the many admirers and friends he had left behind. Eulogio also said that if they asked in San Miguel if we had struck gold, we had to deny it emphatically and claim we hadn't found anything yet and would abandon the search if things didn't improve.

In the next few weeks my companion made two or three trips to the capital. He hid the money on his farm—only he and I and his wife knew where. I thought I had entered into the routine of a miner's life with a fair degree of success and an apparently secure future. At the same time, I began to detect certain warning signs that indicated everything would change, as it always did, and I would find myself back in the uncertain labyrinth of my usual misfortunes. Sometimes I have the impression that everything that happens in my life comes from a marginal, ominous place no one else knows, a place that has always been meant only for me. I've grown so used to the idea that it seems to me I enjoy my brief moments of happiness and well-being with an intensity unknown to other mortals. Those moments restore me, they are necessary to me, and each time they occur I feel as if the world were just beginning. They're not very frequent, naturally they couldn't be, but I know they always come and are sent as compensation for my tribulations.

After one of his trips, Eulogio did not return to the mine. He was so regular in his movements and behavior that there was good reason to fear something had happened to him. And one morning, three days later, his wife appeared, tearful and panic-stricken. Between sobs she blurted out the story: Her husband had been picked up by troops in a mass arrest at a checkpoint just outside San Miguel. They had stopped more than thirty men, all of them campesinos from the area, and taken them to the capital for questioning. She had gone there to see her husband, but it had been impossible. At the barracks they threatened to arrest her too. All kinds of rumors were circulating, but nobody really knew what was going on. Dora Estela had said I should not even consider going down to San Miguel, because in these situations foreigners are the most suspect. The troops think every foreign name means an agitator, an agent with strange ideas who is conspiring against the nation. I told her to take the money we had hidden and use it to pay a lawyer, or somebody with influence, to find out what had happened to Eulogio. She shook her head several times and finally said in a strangled voice, "No, Señor, I'm not going back there. If they arrest me, who'll take care of my children and the ranch? Maybe Dora Estela's willing to go. But

not me. Those people are capable of anything. You have no idea."
But I did have an idea. On other occasions, in other places, I had
seen and personally experienced the systematic, faceless brutality
of the military. I did what I could to comfort her. She had to give
the Governor a message: Ask her please to use our money to help
her brother. She agreed without much conviction and left for the
ranch; at least half a day's travel lay ahead of her. I stopped the
mill, since I couldn't wash the rock myself, and sat at the edge of
the precipice, trying to decide what to do. I heard the thunder of
the torrential river crashing against boulders as a savage but eloquent commentary on the torpor in me produced by the news of
Eulogio's arrest. I could take no immediate steps for the reasons
stated by Dora Estela, which were very persuasive, and this made
me feel useless, frustrated, besieged—emotions as painful as they
were paralyzing. I thought of all the dreadful things that could
happen to my friend, and each was worse than the last. As I said, I
knew what an interrogation by the military can be. If they were
looking for the perpetrators of a crime or for members of the
insurgency, torture was the customary, efficient method for finding out the truth. Eulogio's difficulty in expressing himself would
give them the impression he was holding something back. The
more I thought about it, the more certain I became that Eulogio's life was in danger. Night fell, and the cold wind that began
to blow through the ravine forced me to return to the grotto. I
slept fitfully. With maddening insistence the voice of the wind at
the mine entrance repeated the word that transported me to
other regions, where, on more than one occasion, I had been in
the same kind of danger my friend faced now. "Amirbaaar, Amirbaaar," called the wind, with the persistence of someone trying to
send a message and not succeeding.

A week went by. My growing alarm produced an almost physical sense of suffocation and paralysis, bringing me to the edge of
delirium. At dawn on the eighth day, a shadow blocked the
entrance to the grotto, and I woke with a start. A tall, disheveled
woman, her face distorted by fatigue, began to speak in a hoarse,
broken voice, which I attributed to exhaustion. I couldn't make
out her features or the shape of her body, and her words came to
me from the half-light as if uttered by a sibyl in trance. "The
Governor sent me, Señor, to say she finally got Eulogio out of the
barracks. She used your money to hire a lawyer, and he gave
them proof that Eulogio's record is clean and he really is a farmer
and never did anything against the government. The trouble is

they had already tortured him a few times because he couldn't get the words out. They broke his arms and legs and something inside, because he's spitting a lot of blood and says the pains are very bad. They told her to take him away, but they wouldn't let her put him in the hospital. He's in San Miguel now. The doctor there put him in splints and is waiting to see what happens with the pains. They seem to be getting a little better. He's staying with a family he's known a long time, and right now he's not in danger. Dora Estela says to tell you that if I can help you with anything you should say so, that we're kin and she trusts me. I don't live in San Miguel; I come from higher up. I worked in a place at the top of the Guairo, where the highway is. Tomasito knows me and told me about you too. Think it over. I'm going to rest a little now. I walked the whole way without stopping, and I'm done in." I felt enormous relief at knowing they hadn't killed my friend, and a silent, impotent rage at the brutal treatment an innocent victim had received because of a speech defect. For the moment I couldn't decide what to do about the offer from Dora Estela's relative. I felt overwhelming weariness, apathy, indecisiveness: The sudden resolution of a week's unbearable tension had left me somehow empty and without strength. I told her we'd decide what to do later, and I lay down again on the warm sand. For several hours a dense sleep took me away from the scene of my misfortunes and brought me to calm, deep-blue waters off the Malabar coast. I was on a schooner, its anchor lying on the coral bottom. I was waiting for permission to go ashore from some vague official who was examining my papers on land. A great tranquillity, a sovereign indifference, allowed me to wait and feel no concern for the decision of the coastal authorities. In the event permission was denied, I was perfectly willing to leave. As I dreamed, the self that remains awake and notes every detail of our dreams was wondering where that serene impassivity along the improbable coast of the Indian Ocean came from, when my present was so filled with lurking dangers. When I woke it was past noon. The smell of food came to me like an unexpected presence, something not part of my plans. Then I remembered the early-morning visitor and the news she had brought. The woman had lit a fire at the foot of the grotto wall and was stirring a pot of stew, whose aroma indicated it contained fresh greens she had picked somewhere. The sunlight coming in at the top of the grotto shone directly on her face. She in no way resembled the person I had glimpsed in the morning shadows. Now her black hair with its bluish highlights was pulled back into a heavy knot at the nape of her neck. Her features were vaguely Indian, with high cheekbones and hollow cheeks. Her full, well-delineated lips revealed white, regular teeth that gave the impression of strength. Her dark, almond-shaped eyes had a Mongolian air because of their rather heavy lids and the line of the fold that followed the top of her cheekbones. She squatted on her heels as she tended the pot, her body communicating a sense of robust power that harmonized with the Oriental look of her face. When she stood and walked toward me, I realized she was not as tall as she had seemed earlier. Her solid limbs caused her to appear larger than she really was. She was surrounded by an aura of distance and a certain exoticism, which made it almost surprising that she spoke Spanish fluently and naturally. "I'm fixing a soup that'll give you back your strength," she said. "It has herbs and yucca and some other things I brought from Doña Claudia's garden. It'll do you a lot of good. You'll see." I thought it best to clarify from the beginning the doubts her presence had awakened in me. I asked her name and why she was offering her help and companionship when she didn't know me. The work in the mine was very hard, almost more than Eulogio and I could handle. She smiled, showing her teeth and half closing her eyes in an expression that emphasized her Asian appearance. "My name's Antonia. My parents died when I was a little girl. A flood washed them away along with everything else. My aunt and uncle had taken me to town to see the doctor because I had worms. I used to like to eat dirt. They raised me, but when I became a woman, when I was fifteen, my aunt threw me out of the house because her husband started fooling around with me. I washed dishes at the café in San Miguel, and then Dora Estela came to work there. She told me we were related, I'm not sure exactly how, and she helped me get ahead. One night a truckdriver came into my room at the back of the courtyard, where the cheap rooms are, and he sweet-talked and made promises until I let him spend the night. And so I became his girlfriend, and after a few months he took me to the Guairo Upland and got me a job. Then I found out he was married and had other women on the plain and even in the port on the coast. One day he didn't come back, but I kept on working for the owner, who took a liking to me. Maybe you know her, her name's Flor Estévez. She has a very suspicious nature, but she's a good person. Lucky for me I wasn't pregnant. I'm really scared of that. A fortune-teller in San Miguel told me once if I ever got pregnant I'd die giving birth. Dora Estela came to look for me two days ago and said I should come here and help you while Eulogio's getting better. She talked to Flor. I don't know what Dora Estela told her, but she said okay and here I am. Don't worry about the work. It can't be harder than what I had to do at Flor's. But it's up to you. Don't say yes if you don't want to, because then we'll have trouble later."

*   *   *

Before I go on, I ought to mention that this was the first time I had heard the name of Flor Estévez, that unforgettable woman who would be so important in my life, who took me in years later at The Snow of the Admiral,* the same tavern where Antonia had been working, and cured me of a sickness that was killing me. Nothing in life is gratuitous, everything is connected. It's important to know that. But we're talking now about Antonia and Amirbar, and we'd better get back to them.

*   *   *

I didn't want to make a decision yet about her offer. The soup was ready, and I wolfed it down with a voracious appetite. For several days I had eaten nothing but an occasional piece of corn bread with dried meat. The woman awakened a kind of wary reserve in me that I couldn't concretize into a clear opinion. Her Oriental features certainly had something to do with it. But I've had relations with Asian women on the Malay Peninsula, in Macao, in other places, and precisely for that reason I know they're absolutely trustworthy, and gallant in a circumspect but affectionate way. There was something in her sudden appearance, in the cautious, fearful atmosphere that had surrounded me ever since I heard about Eulogio, something, in short, that seemed to hover over her and kept me from accepting her offer. When we finished eating, she went out of the grotto to wash the pot and metal plates. I had the impression she wanted to leave me alone to consider her proposal. I finally resolved to put aside my hesitation and fear, which I attributed to my partner's brutal imprisonment, Antonia's exotic features, and the week of solitude and uncertainty I had just endured. I decided to accept the help she offered, which I needed to continue working the vein. When she came back I told her my decision. She showed no pleasure or

---

* "The Snow of the Admiral," ed. cit.

surprise, and immediately began to spread the blankets that had been Eulogio's bed and to arrange at one end some things she had brought with her in a large scarf. She placed everything farther from me than the spot my friend had occupied. She was eloquently expressing her desire to establish a tacit agreement: Ours was a working relationship and nothing more. This produced a certain tranquillity in me, and my vague fears receded to some extent.

The woman proved to be a tireless and efficient worker. I was struck by how she washed the rock that came out of the mill. Her movements were so rhythmic and exact that I had to ask if she had done the work before. She replied that a Canadian she had lived with for a while taught her how to wash river sand in a pool a little way down from Eulogio's coffee plantings. "He died of a fever he got from drinking bad guarapo liquor. He insisted on making it himself with pineapple rinds cut under a full moon. When you want to make guarapo, you have to pick the fruit at midday, and the moon has to be on the wane. Otherwise the fly eggs are still alive and give you the fever." Obviously I didn't try to discuss this strange medical theory, especially because she stated it with a conviction that left no room for argument.

In just a few weeks we amassed the same amount of ore sold by Eulogio in the capital, which had been spent to obtain his freedom. Antonia offered to go down to sell the gold. I agreed, and with her I sent a short note to the Governor asking for news of her brother and suggesting she give me more details regarding Antonia. I decided to accompany her as far as Doña Claudia's, where I wanted to leave the animals. They were a good deal of trouble and for the moment were of no use to us. I returned to the mine on foot.

Antonia carried out her mission with the greatest punctuality. I told her to give half the money to Dora Estela for safekeeping and to do whatever she liked with the other half. Antonia brought back a letter from Dora Estela and said she had left the entire sum with her. I asked why she hadn't followed my instructions, and she said her half was for Eulogio, which is what she had told the Governor. "But are you going to work for nothing?" I asked. "That doesn't seem right. You're a very good worker, and I want you to have the wages you deserve." Half closing her eyes until they were almost slits, and turning her face away, she replied, "You don't understand anything, Gaviero." It was the first time she had used the familiar *tú* with me, although I had done so with her from the very beginning. "That money belongs to Eulogio, even if he earns it with my work. They did so much for me, especially the Governor, and I won't let them go without when they need all the help they can get. They have to pay the doctor and buy medicine, and the ranch isn't making any money. Don't talk to me about salaries and stuff like that. The money's mine. Okay, I want to give it to them, and that's all there is to it. Do you get it now?" I said I did, and I couldn't help laughing at how vehemently she expressed her opinion. "It's nothing to laugh at," she declared. "All of us are screwed up, you most of all, or don't you know that either?" I couldn't find anything to say. Two things in her words had struck me: first, the sound of feminine authority kept in reserve, which I hadn't heard for many years— only my friend Ilona Grabowska used that self-assured authoritative tone with me, and it always made me feel a delighted satisfaction; then, as a result of the first, familiar address had been established between us. It hasn't been very frequent in my dealings with women, although it's not a question of any principle on my part. The *usted* form has always seemed spontaneous and natural when I talk to them, no matter what kind of relationship we have.

Dora Estela's letter reflected her unusual, colorful character. Her salutation could only make me smile.

✳   ✳   ✳

Maqroll moved his hand to the breast pocket of his shirt, carefully removed a tattered, grimy sheet of paper, and began to read:

✳   ✳   ✳

My esteemed Señor Don Gaviero:

> *Things here are becoming a little clearer, but not enough to make anybody stop worrying. We finally found out why the soldierboys pulled in poor Eulogio. It seems that down along the big river they blew up a pipeline station and two ships unloading at the terminal called Estación de los Santos. Somebody told them that the people who did it were hiding around here, and for them it's easy to round up men like cattle. Eulogio's fine. It turns out they only broke one leg and his left wrist, the other breaks are hairline and don't go all the way through the bone. He was vomiting blood but that stopped and the doctor says no organs are damaged but one of his ribs was broken and the bone punctured a lung. The poor kid asks for you all the time and he*

worries a lot about the work at the mine since he says you can't do it alone. They'll take him back to the farm next week. The family he's staying with here is hoping he'll leave soon because they don't want problems with his wife who found out one of the daughters is my brother's girlfriend. Eulogio wants me to tell you that the soldiers who questioned him asked a lot about who his partner was at the mine. He doesn't want you to worry, he said it was somebody from the coast who was just passing through and took off when they didn't find anything. They asked if you were a foreigner and he told them no and says they believed him. That wasn't what they were interested in. There's nothing for you to worry about because they found the ones who did it, they were hiding in the river port and they made them talk and that's the end of it. Sending Antonia was my idea but Eulogio didn't like it very much, he says women in mines complicate things and always bring some disaster. You can't prove it by me, I never set foot in those caves because like I already told you I'm no mole. She always lived up on the barrens and I don't think she'll give you any trouble. She's got one obsession and that's how scared she is of getting pregnant and she has her own way of dealing with that. Some men like it and others don't. I told you before that the gold curse is lifted if you're with a woman and do it with love. If you ever want to be with her just say so. Don't worry, she won't take it the wrong way. If she doesn't want to she'll tell you. She's a very good worker and stronger than a mule. I don't know what you think about my idea of sending her to you but for as long as you're up there by yourself, not doing anything and running the risk of the sickness coming back, at least you got company and can get some of the mill work done, and I think that's better. She knows how to wash sand and I bet you know by now how good she is at it. Well, that's all for now. Everybody misses you a lot and you know we're taking good care of the things you gave us to keep. Regards from everybody here and I hope things work out for you.

Sincerely,

Your friend Dora Estela

✳   ✳   ✳

The Gaviero carefully folded the sheet of paper and returned it to his shirt pocket while he explained, "I keep this because it's the only memento I have of Dora Estela and the only letter I still have that was written to me by a woman. I've had to destroy the others when they might have compromised someone if they'd fallen into the wrong hands." He poured himself another beer, remarked that it was unforgivable that the United States had not yet been able to produce a beer like the Danish one we were drinking, and continued his story.

* * *

Getting back to Antonia, I can tell you that she adjusted perfectly to my work routine and my frugal way of life with its long silences and hours of reading, which helped me escape the oppressive atmosphere of the tunnels. I would dig out chunks of the lode with a pick and pile them in a sack. When it was full, Antonia dragged it out and started up the small, rudimentary Pelton wheel, which was powered by the waterfall and turned the mill. From time to time she would go down to the village and bring back provisions and news of Eulogio, whose recovery was very slow. The loss of blood had weakened him considerably, and his rib refused to set and still interfered with his breathing. Conversation with Antonia always focused on details relating to our work, and she never interrupted me when I sat outside the grotto, leaning against the precipice wall to think about episodes from my past and the people I've known during my contrary, nomadic life. I didn't like to spend much time in the grotto. Its atmosphere was saturated with a vague esoteric quality that I found disturbing. As I've said, I liked it only for sleeping, because of the soft, warm sand and the soothing murmur of the waterfall. Something told me that everything could not remain within the confines of a normality that so resembled what I've always rejected as an egregious prelude to death: I mean days flowing by in regular channels, skirting anything unforeseen. Our method of working the lode was so primitive that it barely produced the gold needed to pay my partner's medical expenses and to set aside enough for me to leave the country in an emergency and search for other horizons; as far as I was concerned, these would always be on the sea. For a long time I had dreamed of buying a schooner and carrying cargo between the island of Fernando de Noronha and the coast of Pernambuco. The gratifying possibilities for high profits in this trade had been suggested by a friend of mine, an Egyptian Jew named Waba, who was endlessly resourceful in devising ways to make money without suffering too many hardships. Navigation in that area was calm most of the year, and the prospect of carrying needed supplies to the island, for which the residents were willing to pay extremely high prices, was very promising. I spent hours at the edge of the gorge, making plans and plotting routes in my mind, while flocks of dazzling birds flew out of the hardy dwarf vegetation, their calls resonating between the vertical rock walls with an ominous, melancholy echo.

In the corner of my mind that always sent out warnings of an imminent fall into gray, uneventful routine, there were vague hints of change. As always, it made its first appearance behind the deceptively innocent mask of a predictable, normal event. One night, when I found it difficult to sleep because of the persistent backache that invariably resulted if I had to dig steadily at the vein in an awkward position, Antonia walked over and asked what was wrong. I told her, and she offered to rub the painful area with the palm oil she used for cooking. I agreed, and she began to massage my back and waist with a deep circular motion that brought immediate relief. I asked her where she had learned to do massage, and she said the aunt who had raised her was a bonesetter and knew a great deal about such things. We continued talking and she continued rubbing my body until I realized that this was no longer a massage but a series of intense caresses with a different purpose. I started to undress her slowly, and when we were both naked we began to kiss, not saying a word, becoming more and more aroused. When I was on top of her and ready to penetrate, Antonia turned over abruptly and lay facedown. "Like this, I want it like this," she said. "Go ahead, I'm used to it. I like it this way. I don't have to worry about getting pregnant." I entered her with no great difficulty and realized it was true: She had learned to enjoy a position that presented no risk. As we finished, she gave a series of brief cries that echoed along the grotto walls and blended with the voice of the wind at the mine entrance. It was a strange effect, and I found it very exciting. Her "ay"s alternated with the "Amirbaaar" articulated by the wind with hallucinatory precision.

This embrace with no issue, *contra natura*, became a daily ceremony. On certain evenings, when the wind began to let its voice be heard at the mine entrance as it called for the General of the Seas, desire also began to press with the slow, deliberate pulsing of my blood. Antonia in no way changed the rhythm of her work or the tenor of her normal relations with me, as if what we did at night had no existence in the reality of each day. I often thought of the Governor's sibyline allusion, which I had not understood at the time: ". . . and she has her own way of dealing with that. Some men like it and others don't." This was how the character of the mine changed for me, taking on even more of the ritual, abstruse air that had affected me from the start. My relations with Antonia, marked by the aberrant nature of our embrace, became confused in my mind with the mythic atmosphere of the place. It was like a rite, necessary for invoking hidden forces in the depths of the wind as it whirled through the grotto summoning the Emir of the Sea, and performed amid Antonia's brief cries when her pleasure climaxed. The other, purely real and practical aspect of our relationship, which consisted of taking gold from the seam, merged with the first until it too became part of the ritual of a faceless cult, a blind mystery in which finding gold and sodomizing a female were the way to participate in a single ceremony.

On one occasion, Antonia went to the capital to sell the gold we had accumulated, and took longer than usual to return. They were four days of tension and anxiety, when I completely lost control of myself. The voice of the mine could be heard at night with such clarity that I finally began to answer it. A sharp, almost painful desire tormented my imagination as well as my body, until I thought Antonia had been an invention of my fantasy to fill the solitude of the grotto. On the last night before her return, the voice I always heard woke me, and it seemed to be calling for Amirbar with greater urgency, with a new longing that made me think of Persephone wandering Hades. That was when I raised a prayer to Amirbar in an effort to placate him. Something in the depths of my being told me that my long absence was not viewed favorably by the unfathomable powers of the sea. I still remember this supplication, and I'll say it for you because it forms an essential part of the time I spent in the mines. It goes like this:

> Amirbar, I am here scratching at the entrails of the earth like one seeking the mirror of transformations,
>
> I am here, far from you, and your voice is like a summons to the order of the great salt waters,
>
> the unreserved truth that accompanies a ship's wake and never abandons it.

In the name of the vessels that sink their prows into the abyss and then surface and repeat the ordeal over and over again

and at last, with a shifting cargo pounding in their holds, sail wounded into the calm that follows the storm;

in the name of the knot of terror and fatigue rising in the throat of the machinist whose only knowledge of the sea is its blind assault on the sorrowfully creaking sides;

in the name of the song of the wind in the rigging of the derricks;

in the name of the vast silence of constellations marking the route that the compass repeats with meticulous insistence;

in the name of the men on third watch who murmur songs of forgetting and sorrow to keep back sleep;

in the name of the curlews flying away from the coast in closed formation and calling to console their young as they wait on the cliffs;

in the name of the endless hours of heat and tedium that I suffered in the Gulf of Martaban as we waited to be towed by a coast guard cutter because our magnetos had burned out;

in the name of the silence that reigns when the captain says his prayers and bows in contrition toward Mecca;

in the name of the lookout I once was when I was still a boy, searching for islands that never appeared,

announcing schools of fish that always escaped with an abrupt change of direction,

weeping for my first love, whom I never saw again,

enduring the bestial jokes of sailors in all the world's languages;

in the name of my loyalty to the unwritten code imposed by the routine of a voyage regardless of the climate or the ship's prestige;

in the name of all those who are no longer with us;

in the name of those who sank to resigned graves and lie with coral and fish whose eyes have disappeared;

in the name of those swept away by the waves and never seen again;

in the name of the man who lost his hand trying to attach a mooring line to the shrouds;

in the name of the man who dreams of another man's woman while he paints minium on a rusting hull;

in the name of those who sailed for Seward, in Alaska, where a drifting iceberg sent them to the bottom of the sea;

in the name of my friend Abdul Bashur, who spent his life dreaming of ships while none of the ships he owned ever lived up to his dreams;

in the name of the man at the top of the lateen yard who checks the insulators and talks and laughs with the seagulls and suggests preposterous routes to them;

in the name of the man who takes care of the ship and sleeps alone on board as he waits for the magistrates in their robes to lift the embargo;

in the name of the man who confessed to me one day that on land he thought only of savage, gratuitous crimes, and at sea a longing was awakened in him to do good to others and forgive their offenses;

in the name of the man who nailed to the stern the last letter of his ship's new name: Czesznyaw;

in the name of the man who insisted that women are better sailors than men but have zealously hidden the fact since the beginning of time;

in the name of those who whisper the names of mountains and valleys in their hammocks and don't recognize them when they are back on land;

in the name of the ships that are making their final voyage and don't know it but whose timbers creak pitifully;

in the name of the sailing ship that entered Withorn Inlet and could never leave and remained anchored there forever;

in the name of Captain von Choltitz, who kept my friend the painter Alejandro drunk for a week on a mixture of beer and champagne;

in the name of the man who knew he had been infected with leprosy and threw himself from the deck into the propellers;

in the name of the man who cried, whenever he got drunk enough to collapse onto a filthy tavern floor, "I'm not from around here and I don't look like anybody else!"

in the name of those who never knew my name and shared hours of terror with me as we drifted into the shoals of the Penland Strait and were saved by a gust of wind;

in the name of those now at sea;

in the name of those who sail tomorrow;

in the name of those coming into port now, who don't know what awaits them;

in the name of those who have lived, suffered, wept, sung, loved, and died at sea;

in the name of all this, Amirbar, calm your anger and do not rage against me.

See where I am, in pity move away from the fateful course of my days, let me succeed in this dark enterprise.

I will soon return to your domain, I will once again obey your commands. Al Emir Bahr, Amirbar, Admiral, may your voice bring me good fortune.

Amen.

We were silent for a moment when Maqroll finished his invocation. It was so profoundly of the sea that we felt alien and distant from the world that had truly been his, that would be his to the end of his days. The words of this fierce prayer made us realize that the Gaviero's passage through the subterranean world of the mines had been a kind of self-imposed punishment intended to expiate some obscure failure, some shortcoming in his work as a sailor. No one, of course, had the courage to say anything to him about it, and he went on with his story as if we were not present.

* * *

Antonia arrived very early the next morning. She had walked all night, not even stopping at Doña Claudia's house. She explained her delay only after sleeping for several hours, her slumber shaken by sudden flinching and words whose meaning I could not unravel. Antonia had sold the ore in the capital with no problem, but her luck changed on the drive back in Saturio's "Andean Hurricane." The *chiva* was stopped at an army checkpoint. The ten passengers, who were half asleep, were obliged to get out of the truck and submit to a thorough search. The money Antonia had with her was taken by a sergeant who did not believe it had come from the sale of livestock belonging to some relatives of hers. She had made up the lie on the spot, and it was difficult to sustain. A short while later they released the *chiva* but refused to return the money to Antonia. She returned to San Miguel but left again the next day for the capital in an effort to get back the money that had been taken from her. The Governor tried to dissuade her, insisting that her alibi was dangerously weak. What would she say when they asked who her relatives were and who had bought the cattle? Antonia ignored Dora Estela's arguments, went to the barracks, and with wiles it was prudent not to ask about she persuaded a captain to have the money returned. She came back to San Miguel, determined to leave for the mine right away even if it meant walking all night. "I imagined how you must be having doubts about me, and that hurt so much I decided to get here as soon as I could." I replied that I never had any doubts at all about her loyalty and the only thing I feared was that she had met with an accident, especially when crossing the pass. The path was collapsing and had become extremely dangerous. She looked at me with that expression of distant reserve which her Malaysian features made even more opaque and hermetic. Something about Antonia had begun to disturb me, but I wasn't quite sure what it was. The intimacy of our relations, marked by the physical displacement of the usual seat of pleasure, created in her an attitude of abject submissiveness, of almost animal attachment, which was expressed very clearly in the way she worked at the mill. She even offered to dig the rock out of the seam in order to spare me the painful back spasms that were becoming more frequent. I didn't allow her to, although she already had demonstrated an apparently unbreakable stamina. She continued to insist that no part of our profits should be set aside for her, and became increasingly concerned about what I planned to do when the lode ran out. "I have a feeling you're not going to stay around here even for a day," she said with a touch of sadness. "You don't look like the kind who settles down anywhere. What you really are is a tramp. You're hopeless." I never tried to dissuade her from the idea she had of me: For the most part, it was fairly accurate. But the demand contained in her observations grew sharper, until it changed into anguish tinged with a certain rancor. I felt I had to discuss this with Dora Estela, who might be able to help me, given her independent character and our clear-cut friendship, free of all ties except open, solid affection.

The opportunity presented itself sooner than I expected. One morning the teeth broke on a wooden gear in the mill, due no doubt to our overworking the primitive mechanism. I had to take it to San Miguel, where a Syrian carpenter I had met in the café, who repaired the wooden bodies on the *chivas,* could duplicate it on his lathe, using the same kind of guaiacum wood. I started out at dawn. Antonia would stay at the mine, although she accompanied me a good part of the way along the precipice. She was silent and suspicious, as if she had guessed my intention to talk about us with her friend. She embraced me without saying a word, clinging passionately to my body, and then walked away and did not look back.

It would take at least two days to replicate the gear. I rented my usual room and settled in at my customary table. The Governor sensed that I wanted to talk about Antonia, and on the night I arrived she said as much in her absolutely straightforward way. "Something's eating you, and it's got to do with Antonia. What's going on?" she asked as she added up the checks for her tables on a little pad she always carried with her. I didn't answer right away, waiting for her to finish. "Talk to me," she said. "I'll do my figuring, but I'm listening." I told her, trying to minimize its importance: Antonia was becoming more and more attached to me, and I certainly had no intention of establishing a permanent relationship with her. Not even the mine could keep me in this country for very long. I didn't want to hurt her with an outright rejection, but at the same time I couldn't disclose certain unchangeable quirks in my character and fate: Antonia's sensibilities and background would not permit her to accept them without feeling rebuffed. "First of all," said Dora Estela, "I don't think the problem's got to do with Antonia not making love like other people. I believe her when she says she likes doing it from behind. It was okay with you from the start, so that's not the trouble, but what's happening is that she's in love with you, and that's real tricky because it's never happened to her before. I understand her because the same thing happened to me right after you came here, but I'm not wet behind the ears and I knew how to stop myself in time. The bad thing is that Antonia's with you day and night in that cave, and I don't think she can get free. It's a shame, but Eulogio still needs a couple more months and I don't think this can wait that long. Ah, Gaviero! I have the feeling things like this must happen to you a lot. No woman really believes in feet that itch as much as yours do. Antonia's got a terrible temper, and she doesn't play games. Remember, she's a mountain woman and life's been hard on her."

We turned the problem over and over but could not find a way out. It was to be expected: Feelings have never been controlled or understood by reason. Late the following night, the carpenter sent a message that the gear was ready. I went to pick it up. It was amazingly like the original, and the careful finishing was admirable. I returned to the café, which was almost empty, and the Governor sat down with me. She came straight to the point. "The only thing to do is talk to Antonia in an honest way and make her see she can't expect more from you than what she's got now. Don't you do it; that'll only hurt her and make things worse. The next time she comes to sell the gold I'll talk to her myself. We'll see what happens. You never can tell what women'll do. I hope she doesn't get mad at me: Then we'll really be in trouble, because she won't be thinking straight." It seemed the only sensible solution; after my discussions with the Governor, the problem had acquired more precise and complex proportions than I originally had attributed to it. I set out for the mine, and Antonia was waiting for me on the trail along the pass. Her face was closed and secretive, but she seemed affectionate and talkative, as if she wanted to push away any dark premonitions that may have tormented her during my absence. She helped me install the new gear with such surprising dexterity that it occurred to me again that some remote Asian ancestors had imparted the mixture of patience and skill so foreign to her compatriots. She gathered aromatic herbs on the slopes for a stew of potatoes, yucca, and other bland roots, whose flavor was improved considerably by the seasonings Antonia added to them. That night, after making love twice with more feverish intensity than usual, she whispered in my ear before going back to her bed, "Sometimes I think I could have a baby with you. But who knows. You'd go away just the same and leave me with the kid. Good night, you bum." Her words haunted my sleep and disturbed me in a way I could not define.

We worked very hard for several weeks. The vein was petering out and showed increasing structural differences from the previous sections. We had to take maximum advantage of the rock processed in the mill. Each day we took out more mica and less gold. A sure sign, according to my manuals, that the lode was changing. Curiously enough, this coincided with the point at which it disappeared into the roof. It was necessary to find another seam, and we began digging farther back in the gallery, with no result. The time came for Antonia to leave for the capital to sell the gold. We didn't have much, but even so it was not advisable to keep any at the mine, although no one had come into the area yet. Antonia showed a certain reluctance to make the trip, as if she sensed that some imprecise calamity was waiting for her down below. I did not want to pressure her in any way, because that would increase her apprehension. One night, as if she had come to a decision that had been difficult for her to accept, she spoke to me from her bed just as I was about to fall asleep. "I'm going to the city tomorrow to sell the gold. It can't wait anymore." I heard her turn to the grotto wall and fall asleep, the rhythm of her regular breathing broken from time to time by the deep sighs of a child. And she left at dawn, looking like the victim who offers herself up for sacrifice with a resignation that cancels all hope. Three days later she was back. Her face showed no change. She began immediately to mill the rock I had taken out during her absence. "It's ending," she said after a while, with a thin smile that lent a certain ambiguity to her words, "and if we don't find another vein we can say goodbye to Amirbar." That night she was obliging and affectionate, but after her usual cries at the climax, I heard her choking back the sobs that rose suddenly in her throat.

The vein, in fact, had run out of ore, and there was no point in digging any further to follow it: That would have meant too great an effort for just the two of us, especially with the tools we had at our disposal. And unless another vein surfaced unexpectedly, as the first seam had, searching for one would also entail more work than we could handle. Antonia proposed a temporary solution that seemed very sensible: We could wash sand from the river a little below the pass, on the tiny beaches where the Canadian had tried his luck and enjoyed some success. And we did. You had to take the path along the edge of the gorge until the end of the ravine, and then the king's road, which descended until it ran parallel to the river. You followed the riverbed, making your way through dense growth, half-wild fruit trees for the most part. It took an hour and a half to travel from the mine to this spot. The road was good, and only the section along the cliffs, which was crumbling before our eyes, presented any danger. The return was more difficult and sometimes took almost three hours. Washing sand to separate out the gold is an intriguing process. The gleam of metal appears gradually, and it often seems as if the sand itself were changing into the golden miracle that contains all the light of the sun. When the gold is almost completely washed, it is mixed with mercury, which isolates and then binds with it. The mercury is passed through a fine chamois, and the gold remains in a pure state. The sand was rich in precious ore because the water runs over many sites where lodes cross the riverbed; these erode, and the current carries away the gold. Antonia washed the sand with such dexterity and skill that in the end she panned more than twice as much gold as I did. Some nights, when the weather was clear and there was no threat of rain, we would sleep on the riverbank. We brought down supplies, a Coleman lamp, and a container of fuel for the lantern. Sometimes we stayed for two or three nights without going back up to the mine. Washing river sand at night in the light of the Coleman is fascinating work, and the murmur of water against the rocks was a much more pleasing and peaceful sound than the voice of the mine endlessly calling for the General of the Sea. My invocation to placate his intemperate whims was not necessary there. The days passed, and Antonia made no allusion at all to what she had surely discussed with the Governor. I felt uneasy. The signs of her suffering were becoming clearer and more frequent. Again we had amassed enough gold to justify a trip to the capital. I mentioned it to her one night when we had made love on the riverbank, and Antonia's eyes filled with tears. I asked what was wrong, and her reply was a brusque shake of the head. I repeated the question, and she answered, her voice broken by sobs, "If I go now you can bet I won't find you when I get back. Dora Estela said you wanted to leave, that I have to accept losing you because you never stay in one place very long." I said I would never do anything like leaving without saying goodbye, and I insisted over and over again that I had always been a drifter and it made no sense to think about changing my destiny now. When I did go, I would take her memory with me and keep it always. I thought she was an extraordinary woman, and the unabashed power of her beauty had given me one of the fullest, most exciting experiences of my life. None of this was what she wanted to hear. But I thought it more loyal and honest to tell her what I felt about her and what she meant to me, even though I knew I was causing her a disappointment that was hard to bear. We continued talking, and as my words poured out, she sank into the sullen silence of a wounded animal. When I fell asleep beside her on the blankets we had arranged into one bed, her sobs had become almost inaudible.

I was suddenly awakened by an intense smell of kerosene and the feeling of cold liquid running down my back. I sat up immediately and saw a white form trying without success to light one match after the other. I threw myself into the water just as a spark set fire to the blankets and a good part of the sand. I swam toward shore as Antonia disappeared into the trees, screaming like a madwoman. "I would've had a baby with you, you bastard!" she shrieked, the sound of her voice moving away into the dense woods. "Die, you animal! If you don't have a home you can live in hell!" She ran away, convinced I was in the flames. When I climbed out of the river, the first light of dawn was just breaking. I tried to dry myself with some rags that hadn't burned. I set out for the mine, not really knowing what I was going to do. All I had left were the clothes I had slept in: an undershirt and shorts. My boots were singed, but I could still wear them, although the laces had burned. This made the climb very difficult. When I reached the grotto, I collapsed on the sand. That was when I understood the full significance of what had happened. I had almost been killed in the fire that was still burning when I left the river. The woman had poured the contents of the fuel can, which was full, around the bed and directly on my body lying under the blankets. If the first match had caught fire, I would not be here to tell this story. Her hands were wet with kerosene, which interfered with her lighting the match, and that saved me. Among the items we had left at the mine were a change of clothes and another pair of laces for my boots. Antonia had taken the gold.

I had no choice but to go back to San Miguel, pick up my share of the money from Dora Estela, and leave the region and the tale of gold that had turned into a kind of implacable curse. I hid the tools and some of the mill parts in the gallery and left the grotto, intending to spend the night at Doña Claudia's and continue on to San Miguel the next day. Night was falling when I reached the farm. As I lifted the crossbars at the entrance, a shape emerged from among the trees that formed a kind of fence. It was Doña Claudia, who had been waiting for me. Before I could ask how she knew I was coming, she began to speak in a voice filled with anguish and grief. "That lunatic came by here at dawn, ranting and raving and saying you had died in the flames. It wasn't easy to understand her, but she seemed to be saying she set the fire. That's not the problem, though. The troops came by here this afternoon, and a lieutenant questioned us a long time, me and the owners of the farm, about the mine in the pass and the foreigner who was hiding out there and pretending to be a prospector. They'd just been to see Eulogio and he denied everything, and they beat him again but couldn't make him talk. They're tearing all around here, and I can't believe you didn't run into them. Maybe they're searching upriver before they go to the mine. I've been waiting here awhile in case somebody came by with news about you, because Antonia was so crazy we couldn't get anything straight. Keep out of sight and wait for me here. I'll bring you something to eat, then you better go back along the king's road and stay out of San Miguel. Farther down it crosses the highway, and you can hitch a ride there with somebody and get as far away from here as you can. If those people find you they'll kill you. They never bother to take foreigners to the capital; they break them right on the spot. Don't move from here; just wait for me behind these bushes. It's a miracle you came by here, Chief, a real miracle." And she walked to the house, muttering words I couldn't make out. I hid behind the hedges she had pointed to and began to consider my fate. Once again I had ended up with nothing but the clothes on my back, and the forces of law and order hunting me down without my really knowing why. With luck I could get a message to the Governor and she'd send me some money so I could get out of the country and try my luck somewhere else, but never again, obviously, in a gold mine. Doña Claudia soon returned with a small pot of soup and some corn bread. She also brought me a raw wool poncho and a straw hat, to protect me from the elements and to make me look a little less like a foreigner. Before I left I asked her to try to reach Dora Estela and tell her I'd let her know where I was and to wait until she heard from me.

I walked all night under a sky so brilliant with stars it cast a tenuous light on the road, and so close I felt as if the constellations I had learned to recognize when I was a lookout were accompanying me. The king's road intersected the highway and then continued on its impeccable way, climbing along mountains and ravines, sheltered from time and all its devastation. Several vehicles drove past, but I didn't dare stop any of them. They were private cars, and my appearance could not have been very reassuring. Then a few large trucks carrying freight passed by, but I already knew they never stopped, because the drivers were forbidden to pick up passengers. Two army trucks approached, carrying soldiers who were nodding with fatigue. I saw them in the distance and hid in a viaduct along the highway. When I had lost all hope and had decided to walk until I found a nearby settlement, along came "Maciste," with Tomasito at the wheel, smiling with his perennial air of a man who has just played a trick on someone. Luck had finally come my way. I climbed up beside my friend, and he supplied more details concerning the story Doña Claudia had told me. Antonia came to San Miguel and had to be taken to the mental hospital in the capital that same day. She was raving, flying into rages and attacking people, and she didn't recognize anyone. Antonia even tried to slash the Governor with a broken bottle. Luckily, they stopped her in time. San Miguel was full of troops, and they were questioning everybody. Two more stations along the pipeline had been blown up, and the guerrillas were rampaging through the mountains. They had looked for me at the café and questioned Dora Estela for several hours but didn't torture her. She told them only part of the truth: that she had met me at the café and her brother had given me information about gold mines in the area.

I told Tomasito that I planned to head for the coast, and he promised to help me find the best way to get out of the region and not cross paths with the army. I had been incredibly lucky, he added, to run into him along this stretch of highway, because he almost never used it. His usual route was from San Miguel to the capital. But this time he had a load of coffee beans for the mill in the river port, which is why he was going in that direction. When we reached the port, Tomasito found safe lodgings with people he trusted. He could not have chosen a more unlikely place—a small house on the river, where a widow of a certain age arranged assignations for women who wanted to earn a little money with absolute discretion and secrecy. Almost all of them were married women or widows supplementing their household budgets. The landlady owed Tomasito a few favors and could not refuse his request to take me in for just a couple of days until a few matters could be arranged. It took somewhat longer than the owner of "Maciste" predicted. I stayed out of sight in a back room overlooking an empty lot that ran down to the river. Day and night I

heard the conversations of transient guests and beds creaking
under the weight of couples whose cries reminded me of my
nights at Amirbar.

One morning someone knocked at the door of my room, and
I assumed it was the landlady, but when I opened the door there
stood Dora Estela, who looked at me in astonishment, as if I were
a ghost. She embraced me warmly, her eyes filling with tears. It
was the first time I had seen her like this. "It's a miracle you got
out, Gaviero. When I think it was all my fault, that I sent that
crazy woman to the mine. But who ever thought she'd be capable of something so horrible," she said, wiping her eyes with the
ends of a large scarf that was tied around her head and made her
look like a domesticated Fury. Then she told me about Antonia's
arrival in the village and how she had attacked her in the café.
She was saying things that made no sense, and then she picked up
a beer bottle from a table, broke it against the metal edge, and
went after her, waving the deadly jagged glass. They stopped her
in time, tied her hands, and took her away. They put her on the
first truck heading for the capital, and she was locked away in the
asylum. Antonia had not spoken again; she had withdrawn into
unmoving silence, and it didn't seem likely she would ever come
out of it. I asked about Eulogio, and Dora Estela told me that this
new beating by the soldierboys had almost killed him. He was
recovering very slowly. The problem was who would take care of
his farm and livestock. She couldn't; she didn't know anything
about it. Then she took a roll of bills from the bosom of her dress
and handed it to me, saying it was my share of the gold that
Antonia had sold on her trips to the city. The gold she had taken
with her when she tried to kill me had been confiscated in the
asylum to help pay the cost of her hospitalization. I asked how
much she was giving me. I didn't feel like counting money. It was
a respectable amount and would have bought a schooner to make
the run between San Fernando de Noronha and Pernambuco,
but I couldn't spend money that had brought so much misfortune. I took only what I needed to buy passage on the first ship
out of the closest seaport. I told Dora Estela that the rest was for
Eulogio's family while he was recovering, and for her too, in case
she needed anything for her son. The Governor sat looking at me
with her sibylline scowl that masked an unexpected sensibility.
Then she told me how I'd make my escape. She had driven in
with Tomasito, whose message was that he would come for me
the following week and take me in "Maciste" to a city near the

coast. A friend of his, a truckdriver, would get me to the port. I had to use another name—they had chosen Daniel Amirbar—and say I was part owner of the truck I was driving in. The name was surely Dora Estela's idea. I asked if it was, and she smiled and said yes. We continued talking, recalling episodes in our friendship, until there was another knock at the door. It was Tomasito, who was in a jubilant mood despite the hellish heat that prevailed in the river port and was even worse in my room, which received the full brunt of the afternoon sun. He had come to tell Dora Estela he wouldn't be leaving until the next day, because he had to wait for the launch that was carrying cargo for San Miguel. He looked at her steadily and commented, "Finding a place to stay won't be a problem, Dorita. I don't think the Gaviero will refuse you hospitality for one night."

We slept together, and on that night of farewell to my days as a miner, I embraced the Governor's firm body with the joyful despair of the vanquished who know that our only victory is the triumph of the senses on the ephemeral but true field of pleasure. When I woke the next day, Dora Estela had gone. Like me, she did not enjoy goodbyes. She had protected my sleep with feline care. One more reason for me to be grateful. I spent the days that followed waiting for Tomasito. From time to time the landlady came to chat with me. Her parents were Lebanese, and her husband was also from Beirut. As a girl she had learned a few words of Arabic, which allowed her to communicate with her husband, who had never learned to speak Spanish very well. When he developed heart disease and could no longer earn a living selling trinkets door to door, he was the one who suggested inviting a few of her friends to the house to meet men who were passing through the port city and wanted to spend a nice time there. The secret of her success was that she maintained strict confidentiality and dealt only with men from out of town. Tomasito and other drivers who were friends of hers, and two or three riverboat captains, were her loyal intermediaries, whom she rewarded by offering them the attractive first fruits that appeared from time to time among her female clientele. The woman's stories were fascinating, intertwined according to the delicious Oriental tradition of *The Thousand and One Nights.* She was always amazed at my knowledge not only of her parents' country but of many other places in the Mediterranean that she had heard about as a girl and during her married life. When I told her, for instance, that I carried a Cypriot passport, her enthusiastic response was, "How curious! I have a cousin in Limassol who's named Farida, like me. She's married to a tugboat captain and still writes to me once in a while." I remembered the tugs in that port, always making ships wait, their captains always haggling over fees with the most specious, senseless arguments, and the smell of the Limassol waterfront and its Greek taverns, all with the same dull, monotonous bouzouki music. I almost told her how I obtained my famous passport from a presumptive lawyer in Nicosia, but decided not to cause poor Farida more worry than she already had reason to feel because of my presence in her house. During one of our nocturnal conversations, she offered to introduce me to the wife of the secretary of the customhouse, a very attractive blonde who apparently spoke French. I thanked her but said I didn't have the heart for blind dates. "That's too bad," she said. "A woman always makes you forget your troubles. There's no better cure, I'm telling you." Her words reminded me of my friend the Governor and the old, proven confidence of Levantines in the curative powers of eroticism regardless of the means employed to enjoy it. In Limassol, to be precise, the traffic in young boys from the island was the most common activity in the waterfront taverns. Many a Scandinavian officer paid the price of his own ingenuousness when dawn broke and he found himself naked and tied to a post on the docks.

Tomasito came for me at nightfall on the following Saturday, a day when there was a good deal of traffic and the trip would be safer. We left after dark, having said goodbye to Farida, who told me in Cassandra-like tones, "We'll never see you here again, Gaviero. This isn't the country for you, and if you come back you won't get out alive. I'm telling you." Her words sometimes return to me, like a message I've never deciphered. In any case, returning strikes me as something unthinkable and menacing. The drive in "Maciste" took almost the whole night. We crossed great expanses of rice paddies and sugarcane fields, in heat not even the movement of the truck made bearable. I was lying on sacks of coffee beans that gave off a civilized, delicious aroma. I slept very little, not for fear of the danger that might be waiting for me but because of the smell. It reminded me of my days in Hamburg, in Amsterdam, in Antwerp, days dominated by the aroma of the coffee we drank along canals filled with dark, sleepy water that reflected the bell towers of old Reformation churches and the facades of houses inhabited by a diligent bourgeoisie who carefully nurture the deliberate, mean-spirited hypocrisy of their convictions. A little before dawn we reached the city where Tomasito's friend would meet me and drive to the port on the Pacific. It was one of those typical towns in sugar-growing regions, a place you passed through, a crossroads full of cafés with billiard tables and noisy brothels where bands played all night, a place where nobody ever seems to sleep. The big trucks line up outside the cafés, and the roar of their motors joins the chorus of billiard balls, record players at top volume, and bottles clattering on enameled tin tables: an ear-shattering din that people confuse with happiness. Tomasito went to deliver his cargo, and I waited for him in a place whose name could not have been more of an anomaly: Café Windsor. The beer was still that same liquid with the thin head and the taste that created a kind of nauseating paralysis in the stomach. The rum, on the other hand, was one of the best I've ever tasted in my life, much of it spent in the Caribbean, which I think gives me authority to judge the rum I drank in the Windsor with a good deal of ice and nothing else. A warm, slow wave of well-being washed over me, and the memory of all my misfortunes disappeared as if by magic. By the time Tomasito arrived, I had made the acquaintance of two men, and we were playing a game of billiards that I was losing but enjoying immensely. Tomasito knew my companions, whose professions turned out to be both imprecise and far removed from the penal code. We had understood one another so well that they revealed more than one compromising secret to me. We finished our game, and Tomasito ordered something to eat for all of us. They brought mojarra with rice and fried plantain. I had not eaten fish for so long that the mojarra tasted marvelous. We were on our third bottle of rum, and I was already considering the possibility of joining my new friends in a deal involving contraband fabrics and electrical appliances, which would make us a fortune, when the driver who was taking me to the port came in. He would be leaving in a few minutes and was in a hurry. I said goodbye to the billiard players, we promised to see each other in the port if I didn't find a ship right away, and Tomasito, the driver, and I headed for the truck. The army had set up a checkpoint at the corner and were asking to see everyone's papers. With the greatest casualness, Tomasito suddenly turned into the doorway of a building, and the driver and I followed close behind. My friend crossed a courtyard filled with geraniums and then continued through a yard whose door opened onto another street. It all happened so quickly and naturally that a woman hanging clothes in the courtyard didn't even turn to look at us. We went out the door and found ourselves on a quiet street with buildings like the one we had just walked through, and after two more blocks we came to the warehouse of a customs agency; the truck was parked at the entrance. Tomasito gave me a warm embrace, not saying a word. The driver and I climbed into the cab, and I was struck by its comfort and luxury. Before the truck pulled away, Tomasito walked over to my door, patted me on the arm, and said in a voice clearly filled with controlled emotion, "Good luck, Gaviero, lots of luck. You'll need it." Our encounter with the army and our masterful escape thanks to his sangfroid had brought me back to reality. The strong, aromatic rum, my billiard companions, their chimerical, illegal plans—it all seemed to belong to some vague past. The driver turned out to be a man of few words. I don't know if he really was, or if Tomasito had asked him to maintain a certain reserve with me. We drove almost the entire day. First the highway climbed to the highest part of a mountain chain that ran parallel to the coast, and then it made an abrupt descent to the port. The driver stopped the truck on a deserted street and handed me a piece of paper on which "Travelers Hotel, Mr. Lange" was written in pencil. I was to show the paper to this person, who would take care of putting me up. The hotel was on the docks, just a few steps from where he had parked the truck.

Few things in the world are more similar than waterfront hotels: the same smell of cheap soap in the rooms, the same lobby with furniture of an indefinite color, the same owner, a native of *Mitteleuropa,* who speaks the same thirty indispensable words in every language. When I handed the piece of paper to "Mr. Lange," he looked up for a moment with a sly glance that attempted to scrutinize me without my noticing it. For some reason I spoke to him in the dialect of Gdynia, and he responded in kind with the greatest naturalness. He went upstairs with me, pointed out my room, and as he handed over the key he said, not looking me in the face, "Please don't use the phone or talk to strangers. I'll take care of your passage on the next boat out. It's the *Luther,* bound for La Rochelle, with stops in Panama City, Havana, and the Bermudas. You tell me where you want to get off." I didn't ask about the strange prohibition against using the phone, because I didn't want to hear his evasive reply to my question. I said I would go to La Rochelle and preferred to travel third class or in a hammock with the crew. A pale smile, as imprecise as his gaze, appeared for an instant on his lips and then vanished immediately. "We'll see," he mumbled. "We'll see." I locked the door with the key and lay down on the bed. The faded lilac spread, the unsettling gray of the sheets, were so familiar that I almost found them touching.

So there I was, for the thousandth time, in an anonymous room in an equally anonymous hotel in a port whose smells and sounds, whose ships' horns requesting a tug or announcing their departure, constituted the necessary and by now inevitable backdrop of my days. The tropical heat came in through the window, enclosing me in its gentle, protective presence like an old friend welcoming me with the familiarity of habit. I thought about what had happened, and once again, as always when I remembered, I felt as if someone else had lived the preposterous experiences and met the people who would surely be inscribed forever in memory but who still appeared to me as distant and separate from my wandering fate. What would become of Dora Estela, I wondered, struggling against fate and yet so deserving of better days, and Antonia, whose madness must have grown slowly and silently, nurtured by an ingenuous erotic deviance practiced so obsessively? And Tomasito, who with unfailing intelligence had created an ambience of simple joy all around him, and Eulogio, whose difficulty in expressing himself had unjustly marginalized him from a world he understood and handled with memorable skill? And the whispers, cries, and calls in the galleries of the mines, the voice of the earth penetrating the darkness of a place where man is taken in only in exchange for his renouncing the gifts of the world? Surrounded by these devastating, painful images, and lulled by the horns in the port, I fell asleep. The next morning I opened the window of my room and looked out to see the docks. The scene took away any desire I had to walk around the port. Except for two or three notable differences, there is a certain common denominator in Pacific ports: Almost all of them, from Vancouver to Puerto Montt, have a kind of gray blanket hovering over everything; and brick walls plastered with the remains of posters covered by grime that makes the words illegible; and marshes with melancholy clusters of houses on stilts that remain standing with alarming precariousness, swaying in a lagoon of dirty water where dead chickens, beer cans, and bottles float in slow shipwreck, and there is a stink of excrement, stale urine, misery, and silent, anonymous death. This one was absolutely typical. The overwhelmingly black inhabitants lived in huts made of bamboo and tin that were laid out in rows leading nowhere and connected by rickety planks, along a perpetually flooding river whose waters stagnated beneath the flimsy structures and accumulated all the detritus carried by the current. As I lay on the bed, which gave off an increasingly pungent odor of the sour sweat of countless tenants before me, a slow but inexorable feeling of defeat began to cut a path deep inside me—an old companion who comes at the end of my ventures, when they all empty into the same mudhole of ennui and bad luck. I knew the immense salt sea was the only thing that could free me. I waited for the *Luther* with genuine longing, for I saw how the awful despair I know so well was gaining ground. The owner of the hotel visited my room from time to time and gave me dilatory reports on the ship's arrival. I began to think I would remain forever in that fetid corner of the Pacific coast, but one night he came upstairs to say that the *Luther* had docked that morning and would be ready to sail within the hour. I had to leave right away. I would board as Daniel Amirbar, second machinist's mate, who had been obliged to stay in port during his previous voyage to recover from an attack of fever. When I stood in front of the *Luther,* Mr. Lange said goodbye with extremely measured cordiality. I never found out what my friends did to have him hide me in his hotel and arrange my departure.

The ship's heavy black silhouette did not look very welcoming. It was one of the freighters built in Kiel in the 1920s, at the height of the postwar crisis in Germany, and its snub-nosed appearance seemed to reflect the spirit of those years of hunger and defeat. I presented myself to the captain, who had been born near Heidelberg and had the amiable, slightly ironic nature of people from the Palatinate. He left the sailing of the ship to the bos'n and the first mate, while he devoted himself with excessive meticulousness to financial, commercial, and administrative matters. He received me cordially, asked me to join him in his cabin, closed the door, and invited me to sit down. He knew almost everything about my apprenticeship as a miner. Lange had told him the story without any particular sympathy for me. The captain had said nothing to Lange because he didn't trust those characters who weave extensive networks from the reception desks of their hotels in order to engage in the most outlandish dealings. "I don't understand," he said, "how a seasoned sailor like you, a man who has weathered all the charted seas, could let something like this happen. People like you should stay on land as little as possible. Nothing good ever happens to you there. The sea is often cruel too, but it's never the same." I had neither the desire nor the capacity to explain my motives for attempting that undertaking, perhaps because I didn't know them myself. I answered with some vague, conventional phrases and went to stow my gear next to the hammock that had been assigned to me. I lay down, not thinking about anything, letting my body adjust to its old, faithful shipboard routine. The *Luther's* horn sounded three blasts, and the vessel began to move. The steady rhythm of the rods and the churning of the propellers were gradually giving back to me the relative serenity, the healthy indifference that comes when we entrust our fate to the spirits of the deep. The melancholy ennui of the port soon dissolved. When we entered the high seas and the ship began its slow pitching against the waves, I felt myself becoming who I always had been: Maqroll the Gaviero, without country or law, who submits to the ancient dice that roll for the amusement of the gods and the mockery of mortals. When I disembarked in La Rochelle, after an uneventful month and a half of sharing the captain's well-provisioned table and his spare but solid conversation, I already had in mind several concrete projects involving the teak trade. The mines had passed into the jumbled inventory of what has already happened and cannot be helped.

* * *

We remained silent for a time because we did not know how to respond to this painful sequence of events narrated by a man who seemed almost removed from those events and viewed them as something natural, something to be relegated to oblivion without regret or protest. We finished the last of the beer, said a few innocuous words about the places where Maqroll had tried his luck as a miner, and went to bed when it was almost dawn.

A few days later we returned to the San Fernando Valley Hospital. The results of the examination were satisfactory, and the doctor declared the Gaviero completely cured of the fever. Maqroll asked if he could travel, and the doctor said he saw no reason not to, as long as it wasn't to the tropics. When we left, Maqroll said, smiling as we do when a child makes a clever remark, "These doctors are hopeless. First he tells me I'm cured. He doesn't know that these fevers never disappear completely. They always come back when you least expect them. Then he warns me not to visit the tropics, when I've told him ad nauseam that I spend most of my life there: in the Caribbean, or

Southeast Asia, or sailing between the Lesser Antilles and the
Gulf of Mexico, or cutting teak in Songkhla or Tenasserim. Just
because I'm planning to go to Matarani for a while, the good
doctor forgets everything else. I think that Uruguayan you
brought in the beginning had more sense." I replied that he was
an emergency physician on call at the studios, and we had
required a specialist. "That's a fairy tale," he answered, patting
me on the back. "The Uruguayan had a better eye, and he
never would have been foolish enough to tell me to stay out of
the tropics." I said the tropics were precisely where he had contracted the fever. "But I already have it. There's no cure. With or
without the fever, sooner or later I'd have to go back. Don't tell
me you think I'm going to retire to a little house with flowers
in the windows in Amsterdam, or Antwerp, or Glasgow. Those
are places you pass through, where you cook up deals and the
adventure begins, not places to live in for very long. Those people
don't understand anything." It was useless to argue with him
when it had to do with the secret reasons for his wandering.
That's how he was, how he would always be. The Gaviero
spent the next few days calling shipping companies to find a
boat that was leaving soon for the Peruvian coast. After a good
deal of inquiry and argument, he found a place as a supernumerary seaman on a Danish freighter sailing to Valdivia and
making stops at several Pacific ports. He would have no work to
do and would be paid a token wage. Since the ship had no permit for carrying passengers, Maqroll devised this arrangement as
a way out for the company. I had the impression it was not the
first time he had used this strategem. Naturally, for the plan to
work, he was obliged to prove his long experience at sea.
    Yosip and his wife came to spend time with him on the day
of his departure. They had the desolate air of those left behind
in a strange land where no one remembers the happier years of a
distinguished past. Maqroll went to say goodbye to Leopoldo
and Fanny, and also left them adrift in a kind of anticipatory
nostalgia for the nights of long conversations and the Gaviero's
prolonged silences, which they surely would miss. When I saw
him coming back toward the car where we waited for him, I
could not help being affected by his appearance. He looked like
a homeless convalescent in his light-blue T-shirt that had known
better days, his navy-blue seaman's jacket with the black leather
buttons, purchased at some secondhand-clothing store in a Baltic
port, and the rebellious, graying locks of his unconquerable hair

*escaping at the sides of his black sailor's cap. His slightly pro-
truding eyes had the wary look of a man who has seen more
than humans are permitted to see, and he carried his eternal
duffel bag, with two changes of clothing as threadbare as those
he was wearing, a few talismans, each a reservoir of memories of
indelible sentiments or miraculous rescues from unspeakable
dangers, and the three or four books that always accompanied
him.*A lump came to my throat, and I had to remain silent for
a time to hide my feelings. During the long years of our friendship, one of the Gaviero's most enduring and unchanging traits
had been restraint in demonstrating his affections and loyalties.
He knew better than anyone, perhaps, that time and indifference
inevitably wipe away every trace of the emotions we thought
would last forever. Better, then, to preserve the few that remained
unchanged in an inviolable hiding place. I don't know why, but
until that moment it had not occurred to me to ask what he
proposed to do in the quarries in Peru. After the story he had
told us, I could not believe he was interested in anything even
remotely related to mining. "No, it's nothing like that," he
replied. "I'll be handling the transport of the stone in a couple of
small freighters that I'm going to lease with two Indonesian
captains I've known for many years; they're leaving Guayaquil
this week for Matarani. Transporting stone. What do you think
of that? It's one thing I haven't done yet at sea." I replied that
it didn't seem any more extravagant than many other things he
had tried. He shrugged and said nothing.*

*When we reached the docks in the port of Los Angeles, we
had to leave the car outside the area and walk a couple of kilometers until we found the Danish freighter. The captain stood at
the top of the gangway, giving instructions to his first mate, who
listened from the edge of the pier. Maqroll took his leave with a
silent handshake. As he walked toward the gangway, Yosip's wife
ran after him and embraced him, again in silence, holding him
in her arms for what seemed an interminable length of time. The
Gaviero kissed her on the mouth and freed himself from her
embrace, smiling at her with affection. She returned to Yosip,
who had watched the scene with pained sympathy as he tight-
ened his lips to hold back the tears. Maqroll spoke for a moment
to the first mate, who nodded his head and allowed him to walk
up the gangway. The captain waited for him on deck, displaying*

*See the Appendix, p. 89.

*an astonishment we could not interpret. The two of them went
to the bridge, while Maqroll, barely turning around, waved
goodbye to us with a broad movement of his arm; in it I wanted
to see his assent to the eternally unwritten laws governing our
destiny, and an unspoken, fraternal solidarity with those who
had shared with him a portion of that journey, that celebratory
indifference in the face of misfortune.*

* * *

*Several years went by and I had no news of the Gaviero. This
was customary, and I was used to prolonged silences interrupted
by an occasional report of his death under invariably tragic and
unpredictable circumstances, followed by a denial of the report
and another long period of silence, until one day I received a letter from him or we ran into each other in the most unexpected
place on earth. This time was like all the others. I was in the
Zuidstation in Brussels, waiting for a train to Marseilles. As I
was about to climb aboard and go to my modest, second-class
compartment, a messenger from the Hotel Metropol, where I
had been staying, handed me a packet of correspondence, which
the clerk at the reception desk had forgotten to give me that
morning. Once I had arranged my belongings for the long trip, I
lowered the little table at my seat and began to look over the
mail I had just received. As always, it consisted of news I
already knew, invitations to congresses and conferences that had
already taken place or in which I had no interest, and certain
documents relating to my work, which joined the other papers in
the wastebasket. Only one rather bulky envelope remained. It
was postmarked Pollensa, in Mallorca. When I opened it, I recognized the Gaviero's awkward, uncertain handwriting. The
paper had a prominent letterhead that read: "Munt & Riquer.
Merchants in Navigational Items, Customs Agents, Licenses
Issued. Port of Pollensa, Carrer de la Llotja, 7." The sheets
were yellowed, and the engravings on nautical themes at the top
had an unmistakable fin de siècle air. I began to read the letter,
interested in hearing news of my friend, whose silence had lasted
longer than usual. Maqroll started by bringing me up-to-date
on some unresolved matters involving a savings account I had
opened in his name at the Caja de Auxilio del Marino in
Cádiz. This strange order of precedence was typical of his letters.
He always began with the subjects that were least significant
and, for him, surely the most irritating. Then he wrote of more*

substantive issues, as he did in this case, describing events that
are worth transcribing here in their entirety because they relate
to our encounter in Los Angeles. This is what the Gaviero said
in his letter:

* * *

Regarding my voyage to the port of Matarani on the Peruvian coast to begin working the quarries in Santa Isabel de Sihuas, I think I should tell you what happened in detail, since you're committed to compiling my lunatic schemes with a fidelity and interest I've never understood. The name of the Danish freighter I was sailing on had already stirred something in my memory—I don't know if you remember, but it was called the *Skive,* an obvious enough name for a Danish ship. Still, something told me I ought to recognize it, that it should be even more familiar. At the top of the gangplank stood Captain Nils Olrik, with his Breton pirate's face, one eye staring, as Werfel says, at the third person cross-eyed people always look at, his graying, furiously red hair, the slow corpulence of his body, crouching slightly as if he were preparing to pounce, his sharp blue eyes behind heavy brows—all the outward signs of a sanguine, violent character, hiding one of the kindest, most affable hearts to be found in the intricate routings of the seamen's profession. My Danish is almost nonexistent and his English practically incomprehensible. Despite this we did not stop talking until each had summarized for the other his various incarnations in a life rich in experiences. I had reserved my passage by telephone, and they hadn't understood my name very well, which is something I'm used to, and Nils Olrik didn't pay much attention when he heard it. I had met him many years ago, when I was working as a nurse in the hospital of a miserable port lost in the labyrinth of the Mississippi Delta. Nils came there when his leg was shattered by a derrick on the ship where he was first mate. His recovery was slow and difficult, but they managed to save his leg, and eventually he was able to walk with only a slight limp, which gave him an aristocratic air. Nils was a young man then, an enthusiastic and jovial Dane still in his twenties, who became a devoted listener to the stories of my travels. By the time he was discharged, we were old friends. One of the memoirs of mine that you've published describes the Hospital de la Bahía, with an added dimension that is somewhat lyrical and extravagant, but it is actually a record of my experiences in the hospital.* I don't mention Nils's name, but the environment where he was laid up is described with some fidelity. Life subsequently brought us together again on various occasions. Nils reached the rank of captain in the merchant fleet and became known in almost every port in the world. During one of our encounters he hired me to fill a rather fanciful and unusual position on a freighter: I would serve as an intermediary with members of a Turkish family who were scattered among various Caribbean ports and ran significant import-export companies. The Kadaris were astute and slippery, unscrupulous and aggressive, and feared by all the captains who did business with them. Nils had the novel idea of using my knowledge of Turkish and my familiarity with the quirks in the Ottoman character to help him in his dealings with the fearsome clan. It was a time of amusing episodes, when we repeatedly used our wits in an effort to defeat the millenarian cunning of the Kadaris. If we succeeded, it was reason for uproarious celebrations, when the rum flowed for days. If they scored a point, we had to be content with saving up reserves of rancor for our next encounter. Once, in Port-au-Prince, matters could have been complicated very seriously when Nils Olrik locked himself in his cabin for days on end with a magnificent black woman who was the mistress of Kemal Kadari and whom the Turk loved with an intensity that bordered on dementia. He tried to board the ship with three Herculean blacks who claimed to be her brothers. With the help of some trustworthy sailors accustomed to these kinds of skirmishes, we managed to fend off Kadari and his companions and throw them overboard while we raised the gangplank. The next morning the Haitian authorities came to demand that we turn over the woman, whom we had already lowered in one of the lifeboats and left at the far end of the docks. The intentions of the Tonton Macoutes were obviously not the friendliest, but when they could not find the kidnapped beauty they softened a little, and after we judiciously distributed a few dollars, they left with no further ado. Years later I had the opportunity to put Nils in touch with my friend Abdul Bashur, who employed him as a captain on one of his family's freighters until the Bashurs suffered their first bankruptcy. I could go on endlessly telling you about other experiences I shared with this Dane, whose kindness, as I've said, was proverbial and whose steadfastness and admirable vocation for the

*See note, p. 10.

sea were remembered by all of us lucky enough to work with him.

I told Nils of my plans to transport the output of a quarry located in Santa Isabel de Sihuas. The stone was very valuable because of its coloring and texture, and I would carry it out of the port of Matarani and sell it in San Francisco and Oakland, where I knew people involved in the construction business. The matter of the two ships and my partnership with Indonesians aroused almost as much suspicion in my friend as the quarry project. He told me we would talk about it later, but first he placed at my disposal an empty bunk in the cabin he used as an office. The initial stages of the voyage took longer than expected because we had a breakdown in Panama. Then, in Buenaventura, torrential rains forced us to delay loading on a cargo of dyes bound for Callao, which could not be exposed to dampness. On this voyage the invigorating effect of the sea and its salutary routine, and the companionship of Nils Olrik, who had what seemed to be an endless supply of stories and anecdotes about mutual acquaintances, restored my pleasure in being alive and drove away every trace of the fever that had brought me down in California. But the quarry project also began to blur and dissolve, and deep inside me it became confused with the worst periods of my illness. The skepticism with which Nils viewed the enterprise had a good deal to do with this.

I also spent many hours of the leisure this voyage afforded me in rereading Gabory's work on the wars of the Vendée. The book has accompanied me for years as a memento of the time I spent at Amirbar, and I always profit from it. My copy still shows the marks and stains of my reading by the light of the Coleman in the tunnels of bitter memory, or at the edge of the precipice frequented by birds. A volume more gratifying than most to read again for the rigorous detail and considered historical judgment the author brings to his study of one of the most complex and troubled episodes—and one of those most riddled with strange currents of uncertain origin—in a period rich in such episodes. Now I'd just like to touch on something we began to discuss on the patio in Northridge, though I don't remember going into it with enough detail. It has to do with a curious aspect of the Bourbon character: a taste for the direct exercise of power and the ensuing game of political intrigue that has been a constant trait in the family right up to the present day. An unadorned sense of reality is combined with skill in manipulating the ambitions and weaknesses of their subjects and knowledge of how to maintain themselves on the sidelines or, better yet, above the immediate difficulties generated by the intrigues of their followers. Henry IV, Louis XIV, Louis XV, and Louis XVIII of France are clear examples of this characteristic among the descendants of Saint Louis's younger son. But the curious thing is that another branch of the family has shown diametrically opposed character traits: an alarming political stupidity, a disregard for the most basic concerns driving the ambition of their ministers, an ignorance of what neighbors or rival nations are plotting against their country—in short, a suicidal blindness that always brings them to the gallows or an inglorious exile. Louis XVI and Charles X in France, and Charles IV and Ferdinand VII in Spain, are sorry examples of this grave deficiency. My point is that the Count d'Artois, who was later crowned Charles X, demonstrated even as a pretender to the throne that he was a catastrophic example of this political ineptitude. Imagine; d'Artois held in his hands the most forthright, trustworthy, self-sacrificing instrument that any aspirant to the throne ever had: the Chouans. He was incapable of seeing them this way, and he fell into the most mindless pietism after experiencing every stage of a gallant career in the style of the Ancien Régime. He is responsible for the loss of the throne by the legitimate branch in France and for the shameful rise of the usurper and perjurer Orléans. Someday I would like to do retrospective research to determine if this duality and contradiction in political behavior is also found in the earlier branches of the Capets: the Valois, the Valois-Angoulême, and the first Capets. Since I know you also enjoy these minor great enigmas of history, I leave you with this question in the hope that one day you'll tell me the results of your investigations.

I trust you're not too surprised by this digression in the middle of the story of my voyage along the Peruvian coast. You've transcribed other asides like this one. Since that long ago time when you began to be interested in my travels, you've known that the present offers me nothing but absurd setbacks or continuous displacements motivated by less than reasonable reasons. No wonder, then, that I enjoy digging up comparable destinies and similar misfortunes in the past. I'm not complaining. On the contrary, I think the gods have guessed my secret preferences. You know what I'm talking about. Well, when we finally reached the port of Matarani, the panorama before me was one you're also familiar with: an extension of desert that begins its ascent to the vastness of the Andes, the only green some thornbushes perishing of thirst and a few dust-covered cactus also on the verge of death; and the dilapidated port, the docks eaten away by niter, the derricks always in danger of paralysis, the sun shining without pity or relief, devouring everything in a light that seems created for a planet different from ours. Only one of the freighters was waiting for me at the docks. The captain of the other ship had deserted at the last minute. And the captain of the one in port didn't show very much enthusiasm at the thought of having full responsibility for transporting the stone. I must admit that the scene was not calculated to raise a man's spirits, least of all one from Southeast Asia, where the luxuriant fertility has inspired so much literature, not always of the best. Nils persuaded me to come to an agreement with the Javanese captain and cancel the operation. His arguments were very forceful: Exploitation of the quarry was subject to official permits that had not yet been requested by the owners, who were supposedly going to be partners in the undertaking and so far had shown no signs of life. Selling the stone in San Francisco was contingent on resistance studies, which had been positive but only for a special type of construction that was certainly not the most common in that region of California, where constant seismic movement made it necessary to adjust the building codes periodically. Finally, there was the Dane's lack of confidence in the peoples of Asia, who were naturally disinclined to live up to their responsibilities. Olrik did not have to insist. I spoke to the Indonesian, and without much hesitation he agreed to abandon the undertaking in exchange for a cargo of niter in Concepción, bound for Holland, which Olrik transferred to him with no sacrifice on his part. According to the contract, he would have had to treat the holds with anticorrosives, and as it happened, the Javanese ship had already received that treatment. This was how I became a replacement officer on the *Skive,* serving under my old comrade Nils Olrik, with whom I conversed in half-words. We sailed down to Valdivia and Puerto Montt, where we took on cargo for Cape Town and Dunbar. The years I spent on the *Skive* were, perhaps, the most peaceful time in my life as a sailor. There were no memorable episodes. The usual encounters and farewells in chance ports, the storms that fall upon the ship like a curse from on high, the weeks of dead calm in the tropics, when the heat pours over the deck in successive, slow-moving waves that undermine whatever shreds of will we have left: These were the routine events of a life controlled by the vast, capricious network of the shipping lanes.

One night, as we were coming into Abidjan, Olrik died in his sleep of a massive heart attack. The owners put another captain in charge of taking the ship back to Denmark, and I went my own way. I didn't have what you could call a formal contract with Nils; our agreement was drawn up not in legal terms but according to those established by long friendship and mutual knowledge of our respective strengths and weaknesses. I don't have the will or desire to go into everything that happened before I came to Mallorca and settled in Pollensa as manager of some shipyards that are more hypothetical than real, since they lack the machinery required to perform their work. I'm tired and sick and have lost a good part of my enthusiasm and love for life at sea. Not long ago, during a bout of the insomnia that eats away at my nights, I recalled my convalescence in Northridge, the kind hospitality of Don Leopoldo and his wife, the long nights when all of you had the patience to hear my misfortunes as a miner in the Andes. That was why I decided to write and tell you the outcome of my voyage to the Peruvian coast, and give you my news. I also wanted to transcribe, for you and for the others who listened to me during those nights in the San Fernando Valley, a curious paragraph I discovered in a book I happened to come across when I was going through some volumes that a canon, a good friend of mine, keeps in the attic of the vicarage. It was the title that attracted my attention and brought me back to the time I spent at Amirbar, and I asked Mossén Ferrán to lend it to me. The title is *A True History of the Mines Where the Jews Toiled to No Avail in the Mountains of Axartel*. The author is one Shamuel de Córcega, undoubtedly a coreligionist of the miners. The imprint shows that it was published in Sóller by Jordi Capmany in the year 1776. It's a confusing tale, written in an equal mix of Ladino, macaronic Spanish, and Mallorcan, and the purpose is difficult for the reader to fathom, since the narration is totally devoid of interest and comes to no reasonable or concrete conclusions. It might have been written to validate titles to those lands, which are certainly not very clear, and it isn't even certain whose ownership the book is defending. On the other hand, it may also be meant as an attack against the community of converts; at that time there were many of them on the island. The paragraph I'm transcribing is closely related to Amirbar, the place I described on those hot summer nights in California. It reads as follows:

The profit to be gained from the mines was never mentioned nor was it truly known what mineral could be found there. The only certainty was that a great host of the tribe of Moses gathered there with their women and children and that all went into the tunnels to dig and only a chosen few were privileged to mill the earth that the others brought to houses with sealed doors and windows from which there emerged considerable noise and exceedingly strange odors. As it is a very isolated and solitary region, they made their own laws and no one watched over them. And indeed it was very curious that the authorities received notification that in order to prevent the birth of more infants, who interfered with labor in the mines and required too much care, the elders ordained that henceforth the men and women who were in a state of matrimony or those who lived in concubinage should know each other only in sodomy. So it was, and for several years their numbers did not increase. The profits from their excavations were amassed by the money changers of Alcudia, also of the same religion, until the lands were exhausted and even great toil produced nothing of value. But reports of the sodomy, which apparently was not known with certainty until much later, reached his Excellency Bishop Don Antoni Rafolls i del Pi, a man of great sanctity and discretion, who intervened with his armed men to put an end to the nefarious sin committed there. Women and men who were captured and subjected to interrogation confessed to everything and even admitted to finding great pleasure in the aforesaid sodomies. The lands were confiscated and the dwellings and workhouses leveled and the profits taken away from the money changers, and so ended the labors in these mines where several generations of Jewry had toiled at great cost to their lives and little profit to their purses. The lands were abandoned and there were no reports that anyone ever returned, so great were the shame and fear engendered by the outrage committed there against the natural law ordained in the books written by kings and prophets which we Christians call the Holy Bible.

So. You see by what unexpected channels echoes of the past that we believed gone forever suddenly return. When you see Don Leopoldo and his wife tell them about this, and please say too that I remember them with affection and gratitude. I mentioned that I was ill. It's something very different from the fever that got the better of me in Yosip's motel on La Brea Boulevard.

This time I think it's a question of years, which are beginning to mean more than one would like, along with the Pollensa damp that twists one's joints—like the poor Jews of Axartel twisting in the hands of the hired assassins of Bishop Rafolls i del Pi, who, by the way, I somehow think must have also been a descendant of the twelve tribes.

Well, you'll hear from me soon if the gods are willing. If I leave this place and its ghostly shipyards, I'll let you know where I am. In the meantime, your old friend sends you an affectionate greeting,

Maqroll the Gaviero.

* * *

That was how the letter ended. It had traveled halfway around the world before reaching the Hotel Métropole in Brussels. I've heard nothing since from the Gaviero, and something tells me this is the last communication I will receive from him. He had never spoken before of illnesses or ailments, and his letters always gave me the impression that new undertakings were waiting for him on his endless travels. This time I had no such thought. The concluding paragraphs breathe an air of finality, of a last farewell, and they filled me with grief.

APPENDIX: THE GAVIERO'S READING

This is not an attempt to present the Gaviero as someone who has dedicated particular attention to the world of letters. Nothing could be more foreign to his character; nothing would seem more alien and senseless to him than such an inclination. But the Gaviero was an insatiable reader, a tireless and lifelong consumer of books. This was his only pastime, not for literary reasons but because of a need to stave off somehow the tireless rhythm of his wandering and the unpredictable outcome of his voyages. And therefore it is no simple task to follow the trail of favorite books, the ones that accompanied him wherever he went. Still, I believe I can mention a few: In the many encounters that fate allowed us, he either carried these with him or cited them so often it was easy to deduce a faithful companionship of long standing. By rereading old letters and searching my memory, I have assembled a list of the most notable.

The one I believe I always saw with him, and which he carried in one of the deep pockets of his seaman's jacket, was the Mémoires du Cardinal de Retz, *the beautiful 1719 edition in four volumes published in Amsterdam by J. F. Bernard and H. de Sauzet. One of the volumes was always with Maqroll, and the others lay in his eternal duffel bag. Our first conversation about this famous book by Jean François Paul de Gondi, Archbishop of Paris and Cardinal of Retz, took place in Baltimore. By some miracle we found a bar that was open, and we went in to celebrate our encounter. Maqroll had come there to buy parts for the dredger that he and Abdul Bashur were operating in the Saint Lawrence River. As usual, they hoped to earn a fortune, this time working for the city of Montreal. The dredger of blessed memory finally succumbed to confiscation by creditors, brought on by a delay in payment for work already completed. An oversight caused by the insouciant bureaucratic dawdling of the Quebequois, as Maqroll called them with memorable animosity. To back up some point he was making that night regarding political crime, the Gaviero took out the volume he had with him of Retz's* Mémoires. *I think it was the fourth. I couldn't help asking how he had come by that bibliographical jewel and if it wasn't risky to carry it around without taking special precautions. He replied to the first question with a sibylline smile: "There are women we have known—not very often, unfortunately—who insist on our not forgetting them and consequently are capable of giving away marvels like this."* He said no more and returned to the topic we were discussing. *A little later he suddenly interrupted himself to make this statement: "The only books you lose are the ones that don't interest you. I'll always have this one by the Cardinal. It's the most intelligent book ever written."* A look of astonishment at this outrageous opinion must have crossed my face, because he immediately reassured me: *"No one has lied with so much lucidity in order to defend himself before the judgment of history, and at the same time described the most shameless, dangerous intrigues with a clarity and objectivity that Thucydides might have envied. What a lesson we can learn from Monsieur de Gondi, Archbishop of Paris, up to his neck in the lunatic conspiracies of the Fronde, which were on the verge of ruining France and destroying the noble inheritance of the Capets!"*

Another book I saw regularly and that seemed to be one of his long-standing favorites was Chateaubriand's Mémoires d'Outre-Tombe, *in an ordinary edition with the yellow covers of the Classiques Garnier. It looked as if it were about to fall apart. His enthusiasm for the Viscount's prose was a favorite topic during the high tides of his libations. One night in Bizerte, in a miserable waterfront tavern, he recited almost in its entirety the scene in Córdoba when René meets Natalie de Noailles. He finished and made no comment. He didn't have to. The exaltation born of the Viscount's sinuous, sumptuous prose was written on his face.*

Allusions in his letters, and remarks made during our conversations, indicate that Émile Gabory's study of the wars of the Vendée was one of the volumes he read most devotedly. At the Amirbar mine, and years later, during his voyages with Captain Olrik along the southern coasts of the Pacific, Gabory's work was his inseparable companion. It is appropriate at this point to recall an anecdote that concerns the book and was told to me by the painter Alejandro Obregón. One night in Vancouver, Alejandro and Maqroll found themselves in a police station after a phenomenal bar fight, when they were attacked by a gang of Chinese who claimed they had been offended by something the Gaviero said in a tone they considered cutting. When the officer on duty at the station took down Maqroll's statement and asked him what he did for a living, he replied haughtily, in his awkward English with its Levantine accent, "I am a Chouan lost in

*the twentieth century." That was all he said, and the outburst
cost him twenty-four hours in jail.*

Finally, the book that most helped Maqroll to shake off his
low spirits during the black times when everything seemed to
conspire against him, was the collection of letters and memoirs of
the Prince of Ligne, in a beautiful 1865 edition published in
Brussels. The Gaviero simply could not say enough about the
great Belgian aristocrat. One day, when we found ourselves
together in Antwerp, each because of circumstances as different as
they are difficult to explain, we had to take shelter in a restaurant that served Flemish food. Widespread fighting had broken
out between Walloons and Flemings, and the police were wield-
ing their clubs without stopping to ask about nationalities or
papers. Seated before a majestic waterzooi of salmon that we
had ordered to restore our strength, the Gaviero said in an
admonishing tone, "I don't know if the Belgians are a nation or
one of Talleyrand's diabolical nightmares. But I do know they
can always depend on my unreserved sympathy, because the
most perfect example of a great lord that Europe has ever
known, the Prince de Ligne, was born among them. His funeral
procession in Vienna, on December 13, 1814, while the
Congress was in session, included emperors, kings, ministers, and
the great names of European nobility. They accompanied him to
his final resting place—the perfect honnête-homme of the
Ancien Régime, one of the few times in history when it would
have been worthwhile to be alive."

To conclude these recollections of our friend's favorite readings,
it seems fitting to mention the thesis I once heard him expound
when we were waiting for the train to Naples in the Stazione
Termini. Maqroll was carrying a novel by Simenon—L'Écluse
No. 1, if memory serves. When I saw the book in the café
where we sat waiting to be served, and made some remark about
displays of optimism that bordered on unhealthy ignorance, he
replied with disconcerting naturalness, "He's the best novelist in
French since Balzac." I couldn't help reminding him that I had
heard him say something similar about L.-F. Céline. "No," he
answered, with no change of expression. "Céline is the best
writer in France since Chateaubriand, but the best novelist is
Simenon. And believe me, when I mention Balzac I put aside
certain of my reservations concerning his execrable French." This
was one of the very few literary opinions I heard him express
during the long years of our friendship.

I think these observations on Maqroll the Gaviero as a reader complete the portrait of my friend, which I propose to leave to a posterity that depends, unfortunately, on the highly problematic diffusion that may be enjoyed by the books I have written about his trials and tribulations.

The Tramp Steamer's Last Port of Call

For G.G.M.:
this story that I've wanted to tell you for some
time, but life's uproar did not permit it

and the smell and murmur of an old ship,
of rotten planks and broken tools,
and weary machines that howl and weep,
pushing the prow, kicking the sides,
chewing laments, swallowing, swallowing distances,
making a noise of bitter waters upon the bitter waters,
moving the ancient ship upon the ancient waters.

Pablo Neruda, "The Ghost of the Cargo
Boat," Residence on Earth, I,
Translated by Donald D. Walsh
(New York: New Directions, 1973)

Toujours avec l'espoir de rencontrer la mer,
Ils voyageaient sans pain, sans batons et sans urnes,
Mordant au citron d'or de l'idéal amer.

Stéphane Mallarmé, "Le Guignon"

*T*here are many ways to tell this story, just as there are many ways to recount the most insignificant episode in any of our lives. I could begin with what, for me, was the end of the affair but for another participant might be only the beginning. And it goes without saying that the third person involved in what I will attempt to relate to you could not distinguish the beginning or the ending of what she lived through. For this reason I have chosen to narrate these events from the point of view of my own experience, following the sequence in which they had their effect on me. It may not be the most interesting way for you to learn about this singular love story. From the moment I heard it, I firmly resolved to tell it to a man who has proved himself a master in recounting the things that happen to people. Now that I am writing it for him, since telling it to him in person turned out to be impossible, I have decided to do it in the simplest, most direct way, avoiding the dangers of unfamiliar paths, shortcuts, and detours, which it would not be advisable for me to attempt. I sincerely hope my lack of skill does not destroy the appeal, the strange, painful fascination, of this love story; however transitory and impossible, it has something of the eternal legends that have bewitched us over the centuries, from Pyramus and Thisbe and Tristan and Iseult to Marcel and Albertine.

What I am about to narrate I learned directly from the protagonist, and I have no choice but to undertake the task of writing it down myself, despite my meager talents. I would have preferred someone more gifted to do it, but that could not be: The hurried, clamorous days of our life did not permit it. I wanted to record these reservations, although they certainly will not save me from the harsh judgment of my unlikely readers. The critics, as is their custom, will take care of the rest and return to oblivion these lines that are so far removed from the prevailing taste of our times.

I had to go to Helsinki to attend a meeting of directors of internal publications for various oil companies. The truth was that I went very unwillingly. It was the end of November, and weather forecasts for the Finnish capital were rather bleak, but my admiration for the music of Sibelius and for some unforgettable pages by the most forgotten of Nobel Prize winners, Frans Eemil Sillanpää, were enough to feed my interest in visiting Finland. I had also been told that on days when there was no fog, the far end of the Vironniemi Peninsula afforded a dazzling view of Saint Petersburg, with its gold-domed churches and marvelous buildings. These were reason enough to face the terrible prospect of a winter unlike any I had ever known. And in fact, at forty degrees below zero, Helsinki seemed almost paralyzed inside a transparent, inviolable crystal. Each brick of its buildings, each angle of the railings around its parks buried under marble snow, each detail of its public monuments, stood out with incisive, almost intolerable clarity. Traveling the streets of the city was a mortally dangerous exploit but one that had unsettling aesthetic compensations. When I suggested to my conference companions that I intended to go all the way to the esplanade at the eastern end of the port to see the capital of Peter the Great, they looked at me as if I were a fool whose chances of survival were nonexistent. During one of our obligatory dinners, a Finnish colleague, whose courtesy was not free of a certain wariness caused by my outrageously extravagant plan, warned me of the dangers I would have to face. "When the wind blows there," he explained, "it turns everything in its path into a block of ice, and no overcoat, no matter how heavy or well insulated, can protect you." I asked if on a calm day, one of the very rare days when an ephemeral but brilliant sun puts in an appearance, I could realize my dream of seeing the Venice of the north, even at a distance. He agreed it would be possible, but only if I had a vehicle ready to take me back to the hotel as soon as the weather changed, which could happen in just a few minutes at that time of year. The Finnish representatives of my company undertook to provide the car and inform me ahead of time when a sunny day seemed likely.

The opportunity arose much sooner than I anticipated. Two days later they called to say that a car would pick me up the following day, when three hours of sun without a wisp of cloud were guaranteed by our firm's meteorologists. The next day the car pulled up at the hotel entrance with exemplary punctuality. We drove along the avenue that encircles part of the city and leads to the outskirts where the docks are located. The driver spoke no language but Finnish. Not even my own versions of a few Swedish words allowed me to communicate with him. And I did not really have much to say to this charioteer from the pages of the *Kalevala*. I thought the drive would be longer, but it scarcely took twenty minutes. What I saw when I climbed out of the car left me speechless. The clarity of the air was absolute. Each crane on the docks, each bulrush along the shore, each vessel moving in unreal silence through the still waters of the bay, had such purity of presence that it seemed to me the world had just begun. The city built by Peter Romanoff to satisfy his typical autocrat's delusions of grandeur and his sordid purposes as the cunning son of Ivan the Terrible, rose in the background with the same precision. The white buildings, the gleaming domes of the churches, the docks of blood-red granite, the delicious Italianate bridges spanning the canals, seemed incredibly near, within reach of my hand. An immense red flag waving above the facade of the admiralty building brought me back to a present whose unmitigated folly was inconceivable at that moment and in that awe-inspiring setting with its perfect proportions and translucent, otherworldly air. I sat on the edge of the granite parapet that enclosed the asphalt walk, my feet hanging over the steel mirror of the water, and became absorbed in contemplating a miracle I was sure would never be repeated. That was when I first saw the tramp steamer, a singularly important character in the story that concerns us. This is a term used to describe low-tonnage freighters not affiliated with any of the great shipping lines, which sail from port to port in search of occasional cargo that they are willing to transport anywhere in the world. They earn a poor living, dragging their battered hulls along for many more years than their precarious condition might lead us to expect.

The tramp steamer entered my field of vision as slowly as a wounded saurian. I could not believe my eyes. With the wondrous splendor of Saint Petersburg in the background, the poor ship intruded on the scene, its sides covered with dirty streaks of rust and refuse that reached all the way to the waterline. The captain's bridge, and the row of cabins on the deck for crew members and occasional passengers, had been painted white a long time before. Now a coat of grime, oil, and urine gave them an indefinite color, the color of misery, of irreparable decadence, of desperate, incessant use. The chimerical freighter slipped through the water to the agonized gasp of its machinery and the irregular rhythm of driving rods that threatened at any moment to fall silent forever. Now it occupied the foreground of the serene, dreamlike spectacle that had held all my attention, and my astonished wonder turned into something extremely difficult to define. This nomadic piece of sea trash bore a kind of witness to our destiny on earth, a *pulvis eris* that seemed truer and more eloquent in these polished metal waters with the gold and white vision of the capital of the last czars behind them. The sleek outline of the buildings and wharves on the Finnish coast rose at my side. At that moment I felt the stirrings of a warm solidarity for the tramp steamer, as if it were an unfortunate brother, a victim of human neglect and greed to which it responded with a stubborn determination to keep tracing the dreary wake of its miseries on all the world's seas. I watched it move toward the interior of the bay, searching for some discreet dock where it could anchor without too many maneuvers and, perhaps, for as little money as possible. The Honduran flag hung at the stern. The final letters of the name that had almost been erased by the waves were barely visible: . . . *cyon*. In what seemed too mocking an irony, the name of this old freighter was probably the *Halcyon*. Beneath the mutilated lettering one could read, with some difficulty, its registry: Puerto Cortés. But my limited experience of the sea and the tangled, sordid network of its commerce was enough to keep me from engaging in senseless speculations on the contrasts created by the appearance of a wretched freighter from the Caribbean in the middle of one of the most forgotten and harmonious panoramas in northern Europe. The Honduran ship had returned me to my world, to the center of my most essential memories, and I had nothing more to do there at the end of the Vironniemi Peninsula. Fortunately, the charioteer who resembled Lemminkainen approached and pointed at the sky, where leaden clouds, indicators of an imminent change in temperature, were gathering with dizzying speed. Back at the hotel, my colleagues questioned me regarding the experience I had mentioned so often and looked forward to so eagerly. I extricated myself with a few conventional, reassuring words. The tramp steamer had left me in a reality so alien to this Scandinavian and Baltic present that it was better not to say anything. In fact, there was little to say. In that place, at least.

✳   ✳   ✳

Life often renders its accounts, and it is advisable not to ignore them. They are a kind of bill presented to us so that we will not become lost deep in the world of dreams and fantasy, unable to find our way back to the warm, ordinary sequence of time where our destiny truly occurs. I learned this lesson a little more than a year after my visit to Finland and the encounter I had there, an encounter that became part of the recurrent, inexorable stuff of my nightmares. I was in Costa Rica as press adviser to a delegation of technicians from Toronto, who were studying the construction of an oil pipeline from I don't remember which port into the interior. Two friends I had made in San José, during a turbulent session of itinerant drinking in cabarets of highly dubious reputation, asked me to join them for a sail on a yacht along Nicoya Bay in Puntarenas. I accepted, delighted to escape the inane conversation of my coworkers and the interminable recollections of their successes at golf, a subject that provokes immediate nausea in me. Marco was one of the men who had invited me on the outing. He picked me up in his car, and I remembered that on the previous night he and I had shared quite a few theories regarding alcohol and its effects in various fields of endeavor. The drive to Puntarenas would take little more than an hour. The owner of the yacht was waiting for us there with his wife, who had invited herself along. Something in Marco's words suggested that there was more to say about her but he was keeping it to himself, perhaps to surprise me. I contained my curiosity, and we spent the rest of the time evoking our *non sanctus* pilgrimage of the previous night. When we reached Puntarenas, I found myself once again at the waters of the Pacific—perpetually gray, perpetually about to undergo a change of mood, the same from Valparaiso to Vancouver. The intense, humid heat distended my nerves and disposed me to full enjoyment of the excursion, for which I had many and, as it turned out, eminently justified hopes.

The owner's house had that shabby, welcoming look so frequent along the coasts of our countries. The heterogeneous furnishings were clearly the castoffs of family houses in San José. The refrigerator was filled with beer, tins of caviar, and those inevitable bundles wrapped in plantain leaves, which, under the name of tamales, cover innumerable but equally inedible varieties of corn dough enveloping unpredictable dangers, from the flesh of armadillos to wild turkey meat. We carried it all to the yacht, an imposing presence that cast its shadow over the courtyard of the house. At a signal from the owner, we climbed the gangplank and were helped on deck by a smiling black giant, whose brief comments indicated a very lively intelligence and unconquerable good humor. The engines started up under the command of the owner, assisted by the black man. A woman's sudden shouts— "I'm coming! I'm coming! Wait for me, damn it!"—made us look in the direction of the house. A woman was running toward us, wearing one of the skimpiest bikinis I've ever seen. She was tall, with rather wide shoulders and long, limber legs that swelled to firm, shapely thighs. Her face had the kind of conventional but inoffensive prettiness achieved through carefully applied makeup and regular features, which does not require outstanding beauty. As she came closer to the yacht, the perfection of her almost aggressively youthful body was even more apparent. A boy of six or seven ran behind her. They leaped on board with the agility of deer. She greeted us, smiling and out of breath, and made her son do the same. "If you left me behind you'd have died of hunger, you assholes. I'm the only one who knows where the food is and how to serve it." She laughed with pleasure while her husband, frowning slightly, pretended to be busy at the instrument panel. In a low voice, he gave an order to the helmsman and without any comment went to the forward deck, where he sat at starboard and began shooting with a .45 at the pelicans flying overhead. It was annoyingly clear that the tension between the couple was growing to the rhythm of the shots, which did not hit the mark and only thundered in our ears, making conversation more difficult. "Don't worry," she commented, still smiling. "When he runs out of bullets he'll leave us in peace. What would you like to drink? A nice little beer for the heat, or something a teeny bit stronger?" Those diminutives in the mouths of Costa Rican women have always unsettled me, leaving me in a state of alert somnambulism appropriate to the most disoriented adolescent. We opted to help her fix gin and tonics. She handed each of us

his glass, and I thought the "urgent Golden Aphrodite" evoked by
Borges had come to bless us. Despite that beauty in reach of our
senses, and circulating among us with Olympian naturalness, the
conversation at last managed to flow with some spontaneity. The
mother fussed over the boy, who was becoming seasick, with
what seemed excessive care, as though attempting to use these
attentions as compensation for the guilt she might feel because of
the evident crisis in her marriage. We reached the entrance to the
bay and anchored at a small island, where we had lunch: a memorable lobster washed down with a somewhat less prestigious
Rhine wine from the Napa Valley.

In several asides, Marco told me that the marriage was about
to break up. The owner of the yacht, who would inherit an
immense fortune, worked like a slave all day under his father, an
implacable Asturian. At night, he continued to live a bachelor's
life as if he had never married. Several times his wife had
caught him driving up and down the main street of San José
with his car full of whores and had spent the night at her parents' house. When the young heir had fired all the bullets in his
pistol, he spent the rest of the trip discussing the maintenance
of the yacht with the black man. From time to time he deigned
to talk to us, with a rather forced amiability that left little room
for conversation. His wife, in the meantime, divided her attentions between her son and each one of us, whom she treated
with the spontaneous, cordial courtesy so common in Costa
Rican women of her class and even more evident and marked
in those of humbler station. "They told me you were a writer,"
she said with undisguised curiosity. "What do you write? Nov-
els or poetry? I love to read, but only romantic stories. Is what
you write very romantic?" I wasn't quite sure how to answer
her. The tension was palpable. I decided on the truth. I would
have been an idiot to think our conversation could lead to a
highly improbable outcome. "No," I answered. "My poems and
stories usually turn out to be fairly melancholy." "I think that's
very strange," she remarked. "You don't look particularly sad,
and it doesn't seem to me you've been too battered by life. So
why write sad things?" "That's how they turn out," I answered,
trying to put an end to these questions, whose most outstanding characteristic was not precisely intelligence. "I can't help
it." She was thoughtful for a moment, and a very slight shadow
of disappointment crossed her face. I never dreamed she was
speaking seriously. From then on, without excluding me from

the group, of course, her best smiles were not for me.

It was almost dusk when we returned to Puntarenas. I had to be in San José that night for a meeting at the Economic Ministry. The sun, the artificially scented California wine, the presence, voice, and movements of that female body in the late-afternoon heat, had made me drowsy, and I dozed off but did not fall asleep completely, because I could hear the words of the conversation without really following their meaning. Suddenly there was an inexplicable silence, and I sensed a cool, unexpected shadow invading our surroundings. The noise of the motor began to rebound off a nearby surface with new and irritating harshness. I awoke and opened my eyes, and saw that we were passing along-side a ship whose struggling engines were taking it out of port. At first I did not recognize it, simply because I had never seen it so close. It was the tramp steamer from Helsinki. The same sides covered with streaks of rust and refuse, the cabins and bridge in an identical state of disrepair, and the agonizing death rattle of its engines, emphasized even more by proximity. In Helsinki I had noticed the absence of crew members or passengers moving about. Only a vague form on the bridge testified to the presence of human beings. At the time, I had attributed this to the cold that prevailed outside, and it must have been the reason, because sailors were observing us now from the hatchways and the railing at the prow, with impersonal faces showing several weeks' growth of beard and ragged clothes stained with oil and sweat. Some were speaking English, others Turkish, and a few Portuguese. Each in his own language had made himself responsible for commenting on the woman, who smiled at them with elaborate innocence and greeted them with a wave of her arms that almost exposed her breasts. The remarks became more brutal, and I could not help thinking that this incredible vision would accompany them dur-ing the endless days of whatever rough crossing they were about to make. The sun warmed us again, and once more I read the enigmatic syllable . . . *cyon* at the stern and, under that, Puerto Cortés, in white letters that had almost vanished beneath a coat of oil, dirt, and blotches of minium struggling in vain to win the battle against the rust devouring the structure. "Those poor guys won't make it to Panama City," the woman observed with a cer-tain sadness that was both maternal and childish. "I saw them last year in Helsinki," I replied, not really knowing why. "Where's that?" she asked in some confusion. "In Finland. On the Baltic. Near the North Pole," I finally had to explain when I realized the names meant little or nothing to her. The others looked at me with surprise, almost with disbelief. I felt an overwhelming reluctance to tell them the whole story. Besides, it was not for them. It wasn't theirs. The episode of the freighter, my silence, and our slow digestion of everything we had eaten and drunk ended conversation until we reached land, where we disembarked and went directly to the car. We said goodbye to the couple with the best words we could think of, and as she covered her head with a light cotton scarf, the woman said to me, with a touch of sarcasm, "When you write something romantic you'll send it to me, okay? Even if it's just for the sake of the lobster." The old familiar play, I thought. Nausicaa's and Madame Chauchat's game. Delicious on occasion, more often debilitating and futile. On the drive back to San José, I realized I did not even know the name of our beautiful traveling companion. I decided not to ask Marco. It was better to keep the memory of two anonymous presences that from then on would be inseparable in my mind: the lovely Botticellian figure, who did not worry about foul language, and the crumbling ghost of the tramp steamer. They would complement each other in my dreams, communicating their will to survive along the same channels where poetry also occurs.

Fate still held in store two more encounters with the wandering Honduran freighter. But the first two were enough for its ruined presence to join the family of obsessive visitations behind which are hidden the pulsing, flowing wellsprings of an imprecise game, with constantly changing rules, which we have agreed to call destiny. I cannot say that its subsequent appearances added nothing to the previous ones. Naturally, they brought even more permanence to an image filled with the most secret, active essences of the power that carries all humankind toward its "destination and end": the call of death. For this reason I want to tell you about the last two episodes, which differ from the ones I have already recounted only with regard to the stage on which they chose to play themselves out.

Jamaica had been one of my favorite places in the Caribbean. For a long time Kingston was a stopover on the air route that connects my country to the United States. I generally extended my stay to an entire weekend in order to enjoy the exceptional climate and landscape praised by Admiral Nelson in letters to his family when he was governor of the island. The entire Caribbean has been an incomparable region for me, the place where things happen with precisely the rhythm and ambience that most faithfully and advantageously accommodate the unrealized projects of my life, the place where all my demons are placated and my faculties sharpened, until I feel entirely different from the man who roams cities far from the sea, and countries whose respectable conformity is inimical to him. But certain islands in the Caribbean are exceptional, offering me total submersion in the waters sought by Ponce de León. Jamaica was one of those places. For reasons not worth going into now, I stopped visiting Jamaica for several years. When I returned, everything had changed. A latent aggressiveness that was always close to the surface had turned the inhabitants into people with whom the greatest precautions were necessary in order to avoid an incident. This tension was apparent even in the climate: With no essential alteration, it was accepted differently, and with a different humor, by the Jamaicans. Another paradise comes to an end, I thought. Many others had gone through the same process. One more no longer meant a major sacrifice for me. Just as only two or three ideas can hold and inspire our interest after we reach a certain age, the many places the world presents as ideal can be reduced to two or three, and even that number may be too generous. In short, I swore I would never go back, and I chose other routes for enjoying the restorative bounty of the Caribbean.

In Panama City, several months after my visit to Costa Rica and the outing on Nicoya Bay, I boarded a plane for Puerto Rico, where the association of professors in Cayey had invited me to speak about my poetry. We left at dawn. After half an hour in the air we had to return to Panama City, "to check a minor malfunction in the ventilating system." The fact was that one engine had failed and the other must have been subjected to a strain that the poor, noisy 737 gave no indication of enduring for any length of time. We spent two long hours watching the mechanics who, like voracious ants, pulled parts out of the aforementioned turbine and put them back again. It was announced over the loudspeaker that the minor malfunction had been *normalized* (why, I always wonder, must violence be done to the language as soon as there are any doubts regarding technical matters?) and we could now board. The plane took off without incident. An hour and a half later, as the captain was announcing that in a few moments we would be flying over the island of Cuba, we felt a shudder that left the passengers in a pale silence interrupted only by the rather inconsistent explanations of the stewardesses, who were walking up and down the aisle while trying to hide their own panic. "Due to a mechanical failure in our left engine, we are forced to land in Kingston, Jamaica. Please fasten your seat belts, return your seats to an upright position, and reset your trays vertically. We are beginning our descent." It was the voice of the captain, whose calm not all the passengers took as a good sign. I closed the book I was reading and prepared to enjoy the view of Kingston Bay, which I remembered as a typically Caribbean scene. When the plane began to circle the port, I once again marveled at the dense vegetation that climbed the mountains surrounding the city. It was an intense green, almost black in places, while in others the young bamboo shoots and upright, ceremonious ferns gave it a yellowish cast. Two planes in the airport were preparing for takeoff, and we had to continue circling as we waited for permission to land. With the engines set as low as possible to avoid straining them, the captain was making the descent, preparatory to touching down at the beginning of the runway. I was absorbed in admiring the bay, with the sunken warship at its very center. I never had learned its nationality or how it had been wrecked; I always forgot it as soon as I landed. In one of our passes over the docks, I saw what was unquestionably the tramp steamer, which by now formed an integral part of my most persistent memories. There it lay, like a dog in a doorway after a night of hunger and fatigue. I realized how well I had come to know the freighter, for even from the air, when it was not at eye level as it had been on previous occasions, I could identify it with absolute certainty. It seemed to list slightly to starboard, and when we came around again, I saw that cranes on the pier were loading cargo that must have still been piled on one side of the hold. That may have been why the ship was leaning.

We had to spend the night in Kingston. All the flights to Miami had left that morning, and our only choice was to wait for the engine of our 737 to be repaired. We were taken to a downtown hotel that was not particularly luxurious, but it was quiet and its bar was tended competently by a short, gray-haired black man, who proved to be truly expert in preparing planter's punch, a drink that everybody thinks can be made with canned juice, rum, ice, and the inevitable maraschino cherry. The bartender at our hotel followed the classic, inviolable formula, squeezing the pineapple juice himself and using the canonically correct proportions of rum and ice. It was twelve noon. By my fourth planter's punch I knew that eating lunch would be a grave mistake. By slowing the rhythm of my drinking, I could wait calmly until the sun began to go down, for I had resolved to visit the ship. I felt that if I did not, it would be a serious offense against principles of courtesy and solidarity, as if I knew that an old and dear friend was staying in Kingston and I refused to see him. Some of my traveling companions were making plans for a nocturnal tour of the city's cabarets. I refrained from describing the sordid experience that lay ahead of them. Instead of taking a nap and feeling fresh for a night out, I preferred going to the port, visiting my wounded friend, and coming back to the hotel to try some other possibilities I had begun to explore with the bartender. Without even asking, he offered me a light, perfect tuna sandwich that served as a meal and left room for the evening's alcoholic experiments. When the sun became tolerable, I took a cab to the port. From the air I had located the dock where the freighter was moored. We arrived without incident but found the entrance gates locked. An evil-tempered, arrogant man of black and Indian ancestry informed us we could not go in. The warehouses were locked, and no one was on the docks now. I asked about the tramp steamer, and he said it had been loaded and was about to weigh anchor. Again I felt as if I had failed a person who was dear to me. A five-pound note and some involuted explanations about the need to deliver an urgent message to the captain softened the guard's ill will, and he let me in with a warning that in another half hour, when he left his post and the wharves were locked for the night, no one would be there to open the gate for me. I hurried toward the spot where I thought the ship was docked. Just as I reached it, the freighter began to move, its anchors already raised. The same sailors I had seen in Puntarenas—still unshaven, still wearing the same stained T-shirts and patched Bermuda shorts, cigarettes dangling from their mouths— were looking distractedly into that distance, more interior than external, where seamen lose themselves in order to fend off any trace of nostalgia for the deceptive, ephemeral memories they leave behind on land. The ship had not changed its registry, and the Honduran flag hung, with no great show of enthusiasm, at the stern, where the letters . . . *cyon* continued to pose their faded mystery. It could not have picked up much cargo in Jamaica, because the hull rose conspicuously above the waterline, allowing me to see a section of the propellers as they beat the dark waters of the harbor with obvious difficulty. The ruinous condition of this old servant of the seas was brought home to me with far greater eloquence than before. Once again it was setting out on a bitter adventure, as resigned as a Latium ox in Virgil's *Georgics.* That is how worn, how beaten and submissive, it seemed in its obedience to the enterprises of men whose mean-spirited indifference brought even greater nobility to an effort that had no reward but decay and oblivion. I stood watching as it disappeared over the horizon, and I felt that a part of myself was embarking on a voyage with no return. A siren announced that it was time to leave the docks. The guard was waiting at the gate, slapping a bunch of keys against his thigh to let me know how much trouble I had caused him. The effect of the five pounds had long since dissipated.

I went back to the bar, where the cordial welcome of my expert guide down the road of possible combinations with island rum made it easier for me to bear the painful sense of having betrayed the friend who accompanies me through the dark labyrinth of my dreams: those that night brings and those that occur in clamorous wakefulness. I went to bed as the first couples were returning, disillusioned by their experience of Kingston at night. There was no point in telling them what the port had once been in the days of calypso and hot rum. They would not have understood, and of course it was not worth trying to explain. Dante says there is no greater sorrow than recalling happy times when we are sad. But today we have to do even that by ourselves, and it's probably a good thing.

It remains for me to relate my final encounter with the tramp steamer. I had no idea I was seeing it for the last time. If I had, things might have turned out differently. As I think of it now, what certainly seemed clear at the time was that if the encounters continued, the situation would have taken on the qualities of a mythic persecution, a diabolical spiral that could have ended in one of the superb curses with which the gods of Hellas punished those who transgressed against their immutable designs. But the world is not like that anymore. We barely manage to wreak the paltry quota of vengeance that other human beings impose on us. A trifling matter. Our modest hell-in-life is no longer the stuff of high poetry. In other words, although I did not know it was our last meeting, something told me the game could not go on. It did not lie within the reduced area to which we have relegated the imaginable.

More than ten years ago I visited the mouths of the Orinoco River while I was in Trinidad, enrolled in a training course on the handling of propane gas, where I learned about the dangers of the volatile fuel and the marvels of Antillean music played on oil drums of every size. The entire night and a good part of the day could be spent in a hypnotic trance brought on by the rising and falling waves of rhythm and helped along by the soft, oven-like heat that rules the island most of the year. We sailed, one unforgettable weekend, on a company tugboat to explore the intricate delta where the Orinoco empties its waters into a treacherous Atlantic that seems meek but is full of sinister surprises. I still remember the uninterrupted singing of the flocks of birds whose gamut of colors and sizes kept us in a continual state of astonishment for an entire day. At night, in the thick darkness of a primitive tropical forest, their deafening calls and constant movement did not end.

I returned for another visit, this time as part of a joint mission of the nations that had interests in the rich watershed of the Orinoco. We were six delegates in all, and I, with minimum efficiency, carried out the duties of secretary. I agreed to participate in this bureaucratic exercise only for the sake of returning to the delta; my memory, now tinged with nostalgia, of that landscape's imposing marvels still produced the same wonder in me. We stayed in bungalows on a military post at San José de Amacuro. We enjoyed every comfort, including air-conditioning, whose function was to keep us on the periphery of a climate that affords me a particular sense of well-being, a mental alertness and acuity easily confused with the effects of some unknown hallucinogen. Few pleasures are comparable to unplugging the air conditioner, lying down on a bed protected by a tent of mosquito netting, which has a kind of ceremonial, majestic quality, and letting in the night with its aromas that travel on surges of humid, caressing, almost generative heat. We spent several days exploring the complex delta at Amacuro. They were superficial, not very detailed incursions. It can take years to become familiar with so splendid a labyrinth. We went as far as Curiapo and San Félix, where the abominable signs of our civilization began to make their appearance: plastic, junk food, contraband, and strident music. We returned to San José de Amacuro and spent more than a week preparing a rough draft of the report we were responsible for writing. For me it meant a salutary immersion in the nirvana of the delta. We had to sail upriver to Ciudad Bolívar, to submit a first draft of the weighty conclusions reached by armchair experts, who have a dubious talent for saying nothing worth remembering in a torrent of words that are then laid to rest in ministerial archives until they are unearthed by other, similarly gifted experts, who once again start the cycle of foolishness that allows them to collect their salaries in peace and engage in the gray activity known as "pursuing a career." I did not travel with the others to the capital, on the pretext that I was suffering the early stages of fever and had to undergo emergency treatment at the infirmary on the base. A brief chat with the physician on duty arranged everything, and I was free to explore Amacuro in a canoe with an outboard motor operated by a taciturn, sharp-eyed Indian who knew the delta perfectly. I intend one day to tell the story of those journeys, although there are traces of that time, that gift from the gods, in most of the poems I've been scattering in ephemeral magazines and no less forgettable volumes of poetry. My colleagues returned and said nothing at all about my suspicious recovery. They were too involved in discussing the clauses in the Rio de Janeiro treaties and the hermetic conclusions of the Montevideo conference. Clearly, foolishness can even interfere with the senses and obscure miracles of sight, smell, and hearing like those found in the delta at Amacuro.

A Venezuelan navy vessel was to carry us back to Trinidad. From there we would each take a plane to our respective countries. One morning at dawn we were awakened by the siren of the coast guard cutter that had come to pick us up. Half asleep, with hot coffee still scalding our throats, we climbed aboard in a pouring rain. The cutter weighed anchor and sounded the siren again to announce its departure. Just then we heard a response, a stifled, almost animal moan. "A ship's coming in. As soon as it passes we'll be on our way. The channel's very narrow because of the sandbanks; the current's brought down a lot of tree trunks," an officer explained with the kind of military aloofness appropriate for addressing civilians. Days earlier, something had told me that the tramp steamer was nearby. A vague disquiet, a subdued melancholy at leaving the delta, an anticipatory nostalgia for the wonders I had enjoyed there. And indeed, it was the freighter. The *Halcyon,* as I had grown used to calling it when I pondered its nomadic tribulations. I realized, of course, that by now it was in no condition to leave the Caribbean area. It was going to Ciudad Bolívar. "It must be carrying lumber," the officer said, a condescending smile directed toward the ruined relic of a forgotten age as it moved past us with the same uneven clank of its driving rods, the same pitiable faltering of its single smokestack. The crew was nowhere to be seen on deck, and on the bridge a shadowy figure manipulated the controls with brisk, skilled movements. The countless years of grime accumulated on the windows of the bridge revealed little of its interior except for the dim glow of an electric ceiling light and the brief gleam of an instrument. I was struck by the officer's comment, which echoed that of the half-naked beauty at Nicoya: "I don't know how that ship can risk it under these circumstances. With the rain, the current has terrible force, and sandbanks are forming very fast. It looks like it'll break apart at the first jolt. I've never seen a wreck like it." His remarks wounded my deepest feelings of anonymous partisanship for the freighter I had first seen entering the port of Helsinki with the serene, imposing dignity of great, vanquished men. What could this officer, this dandy encased in the fresh starch of his impeccable uniform, know about the hopeless, secret exploits of the venerable tramp steamer, my beloved *Halcyon,* patriarch of all the seas, conqueror of typhoons and tempests, whose moorings in remote and perilous ports had been sought after in all the world's languages? It moved past us, slow and listing slightly—apparently the problem was not the cargo but a structure giving way to pressures too great to withstand—and now it had a slight tremor that ran the length of the ship, like a hidden fever or a supreme weakness that could no longer be disguised. "At half-speed the engines can't control the rhythm of the propellers," the officer explained as if responding to the question I had just asked myself. Again the prow revealed all its shame, and the same flag hung like a shipwrecked rag. The complete name, *Halcyon,* had finally been painted in. It really had not been too difficult to guess, because the position of the legible letters had indicated room for only one preceding syllable.

The cutter entered the channel at full speed and headed for Trinidad under the agile, efficient power of its propellers. There was something insolent, almost intolerably arrogant, in so much velocity and maneuverability. Obviously, I said nothing. What can people know about these things? Least of all the well-dressed functionaries from the ministries, who are worn away by the monotony of receptions, the inanity of embassy luncheons, the intricacies of protocol as inept as it is vain. I went down to my cabin instead, to sleep before the call for lunch. I felt a heaviness in my chest, an uneasiness with no name or evident cause, a kind of ominous premonition that was impossible to concretize. The image of the *Halcyon* entering the meanders of the delta stayed with me as I slept, with a fidelity that signified something I did not wish to decipher. The bell for lunch woke me with a start. I did not know the time or where I was. Under the lukewarm, slightly muddy water of the shower, I managed to gather the few thoughts I needed to converse with my traveling companions.

*   *   *

And so my encounters with the tramp steamer came to an end. Its memory joined the unadorned collection of obsessive images that merge with the most "mineral and obstinate" essences of my being. It appears in my dreams less and less frequently, but I know very well it will never disappear entirely. In my waking hours I recall it whenever certain circumstances, a certain uncommon ordering of reality, seem to bear a resemblance to its visitations. As time passes, the corner of my mind where those images go to hide becomes deeper, more secret, less visited. This is how we forget: Our affairs, no matter how close to us, are made strange through the mimetic, deceptive, constant working of a precarious present. When one of these images returns with all its voracious determination to survive intact, then what learned men call an epiphany occurs: an experience that can be either devastating or a simple confirmation of certain truths that allow us to go on living. I said I never saw the tramp steamer again, but I did hear of it again, and that was when I learned the full anguish of its history. The gods rarely permit us to move aside the veils that conceal certain areas of the past, perhaps because we are not always prepared for what we will see. I cannot even imagine the happiness of those who "consult oracles higher than their grief."

Some months after my visit to the mouths of the Orinoco, I had to spend long periods of time at the refinery on the banks of the great navigable river that crosses a good part of my country. A long, rancorous labor dispute obliged me to stay there for several months in efforts that ranged from open negotiations with the union to discreet interventions in the region's radio stations and newspapers to present management's views to the public. During periods of calm, instead of taking a plane to the capital, I chose to travel downriver to the great seaport. I made the trip in the company's small but comfortable tugs, which transported long caravans of barges loaded with fuel or asphalt. Each tug had two cabins for passengers, who shared with the captain the food prepared by two Jamaican women whose culinary talents we never tired of celebrating. The pork in plum sauce, the rice with coconut and fried plantains, the succulent stews made of river fish, and, an indispensable and always welcome complement to the meals, the miraculously refreshing pear juice with vodka that left us splendidly disposed to enjoy the constantly changing panorama of the river and its banks; thanks to the magic of that imponderable drink, everything took place in a velvety, contented distance that we never attempted to decipher. (I should mention that whenever the passengers who were fondest of those tugboat voyages attempted to duplicate the combination of vodka and pear juice on land, we were miserably disappointed. We simply produced an undrinkable mixture.) At night, after long conversations on the small deck where we sat waiting for an illusory cooling breeze, we would fall into our bunks, lulled by the laughter of the black cooks and the charm of their incomprehensible but fluid dialect, in which English served as the linguistic canvas.

The strike never did erupt, and negotiations with the union started down a convoluted, byzantine path that would take a long time to travel. I decided to visit the port, and I went to our shipping offices to reserve a place on the next tug. The clerk who always took care of me was talking to a tall, slender man with thick graying hair, who spoke with a slight accent, somewhere between French and northern Spanish, which I found intriguing. "The captain will be traveling with you," the clerk said to me by way of introduction. The man turned to look at me, and with a smile that was amiable but tinged with a kind of gentle austerity, he shook my hand firmly and said, "Jon Iturri. Pleased to meet you." His gray eyes, almost hidden by heavy brows, had the characteristic look of a man who has spent most of his life at sea. They gaze directly at you but seem never to lose sight of something distant, a supposed horizon that is indeterminate but always present. I was given my boarding voucher, and the seaman waited to walk out with me. We headed for the bungalows where the dining room was located. The lunch call had already sounded. His step was firm and somewhat military, but he had the slight roll at the waist of someone who walks on land as if he were still on deck. My curiosity got the better of me, and I asked suddenly, "Excuse me, Captain, but I'm fascinated by your accent. Please forgive me, but it's a deformation of character I find difficult to control." He smiled more openly. His tanned face and heavy black mustache highlighted his perfect teeth. "I understand. Think nothing of it. Besides, I'm used to it. I was born in Ainhoa, in the French Basque country. My parents came from Bayonne. But for various family reasons, I went to school in San

Sebastián and then began my career as a sailor in Bilbao. I'm totally bilingual, but in each language I still have the other accent. My name is another reason for curiosity. The Americans here call me John, and it seems perfectly natural to them." "Well," I replied, "as soon as I heard your name I suspected you might be Basque. A friend of mine in Bilbao is also named Jon. A very good poet too." We continued chatting and had lunch together. He was a typical Basque. He had the distant but open dignity of his people, which has always appealed to me. But along with this national virtue, one could also detect in him an area that he defended with instantaneous zeal against incursions from the outside. He gave the impression of having been in a place like Dante's circles of Hell, where the torments, rather than physical, were of a particularly painful mental kind. During our first meeting we discovered that we shared enough interests and memories to anticipate a pleasant trip together. "Once," I told him, "when I was on my way from Fuenterrabía to Bordeaux, my rental car broke down in Ainhoa, and I had to spend the night in a hotel whose name I've never forgotten, for some reason: Hotel Ohantzea." "It belonged to one of my father's cousins many years ago," he said. Sometimes a detail like this creates full-blown cordiality without our really knowing why. It's not surprising. Sharing a landscape or a town from our youth, even briefly, makes us feel at home. And naturally this is even more marked in those who wander the world with no anchor or permanent home. This was true in our case: He was a sailor, and I had moved frequently from one country to another, always for reasons that had nothing to do with my own desires.

The tug arrived three days later. I went aboard at night. The caravan of barges that had to go downriver to the seaport was ready. I did not see Iturri when I settled into my cabin. I unpacked and went on deck to stretch out on one of the canvas chairs that are always there for the passengers. When I call it a deck I am speaking figuratively. The tiny, three-by-four-meter rectangle on the roof of the bridge did not deserve so generous a name. One climbed a ladder to an area enclosed by a metal railing painted in the company's colors: red, white, and blue. The joke regarding the French flag was inevitable, and no one paid attention to it anymore. No sight can compare to the river and its shoreline from that privileged height. I lay on the chair and prepared to enjoy the details of our departure. I have always thought the skill and coordination needed to guide a string of fuel-laden barges around the curves, bends, and meanderings of the great river are a feat difficult to surpass. Just then I heard someone climbing the ladder. It was Iturri. I must admit I had almost forgotten him in my fascination with the navigational maneuvers on the river. With no greeting, and as naturally as if he were continuing a conversation begun earlier, the captain remarked: "I've never understood why I find river maneuvers mildly irritating. They're like a railroad on water. Water that either moves with you or goes in the opposite direction. It lacks seriousness. Don't you agree?" I had to tell him that on the contrary, it aroused my interest and even my respect. I considered the successful transport of ten barges filled to the brim with flammable liquid a major accomplishment. "Don't mind me," the Basque replied. "Seamen become a little crazed. On land we always feel something like transients and don't really know how to appreciate the things that happen there. For example, I hate trains. I have the impression of too much iron and too much noise for an effort that seems so . . . so idiotic." I had to laugh at the essential honesty, rather brusque but not objectionable, of this sailor suffering the slow dullness of life on terra firma. We continued talking, with long intervals of silence. It was the first time he was traveling on a company tugboat. And he did not work for the firm. He had come to give expert testimony regarding two consecutive accidents that one of our tankers had suffered while docking in Aruba. The insurance company appointed him to represent its interests in the ensuing investigation. He had been obliged to go to the refinery because it was the only place where he could obtain certain data on the transport of combustible materials in leakproof compartments. Now he was returning to ship out on a Belgian freighter that would take him to the Gulf of Aden, where a job was waiting for him as a replacement for the captain of a small ship that transported frozen foods along the coasts of the Gulf nations. The regular captain had suffered an attack of diabetes and would be out of commission for some time.

Our voyage to the seaport would last more than ten days. The tug had to make several stops to deliver some barges, pick up others that were empty, and take them to the company's docks at the storage facility in the great port. Neither of us was in any hurry to arrive. "I could have taken a plane," Iturri explained, "but I thought it would be more interesting and relaxing to sail the river. I've always wanted to make this kind of trip. I don't know any rivers except for a few deltas. The Schelde, for instance, the Thames, the Seine at Le Havre. Not all of them are this passable and safe. Not all of them." I sensed something in his final words. A kind of difficulty in saying them, a dryness in the throat, almost as if a muffled growl had choked him unexpectedly. He remained silent for a long time, and then we talked of other things.

The vodka and pear juice helped to make the journey's routine agreeable, and we decided to give it a Catalan name, calling it *vodka amb pera* in tribute to the loyalty we both felt to the bars in Barcelona, especially the Boadas and the bar at the Savoy, where spiritous wisdom reaches unsurpassed heights of perfection. Many of our individual experiences in the City of the Count were almost interchangeable. The same places, identical encounters, a shared weakness for certain corners of the city, the same devotion to the Greek port of Ampurias and the *rape* served at the yacht club in Escala. It was not surprising, then, that despite his Basque reserve and my desire to respect it, as the days passed the subjects of our conversations took on a more personal, intimate character. Confidences surfaced naturally, and each night, after our third *vodka amb pera,* we would venture into terrains where feelings were warily revealed. We took all the precautions of people who, in that terrain, rigorously avoid vain display or platitudes that contribute nothing to real understanding of the secret catastrophes of the heart, which can be shared so rarely that these occasions eventually are thought of as unimaginable.

One night, when the heat became almost unbearable, we sat on our chairs watching the slow passage of the full moon across an almost cloudless sky—something unusual in those regions. The effect of moonlight on the water and in the forest clearings along the banks had the quality of a Maeterlinck stage setting. Naturally we drifted to the subject of Flanders: its cities, people, and cuisine. Inevitably we talked of Antwerp, a city very dear to me for a multitude of reasons, with a harbor that has the greatest appeal and most harmonious activity of any port, since traffic along the Schelde is a delicate, slow set of maneuvers that turn the entrance and departure of ships into a kind of ballet. As I've already mentioned, we had broken the barrier of sharing confidences, and on this occasion it was Iturri who said something that immediately aroused my particular interest.

"In Antwerp," he said, "I first met the men who would change my life completely. They were a Lebanese who was part pirate and part merchant, clever and charming like most of his compatriots, and his friend and partner, a man of unspecified nationality, who at that time was plundering the Mediterranean in enterprises that did not always respect conventional morality. We met in an Indonesian restaurant along the waterfront, where I was reluctantly eating one of those Oriental dishes that seem prepared expressly to take away one's appetite. The three of us were all protesting at the same time about some irregularity in the service, and in the end we left together, to eat a more normal and abundant Belgian meal at a modest *bistrot*. That's where my life took a direction I never could have imagined."

"But how did that happen?" I asked. "I can't see one of those ninety-degree turns in a person of your character. It doesn't fit the Basque nature. You're all rebellious, of course, and in no way conformist, but you tend to die within your own law, in the town where you were born, practicing the trade you learned as children." I was really puzzled by so radical a change in someone like Iturri.

"Don't you believe it. One must always be prepared for revelations that ripen and break through the surface without our even being aware of the process, things that began long ago. The fact is I had made it an inflexible rule to always work for established shipping lines, to avoid any kind of experimentation or adventures on my own, yet I ended up as part owner and captain of a tramp steamer that looked as if it would go down at any moment. I've never seen a wreck like it."

Something stirred suddenly in my memory and moved me to ask, with an interest that could not help but baffle him, "The ship was anchored in Antwerp? That's where you sailed from? You must know the harbor regulations concerning itinerant freighters, the maintenance standards they require for docking at their piers."

"No, of course, it wasn't in Antwerp," he answered, smiling at my nautical information (this was almost the extent of it). "I took command in the Adriatic, in Pola, to be exact. You had to have seen it. Its dilapidation was spectacular. And the name was just as fantastic and extreme—the mythical bird that nests in the middle of the ocean. Or, if you prefer, the couple who claimed to be happier than Zeus and Hera."

A slight shudder ran down my spine. There are coincidences that violate all possible contingencies and become intolerable because they imply a world governed by laws we do not know, laws that do not belong to the habitual order of things. My voice betrayed how disconcerted I felt, and I could only ask, "The *Halcyon*?"

"Yes," said Iturri as he stared at me, intrigued.

"I'm afraid," I said, "that for me this closes the circle of an enigma that engaged me more than it should have and intruded on a good number of my waking hours as well as many of my dreams."

"What are you saying? I don't understand." Iturri's brows drew together over his gray eyes in a feline expression, not threatening but alert and uneasy.

I gave him a rather hurried summary of my meetings with the *Halcyon* and what they meant to me, the ardent solidarity the ship had awakened in me, and our last encounter in the mouths of the Orinoco. Iturri said nothing for a long time. I had no desire to speak either. Each of us had to reorder the elements of our recent friendship and the dizzying parade of phantoms roused by an almost inconceivable coincidence. When I assumed the conversation would not continue that night, I heard him say in a low voice, "*Anzoátegui*: The coast guard cutter was named *Anzoátegui*. My God! Life follows such strange paths. And we think we're in control. How innocent we are. We're always stumbling in the dark. Well, it doesn't matter." The resignation flowed from him with a nobility worthy of Quevedo. In a more natural tone of voice, as if he were trying to guide the entire matter along a road of ordinary normality, which would make it more bearable, he remarked:

"So the poor tramp steamer that for so many years didn't even have its complete name on the stern became almost as familiar and obsessive for you as it was for me. Except in my case, it was the reason my life went up in smoke. The life I wanted to lead, I mean. The one I live now requires only my body. It isn't that I lost everything: just the one thing that made it worth the effort to go on gambling against death."

There was such desolation, such ravaged distance in his words that I tried to comfort him—it was ingenuous of me—with an innocuous observation. "I think that happens to almost all of us who choose a nomadic, circuitous life." He looked at me again, as one looks at a child who has said something at the table that can be excused only because of his age. "No," he corrected me, "that's not it. I'm talking about the kind of disaster in which everything sinks to the bottom irretrievably. Nothing's left. But memory goes on, tirelessly spinning its thread to remind us of our lost

kingdom. I'm thinking that since you were so closely and profoundly connected to the fate of the *Halcyon,* it's only reasonable
and certainly fair that you hear the rest of the story. One of these
nights I'll tell you all of it. I couldn't now. I have to adjust a little
to the coincidence. It's suddenly brought us closer than the mere
accident of our meeting on this tug. We've been traveling
together a much longer time, a much greater distance." I nodded.
I had no words to add to his. Very simply, he was saying what was
in my mind. Long after the clock in the bridge struck midnight
we went to bed, exchanging "Good night"s in which another
accent could be detected, the accent of a recent, fraternal complicity and the beginning of a new and different stage in our
travels.

That night I dreamed again about the tramp steamer, dizzying,
disordered episodes in which the decrepit ship explained its presence in indecipherable signs that filled me with a vague uneasiness, a silent guilt about something I could not name. At dawn, as
the first light shone on my face through the thin curtains at the
porthole, the *Halcyon* appeared to me freshly painted in brilliant,
vivid colors: the hull a vermilion almost the color of dried blood,
the decks a delicate cream with a blue stripe that ran along all the
cabins, the officers' deck, and the bridge. The smokestack was also
cream, with an identical stripe. "Who could have painted a ship
this way? It's ridiculous," I thought in a brief moment of half-
sleep before I woke completely. That was when the tug began
moving toward shore to dock at a small settlement of thatched
houses and a few buildings with tin roofs. The place was particularly seamy and poor. On what must have been the barracks, the
tricolor waved with a lassitude that made the suffocating heat
even more apparent. Two planes, marine Catalinas painted gray,
were moored at the end of a ramshackle wooden pier. "This is La
Plata," explained the pilot, who was walking past my room just
then. "They've been having a lot of trouble here for a long time
with people up on the barrens. We're delivering a barge of diesel
fuel and getting out as soon as we can." The name of the town
and the pilot's explanation did not mean much to me at the time.
I went back into my cabin to shower before having breakfast
with the Basque, who was in the next cabin, where the noise
of the water made it sound as if he were doing gymnastics in
the shower. I found this especially touching. There was something intimate, almost family-like, in his unexpectedly enthusiastic splashing. It reminded me of morning showers at boarding

school in Brussels. The connections one makes when ruthless, indecipherable fate intervenes!

During breakfast, as brief as it was frugal since we both had only tea and buttered toast, we spoke of inconsequential things— the port, the planes, the perpetual violence spreading up and down the river—nothing, in short, that really affected our lives, which we each sensed were turning toward other horizons, other climates, other people. Which ones? Neither of us could have given a precise answer.

A few days later we entered the final stretch of river, where the water spreads over vast marshes, mangrove swamps, and land that is flooded almost the entire year. It is difficult to determine the current's original channel, and the men who pilot ships down- river to the ocean—most of them learn their trade from their fathers—navigate with extreme caution despite their long years of experience and sometimes decide to stop for the night. Losing one's way in the mangrove swamps and lagoons means the almost certain loss of the ship and great danger for the passengers and crew. The implacable sun shimmers brilliantly on the endless water and blinds the pilots, and there have been many instances of vessels whose occupants, burned by the sun and devoured by insects, have died of hunger and thirst. And if one is also required to bring safely to port ten barges loaded with petroleum prod- ucts, as well as a few empty ones, then the difficulties increase considerably. Dropping anchor for the night along the uncertain bank of the principal channel is an inviolable rule for the tugboat captains employed by the oil companies.

The heat was increasing as we approached the delta. The crew spread an enormous mosquito net that looked like a tent in the desert over the roof of the bridge, where our chairs were located. They knew that with the air-conditioning not operating because the engines had stopped for the night, sleeping in the cabins was unthinkable. And so, almost without realizing it, we changed the order of our life on board: We slept during the day, when the tug- boat was moving, and at night we sat on the small deck, protected from the mosquitoes and waiting for dawn.

During those endless nights, Iturri told me his story. My hav- ing been witness to certain crucial moments in the life of the *Halcyon,* and therefore of its captain, granted me the undeniable right to hear his heartfelt confidences. "This is the first and last time I'm talking about this. You can repeat it to anyone you like later on. That isn't important; it doesn't concern me. Jon Iturri has really ceased to exist. Nothing can affect the shadow that walks the world now and bears his name." He said this with no sadness, not even with the acquiescence of the vanquished, as impersonally as if he were in a classroom explaining a chemical process. He spoke for several successive nights, and my occasional interruptions were intended only to specify a place or reinforce a mutual memory and make it more precise. He did not lose himself in digressions or detailed descriptions, but he often fell into long silences, which I was very careful not to interrupt. At such moments he seemed like someone who breaks the water's surface to take in air before plunging back down to the depths. The tale is worth telling from its real beginning, even though that is merely one more of the many commercial anecdotes that touch on the life of any ship's captain. The fates began weaving their threads from the very start of the affair, and it is interesting to watch the process.

The Lebanese and his associate, the two men with whom Iturri had eaten supper in Antwerp, came to his hotel three days later. The Beirut shipowner, with unhurried manners and words that were courteous but never honeyed, explained that he wanted to make him a business proposition. He had been very favorably impressed by the Basque and had taken the liberty of making a few inquiries regarding his career as a ship's captain, with excellent results. His friend and associate was not involved in what he would propose, but he was like a member of the family and could contribute valuable information concerning the operation he wished to suggest. Could the three of them have a meal together that same day? He agreed, not without some uneasiness. At this point in the story, the Basque again insisted on the characters of the two men. The Lebanese was named Abdul Bashur, and he enjoyed a good reputation in business, customs, and banking circles, not only in Antwerp but in other European ports. True, he had a peculiar range of interests and activities, not all of them as clear or, apparently, as well established as his basic profession of shipowner. This was normal for Levantines, whether Lebanese, Syrian, or Tunisian. Iturri was accustomed to such character traits, and they in no way surprised or discomfited him. The other man, whose name he never understood clearly but who was also called Gaviero, was treated by Bashur with unreserved familiarity and listened to with the greatest attention in matters relating to commercial shipping and the operation of freighters in the most remote corners of the world. The Basque could not determine if Gaviero was a nickname, a surname, or simply a designation left over from the time he was a lookout in his youth. A man of few words, with a rather odd, corrosive sense of humor, he was extremely attentive and sensitive in his friendships, knowledgeable about the most unexpected professions, and, while not a womanizer, very conscious of, one might almost say dependent on, a feminine presence. In this regard he often made fleeting, coded remarks to Bashur, who did no more than acknowledge them with a vague smile.

Here I must make a brief aside before continuing with the captain's story. From the very moment he mentioned the names of Bashur and the Gaviero, I felt obliged to tell him I knew the first by name, having heard about him from the second, an old friend whose confidences and tales I have been collecting for many years, considering them of some interest to those who enjoy hearing about the unusual, contrary lives of people who do not follow the common path of gray routine in an age of mindless conformity. But I also thought that if I let him know of my connection to Maqroll, he would either stop confiding in me or suppress the episodes involving Bashur or the Gaviero. And so I decided to remain silent. I knew I had done the right thing when the Basque seaman finished his story, for nothing would have been gained by telling him something that for him belonged to a past buried forever, if not in oblivion then certainly in the irrevocable darkness of what will never return. Another reason for hiding my relationship with his associates was that it now constituted a second fortuitous circumstance, which might awaken in the hard-pressed corners of his spirit an understandable distrust, or at least some reserve, in the face of so extraordinary yet repeated a coincidence. Chance is always suspect, and much that is fraudulent imitates it. We can return now to the captain of the *Halcyon.*

Their proposal to him was very simple, but as he had already said, accepting it would mean a break with his principle of working only for large shipping companies and always avoiding the tortuous, unpredictable adventures of tramp steamers. They were offering him equal partnership with another associate in the operation of a freighter undergoing repairs in the Pola shipyards, a six-thousand-ton vessel with ample holds and two derricks. The machinery was in good condition although it had been operating for thirty years without a major overhaul. The ship belonged to one of Bashur's sisters, who had inherited it from an uncle.

Warda, which was her name, wanted to be free of the interests held in common by the family. The ship could provide an income that would enable her to reach her goal. Abdul did not go into great detail about this, but it was easy to deduce that Warda was more Europeanized than her two sisters and, of course, her numerous brothers. Abdul did not look askance at his sister's wish for independence, but obviously he wanted it to be achieved with no harm to the enterprises that the rest of the Bashur family managed as a group. Iturri would receive half the profits, less expenses and taxes. He found the proposal interesting, but before he made any decision two basic conditions had to be met: He would have to see the ship, and he would have to talk to the owner. When he mentioned his second condition, the captain saw a shadow cross the Gaviero's eyes. More than a shadow, it was a kind of dark, anticipatory curiosity about what such a meeting would mean to this stranger from the hidden villages of a mountainous land that shelters a singular and unpredictable race. All of this may have been in the Gaviero's glance; that certainly was my traveling companion's a posteriori conclusion. It is more reasonable to assume that what appeared in the eyes of Bashur's associate was a "You'll see," heavy with vague promises.

Bashur accepted the conditions. Travel expenses to Pola would be paid by the tramp steamer's owner. Iturri had several matters to attend to in Antwerp, and they agreed to leave for Italy a week later. During that time Jon gathered information about Bashur and his associates. I have already indicated the results of his inquiries. The manager of a Spanish-French bank, a good friend with whom Jon Iturri played occasional games of billiards, summarized his opinion in words that define the pair precisely. "Look," he said, "they're people who keep their promises and try to meet their commitments. They work together in a lot of things, not all of them exactly within the law. This Gaviero, for example, was involved with a woman from Trieste who was also Bashur's lover, but that didn't affect their friendship. This lady's ability to dream up the most extravagant, risky financial schemes reached lunatic extremes. But the three of them made money, and they were the ones who had the last laugh. As for Bashur's brothers, I don't think they've gone along with excesses like these. They're more settled, more serious, but that doesn't mean they're not implacable if there's a profit to be made. I don't know much about his sister. I think so far they've kept her hidden. You know how Muslims are about things like that. If she wants her freedom now, she must have an iron character. You'll just have to go and talk to her and see for yourself."

That is what he did. From now on I will be obliged to make the most faithful use of my memory in transcribing Iturri's words. If his meeting with Warda on the *Halcyon* is not told with certain elements to which he gave particular emphasis, it risks falling into the stale inconsequentiality of a cheap romance. Nothing could falsify the story more than casting it in that light, stripping it of fatal impossibility. I will try, then, to duplicate what my friend said as closely as possible.

They arrived in Pola at night, after almost two days of changing trains and waiting for hours in stations half paralyzed by the strikes that are endemic to Italy. Bashur and the Gaviero went to the wharves because they wanted to sleep on the ship. The captain preferred to stay in a waterfront hotel. He also had the impression that they wanted to speak first, and in private, to the *Halcyon*'s owner. Jon fell into bed like a log and slept until nine the next morning. When he opened the window he realized that his room overlooked the docks. He had only to cross the street to reach them. Ships were loading and unloading in the port, but none seemed to have the characteristics of the one that might soon be his, or partially his. He remembered they had said it was in the yards for minor repairs. When he went down, Bashur and his friend were waiting for him outside, walking back and forth in front of the hotel entrance, absorbed in a conversation that had nothing to do with the purpose of their trip. "These two characters," he thought, "are involved in things much more complicated and shadowy than the freighter. I'd never want them for enemies." They greeted him very cordially, and the three men began walking toward the piers. Iturri mentioned that he had not seen the freighter from the window of his room. "It's behind the Swedish cruise ship heading for Tiflis," the Gaviero explained, with what the Basque thought was a touch of irony. They continued walking, and in fact, on the other side of the great, spotlessly white ocean liner, the *Halcyon* rested wearily at the dock. It had been given a fast sprucing up that could not hide the marks of its long travels through the harshest climates and latitudes on earth. Iturri, of course, was familiar with all kinds of ships with long histories and notable scars, but this one had fallen further from grace than any he had seen. He felt his heart sink. What would he be getting into, sailing this outcast from port to port in search of hypothetical cargo? The Basques have made silence into a steely, unfathomable weapon. Without saying a word, he followed the two men on board while, in a display of rather questionable manners, they went on with their earlier conversation. They walked to what must have been the captain's quarters. The cabin was freshly painted, and the metal had been polished with acceptable care. But the bunk, the small table (one end had two hinges so it could be raised flat against the wall if more room was needed), and a pair of heavy mahogany chairs revealed an implacable use that could not be disguised, an irremediable wear almost worthy of a museum. They clearly had been built before the Great War. Bashur took some yellowing papers from a small chest of drawers attached to the wall over the bunk and spread them on the table. They were the plans of the ship. Leaning over them, he began to explain the vessel's characteristics to his sister's presumptive partner. "We'll look at the engine room, the holds, everything you want to see. In no way do we want you to make a hasty decision. I know the ship doesn't exactly arouse optimism. But appearances are deceiving, and it's much sounder than you might suppose." Iturri thought: "This is truth and Levantine patter in equal parts," and he concentrated on studying the plans. That is what he was doing when he sensed that the light coming in through the door suddenly gave way to semidarkness. Someone was standing in the doorway, looking at him. He raised his head and was struck dumb. It is practically impossible to put what he saw into words. A wicked gleam in the Gaviero's eyes flashed a silent "I told you so" that was both insolent and kind.

Warda, Bashur's sister, observed each of them in turn. She began with the captain, and now she lingered over Abdul. "She was a vision of absolute beauty"—I'm trying to reconstruct what Iturri said that night on the great river—"tall, and her perfect face had eastern Mediterranean features refined until they were almost Hellenic. Her large black eyes had an unhurried, intelligent gaze in which haste or an ostentatious display of emotion would have seemed an unthinkable lack of order. Her blue-black hair was as dense as honey and fell to shoulders as straight as those of the kouros in the Athens Museum. Her narrow hips, curving gently into long, somewhat full legs, recalled statues of Venus in the Vatican Museum and gave her erect body a definitive femininity that immediately dispelled a certain boyish air. Large, firm breasts completed the effect of her hips. She wore a blue alpaca jacket over her shoulders, and a pleated skirt the color of light tobacco. A classic silk blouse, and a silk scarf in a diamond pattern of green, red, and dark brown, draped simply around her neck, lent her outfit a European or rather a Western look that seemed intentional. Her lips protruded slightly but were perfectly shaped, and they suggested a smile as she raised black eyebrows that were heavy but did not disturb the harmony of her face. 'Good morning, gentlemen,' she said in French, making no attempt to hide an Arabic accent that I thought particularly charming. Her voice was firm, and in the lower register it tended to a slight throatiness that was involuntary yet disconcertingly sensual at times. She kissed her brother on the cheek with a worldly air that stripped the gesture of any familial quality, and she gave each of us a firm handshake but held her arm rather stiffly, as if trying to establish an impersonal yet obvious distance." I should probably warn my readers that the references to museums in this description were put there by me. Iturri said something like "those statues of women in Rome" or "the kouros that's in Athens." Then he told me how they visited every corner of the ship, and how Warda showed fairly authoritative knowledge of the engines, the capacity of the hold, and the operation of the derricks. She walked alongside the men with a step that was firm and decisive yet could never be called athletic. "She was one hundred percent Levantine," explained Iturri, "and her desire to adopt the life and styles of the West in no way altered the unmistakable, essential signs of her people. In fact, as you got to know her, you realized she was not merely content with her Arabic blood but proud of it."

They returned to the cabin to continue talking, and Warda suggested going to the lobby of the hotel where she was staying. "We'll be more comfortable there, and we can have something to drink. Or does the captain wish to see anything else here?" Jon had the fleeting notion of paying her a schoolboy's compliment, something like "There's nothing to see here but you." It was only a passing temptation, which he suppressed immediately, but it was curious that he still remembered it. "No, I've seen enough. We can go now, as far as I'm concerned," he replied, taking refuge in the forthright but impeccable manners of a well-bred Basque. This was when he realized that Warda was looking at him from time to time with an interest free of mere curiosity. Surely she was trying to assess the professional competence of the man on whom so many practical aspects of her future would depend. When he stood aside to allow her to walk down the gangway, Warda glanced at him with a smile that revealed large, regular teeth of an almost marble whiteness. Her skin had an olive cast that was enhanced, with evident intent, by the colors of her clothing. "It was a smile of approval," Jon explained with touching seriousness, "and of acceptance, not only of my skill as a seaman but of something more personal. Yet it did not go beyond showing her satisfaction with some external details of my appearance and behavior. But as for me, I was completely captivated by that combination of inconceivable beauty, solid intelligence, and the strength of character demonstrated by her intention to break every tie that bound her to the familial and secular totems of her people. In the lobby of the small but elegant hotel in Pola where Warda was staying, we continued discussing the venture. She and her brother ordered fruit juice; although not observant Muslims, they seemed to show occasional respect for certain Koranic laws. I had the impression that Abdul would have joined us in something stronger but abstained because his younger sister was present. The Gaviero ordered a Campari with gin and ice, and I asked for the same, forgetting my rule about never drinking before noon. This and other very obvious symptoms were the first indications that something in me was changing forever, and that the change had its roots in the presence of Warda. Another sign was my indiscriminate acceptance, with no serious preliminary negotiations, of the conditions of my agreement with the Bashurs. To this day I still can't remember all the clauses in the contract. My only clear recollection is of the few but categorical interventions by Abdul's sister concerning the ship's commercial operations. 'I don't want you to accept cargo that presents any kind of risk. Even minor run-ins with insurance companies and customs officials have to be avoided,' she declared, casting a meaningful glance at the Gaviero and her brother, who must have been experts in that kind of traffic, because they looked at each other and smiled but made no comment. Another condition imposed by Warda, in an equally peremptory way, is one I'll never forget—you'll see why later. 'I want to supervise, personally and regularly, the commercial operations of the ship. And to that end, Captain, you will please keep me informed of your itinerary, and I'll let you know in which port we should meet. Obviously, in all matters relating to maintenance, hiring, and the *Halcyon*'s routes, you have complete freedom and absolute autonomy.' "

Iturri agreed immediately without even considering what that series of meetings might signify or the responsibility it implied for his giving an ongoing account of his work. They also decided that notarization of the agreement and its required filing in the harbor offices would be completed in Pola as soon as possible. Warda was the first to stand and say goodbye. She wanted to rest for a while, she said, because she had traveled all night on a detestable train from Vienna. When she shook Iturri's hand, she said, smiling and serious at the same time, "I'm sure the *Halcyon* will have an excellent captain, and you a partner who will give you no problems. Tell me, were either of your parents English?" "No," he replied with amusement, because he already knew the reason for the question. "All my ancestors are Basque, and they've lived in the same region for centuries. If you're asking because of my name, it's simply coincidence. Jon is as much a Basque name as Iñaki. It doesn't have the *h* that the English name has." "Fine," she said. "I'll keep that in mind. I would have spelled it with an *h* and made a mistake." Jon merely shook his head as a sign it did not matter. The three men stayed awhile longer, refining certain details of the contract. Then they left to eat in a tavern down in the port. The conversation was devoted to sea stories, told, for the most part, by the Gaviero, whose experience in that area seemed inexhaustible. "My first impression of Bashur's associate changed completely," the Basque explained. "I realized that my own provincial and national prejudices had kept me from seeing the enormous wealth of experience and the solid, warm humanity of this man, whose nationality I never learned, as I never learned the correct pronunciation of his name, which sounded vaguely Scottish but could also have been Turkish or Iranian. I found out later that he carried a Cypriot passport. But that doesn't mean anything, because he himself hinted I should not put too much faith in its authenticity."

Bashur and his friend went back to Antwerp the next day. Warda said she would return to Vienna as soon as the papers she and Jon had to sign were ready. This happened on the day after Bashur's departure. Iturri carried his belongings on board and arranged his cabin with scholarly meticulousness. He would spend an indefinite period of time there, at least two years, according to the contract. He met with four machinists and a bos'n, who had been recommended at the harbor office, and then set out to find the rest of the crew on the lists of available seamen posted on the large entrance gates to the docks. He was examining one of them, when he was startled by the voice of Warda Bashur, who stood behind him and spoke almost in his ear. "I wouldn't trust those lists. But it's up to you. Maybe I'm too suspicious." He turned to look at her, and the fact that she had changed her outfit was somewhat disconcerting in the sense that her beauty once more left him speechless. She was wearing a simple cotton dress with large flowers in various pastel shades. Again a raw wool jacket hung over her shoulders. "I thought you were in Vienna," he said for the sake of saying something. "But how could you think I'd leave without saying goodbye to my partner? Besides, there are still some matters to talk over. Are you busy for dinner tonight?" Warda asked. "No, I'm free. Where would you like to eat?" he replied, excited and curious at the possibility of having dinner with her alone. "I don't know if you're very fond of *fruitti di mare*. I'm a little tired of them. There's a Yugoslav tavern on the street just behind the hotel where you're staying. Suppose we meet there at eight?" He could not control the impulse and suggested coming by for her at the hotel. "You're very kind, but I can take care of myself when I'm alone, and I like window-shopping along the main street. Men don't enjoy that very much." Warda's words always contained a kind of hidden invitation for him to respond with a compliment. Or so it seemed to Iturri, who was about to tell her that rather than boring him, the idea seemed charming. But he didn't. An insightful intuition kept him from such temptations. There was in her a poise, a light authoritive tone in the way she spoke to him, and to Abdul and his friend, that did not allow the kind of easy gallantry many women like to play with. And so Jon did no more than confirm that he would be there at the specified time, and she said goodbye with her usual firm handshake. He had lost his desire to go over the lists, and he went to the ship instead to tell the bos'n—an Algerian with fierce eyes but a gentle nature and slow manners that inspired his full confidence—to take charge of signing on the rest of the crew. At least the men they would need for the first voyage. He wanted to go first to Hamburg, where several friends in the coffee business could give him cargo for the Scandinavian countries and a few Baltic ports.

When he arrived at the restaurant, she was waiting for him. He commented with some irony that apparently the windows were not very interesting on the walk from her hotel. "Not interesting, not anything. There's nothing here. It's a dead city, good only for summer tourists who've lost their way. This kind of place depresses me." Iturri thought that raising the Bashurs' youngest sister must have caused the family more than one headache. The food was excellent, the wine even better: a spicy Bosnian white with a slight fruity aroma that was undeniably natural. They talked about Hamburg, their future projects, and how they would communicate. She would give him a post office box number in Marseilles, and his letters would be forwarded to her wherever she might be. He asked if she planned to do a lot of traveling. "I'm asking because of the mail," he explained, "not for any other reason." "What other reason could there be?" she asked in a tone of cordial defiance. "Curiosity, curiosity plain and simple," he replied in the same tone. "Men tend to be much more curious than women. We're just better at disguising it." She said that in fact she wanted to speak with him about something along those lines. "Until now I've lived under the control of my older sisters; my brothers weren't as strict as you might expect in a Muslim family. My sisters were the ones who took over that job, and they were very conscientious. It made some sense when I was a minor. But I'm twenty-four years old now, and the situation is not only unbearable, it's ridiculous. My sisters are both married—typical, compliant women who pretend to be interested in their husbands' business affairs, take care of the children, and keep house. They've always wanted me to do the same. The strange thing is I'm not a rebel and never have been. Perhaps I do want a life similar to the one my sisters lead, but one that I've chosen, that doesn't conflict with my own tastes and preferences, which aren't very constant yet but I expect they will be after I've lived for a while in Paris, then London and New York. I'm a voracious reader and I love painting. Painting that hangs on the wall. I can't draw a straight line. These are my reasons for asking you not to communicate under any circumstances with my family if you want to get in touch with me, and not to discuss my whereabouts if you ever happen to meet one of them. I have nothing to hide, but if I give them the slightest opening they'll push in and won't let me do things my own way. I don't want to give you the impression that I'm a young girl caught up in being rebellious. I'll say it again: I'm a fairly calm person, and I'm irritated by excess, exaggeration, and grandiose phrases. And I don't hold on to a thing just because I think it's permanent. Nothing is. My short life has been long enough to teach me that. Perhaps you think it odd that I'm spending time on such personal matters, but I know my people and want to be safe from their interfering in my life, at least right now, my period of testing and learning, as I rather pompously call it." Of course Iturri gave her every assurance that he would protect her independence and even ventured to say that he thought her plan showed absolute good sense. He was certain that for someone like her, the outcome of this European experiment was bound to be very solid, very positive, and would surely mean a radical change in many of her ideas and customs. She was quick to say that she did not expect it to be all that radical and did not want to change many things that were part of her life now. "Let's say I'm conservative but want to decide what it is I'm going to conserve without consulting others or waiting for their approval."

Jon was surprised at how Warda talked about herself, with an intelligence and objectivity that not only were not typically feminine—at least that's how it seemed to him—but were completely unexpected considering her age and undoubtedly limited experience of life. Something in her had begun to fascinate the Basque in a very particular way. It was the mixture of serenity, natural assurance, and the composure with which she viewed herself and her future, all of it tinged by something that could not be called tenderness but did have a balsamic effect on him. She had no rough edges, no surprising detours or hidden devices about to explode. Everything was expressed in those features of unearthly perfection and in a body no less harmonious and balanced. It occurred to Iturri that during this conversation, and others they had held earlier, she must have been amused by the expression of astonished admiration and dazzled disbelief that was always on his face; the thought of it made him blush. From the very beginning the beauty and balance in Warda had exercised a profound influence on him, and its ramifications were becoming increasingly evident and decisive. Although it might sound melodramatic and exaggerated, the world had changed for Jon. If someone like Warda lived in the world, then the world was not what he had always thought. He would be fifty years old in a few days, and suddenly everything around him seemed completely new and disquieting. It was extremely difficult to explain. Using the term *love* for so total a phenomenon was simplistic and incredibly superficial. That word almost always meant playing with a marked deck. Something had been awakened, and for the moment it could not be captured in words.

They left the restaurant, and without offering or imposing it, he accompanied her to the hotel. When they said good night, she remarked with a warm, somewhat ironic smile, "Well, *mon capitaine,* I'll be hearing from you soon. Remember that my future is in your hands." He stood for a moment, lost in thought, outside the revolving door through which Warda had disappeared. He returned to the ship, threw himself fully dressed on his bunk, and tried to reconstruct each feature of that face, each tone of that voice; they were plunging him into a spell cast by love potions that once would have had no effect on a man of his race of wizards and hermits, of warriors and sailors with no star to guide them.

* * *

Nights in the swamps, under the warm, throbbing phosphorescence of a star-filled sky, were conducive to Jon Iturri's long confession. Unfortunately, my summary or reordering of it here does not allow for the accents of suppressed emotion that intensified as he spoke. The captain's insistence on Warda Bashur's beauty had something reiterative about it, like the chanting of psalms or ballads. I was moved by his struggle with words, which are always so inadequate, so remote from a phenomenon like a person's beauty when it verges on what is essentially ineffable. There was, for instance, his eagerness to describe how she was dressed each time he saw her. Perhaps Jon thought he could succeed from another direction when he sensed that a simple description of her face and body left little more than a confused, insubstantial image. For other reasons, in this case having to do with the natural modesty and reserve of his people, he also stumbled whenever he described his relations with Warda and their arrival at the *hortus clausus* of an intimacy he could not express, not only for the reasons I've stated but because he was a seaman with little experience in navigating the representations and stratagems typical of stories about those who live on land. I will try to follow a straighter, simpler path than the one taken by Jon during our nights in the swamp where he told me about his affecting experience.

In Hamburg he took on a cargo of coffee and heavy machine parts destined for Gdynia and Riga, and then returned to Kiel, where he loaded on more cargo, bound for Marseilles. He informed the *Halcyon*'s owner of his route in the manner they had arranged. He experienced a very curious phenomenon with regard to the tramp steamer: He was growing accustomed to the ship's deplorable appearance, which was, as Bashur had said in Antwerp, rather deceptive. The machinery, even though it dated from the early years of the century, had been maintained with such meticulous and conscientious regularity that it worked a good deal better than its arrhythmic, grumbling intermittency led one to suppose. The lack of paint, the rust that little by little was conquering even the most secret corners of the ship, and its ungainly shape were defects that could be corrected, at least in part, and he proposed to attend to them at the earliest opportunity. The derricks still operated with no major setbacks. They were slow and hesitant, which enraged the stevedores on the docks, but they never failed completely. Jon came to feel a warm solidarity for his ship and was unwilling to listen to the observations, some humorous and others openly insulting, of his colleagues or the dockworkers. Each time this happened, his innermost thought was: "If they only knew the owner they'd change their tune, they'd have to see the *Halcyon* with different eyes."

A brief message from Warda, announcing her arrival the following day, was waiting for him in Marseilles. She did not mention her hotel or what transportation she was using. At noon the next day, as the ship was being unloaded under a June sun burning in a cloudless sky, Jon saw her appear at the foot of the ladder. She had arrived in a taxi, which left immediately. Warda greeted him with an unexpectedly familiar wave of her hand and quickly walked up the swaying gangplank. He was in his shirtsleeves, without the sailor's cap he usually wore, and part of his attention was focused on a derrick that was seizing up constantly. She looked splendid, and again he was struck at how each change of outfit glorified her beauty as if it were a vision he had never seen before. "I could have smashed that damn derrick," he told me, "for distracting me when I wanted to concentrate on my beautiful visitor. It's at times like these that machines behave with the dull-witted, irritating unpredictability of human beings. The bos'n came to my aid, and I put him in charge of overseeing the operation." Warda suggested going to a restaurant in the Canebière district owned by compatriots of hers who knew her family. "I can guarantee two things: an honest wine and a bouillabaisse like the one they served to Marshal Masséna when he stopped here. At least that's what the owners say. They think Masséna fought in the Great War. Don't tell them otherwise: It would be fatal to the bouillabaisse." She waited on deck while Jon took a quick shower and changed his clothes. The restaurant turned out to be truly exceptional. The white wine had an intelligent freshness that allowed the aromas of the food, barely masked by the fruity, earthy aura of the previous year's *clairette de Die,* to expand on the palate. Jon briefly summarized his activities and informed Warda that their profits, without being brilliant, more or less met her estimates for becoming independent. The tone of the conversation had a warmth and spontaneity that had not existed before. Now it was as if they had both worked on their memory of the other's image, which had established a common ground, unspoken but always present. Jon asked how her experience in Europe was going and what conclusions she had drawn during the past few months. "I'm asking," he explained, "because I felt you had great hopes and I didn't want to say anything that could have had a negative influence. You're too intelligent to overlook certain obstacles that contact with the West presents to people whose sensibilities haven't been blunted and who don't see things with a tourist's eyes. Of course, for you, Europe seems a fairly recent continent, like a more sedate America. Or am I wrong?" "Yes," she answered with a smile, "you're completely wrong. I don't know why you attribute more than normal intelligence to me. But in any event, we do come to Europe with very ingenuous eyes. A long time ago our maturity turned into a kind of exhaustion, a decline caused by customs and ideas we can no longer live by even in our own country. But if you want me to tell you what I've been experiencing in Europe, I'd say it's a slow but growing disillusionment. I feel I belong in other environments, other climates. Which ones? I don't know; I can't say yet. It's certainly not nostalgia for my country or my culture. It's as if I already knew and had been bored by everything I'm trying to see and absorb now in Europe. Perhaps that seems obvious to you: You lead a sailor's life and have no permanent home. I don't know. I wish you'd tell me." Her deep eyes had tears in them as she looked at Iturri, waiting for him to speak. "I knew very well what I was supposed to say," the Basque told me, "but at the same time I knew we were talking not only as old acquaintances but as accomplices in a nascent feeling, not yet explicit but certainly evident in the direction our conversation was taking. The white wine contributed a good deal to lowering our mutual defenses and calming our fears. This was another matter, another kind of relationship. When we recalled our first meeting, we seemed strangers to ourselves. We didn't say so. We didn't need words now. At least not the ones that would allude directly and brutally to the change. We sensed it, and that's what mattered. Under those circumstances, it was useless to go on stringing together general platitudes about Warda's 'European experience,' and besides, that wasn't what she wanted to hear. I told her I thought the important thing was to keep her readiness, her openness of spirit. The answers, experiences, and changes would come inevitably. The *Halcyon* promised to produce enough for her to continue her 'sentimental education,' a term that made Warda frown for a moment with those black brows that were almost always tranquil and still. I explained that it included areas much vaster than the simple field of love. Suddenly she confessed something that signaled our definitive entrance into a common history. 'I know what you mean,' she said. 'As for what you call the "field of love," I've already been there, more times than you might suppose for a woman my age. Don't put too much faith in what you hear about Muslim vigilance. I've had several men in my life. *Je ne regrette rien.* But I have no memories worth saving either. Having said that, let's go on with my "sentimental education." I'm counting on your help.' I told her she'd always had it. 'But I don't know if a fifty-year-old man can contribute anything valid or positive,' I added. 'You already have, and it's duly noted,' she answered with her first openly and jubilantly flirtatious look, which left me feeling like a cat that's fallen off a roof and doesn't know for a moment exactly what's happened or where he is. It was past midnight when we left the Lebanese tavern. Abruptly she hailed a taxi, and telling me good night with some haste, she said, 'I'm going to the hotel to catch up on my sleep. I didn't sleep at all on the trip. I suppose the docks are just a few steps from here, aren't they?' No, the docks were much farther than her hotel, but I didn't tell her so. She obviously did not want to continue our conversation; she was protecting herself from something, from some impulse, perhaps from a prolongation of talk in that intimate tone. When she was in the taxi she lowered the window and asked where I planned to go after Marseilles. 'To Dakar, to pick up cargo for the Azores, and from there I'll be carrying freight to Lisbon.' 'We'll see each other in Lisbon,' she said, her eyes very wide as if she were pondering some secret joy in that city."

Iturri nodded his agreement and waited for another cab, to take him to the docks. He was paying the fare and counting out the tip when he realized he was definitively and deeply in love. "Like a schoolboy," he said, "like a poor defenseless schoolboy, shy and afraid. I hadn't felt that way in years." He did not sleep that night, and the next day he had a blinding headache as he set out for Dakar in the middle of one of those summer rainstorms that turn the Mediterranean into a steam bath. He thought the moment had come to paint the *Halcyon.* The frivolity of the idea made him blush. There would be no time to do it. Old friends who believed in his seriousness and wanted to help him had contracted with him for the rest of the year. The loading operation in Dakar took much longer than expected. By the time he reached the Azores, autumn had begun. He remembered that Warda had mentioned plans to visit the great Russian Orthodox sanctuaries, including Zagorsk and Novgorod, late in the fall. The idea of not seeing her soon in Lisbon began to torment him. This was another emotion he had not experienced for a long time: anticipation of a joy that we feel cannot be postponed but that becomes less certain with every passing day. A minor hell that deprived him of sleep and kept him from working with a clear mind. A dead weight, an oppressive feeling in the pit of his stomach, took away his appetite. The voyage from the Azores to the Portuguese capital was absolute torture for him. At times he thought he had a fever. He reflected, to no avail, that at the age of fifty, when he thought experiences like these had been canceled out a long time ago, it was somewhat disconcerting to run headlong into a dead end when all he could hope for, if he risked going ahead, was the icy water of a well-deserved rejection. As he sailed into the mouth of the Tagus, his heart pounded as if he were an adolescent waiting on a park bench.

There was no message for him. He met with some clients to arrange a shipment of olive oil and fine wines to Helsinki. Autumn was slipping away, and Lisbon showed the opaque, melancholy face so attuned to the fados that tourists pretend to enjoy in the taverns. He returned to the ship with an overwhelming exhaustion grinding inside him like the beginning of a tropical disease. He had lost all interest in the *Halcyon,* and when he saw the tramp steamer lying at anchor in the middle of the bay as it waited for a berth at the docks, its graceless figure awakened in him a combination of irritation and apathy. As he was about to climb down to the launch that would take him out to the freighter, he heard a woman's voice calling from a distance: "Jon! Jon! Wait for me." Warda was running along the street that led down to the waterfront. She wore cream-colored slacks and a red blouse, and waved a light-beige sweater to attract his attention. He stood, not moving, on the dock, while an uncontrollable joy exploded in the middle of his chest. When Warda reached his side she kissed him on the cheek; he could barely respond with a light brush against the slightly moist skin of the face that had obsessed him for so long. Without saying a word, she put her arm through his and led him toward the center of the city. They crossed the Avenida Vinte e Quatro de Julho and walked along the Rua do Alecrim. She said that surely some bar would be open in the narrow streets of the Bairro Alto. "I thought you weren't coming. I imagined you on your way to the Orthodox holy places." "For now there's another orthodoxy that has to be taken care of," she replied with a meaningful glance, amused at the expression that must have been on Jon's face. Iturri had that intrinsic Basque inability to hide his emotions. "We found a bar, and there we revealed our feelings, slowly but implacably. I admitted that if she hadn't come I would have gone to Australia to work on a coastal trader," Jon said in a voice that after so many years still betrayed an unexpected despair completely foreign to his upright, reserved character. He recalled very little of their conversation. Warda, without losing the serenity and balance that lent so much charm to her youth, confessed that her presumptive European education had been an unmitigated disaster and that all she cared about now was to be with him. Something in him filled her with a plenitude she had never known before. It was all she wanted. She did not believe the future offered any chance for them to build a life together. She didn't care about that either. What she needed now, needed like the air she breathed, was to live fully in the present. Jon stammered something about the difference in their ages, their nationalities, their customs. Warda shrugged and with the certainty of a clairvoyant replied that he didn't believe a word he was saying and none of it mattered in the least. It was six in the evening and they had consumed several bottles of vinho verde along with some perfectly unmemorable fried fish. They went to her hotel on the Avenida da Liberdade and tried to walk in with firm, natural steps. Jon registered as Warda's husband, and they rode up to the room in an embrace so close that the elevator operator turned around a few times to see if they were still breathing. Every article of clothing they were wearing lay scattered on the floor between the door and the bed.

"We made love again and again, with the slow, meticulous intensity of people who don't know what will happen tomorrow. Warda's obsessive desire to fill the present with meaning was based on her intelligent and accurate assessment of the limited possibilities and hopeless obstacles our relationship offered. As I had said in the bar, I couldn't see where it would lead either. And so, with a surrender that bordered on desperation, we took refuge in the pleasure of our bodies. Warda, when she was naked, acquired a kind of aura that emanated from the perfection of her body, the texture of her moist, elastic skin, and that face: Seen from above, when we were in bed, it took on even more of the qualities of a Delphic vision. It's not easy to explain or describe. Sometimes I think it never happened. The only thing that has stopped me when I've wanted to die is the thought that this image would die with me." When he reached these barriers to communicating his experience, Iturri would fall into long silences in which profound despair stirred up its bitter dregs. Then he went on. "We spent three days in the Hotel de Lisboa and never left the room. We had turned it into a kind of private universe, a slow alternation between almost wordless lovemaking and an exchange of confidences about our childhoods and our discovery of the world. Warda possessed a very peculiar idea of a sailor's life. I had little to tell her about my own experience at sea. Nothing unusual had happened to me in a profession filled with gray tedium relieved only by the changes in climate and landscape that constant travel necessarily imposes. I can't reconstruct our conversations now. I do remember that her character made them serene and full, and that anecdotes and surprises gave way to the examination and assimilation of our personal visions of the world and its people. As I've said, Warda had something of the sibyl about her. She moved through the half-trance of her sensations with the confidence of a sleepwalker. In this she was as fully Oriental as any genie in the *Arabian Nights.*"

Jon finally had to return to the ship and attend to certain customs transactions prior to the freighter's departure. He had used the hotel phone to close the contract for Helsinki, where he was to pick up an important shipment of paper for Vera Cruz. Warda stayed with him during these negotiations, which she followed with discreet but intense curiosity, attributing to the transactions a mystery that made Iturri laugh. Neither of them wanted to mention the moment when they would say goodbye, and when it arrived she would only promise in a voice that did not quite succeed in its attempt to be natural, "I'll see you in Helsinki. I'll wait for you in the port." Jon explained that he would be forced to make a stop in Hamburg to replace some engine parts, which would take at least a month because he would have to wait his turn at the shipyards. By the time he reached Helsinki the temperature would have fallen to well below zero. "As soon as you find out, let me know the exact date of your arrival. I'll be in the port." This kind of certainty, this unwavering firmness, was one of the traits that Jon found most attractive in Warda, who had, as he put it, "the wisdom of the matrons at home in Ainhoa, and the body of Aphrodite. Too much for the poor life of one man." When we reached this part of the story, he fell into one of his silences, perhaps the longest of all those that had interrupted his confession over the course of several nights.

*   *   *

When I thought he had finished talking and was ready to go back to his cabin, he began to speak again. "Now my story intertwines with yours. I must admit that what surprised me was not your encountering the *Halcyon;* that's just ordinary chance and easy to understand. What really intrigued me and was, in fact, the reason for telling you my story is another coincidence. This one is absolutely unsettling, and I listened to it as if you were transmitting a covert sign from a secret brotherhood: Every one of your encounters with the *Halcyon* coincided with a decisive, critical moment in my love affair with Warda. There were other memorable times, happy times, but a combination of circumstances made each of those ports of call—Helsinki, Puntarenas, Kingston, the delta of the Orinoco—a place where our future would either be defined or disappear forever. The only thing left for me to tell you is what happened on the *Halcyon* and what our feelings were each time the old ruin of a ship showed up when you were least expecting it. You're the only witness who has a right to know the facts. In a way that I'll never be able to explain, you're also a major protagonist."

Then Iturri proceeded to explain details of the repairs in Hamburg, where the ship was also registered at the Honduran consulate, since its Italian license had expired and could not be renewed. By the time the freighter steamed into Helsinki, winter had settled in with the severity I described when I told about my first encounter with the *Halcyon*. Warda was faithful to her promise. When the ship docked, she walked up the gangplank along with the harbor officials. She shook the captain's hand and took refuge in his cabin while the authorities were on the bridge verifying the vessel's documents. When at last he was free, Jon went to his quarters. Warda lay on the bed in a hieratic posture, looking at the ceiling. A smile played over her lips when she saw his face. The heat was turned up as high as it would go, and the room smelled of toothpaste, aftershave, and objects lined in leather, the characteristic scent of certain exclusively masculine places where a military discipline prevails. "Come, give me a kiss and don't look that way. I'm staying here as long as the ship's in Helsinki. I suppose you have no objections? None of those superstitions about women on ships and all the rest of that nonsense?" Iturri replied that he had no such objection, that on tramp steamers it was common for the captain to travel with his wife or with a friend who pretended to be his wife. What concerned him was the obvious discomfort, the lack of space and other things a woman found indispensable. But more than anything else, he was intrigued by her preferring the *Halcyon* to the luxurious hotels in Helsinki, which were famous for being the most comfortable in northern Europe. They could just as easily stay in one of them as in this shabby, ill-equipped cabin. Warda explained that she had several reasons for making this decision. "In the first place," she said, "I can't abide these Nordic types. They make me think of rag dolls that move like humans, and it throws me into a panic. They drink badly, they eat badly, and from the little I remember of a short-lived affair, they love with all their Protestant guilt intact. Imagine what that means for someone from Beirut." Second, she had taken it into her head to live with him on the ship, to watch him work when they were loading and unloading cargo, to see a Jon she did not know. "I've brought the right clothes; don't worry, I'll be fine," she said in anticipation of any further objection. Finally, she wanted to spend time with him in the bars and little restaurants along the waterfront, where the atmosphere was bound to be warmer and more relaxed than in the hotels, which reminded her of California funeral homes that had been transported to the Arctic. Iturri was delighted with the idea, and he told Warda so. They would pick up her luggage at the air terminal and then come back to the ship.

The days in Helsinki were brightened by a flood of optimism and the confirmation of their experience in Lisbon, which had possessed the sort of completeness that leads one to think it can never be repeated. Making love and sleeping together in the narrow space of the bunk gave rise to the kinds of gymnastics that made them laugh uncontrollably. Their love grew strong in the firm, clear agreement not to burden it with ulterior consequences or attempt to direct it toward a lasting commitment. "As long as this lasts it will be the way it is now. It can't be otherwise, and we both know that. The important thing is not to try to alter the situation or let others interfere in an effort to change it.

Everything depends on us, and let's not talk about it anymore—it's tiresome and doesn't get us anywhere." She made this analysis while they were attempting, with some reservations, to consume a reindeer fillet prepared with herbs from the tundra and accompanied by iced Finnish vodka flavored with pepper and ginger. They had grown fond of this small waterfront tavern, which had a large tiled chimney in the middle of a tiny room where six tables were served by two smiling women of a certain age, who spoke nothing but Finnish and consequently had absolute control over what they ate. When Jon saw her drink one small glass after another of the vodka that freezing had turned to slow-moving syrup, he reminded her of how, in the hotel bar on the day they first met, she and her brother Abdul had both abstained from alcohol. "And there you have," she explained with almost doctoral gravity, "the whole key to my problem, and the one that faces many Muslims: We submit on the surface to rules that we've grown used to bending, while we ignore certain essential truths." He observed that now she seemed to drink alcohol with no hesitation. Jon would later remember her reply as an early warning that he had disregarded: "Yes, now I drink vodka and make love to a *rumi,* but every day I feel more alienated from Europe, more disinterested, and every day I have a deeper understanding of my brothers and sisters who make their pilgrimage to Mecca without knowing how to read or write, who have never tasted wine, and are resigned to the punishing life of the desert."

After Helsinki there were other meetings, in Le Havre, Madeira, Vera Cruz, Vancouver. Warda had grown accustomed to living with Jon in his cabin when the ship was in port. They almost never visited the cities, and they spent their time, as they had in the Finnish capital, in harbor restaurants and bars, where Warda's entrance was a spectacle that always followed the same pattern. When she appeared at the door, all the patrons turned to look at her in almost religious silence. Then came a wave of whispers that began to die down as the couple concentrated on their conversation without paying attention to those around them. After that, there were only discreet glances at Warda over the newspapers of some who could not resist the allure of beauty like hers. What amused Jon was how her response to this scrutiny never varied. Blushing faintly, she became even more involved in talking to him, as if she was trying to escape the curiosity of others. He never saw the slightest look or gesture to indicate that she was conscious of the eloquent astonishment she caused, or used it in any way. It might have been occurring in another dimension of the world, one that was completely foreign to her.

Their relationship stayed within the guidelines established in Lisbon the first time they went to bed together. They had discovered a certain kind of humor, certain verbal keys and caresses that invariably occurred to them at the same time and helped them avoid any allusion to a future commitment. The most they would do in that area was to choose the port where they would next meet. This was how they spent a long year, until the day Iturri arrived in Puntarenas.

He had arranged to meet Warda there. She wanted to travel with him through the Caribbean, an itinerary some old friends of his on the islands had made possible. They were short, well-paying runs involving cargo that was easy to handle. When he anchored at the docks of the Costa Rican port, instead of Warda waiting for him he found Abdul Bashur, leaning against a mooring post. "The truth is," Jon commented, "I wasn't particularly surprised to see Warda's brother, no matter how unusual his presence might seem in a place so far from where he usually transacted business. I was acquainted with Levantines well enough to understand that sooner or later they would want to know what kind of life their younger sister was leading. This was a kind of tribal principle that not even the most Europeanized can escape. Abdul's manner was reserved but cordial. He came on board, visited the hold and engine room with me, and seemed generally satisfied with the *Halcyon*. When he commented on the really lamentable condition of the paint, I explained that no matter which shipyard I took it to for painting, it would bring in no money for at least a month, and if I had the crew do the painting while we were at sea, I would be obliged to hire more men. In either case, earnings would be significantly reduced, which meant there would not be enough to make the minimum payments fixed by the owner as her share of the profits. I had given Warda the same explanation, and she had made no comment. Bashur looked at me with a mixture of curiosity and amusement. Then he asked me to accompany him to San José while the ship was being loaded. He had matters to discuss with two clients who were in the coffee-roasting business. We would have lunch in the city, and I'd return to Puntarenas in the afternoon. He was taking a plane that night from San José to Madrid. I gave instructions to the bos'n and left for the capital with Bashur. It was clear that he wanted to talk to me about my relationship with his sister and this was the pretext he had found for doing so. As he drove the car he had rented at the airport, he led the conversation around to the subject with absolute discretion and even with a delicacy for which I was grateful. Before he could go on, I informed him, with a frankness that was somewhat brutal but seemed necessary to me, that neither Warda nor I had any plans other than to keep our relationship at its present level and within its current parameters. It was something we had established with absolute clarity. We were free to make our own decisions, and there was no place for demands or diffidence of any kind. This seemed to please Bashur, who made some observations on how his people viewed these problems and on the effort to emancipate women in the Middle East. Nothing I didn't know already, but I listened attentively because I felt he almost wanted to excuse himself for interfering in our affairs. Then he alluded to Warda's distinctive character. Until recently she had seemed the most submissive of his sisters, the one who showed least interest in learning what the Western world had to offer. But since she was also the most reserved, imaginative, and sensitive of the three, Abdul interpreted her desire to experience Europe as natural and rational. In a confidential tone, as if it were a sign of his faith in me, he said he thought Warda would return to Lebanon and become the most devout Muslim in the family. Then he uttered the words that would have such profound repercussions on our destiny, on Warda's and mine: "What you two have will last as long as the *Halcyon.*" I made no reply, but a brief panic ran the length of my body. I knew Bashur was right; I had known it from the first moment I realized his sister no longer saw me as only a business partner. This unappealable sentence had been hanging over our heads for a long time. After a prolonged silence, all I could think of to say was, "Yes, perhaps you're right. But it's also true that within the absolute present we've imposed in order to maintain our relationship, what you're saying doesn't mean a great deal." Bashur gave a slight shrug, and we changed the subject.

I accompanied him to his meetings in San José, and we ate at Rías Bajas, a restaurant with a pleasant atmosphere and a very beautiful view of the valley in which the city is located. The menu attempted, not always with success, to re-create the inimitable magic of Galician cuisine. I went with Bashur to the airport, where we said goodbye. As he shook my hand, he placed his other hand on my shoulder and said with sincere warmth, "Take care of the ship as if it were your guardian angel. Good luck, Captain."

When Iturri returned to Puntarenas, he found Warda in his cabin. She had arrived shortly after Abdul and, seeing them on the bridge, had waited until they left before coming on board. "I suspected he would come. That's why I decided to leave the two of you alone. Abdul is very much a knight errant. We've always been very fond of one another. He can be implacable in business, but he's an exemplary friend. There's something of the ascetic in him. The Gaviero, who's been going around with him and the Triestine woman for many years, claims that if Abdul ever goes to Mecca he'll be kidnapped and made into a saint in his own lifetime." The next day they set out for Panama City, where they would enter the Caribbean. Jon reminded me that while they were leaving Puntarenas, Warda had mentioned a stunning woman in the smallest bikini she had ever seen in her life, calling to them in Spanish from a yacht that crossed their path as they sailed out of port. He too had heard her, from the bridge, and was glad his friend did not understand the language very well. The first thing he had done on his return from San José was to tell her what Bashur had said about the fate of their love being tied to that of the tramp steamer. When the woman in the bikini expressed her doubts about whether the ship would ever reach Panama City, Warda, who was not superstitious but was certainly a fatalist, would have related her words to Abdul's and taken them as an ominous confirmation of her brother's prediction. "Luckily," the captain said, "fortune doesn't usually weave such tight nets and is more merciful than we tend to admit."

For Warda, their passage through the Caribbean was the revelation of a world filled with affinities and suggestive coincidences that appealed to her Eastern sensibility. "Sinbad must have come through here," she exclaimed, intoxicated by the climate of the islands, the exuberant vegetation always in bloom, and the mixture of races in the inhabitants, which was so like the melting pot of the eastern Mediterranean. For more than six months they sailed the Antilles and the coastal ports. Along with Warda's enthusiasm, two other phenomena became increasingly evident: The structure of the tramp steamer was finally starting to weaken, giving signs of obvious fatigue, and a longing for her own country and people began to grow in Warda's spirit as she became more familiar with the delights of the Caribbean. These were manifested in subtle ways. It was not in Warda's character to hide her feelings. When she realized at last that something inside her was changing, that images and memories of the Middle East she longed for were appearing not only in her dreams but during her waking hours as well, she immediately discussed it with Jon. He had noticed certain vague signs, and he listened with fatalistic resignation. When they reached Kingston, the end of their Caribbean voyage, they had a long conversation. This is how Iturri summarized Warda's words for me: "I think the time has come to return to my country and see my people. I'm not going with a specific purpose or any definite plans. It's something I feel in my skin; it's as simple as that. I've been coming to some conclusions: I don't want to be a European, and I could never really be one; the kind of itinerant life we've been living these past few months, and earlier too, but less intensely—I feel as if it's wearing me away inside, destroying the hidden currents that sustain me and are connected to my people and my country; you're the man I always thought I could live with, you have the qualities I most admire, but you've been a wanderer most of your life and nothing can change that now." Jon could not resist asking the question that has been inevitable for as long as there have been lovers: "But does that mean we won't see each other again?" Warda answered immediately with a dismay so spontaneous and sincere it brought a lump to his throat. "God, no! It's not anything like that! I couldn't bear the thought of not seeing you anymore. I have to feel the land under my feet, but I'll have you with me. You understand, you know exactly what I mean. I don't want to talk about it." These thoughts and others like them became the constant topic of their conversation as they approached Kingston.

And here Jon fell into one of his interminable silences. It was clearly difficult for him to think about their separation in Jamaica. He said so little about this episode that it is not easy for me to put into writing. I think one phrase, lost in a welter of awkward explanations and repeated evocations of a single detail, best reflects his feelings: "That listing ruin of a ship you saw docked in Kingston is the most faithful portrait of her captain's state of mind. We were both beyond help. Time's bill had to be paid. The days of wine and roses were over for both of us." Warda said goodbye to Jon at the Kingston airport. She was flying to London and from there to Beirut. The last thing she said as she cupped his face in her hands and looked at him with the steadiness of a sibyl was: "You'll hear from me in Recife. Let me put my inner life in order, and I'll see you again." Jon returned to the freighter, his spirit shattered, but also accepting his fate with a good amount of stoicism and even more of an Iberian acquiescence to what the gods decree.

His plans included an attempt to repair the freighter, however provisionally, at the New Orleans shipyards. Then he would stop at La Guaira to load on oil-exploration equipment bound for Ciudad Bolívar, and from there he would sail to Recife with a cargo of lumber. The report from the yards in New Orleans was fairly pessimistic. General repairs to the framework of the hull, and to the hold, were prohibitively expensive, and in any case the engineers would not take full responsibility for their work, given the condition of the rest of the ship. Exterior painting would cost more than the total value of the *Halcyon*. Recent adjustments to the engines had extended her life, but the mechanics refused to say for precisely how long. Jon had to settle for cutting her cargo capacity by half to avoid putting stress on the sides of the hull and the walls of the hold. As a consequence, when he reached La Guaira he could accept only part of the cargo waiting for him at the docks.

* * *

The tugboat had left the swamps behind and was now in the last stretch of river before the port. This section had been dredged and maintained since colonial times in order to facilitate heavy traffic between several cities along the Caribbean coast. These were connected by a canal that began at a bend of the river and ended in Villa Colonial, with its heroic tradition of resistance to the incursions of buccaneers during the seventeenth and eighteenth centuries. The passage through the vast extensions of marsh is devastatingly monotonous. I must confess that this time I did not even notice. Captain Jon Iturri's story had all my attention, and since we spent the nights talking on deck, we slept almost the entire day in our air-conditioned cabins; the artificial coolness reminds me of a morgue, but in those regions it brings undeniable relief. The last portion of the river had stone and masonry walls along both banks, creating the impression that one had entered a canal like those in Belgium and Holland, which cross the countryside in all directions. We had two more days of sailing before we reached our destination. On the next to last evening, Iturri suggested we continue our custom of staying awake at night. His story was reaching its conclusion, which I had partially witnessed without realizing it. We went up on deck at nine. The Jamaican cooks brought us a large pitcher of *vodka amb pera* with pieces of ice floating in it to keep the drink cool. Jon began to speak in an impersonal, opaque voice that indicated a certain reserve, a certain difficulty, the reasons for which were overwhelmingly apparent as the story came to an end. "You're familiar with the mouths of the Orinoco. An infernal labyrinth in one of the most debilitating climates I know. To make matters worse, in those days the region was fairly desolate, and the lack of supplies was cause for alarm. I had never been there before, but the Algerian bos'n and the pilot did seem familiar with the place. The pilot was Aruban and had sailed upriver several times to Ciudad Bolívar, which is where we were heading with our cargo of machinery. He didn't seem particularly concerned about the difficulties detailed on the navigational chart. "The only thing you have to be afraid of," he claimed, "are sudden floods during the rainy season, when the current carries down huge mud deposits and roots and tree trunks that can block the channel in a couple of minutes. But the port radio in Ciudad Bolívar usually broadcasts weather advisories. We won't take any chances. Don't worry." That was when I did begin to worry. I know exactly what "Don't worry" means in these countries. It's really saying, "If something happens there's nothing we can do anyway, so there's no point in worrying about it." It was dark when we drew opposite San José de Amacuro, and I decided to anchor in the small bay and not try to enter the delta until it was light. It rained all night. The pilot reassured us, explaining that this did not necessarily mean it was also raining in the interior, where the swollen waters of its tributaries flowed into the Orinoco. At five in the morning, we entered the arm of the delta that was most navigable, according to the chart. This was where we passed the *Anzoátegui*. The torrential rains continued. We had our radio tuned to the harbor station, which did in fact broadcast periodic reports on weather conditions in the area. At half past eight, it announced the first flooding but said it posed no danger to vessels entering the delta: The water was moving along one of the arms that emptied into extensive mangrove swamps. A few minutes later the station went off the air. On the horizon, over the spot where we calculated the city was located, a cumulonimbus cloud mass was growing into the usual anvil shape, and lightning flashed from it almost continuously. We moved slowly along the narrow channel, which was partially marked with buoys. Suddenly the ship began to vibrate, at first almost imperceptibly and then with growing intensity, until the metal plates of the hull were rattling with a deafening noise. The pilot announced that it was a flood, but because of how the water was moving it did not seem to be carrying mud deposits. The bos'n was not as confident, and he ordered the crew to take certain precautions and ready the lifeboats. Suddenly the ship struck something on the bottom and went into a violent spin, until she was at right angles to the current and taking its full impact across the beam. I ordered the engines to full power in an effort to bring her around, and we had almost succeeded when something hit us with so much force that we were left listing with our propellers out of water. I stopped the engines and ordered everyone on deck. The ship was taking on water very quickly. It had split down the middle and was stranded on a huge deposit of mud and vegetation that grew larger by the second. One of the two lifeboats lay smashed beneath the ship. We managed to crowd into the other, and the current carried us away in a whirlwind of mud and rain. Fortunately, the same mud that had collided with the *Halcyon* also held back the waters. After half a mile we could control the lifeboat. The tramp steamer, shaken by the current's savage blows, was breaking apart before our eyes. It was like watching a prehistoric beast being torn to pieces by a voracious, inescapable enemy. At last the two sections of the ship were carried away in opposite directions toward the banks, and then they suddenly disappeared into the channels that are formed near shore by the pressure of the water on a soft river bottom. We reached Curiapo at six that evening. The authorities put us up at the military post and gave me permission to communicate with the underwriters in Caracas and begin the process of repatriating the crew. And that was the end of the tramp steamer that still lives in your dreams . . . and in mine."

I was silent for a time, thinking about how right Iturri had been when he said I had witnessed the decisive moments in the story of the *Halcyon* and its captain. I had even seen it a few hours before it sank, when we were on board the Venezuelan coast guard cutter waiting for the freighter to pass so we could enter the open sea. I did not want to ask more questions just then. We still had one more night before we reached our destination. On the other hand, it was fairly easy to imagine how it had all turned out for him. And so not to satisfy my curiosity, but to give him the opportunity to exorcise the demons tormenting his introverted, sensitive Basque soul, I asked him to tell me the end of the story on the following night. He replied, "Stories don't have an end, my friend. What happened to me will end when I do, and then, who knows, maybe it will go on living in other people. We'll talk some more tomorrow. You've listened very patiently. I know that each of us carries his own share of hell on earth, and that's why I am much obliged for your attention, as my grandfather who was a teacher in San Juan de Luz used to say." When he passed in front of me to climb down to his cabin, a grim shadow on his face made him look older. The light of the full moon on his hair seemed to turn it white, and made the image of sudden aging even more poignant.

The next night, when we met on the small deck, we could see the reflection of the city's lights on the horizon, like an unmoving fire that filled the scene with unexpected drama. Iturri began speaking with no preliminaries. I had the impression he wanted to finish quickly, as if narrating his own misfortune was like walking on burning coals. As always, he avoided any turns of phrase that could be interpreted as self-pity. There was, of course, not the slightest trace of pride in this. He did it out of simple decency, what the French in the eighteenth century so beautifully termed "gentility of the heart."

"The underwriters met with me in Caracas to study the *Halcyon*'s policy and indemnify the officers and crew. While I was there I sent telegrams to Warda and Bashur, informing them of the wreck. I waited a reasonable time for an answer. Their absolute silence began to worry me. In the meantime, the idea of going to Recife became an obsession that never left me. It was even more urgent and pressing now. Whatever Warda might decide about the future, I could not bear the thought of never seeing her again. Our goodbye in Kingston could not be our last. My mind filled with all the things I hadn't said to her when we were together. Then they had seemed unimportant, almost unnecessary: Our gestures, our lovemaking, our shared likes and dislikes, had made words superfluous. Now they were in control again, insistent and demanding. They were the links that could create a new connection between us or prolong the old one on different terms. And so, when my work in Venezuela was finished, I took a plane to Recife. Do you know Recife?" I replied that I had been there twice and found the half-Portuguese, half-African city unforgettable. It appealed to me in a way I could not define. "It attracted me too the first few times we put in there, when I was on a tanker transporting chemicals from Bremen. But this

time the beauty of the city, its bridges, plazas, and buildings,
everything slightly eroded and crumbling, made the days I spent
waiting for a message from Warda even more intolerable. And I
insisted on waiting, more from the force of my desire and longing than for real, tangible reasons. She had told me we would
meet there, but implicit in her words was some reservation
regarding what would happen when she returned to Lebanon. As
I remembered and reconstructed each of her words and gestures,
our appointment in Recife seemed an obvious illusion, a consolation she had devised so that our parting in Kingston would not
have the melodramatic qualities of definitive separation. I no longer
knew what to think, or how much my imagination was construct-
ing with no more foundation than my own dreams and how much
was real. I haunted the hotels where I supposed Warda might stay. I
became an eccentric, even a suspicious character, to the bartenders
and the clerks at the reception desks. They would see me come in
and shake their heads with a smile in which an increasingly evident
pity mixed with the kind of annoyance provoked by maniacs or
crackpots. I started to hate the city and blamed it for everything.
The heat was becoming intolerable, and I didn't bother to look
for another job, although I needed one desperately because I was
beginning to run out of money. The insurance would not be paid
in its entirety for another year, not until a detailed investigation
of the wreck had been completed.

Finally, there was something for me at the post office. It was a
long letter from Warda. I won't read it to you. There's nothing in
it that I haven't told you already, but her writing is so fluid and
natural that reading it aloud would be a little like hearing her
voice. I couldn't bear that. It's easy enough to summarize. She
described her arrival in Lebanon and her immediate adjustment
to her society and her family. Her dreams of Europe, and of other
things, vanished instantly, all their reason and solidity gone. What
remained were the feelings that joined her to me. These were
intact but could not serve as the basis for building anything or
hoping for anything but a senseless experience that would turn
our love into a tangle of repressed demands and hidden guilt and
frustrations: the inevitable result, in short, of starting out with a
distortion of reality and mistaking our desires for incontrovertible
truth. She would not go to Recife and did not intend to see me
again, not there or anywhere. It made her terribly sad if it seemed
that the wreck of the tramp steamer had influenced her decision
to stay on land and submit to the laws and customs of her people,

as if Abdul's words had come true, but that was not the case and I mustn't think it was. The ship, she had to admit, had been on the verge of expiring. It was almost a miracle that it endured as long as it had, doing work so much greater than its strength. Then there were some thoughts about me and the virtues and qualities Warda attributed to me, which were obviously magnified by her memory of the good days we had spent together and the nostalgia she felt at knowing we would not meet again. I've never had much success with women. I think I tend to bore them. What she may have seen in me is a certain order, a certain protective distance that I put between myself and other people's foolishness, which proved immensely helpful to Warda in dissipating her obsession with Europe. With me she learned that human beings are the same all over the world, that they are moved by the same mean passions and sordid interests, as ephemeral as they are identical in every latitude. When she was thoroughly convinced of this, the return to what was hers was easy to predict and showed a maturity that is very rare in a woman of our time.

In Recife I agreed to captain a tanker going to Belfast for repairs, and so I returned to the life I had before I met Bashur and the Gaviero in Antwerp. But Warda had so filled my life, the secret fibers of my body, that her absence left a void nothing could ever fill. I told you at the start: I perform the function of living as if I were a robot. I let things happen as they come, without looking for consolation or relief in the disorder they often create to deceive us. And as I warned you at the beginning, I also know that this story may be rather trite and simple. But if you had seen Warda, even for an instant, if you had heard her voice, you would see how everything has a very different meaning. Something in her was like an inconceivable vision that can't be expressed in words; only if you experienced it yourself could you explain the incredible joy it was to be with her, the unspeakable torment it is to have lost her."

We remained, as usual, in silence for over an hour. Then Iturri suddenly stood, offered his hand, and gave me a long, warm handshake that attempted to replace the words his reserve kept him from saying. "I don't know if we'll see each other tomorrow. I have to be at the docks very early to board the Belgian freighter leaving for Aden. It was a great pleasure meeting you and knowing that your sympathy for the poor tramp steamer that first appeared to you in Helsinki will unite us forever. Good night." I responded with a few disjointed phrases. The emotional impact of his goodbye, which I felt immediately, did not allow me to tell him how much it had meant to learn the other part of the story of the *Halcyon* and its captain. Dawn was breaking when I went to bed. The company's car would not come for me until noon. Before falling into the sleep I needed desperately, I pondered the story I had heard. Human beings, I thought, change so little, and are so much what they are, that there has been only one love story since the beginning of time, endlessly repeated, never losing its terrible simplicity or its irremediable sorrow. I slept deeply and—this was quite unusual for me—dreamed of nothing at all.

Abdul Bashur,
Dreamer of Ships

To the memory of my brother Leopoldo Mutis, who, before he left us, listened with interest to my plans for this book and commented, in a voice no longer of this world: "I'm glad. It's the least Abdul deserves."

Years, years spent pouring words we couldn't fathom.
Only through death we speak in honest fashion.

Peter Dale, *"He Addresses Himself*
to Reflection"

Monody shall not wake the mariner.
This fabulous shadow only the sea keeps.

Hart Crane, *"At Melville's Tomb"*

*F*or some time it has been my intention to collect certain episodes in the life of Abdul Bashur, who, for much of his life, was the Gaviero's friend and accomplice as well as a protagonist, and by no means a secondary one, in many of the ventures in which Maqroll became embroiled with suspicious ease. Thanks to the astute patience that constitutes a predominant trait in Levantines, Bashur often played the role of savior, rescuing Maqroll at critical moments. At last, motivated by an incident that typifies the shifting fortunes and unforeseen events that filled the Gaviero's existence, I have resolved to undertake the chronicler's task I had put off for so long.

I was en route to Saint-Malo to attend a meeting of friends devoted to preserving the tradition of adventure and travel books, and had to change trains at Rennes, but I missed my connection and was obliged to wait for the next train to the illustrious Breton port. An insistent, icy rain was falling, and I decided to sit quietly in the waiting room and read Michel Le Bris's book on medieval Occitania. Waiting rooms are the same everywhere in the world: They have the air of a no-man's-land; a shabby bar serves predictably insipid coffee with an undefinable taste of neglect, or cloying regional liquors of improbable colors and flavors; a kiosk sells weeks-old papers and magazines, which no longer attract anyone's attention because the news is out-of-date and the photographs dull and faded. The travel posters on the walls always display beach resorts tinged with sickly decadence, or snow-covered mountains whose names mean nothing to us and in no way tempt us to anything so foolhardy as trying to climb them. On invariably hard and unsteady benches, anonymous passengers wait for their trains with the fatal acquiescence of those who have lost all hope of sleeping at home that night. In waiting rooms, people are resigned to whatever may come, no matter what it might be.

Suddenly someone called my name from the corner where a gas stove struggled in vain against the pervasive cold and damp. I could not see who it was, and feeling a combination of curiosity and annoyance, I walked to the other side of the room, intrigued that anyone in the station at Rennes, where I had never been before, would know me. Sitting next to the stove and holding a boy of about ten in her lap, a woman who still retained her Middle Eastern beauty smiled at me with interest and a certain apprehension. Her features, her Lebanese accent, something in her expression, stirred a flood of vague recollections in a corner of my memory.

"I'm Fatima. Fatima Bashur. Don't you remember? We met in Barcelona when I brought the money to get Maqroll out of prison," she said with a rueful smile. I leaned over to kiss her cheek and sat down beside her, mumbling some hurried excuse for not recognizing her immediately.

Fatima Bashur. Why does chance so often take on the accents of a fearsome call from the gods? The entire episode of our meeting returned to me with the unruly haste of those things we have relegated to oblivion in order to protect the precarious equilibrium of our days. Fatima, Abdul's older sister, had indeed come to Barcelona, bringing money from her brother to meet the expenses of legal proceedings that almost sent Maqroll to prison for many years. At the small Catalonian port of La Escala, the harbor police, undoubtedly advised by one of their paid informers, arrested the Gaviero as he was unloading a shipment of weapons and explosives that had been hidden in crates of replacement parts for a fish packing plant. Abdul and Maqroll had arranged to transport the cargo in Tunis, with a couple who pretended to be on their honeymoon but in fact belonged to an anarchist group that had made Barcelona their headquarters. The couple had followed the routes of the Cypriot freighter that the two friends were operating in the Mediterranean and concluded they were the ideal types for smuggling arms to the Costa Brava. Bashur had gone with them to Bizerte as a hostage. When they learned that the ship, the weapons, and Maqroll had all been taken, the couple disappeared as if by magic. Abdul left for Beirut and raised what little money he could in an attempt to save his partner, who was insisting to the Spanish police that he had been the victim of a deception and did not know the real contents of the crates he had carried to La Escala. Abdul assumed, and with reason, that instead of going himself, it would be more prudent to send one of his sisters, and he entrusted the mission to Fatima, whose seriousness and good judgment were perfectly suited to the task. Abdul had three sisters: Yamina, a married woman whose son suffered from a strange disease that the doctors repeatedly diagnosed as leukemia; Fatima, still single at the time, whose serene, rather hieratical appearance tended to go unnoticed at first but then became, as it did for me, an obsessive, enigmatic image; and the dazzling, unconventionally beautiful Warda, part of whose story I have told elsewhere.

Bashur informed me of Maqroll's imprisonment when we met in Paris, where I was spending a few days on my way home from Hamburg. I changed my plans immediately and left for the City of the Count to see what could be done for our friend. When I visited him in prison, I found him sunk into the peculiar apathy that tended to overwhelm him in situations like these. I told him of Bashur's plans and Fatima's imminent arrival with money to pay a lawyer to handle his case. He shrugged, smiling vaguely.

"I don't think they should spend money they really need now. Either the police will decide to believe my story, which I admit is a little hard to swallow, or they'll bury me here for as many years as they want. I'm sick of moving from place to place and getting caught up in schemes that don't even interest me very much. I've been thinking recently that maybe it's time to stop spinning the wheel, to stop tempting fate. I don't know. We'll see." I did not want to remind him that I had heard him say the same words, or ones very much like them, on previous occasions, and yet he always returned to his wandering: He was in no frame of mind for such reflections. I merely said I would stay in Barcelona until Fatima arrived and I knew what steps were being taken to obtain his release. He made a gesture of resigned assent, then stood up and waved goodbye as he threw his jacket over his shoulder and walked through the door of the visiting room at the Modelo Prison.

Two days later Fatima called from the airport. She had taken an earlier flight than planned, but no one had remembered to tell me. I gave her the address of my hotel and called reception to change the date of her reservation. Sometime later, a timid knock pulled me from a sleep I was falling into without realizing it. I opened the door and saw a tall woman with firm, slender limbs and straight shoulders that gave her a somewhat martial air; the proportions of her head and face reminded me of Indo-Hellenic sculptures. I asked her to come in, and she sat down with a simple familiarity I found somehow touching. She spoke the kind of correct French that almost no French person speaks anymore but that is common among certain Lebanese and Syrian merchant families of the upper middle class. I told her of my conversation with Maqroll, and she remarked very simply, "It's natural for him to feel that way. He always does. But we'll get him out somehow." Her words held so much conviction that my opinion of the Gaviero's future became tinged with an optimism no less unshakable for being gratuitous.

The following day we began the process. That same afternoon we saw a lawyer whose reputation was based on his successful defense of foreigners facing legal difficulties in Spain. For several weeks Fatima and I, accompanied by our diligent attorney, carried briefs from one office to another and talked to every imaginable kind of official—a series of circumspect, hermetic, distant faces that did not sanction the slightest hope. At the same time, I began to realize that the presence of Fatima Bashur lent a peculiar charm to these negotiations, although I must confess I am repelled by any contact with the world of legal bureaucracy. In a rapid examination of conscience, following a supper with Fatima in La Puñalada, when we broached more personal subjects having little to do with our friend's case, I concluded that I was probably beginning to fall in love with Abdul's sister. It was a difficult situation. By then I knew Fatima well enough to understand that she was not a woman given to superficial flirtations: I realized, fortunately, that her interest in me did not go beyond a normal friendliness invariably associated with the responsibilities her brother had entrusted to her, and I resolved not to even hint at my feelings.

The solution to Maqroll's difficulties was found in the most unforeseeable and unexpected way. One night at the Boadas bar, where my friend Luis Palomares had introduced me to the bartender with the recommendation that I receive very special attention, I was attempting to find, for the thousandth time, the formula for the perfect dry martini, when I was approached by an Englishman who was clearly an official at Her Majesty's consulate in Barcelona. He proposed a few variations that might help us reach the paradigm of that unattainable cocktail. The results were positive but not conclusive, although the experience did establish a relationship between us that was as amiable as the inhabitants of John Bull's island can allow. I don't know why it occurred to me to mention the reason for my visit to Barcelona, without going into specific details, of course. He showed immediate interest but, with characteristic impassivity, would only say: "Come see me tomorrow at the consulate. I think perhaps something can be organized to help your friend. You did say he was traveling with a Cypriot passport, didn't you?"

I confirmed that he was, and in a little while we said our goodbyes, promising we would try again to discover the recipe for the perfect dry martini.

The next day I went to the British consulate. My companion at the Boadas had not lost his earlier cordiality, although it had acquired a more official and somewhat distant accent. He took me to his office, closed the door, and came straight to the point. Maqroll's passport had been issued in Cyprus during the time of the British mandate. Because of a series of circumstances that he did not explain in detail, his government was particularly interested in having Spain release this English subject so that a Spanish citizen, who was being held in Gibraltar because of his suspicious associates, could be freed and thereby satisfy Madrid's insistent demands. It was a question of making a fair exchange in order to avoid establishing an unacceptable precedent. I thought I was in the middle of an intrigue worthy of a novel by Eric Ambler, but the final outcome could not have been more gratifying. Maqroll was released after spending almost three months in the Modelo Prison. He was to return to Cyprus and report to the authorities. His ship would be confiscated and the customs officials would decide how to dispose of it.

Fatima had spent only a small portion of the money she had brought with her; this helped to reassure the Gaviero, who was well aware of the rather difficult times that both Abdul and his family were experiencing. Maqroll sailed for Cyprus on a Greek ship, carrying the passport that had saved him, although there was good reason to harbor the gravest doubts regarding its authenticity. As the Gaviero said goodbye to me on the dock, he smiled mischievously and remarked:

"Thank you very much for everything. I'm glad this didn't cause even more trouble for all of you. Life is so strange: I walk away a free man and you were almost caught, in a charming prison, it's true, but one filled with unpredictable consequences. Always remember, my friend, that Allah protects his women. It's important to keep that in mind when you're traveling through the lands of Islam."

That same afternoon Fatima took a plane back to Beirut. I

stayed with her through all the formalities, and when she was ready to pass through Immigration she stared at me for a moment and, after offering me her cheek for a farewell kiss, said in a voice made opaque by her natural shyness:

"It was a great pleasure meeting you, and I want to thank you for being a gentleman; that kind of tact is certainly not very common among Western men. My compliments to you; I'll always be grateful. *Adieu.*"

She spoke with such finality that her goodbye was etched in my memory for a long time afterward. I often wondered what would have happened if I had adopted the tactics of the Knight of Seingalt with Fatima. Moments like these always leave us in doubt. That women are inscrutable is by now a cliché that does not bear repeating, but it is obviously less of a commonplace that men are a vain and fickle species, which is why we invariably lose the game.

What remained of my encounter with Abdul's sister in Barcelona was a face whose harmony belonged to the time when Hellas penetrated the East, a warm, velvety voice, a Byzantine serenity of movement and response—all of it perceived as something not meant for me, something that could never be mine. Now, many years later, in a freezing train station in the middle of rain-swept Britanny, I had met Fatima once more. She had succumbed to the fleshiness that characterizes Mediterranean women as they approach fifty; her face was still beautiful though marked by signs of weariness, and her serene smile displayed a certain rigidity at the corners of her mouth, indicating years of slow disillusionment and small daily griefs. She looked at me with a mixture of disbelief and cordiality, and I attempted to string together a series of trivial questions: What had she been doing all these years? Who was the child she was holding? How were her sisters? So much had happened since those long ago days in Barcelona that each answer would have required many hours. Although several lay ahead of us, she limited herself to succinct but amiable answers. Shortly after her trip to Barcelona, she had married a distant cousin to whom she had been betrothed since childhood. He was a prosperous, methodical cloth merchant, who always treated her as if she were a little girl. They had three children. The boy in her lap was her grandson. She was taking him to Paris to have a spinal injury treated. His parents lived in Brest, where Fatima's son, a second officer in the Lebanese merchant marine, was studying naval communications. The boy had fallen while playing on the jetties and suffered pain all along his spinal column. Fatima had been a widow for more than ten years and was completely devoted to her grandchildren. Her other two sons had completed their education; one was a lawyer, the other an optometrist, and both were married. Her older sister, Yamina, had died soon after Abdul. Warda was still leading her withdrawn, quiet life, working for the Lebanese Red Crescent and helping Palestinian refugees. We moved on to other subjects and the people with whom we had common bonds. Neither of us had heard from Maqroll in a long time. My last news was from Pollensa, where he was caretaker at some abandoned shipyards. I noticed that her face colored slightly and her voice took on a different intensity when I mentioned the Gaviero. I wondered if she had once been in love with him. Inevitably we talked about Abdul. He had been her favorite brother, the one she was closest to in age and affection, and they had grown up together.

"Abdul's goodness," she said, "was of a very special kind. It wasn't on the surface, it wasn't expressed in obvious acts. He carried it hidden, deep inside, but always ready for use. He loved us all, including his friends, with a kindness that was unchanging, watchful but discreet, making him indispensable, like a guardian angel, though it was never very clear for what. His absence has been painful. He was a nomad who became involved in the most contradictory situations and never cared if they were legal or not. The only law he recognized was the one dictated by his feelings. Well, you knew him fairly well. I don't know why I'm telling you all this."

I replied that I had never really been very close to Abdul, that a good part of what I knew about him came from the Gaviero, who was certainly his inseparable comrade and accomplice in every kind of enterprise. We had met a few times, enough for me to confirm that his devotion to the people he loved was a constant in his character. Maqroll always spoke of him in the affectionate, amused tone with which we refer to a younger brother, and mentioned him in many of the letters and stories he had given to me when I began to record his adventures.

"Well, I can complete the information you have," Fatima said with emotion. "I've kept many of my brother's letters, and other documents related to his travels and adventures. If you're interested, I'd be happy to send them to you. I'm sure you'll make better use of them than we can. We keep them in a trunk for love of his memory."

I accepted her offer and wrote my address on a card so that she could send me the papers. They would undoubtedly provide the information I needed to give a full accounting of certain incidents in the life that for so long had run parallel to the life of my friend Maqroll the Gaviero.

We continued our talk, returning to the same topics. Fatima had retained her charm. Difficult to describe, it combined acceptance of life and its surprises with a deep-rooted sense of reality that excluded all exaggeration and fantasy, for they ultimately diminished each day's unadorned truth. Yet Fatima admired her favorite brother, who had led a turbulent and erratic life. I remarked on this, and she responded in the tone of someone attempting to define an issue that had not been raised before.

"We know that Abdul was always very restless. He was never resigned to accepting what life offered in the way it was offered. Still, he was not moved by a genuine yearning for adventure or a longing for uncommon experiences. He was practical and methodical in his endless desire to modify the course of events, to amend what he always considered the unacceptable arbitrariness of a few people, the same ones for whose sake the rules and regulations governing everybody else's behavior are made. His favorite phrase was 'Why don't we try this instead?' and then he would propose the radical transgression against what had been presented to him as immutable law. But this was always rooted in a judgment of people that was in no way indulgent. He never had any illusions about anyone, yet he believed with unyielding certainty in the ties of affection that joined him to his family and friends. One thing did not cancel out the other. It's difficult to explain and even harder to understand, but that's how he was."

I was surprised by Fatima's intelligent assessment of the nuances and apparent contradictions in her brother's character, which I had observed but never could define with any precision. We returned to the Gaviero, and I asked if her family thought Maqroll might have been a factor in Abdul's choosing the wrong path, especially toward the end of his life, when he traveled the grimmest roads of the Middle Eastern underworld. Fatima looked at me in astonishment and quickly replied:

"We never thought any such thing. Abdul was not a man to let anyone lead him astray. From the very beginning we knew he had simply met someone who shared many of his views on life. That's why they traveled together for so long. In a sense, they complemented each other. Maqroll was a good friend of ours, and his memory is as present as Abdul's." My intention in asking the question was to further explore her feelings toward the Gaviero, but I had clearly missed the mark.

When it was time for me to board the train to Saint-Malo, we both stood, although she was still holding her grandson. Our goodbyes were brief. That was when we knew we had raised a cloud of delicate memories difficult to control under those circumstances and after so many years. I kissed her on both cheeks, and Fatima did the same, with a spontaneous effusiveness she made no effort to conceal. From the train window, through glass clouded by soot and rain, I watched her still waving goodbye. Several hours passed before I could impose any order on the whirlwind of memories and conflicting emotions awakened by my meeting with Fatima.

Less than a month later I received a bulky package of letters and a few photographs from Cairo. In an accompanying letter Fatima explained that she had moved to Egypt because of the crisis of violence in her country. This was how I obtained the documentation needed to carry out my long-standing intention of re-creating, for my unlikely readers, certain episodes in the unorthodox and troubled life of the Gaviero's oldest, most faithful friend. Mercifully, our memory has the ability to set certain images aside, to keep them above the disenchantment that the years can inflict with surprises like the one I had in Rennes. And so when I think of Fatima now, what comes to mind is the girl with the face of an Indo-Hellenic medallion, the girl with firm shoulders and slender limbs who came to Barcelona to rescue Maqroll the Gaviero, and not the mature, robust woman holding her grandchild in her arms, with whom chance brought me face-to-face in rain-swept Brittany.

I began at once to examine the papers sent by Fatima, which, as I have mentioned, included photographs of Abdul at various times in his life. One in particular attracted my attention. It showed a boy looking with rapt interest at a smoking heap of twisted, charred metal. The portions not destroyed by fire indicated a plane that had crashed moments before. The boy regarded the scene with great dark eyes, one of which had a slight squint; equally dark curly hair completed his typically Levantine appearance. The snowy mountains of Lebanon were visible in the background. "Abdul at the age of eight" was written on the back of the photo in a meticulous Arabic hand. I began classifying the papers and, as far as possible, arranging in chronological order those that referred directly to Bashur's travels through the most diverse and remote regions on earth. Naturally, I set apart those that alluded to family matters or the business dealings of his closest relatives. It seemed to me that with these documents, and my own recollection of the various times I had seen Abdul, I had enough material for a tale of moderate length that might interest those who have followed the peripatetic life of the Gaviero and are already familiar with certain episodes in which his Lebanese friend and associate appears as coprotagonist. For this narrative of mine has to be written within a framework that in no way conforms to the conventions of how a story should be told. It is absolutely impossible to give it chronological unity. When there are any dates on the papers in my possession, they are not reliable. In most cases, their absence makes it impossible to determine precisely when events occurred. In addition to these documents, which are partial and not always rich in details, I have been obliged to turn to the written accounts of Maqroll himself and to my memory of our numerous conversations. But I do not believe these chronological irregularities are of major importance. The rigor demanded by historical biography becomes excessive when dealing with "ordinary cases of humankind." It does seem appropriate, however, to begin by relating the circumstances of my first meeting with Abdul Bashur and then allow events to follow in their own order, for even life does not always adhere strictly to the routine sequence of days but often prefers the inconsistencies and repetitions that make its very essence unpredictable and capricious. This, then, is how I first met Abdul Bashur.

I

I was working as head of public relations for the subsidiary of a large international oil company in my country. One morning, when the day promised to be calm and uneventful, and I consequently decided to visit a used-book dealer who had been tempting me with rare titles by Ferdinand Bac, the grandson of Jerónimo Bonaparte, I received a phone call from the director of the company. His voice betrayed unmistakable anxiety, and so farewell to the gardens of Bac and his turn-of-the-century memories. When I walked into the director's office, he was speaking on the phone to the minister of public works, a man of tyrannical temperament and draconian decisions, who at that time figured as a future president of the republic. My superior repeated two sentences over and over again in a kind of litany: "Yes, Minister, we will" and "I don't see any problem, Minister, don't worry, sir, we'll take care of everything." Life looked bleak for whoever had to turn those promises into reality. If I had any doubts as to who that man might be, the director dispelled them when he hung up the telephone.

"Listen carefully. In ten days' time, in exactly ten days and not a day longer, we have to have everything, and I mean everything down to the last detail, ready for the opening ceremony at the pipeline terminal in the port of Urandá. Our minister of public works and the minister of mines will be there, as well as ministers and the company's regional directors from neighboring countries, and church and civic leaders from the provincial capital and from Urandá. The good news is that their wives will not attend. You have to stay on top of the situation at the Urandá airport and arrange accommodations for the guests in the event their return flights are canceled at the last minute. They'll be flying in on government or company planes. After the ceremony at the terminal and the bishop's blessing, a first-class luncheon has to be served, of course. Don't forget that church dignitaries will be there. You studied with the Jesuits. I don't think you'll have any problems on that score."

Although by now my assignment came as no surprise, I must confess that my prospects were fairly grim. A series of adverse factors combined to make the task almost impossible. Urandá is a port. Half of it is built over marshes that flow into the sea through an impenetrable tangle of mangrove swamps; the other half is on a hill and consists almost entirely of a red-light district. The region boasts the highest rainfall on the planet, and as a consequence the airport is closed for most of the year. The heat is suffocating, and the prevailing atmosphere of a Turkish bath exhausts all initiative and undermines all enthusiasm. At dusk, the occasional visitors, who by this time have been turned into true zombies, desperately seek a little cool shade and the glass of whiskey that perhaps will revive them. Both can be obtained without too much difficulty. Shade is taken care of by the night, which falls all at once and brings its entourage of mosquitoes and aberrant insects that seem to have escaped from a science fiction nightmare: Great hairy, slow-moving butterflies with black wings insist on attaching themselves to tablecloths and bath towels; horned beetles, their color an iridescent, phosphorescent green, crash endlessly against walls until they plunge into the glass you are drinking from or fall onto your head, where they struggle until they are trapped in your hair; pale, almost translucent scorpions display their expertise in complicated couplings and deliriously erotic ritual dances. As for the glass of Scotch, it can be obtained at the bar of the only habitable hotel in the port, which bears the strikingly original name of Wayfarers Hotel. A ramshackle cement structure streaked with mold and rust, its three floors constantly ooze an evil-smelling, oily mildew on the inside and outside walls. This is a typical building designed by an engineer, with gratuitous spaces that are either outsize or far too small, depending on the mood of the capricious foreman in charge of construction: an immense dining room, with high ceilings stained by suspicious leaks from ill-fitting pipes; a long, narrow reception area, where the asphyxiating atmosphere, heavy with vaguely nauseating odors, brings on instant claustrophobia; each room with the most absurd proportions and shapes, and many, for some reason, ending in an acute angle that can disturb the most peaceful slumber of any guest. The bar runs along a cramped, windowless corridor that leads from the reception area to the patio, where a pool of murky greenish water is visited by indefinable fauna, creatures that are part fish and part bulging-eyed dwarf reptile. A row of tables fastened to the wall faces the bar made of tropical woods carved with indigenous and African motifs, all as spurious as they are hideous. The solace that could have been derived from whiskey, despite the ice of an unsettling brown color floating in the glass, vanishes immediately in the tainted ambience of that passageway, worthy of a police station, which some administrator with a macabre sense of humor named the Glasgow Bar. The hotel was surrounded by a sprawling extension of shacks built over a marsh that gave off the fetid smell of decomposing animals and garbage adrift in dead, muddy waters.

Urandá also had a district of buildings constructed on the solid ground of a small hill, where a merciful but short-lived breeze passed by from time to time. As one might expect, the madams lost no time moving in and establishing their brothels, in which visitors familiar with the port would frequently take a room with air-conditioning and a few relatively predictable hotel services in order to avoid the sinister Wayfarers Hotel. The prostitutes were not too insistent about offering their companionship; their preferred clients were sailors who brought the dollars, marks, or pounds they longed for, not guests carrying a devalued national

currency. Furthermore, the houses were staffed by undernour-
ished, anemic, toothless creatures, many of them suffering from
exotic tropical diseases, the most prevalent of which was pian, a
terrible vitamin deficiency that eats away the face so that the victims never show themselves by day and at night avoid electric
lighting. The women, their faces covered by improvised handker-
chiefs and whimsical veils, attend to their clients in semidarkness
and dispatch them with so much skill that the men never suspect
anything, especially after a few glasses of adulterated rum.

And so planning a six-course buffet with three different fine
wines, the kind found in any hotel along the Riviera, and serving
it in Urandá, was a feat that exceeded the limits of the possible
and moved into the realm of the utterly lunatic. Then there was
the problem of landing and takeoff at the airport, where the precarious control tower usually lost its electrical power at the first
drizzle, even though it was located in an area with almost permanent rain, a fact that also accounted for minimal and ephemeral
visibility on the highway. It is easy to imagine my state of mind
when I left for the provincial capital, where I checked into a
hotel I knew very well. It was run by a couple from Luxembourg, who gave the establishment a special appeal and provided
impeccable service. The capital of a prosperous sugar-producing
region, the city enjoyed a moderate, pleasant climate, a certain
lively, cosmopolitan atmosphere, and a life free of serious alter-
ations or surprises. It was like an island in the storm of unre-
strained political passions that devastated the rest of the country
and kept it submerged in blood and mourning. I enjoyed spending long hours at the hotel bar, located on a veranda cooled by a
breeze heavy with intoxicating vegetal aromas. The days passed,
and I found no solution to my problem. My visits to the city's
private clubs produced nothing but incredulous looks from dining room managers, who listened to me as if I had lost my mind.

A new bartender, also a subject of the grand dukes, was working at the hotel, and as I evoked the years I had spent in Belgium,
and my frequent visits to Luxembourg, I easily established a
friendship with him. He was much more imaginative and enterprising than most of his compatriots. One day when I happened
to be in a mood for confidences, I told him about the critical situation I was facing. After listening to me attentively, he walked
over to the bar without saying a word, brought me a Scotch that
was somewhat more generous than usual, and stood beside me in
a meditative attitude. He finally broke his silence to ask:

"Do you have any budgetary constraints for this piece of madness?"

"None at all," I replied, intrigued. "I have carte blanche."

"In that case, I'll take care of everything," replied my savior, who was named Leon.

When he saw what must have been my expression of astonishment and disbelief, he unfolded his plan with the utmost naturalness.

"Look, my friend. I've worked in places on the coast of equatorial Africa that make Urandá look like paradise. And I've served buffets there that the guests still remember as something extraordinary. The problem is simple but very expensive: It's merely a question of having adequate, reliable transportation, lots of ice, and perfect coordination. Every minute is decisive. The highway to the port is hellish. I came in on it, and it's not easy to forget. We need three trucks to stay in Urandá, with their motors and tires in perfect condition, prepared to replace the three that will leave here with the food, wines, dishes, and flatware; we'll install two-way radios in both fleets of trucks, and if there's a landslide on the highway, or one of the vehicles breaks down, an emergency call to Urandá will bring assistance. As to the menu, for a varied and elegant buffet I suggest six dishes, most of them cold. I can prepare the sauces and the aspic when I get to Urandá. Don't worry, I have a good amount of experience doing this kind of thing. As to the cost, I can give you a detailed list of expenses to present to your director. You can tell him as of now that everything's been arranged. Trust me, I won't make you look bad: Urandá is no more difficult or dangerous than Loango or Libreville." I confess I felt an impulse to kiss this loyal Luxembourgian on the forehead. I stopped myself in time and drank to his health instead, draining the glass he had brought me.

My director approved the budget, raising absolutely no objections. Things began to move ahead with the precision of a commando operation. There was still the problem of air transport. Six planes had to land and take off with strict punctuality. I left for Urandá four days before the ceremony to coordinate the unpleasant task of making this uncertain aerial bridge viable. I had to stay at the Wayfarers Hotel, since it was the only place with a long-distance line and a telex. I met with the airport personnel who would direct the operation. We sat at a table that I had the hotel set up for us in the patio where the alleged pool was located. We discussed at length all the possibilities for bringing a difficult situation to a successful conclusion. I had asked my company to send three meteorologists from the refinery as reinforcements, and they helped to maintain the morale of the local technicians, who were very prone to discouragement.

One night as I sat alone at that conference table where all the possibilities for incalculable disaster had been shuffled and dealt, drinking a whiskey I had delivered from muddy ice by adding only chilled soda, I saw a man walking toward me. He was wearing a dark sailor's cap, a denim shirt with shell buttons, and a linen suit of undeniable quality that must have seen better days in the cafés of Alexandria or Tangier before coming to this miserable Pacific port. His appearance was utterly foreign to these surroundings, yet he moved through them with disconcerting familiarity. When he stood in front of me, he raised his hand to the visor of his cap in greeting and said in fluent French with a slight Arabic accent:

"If you'll permit me. I am Abdul Bashur, and we have a mutual friend, Maqroll the Gaviero, whom we both esteem highly. Perhaps you've heard him speak of me."

I stood to shake his hand and invited him to sit down, which he did with ceremonial slowness. He was a tall man with long, sinewy arms and legs that gave an impression of energy controlled by a critical, agile mind. He walked with a slight hesitancy that I immediately attributed to caution more than timidity. His fine-drawn face with its regular features might have had a somewhat conventional Eastern handsomeness if not for a slight squint that gave his eyes the expression of a recently awakened sleepwalker. His strong, bony hands moved with a singular elegance that had nothing to do with affectation, although these movements never corresponded to his words. It was vaguely disconcerting, as if his double, crouching there inside him and obeying an indecipherable code, had decided to express himself on his own. For this reason, Abdul Bashur's presence always aroused disquiet combined with sympathetic feelings for the captive who could make his presence felt only in gestures of a rare distinction, which were not those of the real person talking to us. His thick, curly hair had turned a rebellious, intense white at the temples. He smiled with spontaneous ease, displaying teeth slightly stained by his perpetual cigarettes. Abdul, who could express himself abundantly and fluently in some ten languages, among them Turkish, Persian, Hebrew, and of course his own, which was Arabic, moved from the French in which he had greeted me to a Spanish that he spoke with a peninsular accent, obviously learned in Andalusia, a fact I subsequently confirmed.

"So this is the famous Abdul Bashur," I thought—the inseparable comrade of Maqroll the Gaviero in his most daring incursions, the man with whom he shared the love of Ilona, a tale I heard in Marseilles from the Gaviero himself when he was engaged in an improbable undertaking involving antique carpets. Bashur sat down across from me, there on the filthy patio of the Wayfarers Hotel, and the first thing I could think of to ask was what had brought him to this vile hole on the Pacific, a place I would not think was worth his time.

"I came to meet you personally and to speak to you about a matter that interests me very much," he replied, still smiling affably as if trying to allay any misgivings I might have.

He then explained that he had come from New Orleans, where he had met with the head of our company's fleet of ships, who had been invited to the opening of the oil terminal. He had mentioned to Bashur that he knew me very well, since we had made several trips together to the Caribbean islands, and had urged Abdul to accompany him to Urandá. Bashur had—in his own words—two reasons for accepting: to meet me (the Gaviero had told him I had been tracking him for some time and intended to write about his unsettled existence) and to explore the possibilities of our firm's leasing two of his family's tankers now operating in the Caribbean area. He thought I might be the person to orient him and introduce him to my director, with whom the decision rested, according to his friend the head of the fleet. They had arrived this morning on the tanker that would unload the first fuel at the terminal. He had wanted to make my acquaintance and to talk awhile before discussing business.

His words, and especially his tone, as familiar as those of an old friend, blended with an unmistakable commercial nuance that was characteristic of his people. Naturally, I offered to put him in touch with my director, and then warned him that this executive was jealous of his prerogatives and responsibilities, and always apprehensive about interference by officials from other departments in the company. I promised I would speak with him to prepare the ground and assuage any suspicions he might have. As for Alastair Gordon, the head of the fleet in the Antilles, we were old friends and in fact had consumed countless liters of Scotch as we sailed between Aruba, Curaçao, and the mainland. He was an amiable Scot with an often eccentric and explosive character, but he was a good friend and a man who gave signs of being a repressed sentimentalist.

Then Abdul and I began reminiscing about our friendship with the Gaviero, and we would have kept it up the rest of the night if Alastair Gordon himself had not appeared a few hours later, with his eternal cherrywood pipe, his stony Scots accent with *r*s that rolled like boulders down a rocky slope, and his insatiable thirst. He and I decided on the approach Bashur's proposal ought to take, and Gordon agreed that he should proceed with utmost caution. It was close to midnight, and Gordon and I had finished the second bottle of whiskey, when Abdul suggested going to the dining room, and I had to explain that it was advisable to avoid that experience, at least for now. We would go to the hill instead, to the house of a madam from Toulon, a good friend of mine named Suzette, who would prepare a shellfish stew of her own invention, not very orthodox, it's true, but worthy of our confidence. I said we would have to show a certain patience with her mediocre Chilean white wine, because it was the only drinkable wine in Urandá. They agreed to my suggestion, and we drove to the hill in a company jeep so battered it must have been used in Clark's invasion of Sicily. Suzette agreed to cook her favorite dish for us. When it had been consumed, along with the wine, which we tolerated with equanimity, I told my friends we should sleep there. They had no idea what might be waiting at the hotel. The women in the house circled around, looking at us with inviting glances that brought a poignant expression of panic to Abdul's face. I had already warned him about the surprises that the effects of pian might hold in store. Suzette imposed order among her staff, and I explained to Bashur that we were under no obligation to take anyone to bed.

"I've frequented, and even lived in, the worst dives in Tangier, Marseilles, Tripoli, Alexandria, and Istanbul," said Abdul, "but I never thought anything like this was possible."

In view of Bashur's reaction, Alastair proposed sleeping on the ship. I accepted his invitation. We paid the owner generously, left a few dollars for the girls, and set out for the dock. Abdul's face reflected his obvious relief.

In the days that followed, my relationship with Abdul became closer, our common sympathies and experiences more apparent. He found it hard to believe that fate had so miraculously furnished me with the *maître* from Luxembourg, and he carefully followed each step in the drama of Leon's incredible gastronomical feat, which was going smoothly, just as we had planned. What continued to present apparently insuperable obstacles was what Abdul called, always with a touch of uneasiness, the damned weather. Still, the flight controllers I had requested from the refinery gave me a certain margin of confidence, compared to those from Urandá, who vegetated at the airport in subhuman conditions. In any event, the element of the unknown created by the region's sudden changes in weather continued to hang over our heads like the sword of Damocles. I ordered the runway to be leveled and had emergency drains built in an attempt to keep the ground solid. The steamroller filled the runway with gravel and rubble from buildings that had been destroyed by weather and floods. But all of this was secondary. *Cette putain de météo,* as Abdul said scathingly, was our real concern, yet there was nothing we could do about it, since it obviously did not depend on us. Arrival and departure of the six DC-3s carrying the guests had to be scheduled for the hours of the day that had the least risk of bad weather. And the meal had to be served in the interval.

The day arrived without incident. The weather was good, and the planes landed with absolute punctuality. The blessing of the dock and the speeches by the minister of public works and the director took as long as we had estimated. By the time the buffet was served, the back of my neck, and of Abdul's, ached with so much looking up to detect the slightest change in the clouds moving peacefully across a suspiciously innocent blue sky. Bashur had displayed complete solidarity with me and followed the progress of the affair with an interest and concern equal to mine. I managed to speak for a moment to my director, and with this recommendation his manner toward Abdul was pleasant, but he said he preferred to talk in the provincial capital, where he planned to spend a few days. Now he had to attend to all these people and could not think of anything else. Bashur understood completely, and we arranged for him to travel with the firm's personnel in the company plane, which would also be carrying the ministers and their aides.

The buffet was a success. Leon was congratulated by the minister of public works himself, who mentioned the coincidence that he too had studied in Brussels and told the *maître* in French that he would never forget the exquisite quality of the food that had been served and enjoyed in the last place on earth where he would have dreamed it possible. We were about to climb into the cars that would take us to the airport, when we heard the first clap of thunder announcing a storm; it sounded to us like the crash of the apocalypse. Our elation, and with it the notable success of the banquet, vanished on the spot.

The director walked over to me and in a low voice instructed me to take the foreign delegations to the airport without delay. The company plane, carrying our ministers and the bishop, would also leave immediately. We would travel in one of the three limousines he had standing by for just such an eventuality. I left for the airport with the foreigners, leaving Bashur, who was both disconcerted and amused, to ride with the director and his colleagues. The last plane took off as the storm broke at the far end of the runway. The passengers wore expressions of panic that they tried to control with jokes as stupid as they were useless. The pilot of our plane, a former ace in the Air Transport Command, told me he was sure he could get out with no danger. Everyone decided to leave with him except the minister of the economy and the head of the presidential guard, who chose to drive with us on the highway. Obviously, I made no objection, and even thought the director might want to take advantage of the endless trip overland to discuss a few matters with the minister, Dr. Aníbal Garcés, a small, plump, rosy individual who was almost completely bald and wore a meticulously trimmed reddish mustache just above his lip line. His almond-shaped, rather feminine eyes stared at people with insolent authority, as if attempting to compensate for his short body, as round as an abbot's. He was one of those men who know everything, explain everything, object to everything, anticipate everything, with a cutting speed that brooks no reply. Their political careers always culminate in cabinet ministries: Appearing at public forums, which is indispensable for achieving the presidency, is unimaginable.

We left in the limousine, not waiting for night to fall. We found our places, the minister and the director in the back seat, Abdul and I in the pull-out seats in the middle, and the brilliant colonel of the presidential guard sitting beside the driver. This representative of the armed forces, whose presence no one really understood, was a memorable sight in his dazzling white dress uniform, his chest covered by decorations that were impossible to identify. At the last minute the director had insisted on Bashur's riding with us. It was clear that a current of sympathy already existed between them. Later, during the drive, I remembered that he had been the company's chief of operations in Ras Tanura and was proud of having learned Arabic and speaking it with relative correctness. That may have been the origin of his fondness for Bashur. We said goodbye to Alastair, who came over to the car as we were about to leave to remind Abdul that the ship would sail in three days, after unloading its cargo of fuel at the recently inaugurated terminal. Abdul assured him he would be there, and we drove away from the Scot, who made his farewells by shaking his head in a gesture of open disapproval that only the driver and I fully understood.

The highway that connects the port of Urandá to the provincial capital has been a rich source of stories, most of them macabre, the others maniacally absurd. This is understandable only after driving the road, at any season of the year. It leaves the port and passes through some twenty kilometers of flat, monotonous terrain where plantains and other fruit trees with barely pronounceable names are grown. At this point the road begins to climb in a tight zigzag to an altitude of three thousand meters. Then, in dense fog that appears without warning and makes it almost impossible to proceed, the highway starts its slow descent along the edge of precipices whose depth cannot be calculated because a relentless wind drives the fog between the steep walls of the ravine. Far below, the torrential river plunges downward, crashing with a terrifying roar into the boulders strewn across its path. The engineers responsible for keeping the highway passable—the only road connecting one of the richest sugar-growing regions in the world with the ocean—have found it impossible to avert the constant cave-ins and great mudslides caused by incessant rains, and on countless occasions, in order to open a new route and keep traffic moving, they have had to bulldoze and bury entire fleets of trucks along with their drivers. The vehicles waiting to continue on their way run the risk of being buried too, which means there is no time to recover the bodies of the victims or the freight they were carrying. Lines of crosses, placed at the sites of the catastrophes by drivers' families, are the only memorial to the men who died there. Sometimes, after months or years have gone by and the earth has continued its advance toward the precipices, the river carries anonymous remains down to the valley, where they sink slowly into impassable quicksand along the muddy banks.

Our limousine drove through darkness, for night had fallen all at once as we were beginning the ascent into the cordillera. The minister and the director talked quietly, while Abdul and I, maintaining a discreet silence, tried to keep our balance on precarious seats. Up front, next to the driver, the colonel emitted thunderous snores. We had seen him pursuing waiters at the banquet, demanding that they refill his glass with white wine, and then with champagne, with the insistence of a man who wants to take advantage of an opportunity he apparently has not enjoyed very often in his life. The first few hours of our journey went by in this fashion, until we reached the top of the mountain. Our companions on the back seat had stopped talking, their silence filled with the opaqueness that typically emanates from people deep in thought about problems that have arisen during their conversation and for which they can find no solution. We began the descent, again in a tight zigzag that forced the chauffeur to drive with almost ghostly slowness through fog illuminated by the headlights into milky, blinding brilliance. We were obliged to stop frequently. From time to time, on curves taken with extreme caution, the lights revealed the edge of the abyss, where the fog swirled, curling up the mountainside as if trying to escape the depths in which it had been imprisoned. Every time I traveled this road I was reminded of Doré's engravings for *The Divine Comedy.*

The minister suddenly broke his long silence and told the driver to stop because he needed to urinate. The driver complied, and the minister left the car without saying a word. The director began talking to us, launching into a series of nostalgic recollections of his life and experiences in the Middle East. He and Bashur traded names of places, political personalities, and businessmen, the two of them creating the kind of *hortus clausus* that encloses people who share the same longing for places where they think they have been happy. After some time had passed, I interrupted to say that Minister Garcés was taking too long to relieve his bladder, and I thought it prudent to go out and find him. We got out of the car and realized we were only a few meters from the edge of the chasm. The director turned to rebuke the driver, but I intervened, explaining that stopping at the foot of the cliff wall would have been more dangerous due to frequent rock falls caused by the rain. We began to look along the edge of the precipice, but there was no sign of Dr. Garcés. The driver helped us in our search and finally offered a suggestion: We ought to feel the ground with our hands to find the place where the minister had urinated, which should still be warm even though a merciless drizzle continued to fall. Resigning ourselves to the task, we found nothing and finally decided to call the minister's name. The only response to our shouts of "Dr. Garcés! Dr. Garcés!" was the distant, muffled thunder of the water crashing violently against the rocks. Suddenly the white phantom of the colonel of the presidential guard was upon us, yelling hoarsely and waving a .45 pistol.

"Listen, damn it, what the hell did you do to Dr. Garcés? I'll pull you all limb from limb if anything's happened to him!" He assailed us in the booming, sputtering voice of a man who has wakened from a surfeit of badly digested wine, champagne, and lobster.

That was when another facet of Bashur's character was revealed to me. While the rest of us stood there paralyzed at the sight of the frenzied colonel aiming his pistol at us with an unsteady hand, Abdul began walking until he stood directly in front of him and, in a quiet but audible voice, in the tone used with a subordinate, said simply:

"Listen, friend. Stop shouting and put away that pistol. You'll probably have to use it on yourself if your minister doesn't show up."

The man stood for a moment, not knowing what to say, then returned the gun to its place under his uniform and went back to the car with the air of a reprimanded mastiff.

We continued calling Dr. Garcés for some time until, in a silence created by a shift in the wind, a muffled groan came from the edge of the abyss. The driver immediately went to the car and moved it so the headlights were directed toward the darkness where the faint moaning could be heard. At last we saw Dr. Garcés, his body cradled in the thick branches of a tree growing out of the side of the ravine just below the rim and not far from the place where the limousine had stopped. Using the tire chains carried in the car in the event it had to drive through mud, we managed to rescue the minister, who was miraculously unharmed except for a few small scratches on his face. Once he was on solid ground, he stared at us with the befuddled look of someone who still does not understand what has happened. Then, in a calm, official tone, he said, "Thank you very much, gentlemen. I'll just be a minute. Excuse me," and he walked to the foot of the rocky cliff at the other side of the highway and urinated copiously but with modesty.

We went back to the limousine and continued our journey, saying nothing about the ministerial accident. The colonel resumed his pitiless snoring. The minister referred briefly to the providential miracle of a tree growing at that unlikely spot. The director said something in Arabic into Bashur's ear. His growing exasperation with the distinguished cabinet member was apparent. Speaking to Bashur in a language the rest of us could not understand, and saying something that obviously alluded to the accident, meant he either did not expect much from Dr. Garcés or already had what he wanted. There was no further incident, and six hours later we reached the city, exhausted, depressed, and in desperate need of a bed. The director, Abdul, and I were staying at the hotel where Leon worked as bartender. The minister and the colonel were taking the company plane to the nation's capital. Our farewells were rather brief and just civil enough to maintain necessary relations in the future. Before we went up to our rooms, the director put his hand on Abdul's shoulder and said, "You can count on that contract for your tankers. I'll send Gordon a telex from the capital. I have two days of meetings with departmental heads, and I don't know if we'll have a chance to see each other again while we're here. If not, I wish you luck. I'm sorry you had to suffer this car trip, but it did give me the chance to get to know you. Believe me, it's been a pleasure." He turned to me and winked. It was his way of saying goodbye when he was satisfied with my work.

After a night of restorative sleep, Abdul and I met on the hotel veranda at about eleven in the morning. Leon, fresh and smiling, greeted us with a Tom Collins of his own devising that would have revived a hussar. He had arrived at dawn, after sleeping like a baby in the truck carrying the dishes and kitchen equipment. *"J'ai trouvé votre ministre un type trés malin,"* he said to me, referring of course to the minister of public works, who had congratulated him so warmly. Then Leon served us a delicious meal prepared according to the canons of Belgian cuisine.

Later we went out for a stroll through the town, justly famous for its beautiful women. On the bridge over the river that crosses the city, we waited for the appearance of the women who work in the downtown offices and shops. The most beautiful girls pass by in a kind of ritual that has been repeated for many years. It was, in fact, an overwhelming sight. Their elegant walk, the svelte proportions of those young, elastic bodies, their great dark eyes, the smooth, velvety skin that seems to invite a touch, all make the women of this region a kind of race apart, a species of mysterious origins. As if he had read my mind, Abdul said:

"They're very similar to Andalusians, and to Levantines too.

But when you see them you know that time won't ruin them the way it devastates our women when they reach thirty. It's as if their bones were made of something stronger yet more flexible. They're mutants."

As it grew dark, we returned to the hotel. Abdul hired a taxi to take him to Urandá at dawn. We had a few aperitifs at the bar, and Leon served us a frugal, impeccable supper. We went up to our rooms, and I said goodbye to Abdul at his door.

"I'm certain we'll meet again, and often. When you see the Gaviero, please tell him that I always look forward to hearing from him, and be sure to tell him about Dr. Garcés and his incredible rescue. I know he'll be amused." He replied that by now Maqroll was probably sailing on a Danish ship from Java to the Malabar coast. He had a friend there who made incense for funerals, and he usually stayed at her house when he decided to take time off.

"We'll see each other," Bashur added, "and sooner than you think, I'm sure. My tankers will begin working for the company in a few weeks, and by then I expect to be in Aruba."

He took his leave with a firm handshake, confirming the mutual fondness that would unite us for some time to come and that began in our unforgettable first meeting in Urandá. Other encounters would follow over the course of many years, but not the one in Aruba. The gods willed otherwise. At about that time I began traveling to other lands and having new experiences, not all of them pleasant.

Abdul Bashur went on to join the small band of my friends who have lived their lives under the sign of chance and adventure, and at the periphery of laws and codes created by men who, like Tartuffe, wish to justify their own paltry destinies. During the days I spent with Bashur in Urandá and in the city of unimaginable women, I discovered some of the exceptional characteristics of his spirit. He possessed an extremely refined and profound sense of friendship and was capable of sacrificing all thoughts of his own well-being for the sake of a friend. His response to the secret laws of chance often reached the extremes of ritual. Only the unknown awakened his interest—in this he was similar to the Gaviero—but deep inside, Bashur maintained an inexorable core, and any effort to curtail his independence, the inclination of his feelings, or his most personal desires would shatter against it. When this happened he displayed an implacable, icy ferocity that surfaced when an attempt was made to impose on him even the slightest obligation if he had not accepted it beforehand, either for emotional or for purely pragmatic reasons. When I saw him subdue the frenzied colonel of the presidential guard, I learned how far his tolerance could be pushed. I had already heard a good deal about his friendship with Maqroll; when I met Bashur, it was easy enough to understand. It was rooted in an interplay of their ways of behaving, some contrary, others complementary or consonant, but in their totality creating an unbreakable harmony between the two men. Maqroll acted on the conviction that everything was already hopelessly lost. We are born, he would say, with a vocation for defeat. Bashur believed that everything was waiting to be done and that those who lost were the others, the irredeemable fools who undermine the world with sophistry and camouflaged ancestral weakness. From women Maqroll expected friendship without commitment or any trade in guilt, and in the end he always left them. With infallible regularity Bashur fell in love as if for the first time; he accepted, without analysis or judgment and as though it were an inestimable gift of heaven, everything that came from women. Maqroll only rarely confronted his adversaries; he preferred to leave punishment and reprisals to life and its changing fortunes. Abdul reacted immediately and brutally, not calculating the risk. Maqroll forgot offenses and therefore never thought of revenge, but Bashur cultivated vengeance as long as necessary and took it without mercy, as if the offense had just occurred. Maqroll had absolutely no money sense. Abdul was immeasurably generous, but at bottom he kept a running balance of profits and losses. Maqroll called no place on earth home. Abdul, a distant descendant of Bedouins, always yearned for the nomadic encampment where he would be welcomed with familial warmth. Maqroll was a voracious reader, especially of history and the memoirs of illustrious men, liking in this way to confirm his hopeless pessimism regarding the much vaunted human condition, concerning which he held a rather disillusioned and melancholy opinion. Abdul not only never opened a book but did not understand what possible use such a thing could have in his life. He had no faith in humans as a species but always gave each person the opportunity to prove to him that he was wrong.

This is how the two friends traveled the world together, engaging in the most outlandish enterprises, sowing both intimate and legendary memories in their wake. I have attempted to record this unusual saga, if not with absolute success, at least with the hope of delaying, to the limited extent of my ability, their fall into oblivion.

A good deal of water has gone over the dam since Bashur and I first met. Abdul is no longer among us. I have not had news of Maqroll the Gaviero for almost two decades, not since a long letter he sent from Pollensa, on Mallorca. The world has changed so much that many of their adventures are inconceivable today. As for the tramp steamers they sailed on, the source of the Bashur family's limited fortunes, there are only sixteen left on the seas, and these have become museum pieces that are displayed in books as if they were exotic survivors from a remote past.

Having selected some documents from those sent to me by Fatima, and others from Maqroll's papers in my possession, I will now attempt to revive certain moments in the life of Abdul Bashur. I confess to misgivings regarding the interest my readers may have in these adventures, so many of them anachronisms in the lackluster present we have been condemned to inhabit. Yet I have resolved to proceed, hoping that by salvaging the past of my two friends, I will not only perform an act of simple justice toward them but help to prolong my own memories; at this stage of my life, they represent a very large portion of the reasons I go on living.

II

The story of how Maqroll and Bashur first met, in Port Said, has already been told. Even though the Gaviero himself recounts the tale in his Xurandó Diary (I found the pages in an old book on the assassination of the Duke of Orléans, which I bought in Barcelona), certain points are not at all clear in his description of the episode. I have always believed that the Jew from Tetuán who walked away cursing the two friends was the victim of something more serious than having to sell his gems at a price lower than he had anticipated. Certain aspects of Maqroll's version are open to serious doubts. The Gaviero, for example, addresses the Jew in Spanish and Bashur in Flemish. How did he know Abdul spoke that language? And the Jew eventually curses them with so much fury, it is logical not only to assume that the poor son of David suffered another kind of deception at their hands but to wonder as well if they had not met before and if the owner of the stones was not someone other than Bashur. I never attempted to clarify this with either of them, since imprecisions and emendations like these in their stories are constants in the letters of both men. And so we will pass over this presumptive first meeting and go directly to what appears to be the earliest chapter in their Mediterranean adventures.

At that time Marseilles was the major drug distribution center for Europe and Asia Minor, and represented, along with Shanghai, the greatest focal point for crime in the world. Pursued by creditors, Abdul Bashur found himself obliged to sell the small freighter he had operated between Morocco, Tunis, and the Mediterranean ports of France and Spain. Although they surely would have come to his aid, he did not want to ask his family for help, for their businesses were not prospering either. Moreover, the last time he borrowed money from them, they had refused to cash the checks he signed to repay the loan. He was in Marseilles, living in a pension on the rue Marzagan, a few steps from La Canebière. The owner of the establishment was a Frenchwoman born in Tunis, who had a rather checkered past. She had been Bashur's lover when he worked for the shipyards his family owned then and had begun visiting the ports in the region. She later married a wine merchant, who died after a few years, leaving her a modest inheritance that she used to establish the pension in Marseilles, which was frequented for the most part by the couple's old friends. The place was discreet, and Arlette, the landlady, knew how to maintain good relations with the police. Some of her guests were engaged in dealings that did not always fall within the parameters established by law. In each case she knew whether to offer her protection or simply allow the authorities to take action. The prosperity of her business rested on this balancing of loyalties.

For some days Bashur had been planning a project and refining the details, and now he was looking for an associate to help put it into effect. It was a delicate matter, and he did not think it wise to discuss it with anyone who was not totally reliable. He visited the cafés on La Canebière and the adjacent streets, turning the idea over in his mind as he sat on the terraces, trying to keep his expenses to a minimum. One night, when the heat in his room had become unbearable, he decided to go out to find a breeze and drink an iced coffee that would have to last until dawn. He was an expert in the technique, which he had learned in his youth and could employ with an impassivity that disconcerted waiters. At about three in the morning, when the only people on the boulevard were some aging prostitutes watched over by pimps who could have been their grandsons, he saw a man jump off a moving bus and signal to him. The unmistakable form of the Gaviero, with his seaman's duffel bag on his shoulder, emerged from the darkness, came onto the lighted terrace, and walked over to Abdul's table. They exchanged greetings as if they had seen each other the day before, and Maqroll ordered an iced coffee and a cognac on the side. Bashur shuddered when he thought of his meager budget. Each man gave a brief accounting of recent events in his life and his reason for being in Marseilles. Maqroll had just left his position as bos'n on a Norwegian fishing vessel because of a dispute with the first officer, who suffered from a persecution complex that had turned into frenzy. He had declared Maqroll a messenger of Beelzebub, his mission to bring the Black Death back to Europe. The man was the owner's nephew, and there was no way to rid him of his obsession, typical of a stern Lutheran fanatic. Maqroll had arrived that morning on the train from Genoa and left his suitcase at the Gare du Prado. Without a moment's hesitation, Bashur invited him to share his room at Arlette's pension and then made a sibylline statement that intrigued the Gaviero.

"Don't worry about looking for work. We'll have plenty to keep us busy, and in a few weeks' time we can have all the money life owes us."

Before going on with the story, I think it would be helpful to clarify one aspect of their friendship: They had never used familiar forms of address with each other. I once mentioned this to the Gaviero, who gave me a characteristic reply.

"When we first met, each of us had already had more than his share of experiences. These we subsequently shared have been so varied and unusual that using *tú* would have seemed like an unwarranted change, something foolish and inappropriate to our ages and circumstances. We've been through too much together to do anything so frivolous."

But let us return to the Café des Beges and the conversation that would become the subject of so many vivid recollections on the part of both protagonists.

Bashur's words held a promise that awakened a kind of unconditional readiness in Maqroll, a renewed, untrammeled enthusiasm that he immediately communicated to his friend. He leaned his elbows on the table, rested his chin on crossed hands, and prepared to listen.

"A few weeks ago," Abdul said, "Ilona Grabowska called me

from Geneva. Yes, she's trying to organize a project there, and if it works, it could be incredibly profitable for the three of us. She has a friend who is the private secretary to a Persian Gulf emir; they've known each other since she was a girl in Trieste and he was a talented young lawyer. Thanks to their friendship, Ilona has been commissioned to decorate the new building of the Banque Suisse et du Proche-Orient in Geneva. The directors of the bank have requested extremely valuable antique Persian carpets for the reception areas, the meeting rooms, and the offices of the managers and department heads: Princess Bukhara, Tabriz, things like that. And our dear friend's first thought—you know how she is— was to call me so that I, as a Muslim and a Lebanese, could advise her. I explained my current situation, and she ignored the problem as if it had absolutely no importance. She asked me to telephone when I had concrete news. She's called me two more times. The bankers are pressuring her; they want to have everything ready for the next visit of several emirs who are their principal clients. I didn't know what to say to her. Then, two weeks ago, I thought of the perfect solution. All I needed was a partner. Now you're here, and everything's settled. In Arabic that's called—"

"*Baraka*," Maqroll said without hesitation. "What I don't understand is the first stroke of *baraka,* the one that brought you the solution, because I was about to suggest that we talk to Ilona and tell her to look somewhere else. Our present circumstances put us a long way from Princess Bukhara, Tabriz, and all the other carpets of Harunar-Rashid."

"They're within our reach. You can consider them ours. Let me explain," replied Abdul. Maqroll held up his hands as if to stop someone, and interrupted his friend.

"Wait a minute, Abdul, wait a minute. You know we can't do anything with fakes or copies, no matter how faithful, because our friend from Trieste is involved and can land in jail, and she'd never forgive us for that."

"And she'd be right not to," Abdul declared. "But that's not the plan. Ilona and her emirs will have the most authentic, the most original, the most certified antique Persian rugs in the world. Listen carefully, and you'll see what an unbelievable stroke of *baraka* this is. Do you remember Tarik Choukari, my compatriot with the French passport, the customs official who helped us here when we were doing the signal flags?"

"Good God!" the Gaviero exclaimed, holding his head in his

hands. "Of course I remember him. I still dream about him. Don't tell me he's the solution."

"Yes. A man like him is exactly what we need now. Well, the other day I ran into him at a club in the Vieux Port, where they have the best belly dancers in this part of the Mediterranean. You know the calming effect this erotic ceremonial dance has on me when it's performed by authentic practitioners of an art that's much more difficult than Europeans suppose. We were there until dawn, drinking a vile mint tea. When the place closed, we went for a breakfast of fish fresh off the boat. I told Tarik about losing my ship to the banks, and in passing, not giving it too much importance but merely to highlight the ironies of life, I mentioned that now I was looking for superb antique Persian carpets. He stared at me, obviously suspecting I had an ulterior motive in bringing this up.

"'I don't know why you're so shocked,' I said. 'Believe me, it was a completely innocent remark. What is it? I don't understand.'

"Finally, Tarik was convinced I knew nothing, and as we walked along La Canebière on our way to the pension, he filled me in. Tarik still works in customs. He's now head of the night watchmen at the warehouses of the customs police, and he maintains the same connections and arrangements with certain of his superiors that proved so useful when we were doing the flags. Well, here comes the incredible part: For several months there's been a collection of twenty-four carpets lying there in those warehouses. They came directly from Bushire, in Iran—you know, the port that connects with Shiraz."

"I know it," said the Gaviero. "It's a hole where you can die of boredom."

"That's the one," continued Abdul. "Well, these antique rugs are exactly what Ilona is looking for. And there they are, not because anyone tried to smuggle them in but because the owner was killed in a brothel fight that somehow involved drugs. The crime hasn't been solved, and so far no one has claimed the rugs. But that's not the end of the story. A customs inspector, a friend of Tarik's who's already cooperated on a few operations with him— you can imagine what kind—said that the owner described the rugs as ordinary and modern in his customs declaration and put a very low value on them to avoid high import taxes. Through an unusual but understandable oversight, none of the inspectors has caught on to the swindle. Perhaps they've been distracted by the mystery surrounding the owner's death. In any event, the rugs are there. All we have to do is replace them with others that roughly correspond to the description on the customs declaration, and that'll be it. So it's a question of making the switch, getting the authentic rugs out of here as fast as we can in case anything's discovered, taking them to Rabat, and shipping them from there to Geneva. That's all. In case any of it comes to light, it'll be easy to prove it all happened a long time ago, and suspicion will fall on customs employees who are now in jail paying for other crimes. You can imagine how I felt when I heard Tarik's story. I needed a partner to set in motion the various mechanisms that this venture requires. I thought you were in Malaysia, submerged in funeral incense, which is why I didn't even think of you. And now you show up in Marseilles, and this is the second stroke of *baraka* that reveals the hand of the Prophet."

"Let's not exaggerate, Abdul, let's not exaggerate. It's better to leave the Prophet out of operations like this," said Maqroll with a smile. Then he was silent for a long time, absorbed in digesting what Bashur had just proposed, and finally he said:

"All right. Let's get to work. The first thing is to buy the ordinary rugs. That can be taken care of in Morocco or Tunis. I volunteer to do it. I know people in both countries who can help me. The second thing is to get the authentic ones out of France, into Morocco, and on to Switzerland with all the papers in order. You ought to take care of that. It sounds much more logical, given your nationality and your family's commercial background. Don't smile, Abdul. I'm serious. You know I am. It seems to me we're missing only one thing: money to travel and to buy the ordinary rugs. And we'll need an advance for Tarik so he can grease his colleagues' palms when it's time to switch the merchandise. When that's been arranged, we'll be ready to move. You can count on me."

"Ilona has enough money to cover those expenses," explained Bashur. "The people from the bank have already advanced her a sizable sum, and that's one of the reasons she's in a hurry. As for the rest of it, I agree with everything you've said, but you've overlooked one detail: Somebody has to go to Geneva to explain the operation to Ilona. Obviously we can't use the telephone. I think this is something you ought to do."

"Agreed. We'll call Ilona today so she can send the money I'll need to go to Switzerland. We can tell her everything's arranged and that I'll explain it to her in person."

It was seven in the morning, and they still had an hour or two of relatively cool temperatures for sleeping before the heat returned. They walked back to the pension in high spirits. Deep inside, each man could feel the stirring of those wings that respond to the unknown and the proximity of adventure, and portend something akin to youth restored, a world that seems newly created. The landlady welcomed the arrival of Maqroll; her former lover had told her about him. Later that day they telephoned Ilona from the pension. Arlette authorized the long-distance call: An ember of her past love still glowed. When she heard the Gaviero's voice, Ilona could not help exclaiming:

"Where'd you come from, you ungrateful bum! I can just imagine what you two are cooking up. Good Lord, what a pair!"

Ilona promised to send a money order that same day; she was consumed with curiosity to hear Maqroll's explanation of the unexpected and apparently miraculous solution the two old friends had devised for the problem of finding rugs loaded with antiquity and dangers she could not even imagine.

In the afternoon they looked for Tarik in the club with the belly dancers, the place where he handled his affairs during the day. Choukari stared at the Gaviero.

"We know each other, don't we? Sure, now I remember . . ."

"The signal flags. That's a long time ago."

Maqroll was going to say something else, but just then the first dancer came on, playing her finger cymbals and swaying her hips with the dreamy slowness that begins the dance. The Gaviero was also a devoted fan of this ritual, which he considered propitious for good fortune and mental health. Abdul hurriedly informed him:

"Here the first ones aren't the best. It's not like Cairo. Let's talk to Tarik now; the authentic dancers from Damascus come on later."

Maqroll smiled tolerantly and paid attention to what Tarik was about to say. It would be fairly brief, because informers would soon be coming in, along with the first patrons of the evening. Police did not show up at the club too often, but this did not mean he could throw all caution to the wind. Choukari agreed that Bashur was the one to take the genuine rugs to Rabat. Ilona would meet him there and then go on to Geneva with the merchandise, which would now be legally purchased and have a legitimate bill of sale. This could be prepared and printed in Marseilles, with a letterhead reading: "Abdul Bashur. Authentic Persian Rugs: Beirut, Rabat, Tehran, Istanbul." When the valuable rugs had been replaced by the ones Maqroll bought in Tangier, they would be removed from the customs warehouse at night. Bashur would take them to Melilla, a Moroccan port where a friend of Tarik's would facilitate the procedures for reexpediting the rugs to Morocco because of the owner's death. Tarik would take care of those papers, but of course he would have to pay a substantial sum to one of his coworkers.

Rather than mistrust, Choukari awakened a kind of uneasiness in the Gaviero. It was caused by the man's rachitic appearance: his face twisted and tortured by disconcerting tics, his pallid skin, the constant, feverish movement of his eyes, all of which reminded Maqroll of spies in silent films. But he also knew that these purely external symptoms could hide, as they frequently did among Choukari's people, consuming energy and infinite ingenuity in discovering the least dangerous ways to break the law. As Abdul followed Tarik's explanations, he stared at an uncertain horizon, which in squint-eyed people indicates intense concentration. Tarik left abruptly, almost without saying goodbye, when a new group of patrons walked into the club. Abdul and the Gaviero stayed until dawn, enjoying the dancing, which grew in quality and dramatic tension in a way they had rarely seen before. As always, the outstanding performers, the ones who surrendered to the kind of ecstasy experienced by dervishes, were the oldest women, whose bodies betrayed the ineluctable ravages of time.

Maqroll traveled by train to Geneva, where Ilona met him at the station. Each was surprised at the other's appearance. The Gaviero saw a slimmer, tanned Ilona who breathed an unexpected air of prosperity and well-being. To Ilona, Maqroll seemed even more tortured by his nomadic fever, more driven by internal storms of uncertain origin; after his many years without a direction or a home, these had grown old but could be seen now in his eyes, which were those of a prophet who brings no word, no message. Ilona thought she had probably idealized him during long nights of alcohol and erotic excitement in the shabby boardinghouse in Ramsey, on the Isle of Man, and in other places, even less respectable and circumspect, where they had been together after that first encounter. They both admitted to their discomfiture. Ilona said she usually sunbathed nude, lying in a canoe in the middle of the lake, to the horror or delight of puritanical functionaries, steeped in Calvinism, who passed her as they rode the ferry to their spotless houses or aseptic offices. She had more money now and had spent considerable amounts to refurbish her wardrobe. Maqroll agreed that although the demons pursuing him were the same, the trials they had recently inflicted on him had gone beyond the limits of his tolerance. Yet, at the core, he did not believe he had changed much.

Ilona was living in a small apartment with hotel service and a view of the lake, and the Gaviero came to stay there after they had eaten a generous supper, preceded by tolerable dry martinis. They made love as if they had just invented it. Later, as they lay naked in bed, the Gaviero explained how their plan for acquiring the rugs and taking them to Geneva would work.

Ilona had first met Bashur in Cyprus, during the episode of the signal flags. They became lovers there. After that, the three of them shared other experiences, always at the outer limit of conventions when not in open violation of them. Some have been recounted elsewhere. Ilona worried about Abdul as if she were his older sister and attempted, usually in vain, to protect him from the dangers he often faced, for he was motivated by a curious mechanism that Ilona herself analyzed with her customary eloquent lucidity after she heard the Gaviero's explanation of the plan.

"It's so typical of his nature. You can be sure there's a way to get those rugs without breaking the law. But that doesn't interest Abdul. His Bedouin genes move him to establish his own laws, and the easiest way to do that is to ignore the ones that have already been written. Remember what he always says: 'Instead of that, why don't we . . . ,' and off he goes down the most baroque and dangerous paths until he gets what he wants and has the police at his heels. The strange thing is that when his family's interests are involved, he never tries anything that isn't absolutely legitimate. Well, since you and I are his good friends as well as the accomplices he needs for all his villainies, I'll be there in Rabat to take the rugs to Geneva. Have you any idea what rugs like that are worth? I'm sure you don't, that it hasn't even occurred to either one of you to find out. A fortune, Maqroll, the kind of fortune you can't even imagine. With 'Operation Princess Bukhara,' we're on our way to becoming millionaires, in Swiss francs. This all sounds like a bad thriller."

Ilona was correct in her analysis, but she did not have a moment's hesitation in joining her friends and lovers with a feverish enthusiasm identical to theirs.

Maqroll returned to Marseilles with the money required to

initiate the plan. A week later everything was arranged. Tarik, who had advanced his coworker in customs half the sum the man had been promised, was reimbursed. The Gaviero traveled to Tangier. In Tarik's opinion, the inferior rugs needed to replace the valuable ones would be easier to find there. Maqroll returned in just a few days. He had been so fortunate in his purchases that, except for some minor differences, the merchandise matched the descriptions on the customs manifest. The bills of sale that would be turned over to Ilona in Rabat had been printed and were in Bashur's possession. Now it was Tarik's turn. The switch would be made on the following Sunday, the least risky day of the week. On Saturday night, a woman's voice on the telephone informed Bashur that Choukari had been detained by the police. When Abdul gave him the news, Maqroll, who was less inclined to lose heart at this kind of setback, reassured his friend.

"If they're holding him, it's for something that doesn't have anything to do with us. As of now we haven't even moved a finger in Marseilles, and nobody can know about something that's only been a plan so far."

But Abdul was more familiar with the complex labyrinths that connected the Marseilles police with the underworld. He thought about the informers in the club frequented by Tarik and did not feel quite so certain that his arrest had nothing to do with the Persian rugs. At this point Arlette came in to change the sheets and bath towels. When she saw how preoccupied they were, she asked what was wrong and if she could help in any way. Suddenly Abdul leaped up and exclaimed, "Arlette is our salvation!" She stared at him in stupefaction as Abdul threw his arms around her and gave her resounding kisses. Then he asked her to sit down and explained that a friend had been detained by the police, and they could not go in person to find out what had happened because neither one had his papers in order. But she could. Arlette sat watching them with the expression of someone who knows more than anyone supposes, and said:

"It's Choukari, isn't it? That's what I thought. You're planning something with him. I've seen him hanging around here, and I know him better than you do, and for a longer time. You can trust him, don't worry. He's no stool pigeon. But he's done things in the past, and the police have had an eye on him for a long time. I'll go and find out what's happening. I'll say he lived here for a while, which is true, and that I'm fond of him, which isn't. Wait here, and don't go out until I get back." As she spoke, Maqroll scrutinized Arlette as if he had never seen her before. She had a soft, fleshy body and an aura of health and abundance that was centered in her face, where her violet-blue eyes and a certain Celtic regularity in her features attested to a beauty that must have been remarkable. She radiated a sly coquettishness, which was very French, together with authority in her gestures and words, a combination that has inspired several centuries of the kind of amorous literature and gallant painting known only in France. The Gaviero rose to his feet, took one of her hands, kissed it in a courtly manner, and declared in a French copied from the plays of Marivaux:

"Madame, allow me to express my warmest feelings and deepest gratitude. I pray that from this moment on, you will count me not only among your sincerest friends but also as one of your most humble admirers." The landlady looked at him with amusement and curiosity, as if asking herself, "What's wrong with this one?" Bashur gave the restrained laugh of a man who has understood everything, and turned to look at his former lover in anticipation of her reply. She, in turn, gazed deeply into the Gaviero's eyes and, with a wide smile, answered:

"From the first day I saw you it seemed to me that lurking behind that air of a wizard on vacation there was something to worry about, a comrade worthy of this lunatic from Lebanon."

As she spoke, Arlette caressed Abdul's cheeks with the inimitable grace and tender wisdom of a woman whose fires are still a long way from being damped. She walked out of the room without another word, leaving the two men to wait for the outcome of her efforts. Shaking his head in disbelief, Bashur remarked to his friend:

"I can't believe my eyes. I never thought I'd see Maqroll playing the *chevalier servant* with Arlette. There's no hope for you either, my dear Gaviero."

"Listen to me carefully, Abdul," replied Maqroll. "If I ever decide to stop this wandering and settle down, I'd want to do it with a woman like Arlette. She's what Apollinaire called *une femme ayant sa raison*. What else can you ask for in life?"

Abdul shrugged and stretched out on his bed to wait for the news. He was still worried, despite the Gaviero's ruminations.

It was almost midnight when Arlette returned, practically dragging Tarik behind her. She let him go in the middle of the room and said:

"Here he is. The next time you two decide to use him for

something, tell him that at least for the time he's working with you, he should refrain from hitting his wife." They had not known he was married but were so relieved to see him they forgot to reproach him for the anguish he had caused. As Tarik tried to straighten the disarray of his clothing, which proclaimed his passage through the police station, he explained what had happened.

"I couldn't help it. I caught her in bed with our neighbor Gaston, the streetcar conductor, both of them naked and having their fun. He managed to get back to his room, and she stared at me as if she'd seen a ghost. I taught her a lesson, but it seems I lost control. Gaston called the police. He thought that was a way to get rid of me."

Arlette led Tarik to the porter's room, which had been empty for many months. As she left she motioned to them, putting a finger to her eye to indicate they should not lose sight of him.

The incident revealed the rather precarious foundation on which their plans rested. But there was nothing they could do; they had to move ahead. The next night, after repeated apologies and promises of loyalty and discretion, Tarik switched the rugs in the customs warehouse. The valuable ones, along with Bashur's baggage, were put in a launch, and Abdul sailed for the port of Melilla in Morocco. Maqroll remained in Marseilles, wooing the autumnal plenitude of Arlette.

Ilona was waiting in Melilla, and as she greeted Abdul she could not help congratulating him for how efficiently the plan had worked so far. Bashur protested her lack of faith in the criminal talents of her two lovers, and Ilona's response was immediate:

"Ah, my dear Abdul, the two of you will never be real professionals. You, because all you care about is breaking the law, and Maqroll, because in the middle of a job he can drop everything and start thinking about a new scheme on the other side of the world. Being a criminal is very serious work, darling. Amateurs like us always end up as mere onlookers."

Abdul said that this time, at least, everything was moving along without a hitch. The papers Tarik prepared for bringing the rugs into Morocco as unclaimed merchandise had worked perfectly. Choukari's friend in Melilla had expedited the operation and been paid by Abdul. Bashur handed Ilona the bills of sale that confirmed the purchase of the merchandise, making her the undisputed owner of twenty-four extraordinary antique rugs. When they reached Rabat, they registered at different hotels to avoid arousing suspicion. But Ilona could not resist taking Bashur up to her room, where they made love with the excitement of those who have successfully completed a very dangerous mission. They arranged to meet later at a small restaurant that served Berber food and played music from the time of Al-Andalus. They had discovered the place during the famous episode of the signal flags.

The next day Bashur stopped for Ilona at her hotel and went with her to the airport. The rugs were declared accompanied freight covered by Ilona's ticket on the direct flight from Rabat to Geneva on Royal Air Maroc. When it was time to say goodbye, she reminded him that in two weeks she would be expecting them in Geneva to divide the profits. Abdul gave her a kiss so brief and conventional that Ilona whispered in his ear:

"You see? We'll never be as spontaneous as the truly wicked. We're amateurs, which is just as well, I'd say. See you soon."

The exchange of rugs was never discovered. Tarik, looking like a malaria-ridden fakir, still frequented the taverns of the Vieux Port, cursing the streetcar conductor who continued to replace him in his conjugal bed whenever the opportunity presented itself. Abdul and Maqroll said goodbye to Arlette and paid their bill with a punctuality that brought a complicitous smile to her face. As he was leaving, Maqroll gave her a resounding kiss on the mouth and promised to return.

Ilona was waiting for them in Lausanne, wearing a very stylish spring dress. She radiated a provocative, playful optimism. They sat on the terrace of the Grand Palace Hotel, where they were staying, and ordered a bottle of the delicious, slightly carbonated regional wine. When Ilona handed each of them a check, they were astonished to see the figure with six zeros that was written there, surely the first and last time they ever held so much in their hands.

"Wipe that stupid look off your faces," said Ilona, laughing, "and tell me instead what you're going to do with all this money. I'm curious to know your plans."

"I don't make plans," was Maqroll's immediate reply. "I really don't know what to do with it."

"And you, Abdul of my sins, what will you do?" asked Ilona, caressing Bashur's hair as if she were petting a Siamese cat.

"I'm going to Istanbul to buy the ship I've wanted all my life. It's called the *Nebil* and was built in Sweden in 1914. It has an English Crosley 8/480 diesel engine, four cargo holds with a total capacity of six tons, and a nine-man crew. The elegance of its lines is perfect. An expert in these matters, Michael J. Krieger, called it the Bugatti of old freighters." He pointed to the check with fervent devotion. "With this I can cover the first three payments of the six I have to make to become the owner of that jewel."

"Here are the other three," said the Gaviero. "It's nothing compared to the pleasure of becoming the co-owner of the *Nebil*. I saw it last year in Galata, and it inspired me with almost religious respect. Let's order another bottle of this well-behaved wine to celebrate." Maqroll called the waiter, while Ilona looked from one to the other with the expression of someone overwhelmed by events.

"I don't know which of you is the bigger lunatic," she finally exclaimed. "You risk twenty years in jail, and now one wants to buy a paleolithic boat and the other hands over his money to help pay for it as if the check took up too much room in his pocket. You're hopeless, both of you. I, on the other hand, am going to buy an apartment in Trieste and live there in the summer. That's another old, unrealized dream."

"Very sensible, very sensible," observed Bashur as they all laughed, and with that the subject was closed.

At this point I think it appropriate to mention a lifelong dream of Bashur's, which he never achieved. A constant in his destiny, more tenacious than any other and, for his friends, the most moving, it was his endless search, in every port on earth, for the ideal freighter: its design, size, and engine were always on Abdul's mind. He wanted to spend the rest of his days on the ship, sailing all the world's seas with a captain who, like Bashur, could appreciate the vessel's svelte lines and perfect seaworthiness. Our friend spent a good part of his life pursuing this unlikely dream. Both Ilona and the Gaviero had long since given up their joking allusions to Abdul's mania. There was no humor left to talk about it. They had heard him describe too often how he had found the ship of his desire, suffered dangerous, foolhardy tribulations to obtain the money to pay for it, only to learn when he went to buy it that it had already been sold or was in a shipyard being dismantled for scrap. This last eventuality caused him the most pain; the sadness could last for months, and he spoke of what had happened as if he had lost someone dear to him. The fact that anyone could turn a work of art into scrap metal made him curse the entire human race, and shipowners in particular, although his family were counted among them. In this perpetual search for the perfect freighter, Bashur had missed every opportunity for making a fortune offered by his apparently bottomless ingenuity and his notable gift for friendship, never far below the surface. One day when Maqroll was talking to me about this characteristic of Bashur's, he made a revealing comment:

"Abdul knows very well he's pursuing an impossibility. His ideal ship always slips between his fingers at the last minute, or he discovers certain features that don't match the dream just as he's about to close the deal, and he pulls out. I think he must have invented this diabolical illusion when he was a boy trying to correct and improve his father's models; he was a shipbuilder, as you know, highly respected all over the Middle East. Abdul tried to surpass his father's reputation by creating a prototype of an unattainable ship that he would make both his home and his source of income. But we pay the rest of our lives for every rebellion against the magnified and oppressive image of the father. The only way out of the labyrinth we all enter at one time or another is to become convinced that rather than replacing him, we must attempt to prolong his life to the extent our own strengths and demons will allow. It isn't easy, and it's usually not pleasant, but there's no other way to face the challenge of living our own lives."

Since I could not remember ever hearing the Gaviero speak in those terms before, I concluded that the ties joining him to Bashur were stronger and much more complex than those of simple camaraderie. Once again the complementarity of their friendship—patently clear to those of us who knew them well—was revealed to me. Ilona, who could maintain a crisis-free intimacy with both of them, once remarked:

"They're like brothers but are composed of contrary elements. The Greeks said something about this, but I can't remember the name of the god or the myth that exemplifies it."

If one knew this, one could also foresee that when he reached the Bosporus, Abdul Bashur learned that the *Nebil* had just been sold to a Turkish shipowner, who guarded it as if it were a treasure. Maqroll returned to Marseilles, moved into Arlette's pension, and established an intimate relationship with the landlady that left her in a kind of erotic limbo filled with sensations that she had thought were wiped out years before.

Abdul arrived several months later. He tried to return his money to Maqroll, but the Gaviero convinced him to keep it. As always, Bashur eventually acquired a perfectly ordinary freighter, which was offered to him in Marseilles at particularly advantageous terms. Half the ship's profits would go to Maqroll, who knew that a good part of his share would be returned to Bashur to cover the cost of repairs and maintenance.

"I don't know," said Arlette, a good French proponent of the art of thrift, "what the hell you two have against money. You don't know how to put any aside for the bad times, and it slips through your fingers as if you hadn't worked hard to earn it."

"We've already lived all our bad times, my dear," replied Maqroll. "Now we're going through what our friend Paul Coulaud once called *la misère dorée*."

"I really don't think that's funny," Arlette concluded, while the Gaviero explored the opulent décolletage of a well-fed Flemish woman.

III

I have not been able to determine exactly when Abdul Bashur met Jaime Tirado, the Mirror Breaker. In order to tell about their encounter, I have made use of Bashur's letters to Fatima, where the incident is mentioned without too many particulars, and of my notes on conversations I had with Maqroll, which are certainly much more explicit and detailed. Bashur mentions the tramp steamer that he bought in Marseilles and named the *Princess Bukhara,* displaying a sense of humor more easily ascribable to the Gaviero than to Abdul. It was on this ship that he sailed to meet the Mirror Breaker. But many events occurred before this, and many others came later, judging by the information I received from Maqroll—almost all of it undated, for chronology was never one of his strong points. Ultimately, however, the vagueness is not very important, since it has not been my intention to adhere to any strict temporal sequence either in this recounting of Bashur's life, which is certainly partial, or in my earlier narratives dedicated to the Gaviero. With regard to the episode of the Mirror Breaker, the presence of the Vacaresco twins interfered with my establishing precisely when it occurred, for I thought the two women had disappeared long before Bashur and Tirado met. The error was surely mine: In the information gathered from both Bashur and Maqroll, the famous sisters are there at the very beginning of events on the Mira River and the encounter that almost cost Abdul his life.

Maruna and Lena Vacaresco performed at a cheap cabaret in Southampton. Their erotic number was rather primitive but acquired added prurience because they were twins engaging in a series of acrobatic lesbian acts, with a complete gamut of moans and spasmodically rolling eyes—not particularly convincing, it's true, but sufficiently believable to hold the morbid interest of an audience composed almost entirely of sailors of the most diverse nationalities, who did not demand rigorous realism in the twins' performance.

One night, when the *Princess Bukhara* was unloading Egyptian raw linen at the English port, Maqroll and Abdul decided to leave the ship and visit the bars near the docks. The gray monotony of Southampton's streets, the looming massiveness of its factories and harbor installations, depressed their spirits more than any other port in England.

"A good whiskey can erase two-thirds of all this colorless cement, all this brick and soot, and all these obtuse and badly fed Englishmen," said the Gaviero, trying to convince Bashur to join him in his escape from the syncopated, implacable din of the cranes.

This was how they came to the Pink Surprise, which was the rather gratuitous name of the club where the Vacaresco twins were performing. They had visited enough bars for the Scotch to fulfill Maqroll's promise, and everything seemed more tolerable. For some unfathomable reason, the sisters' act was accompanied by Spanish music, which delighted Bashur more than the Gaviero could understand. It began with the introduction of the sisters, one on each side of a small stage that held a round bed decorated with pink bows and pom-poms, which also adorned the sheet that covered it. To the left stood Maruna, with her deep-black hair, eyes heavily lined in kohl, and a plump body covered by a brief, sky-blue baby doll. Lena appeared on the right, with her abundant platinum-blond hair, eyes lined in an intense lilac, and a pink outfit as skimpy as her sister's. The action began with the paso doble "*El Relicario*," followed by other, equally famous pieces, and ended, as the sisters reached their ecstasy, with "*España Cañi*." The routine of intertwinings, kisses, caresses, and noisy lickings, to a steady accompaniment of exaggerated moans and sighs, was, as I have said, both unconvincing and tedious, but Abdul was so amused that he invited the twins to the table and ordered a bottle of champagne. The Gaviero watched him, intrigued by an enthusiasm that was not warranted by either the place or the Vacaresco twins.

"Only the English," said Abdul in explanation, "are capable of producing rubbish as absurd and tasteless as this. It's the most deliciously grotesque thing I've seen in a long time. And the twins have something—what you call 'Danubian spirit.' Wait and see."

And in fact, the Vacaresco sisters turned out to be quite different from what one might imagine after seeing their performance at the Pink Surprise. First, predictably enough, their names were not Maruna, Lena, or Vacaresco, but Estela and Raquel Nudelstein. Their father had been a Jewish tailor from Bessarabia, and their mother, who acted as their agent, was the daughter of a Hasidic rabbi from Lvov. In her youth, this imposing matron, Doña Sara, had seen a photograph in an old French magazine of the Romanian poet Hélène Vacaresco, who enjoyed a certain notoriety in Paris during the years immediately preceding the First World War. It seemed to her that the name Vacaresco went very well with the profession she had planned for the twins given to her by Jehovah as an infallible source of income. Their father had been killed in one of the first Stalinist pogroms. All of this was recounted by the sisters after their second glass of champagne, with a spontaneous wit that, as Bashur had foreseen, they kept to themselves and never displayed onstage. Without their makeup and elaborate wigs, they had interesting faces and lively, mischievous expressions, confirming Abdul's prescience when he had cited Maqroll. This was certainly a characteristic of many Jews from *Mitteleuropa,* who were often more Viennese than the Viennese, or more Magyar than the Hungarians. One need only consider Erich von Stroheim, a Viennese Jew whose film roles were perfect characterizations of an officer of the guard in the time of Emperor Franz Josef, or an authentic Prussian Junker. The first thing Abdul asked the twins when they sat down was what had given them the idea of using such irresistibly vulgar Spanish music. Maruna, who began to show a marked preference for the Gaviero, explained that the club owners had probably assumed that Vacaresco was a typical Andalusian name and put together this dazzling potpourri of paso dobles to make the act more interesting. With great satisfaction, Bashur said, "I told you so. Only the English could do something so marvelous. They're priceless."

Lena, who was showing interest in Bashur, suggested they express their opinions in French. People at other tables were already showering them with openly disapproving looks. The four of them left the Pink Surprise after the second show, when the Vacarescos' indifference and fatigue were almost insulting to the audience. They stopped in at two or three other clubs, then walked to the port for a breakfast of oysters, fresh fish, and white Portuguese wine sold by a Lisboan at a tiny stand near the exit of a garage. They returned to the ship, and the couples walked to their respective cabins as the twins sang spurious fados without knowing a word of the language of Camoëns.

After the cargo of raw linen was unloaded, the *Princess Bukhara* underwent an urgently needed hull cleaning. The ship was in dry dock for five days; with the rather reluctant consent of Doña Sara, Maqroll and Bashur stayed with the twins in their hotel. The sisters turned out to be an apparently inexhaustible source of entertainment. Their natural predilection for instantaneous, caustic humor, directed at the most trivial daily events, turned the time the two men spent in Southampton into a memorable celebration. The sisters had entirely dissimilar personalities. Maruna, Maqroll's friend, had a concentrated character that leaned toward melancholy and transient melodrama. In bed she compensated for a certain tendency to frigidity by miming sudden ecstasies that were much more convincing than those she faked onstage. This simulation, in an intimate setting, awakened an excitement in Maqroll that he had not known before. When she was seriously aroused, Maruna would fall into a Madonna-like trance that he found equally exciting. Lena, who was extroverted, superficial, and disorderly, had the ready sensuality of women for whom only the present exists, who prefer instinctive men, the ones who reject "any intellectual complexity or metaphysical anguish," as she herself defined them. "The only anguish I know is when someone doesn't like me," she would say as she tossed her hair in a provocative gesture that had become habitual. The Vacaresco sisters became a kind of calculus for Maqroll and Bashur when they judged a place or an experience. A Vacaresco night, or a woman who was not at all Vacaresco, was an indicator of how much they had enjoyed themselves.

But the incident that made this time unforgettable, especially for Bashur, took place the night before the *Princess Bukhara* was to leave. Lena wanted to give Abdul a memento of their meeting. She had taken a pile of photographs from an empty biscuit tin and was searching through them for one that displayed her allure without being trite. Suddenly Bashur saw a picture of her standing beside a prosperous-looking man with a somewhat disquieting face and an athletic air. They were leaning against the railing at the stern of a freighter with a notably elegant line. The forecastle reminded him of the *Nebil,* but the design was even more classic. He picked up the photo and became engrossed in looking at it, trying to identify the ship. Lena could not understand Abdul's interest and asked what attracted his attention in that particular snapshot. Instead of replying, Abdul asked with evident excitement, "Where's the ship now? Is the owner the man in the photograph? Who is he?"

Lena looked at him, surprised by the flood of questions, and answered with the patience of someone trying to bring a man back to his senses.

"The ship is named the *Thorn,* and it's rotting there in the mouth of the Mira River on the northern border of Ecuador. The owner is the man in the photograph." She hesitated for a moment before continuing. "There's not much to say about him. At least I don't know very much. He made a lot of money in some kind of agriculture—he owns fields upriver, a couple of hours away."

"What's his name?" Abdul interrupted her impatiently.

"What's the matter with you? The guy's name is Jaime Tirado, but they call him the Mirror Breaker. Don't tell me you're jealous! That's the last thing I expected from you." Lena could not understand Abdul's feverish interest in someone so distant.

"Good God, no," Bashur replied. "It's the ship I'm interested in. It has a marvelous line. Do you think it's still there?"

Reassured, Lena answered, "Probably. I'm afraid it doesn't go to sea anymore. I seem to remember that the owner once tried to sell it."

"The Mira River, did you say?" Bashur insisted.

"Yes, the Mira River, on the border with Colombia," she replied. "But you can't be thinking of going there! It's the end of the world. I went there with the Mirror Breaker on a yacht; we sailed from Panama City. It's hot as hell, the mosquitoes eat you alive day and night, and the desolation and misery all around you are hard to believe. He lives like a marquis, of course, but that's upriver, and trying to get there is more dangerous than it's worth."

"I know places much worse and a thousand times more dangerous. Don't worry," said Abdul, placing the photograph in his wallet.

Lena handed him another snapshot: It showed her with a defi-

ant smile, opening her blouse and offering her breasts to the photographer.

"Take this one too," she said, "even if it doesn't have a boat.
Keep it as a souvenir of our nights in Southampton."

Abdul put it next to the first photograph and changed the
subject. Later they picked up Maqroll and Maruna, and they all
went to have supper at a Pakistani restaurant that had been recommended by Doña Sara, a lady of imposing flesh, who was endlessly clever and knew how to stay on the sidelines, giving her
daughters an apparently absolute freedom that was really no more
than the time-honored game of the fisherman and the bait. The
twins never mentioned her, but the two men had already detected
certain signs, imperceptible to others but, it was easy to surmise,
reflecting strict instructions from the Lvov matron, which they
never disobeyed.

They did not sleep that night but spent the time making accelerated, feverish amends for saying goodbye. They visited the few
passable bars in the port, went back to the hotel, and made love
with all the driving force of those who know they will not meet
again. They walked to the *Princess Bukhara,* and at the foot of the
gangplank, before their final farewell, Maqroll said, with an
emphasis that was unusual for him:

"From now on, when the black days come, and they always
do, the memory of the Vacaresco sisters will help us recall that
happiness is not something the naive invent in order to deceive
themselves. It clearly exists, because we have known it with you."

As tears ran down their sleepless faces, the sisters tried to grasp
what the Gaviero was saying, but it was obvious they had understood nothing. When the ship began to move, Maruna and Lena
were still on the dock, waving their arms and crying with a forsaken
air that brought a lump to the throats of the Gaviero and Bashur.

When they were on the high seas, heading for Danzig, where a
cargo of agricultural machinery bound for Djakarta was waiting
for them, Abdul showed Maqroll the photograph of the *Thorn*
and mentioned his interest in finding out if the ship was still for
sale. The Gaviero, long accustomed to sympathizing with his
friend's mania, proposed that in their ports of call they find cargo
destined for Panama City or Guayaquil. Then Abdul could see
the ship that had made him so restless. Maqroll acknowledged in
passing that the design really was notably elegant and simple, but
Abdul had to find out what kind of engine it had and what condition it was in. As for the owner, he declared frankly:

"A piece is missing in Lena's story, but she's clever enough to assume we'll find it on our own. One thing I'm sure of: This famous Mirror Breaker didn't make his fortune exporting bananas, the crop that's grown in the region. His money comes from something more valuable and much riskier. He has the look of a rich kid who's a little stupid, but he seems very suspicious to me. There's no breed worse than these playboys who break out and defy the rules and conventions of their class. They're extremely dangerous: They abandon the principles they were born to and never respect the ones established by the under-world. That means they're capable of anything. Nothing holds them back. Well, we'll see. We'll pick up cargo for Panama or Ecuador, and then we'll see."

Abdul put away his photograph, satisfied that his friend and partner still supported him in his search for the ideal tramp steamer.

Maqroll decided to stay behind in Djakarta, travel through the Malay Peninsula, and resume relations in Kuala Lumpur with the widow who sold funeral incense; her charms still held consider-able fascination for him. Before the Gaviero left the *Princess Bukhara,* he offered Bashur a final piece of advice. "Abdul, watch out for the Mirror Breaker. Remember what I said about those playboys. Let me know what happens. You know where to write."

"Don't worry. I'll remember. Everything will be fine," replied Bashur, watching Maqroll, whose gait was as cautious as a weary cat's, walk down the gangplank and into the motley crowd in the port, his head raised and alert as if he were calcu-lating when the world would attack. Again he felt the affection-ate solidarity, the unshadowed friendship, austere and warm at the same time, awakened in him by this unique man, this inde-fatigable tester of the sands where destiny and chance combine to ensnare humans and confound them with the empty illu-sions of ambition and desire. He would remember the Gaviero's warnings regarding the owner of the *Thorn* at precisely the moments he would have most liked to have his friend with him, but that he had to face alone in the harsh solitude of the unforgiving tropics.

From Djakarta Abdul sailed to Tripoli, and from there, carrying a cargo of explosives, to Limassol in Cyprus, where he delivered the compromising shipment to a man with a long, carefully combed reddish beard and hair the same color hanging down to his shoulders. He looked exactly like a priest of the Greek

Orthodox Church, and his small hands, worthy of a perfumed lady, moved as if giving a blessing. He was clearly a cleric in civilian disguise, involved in the intricate conspiracies that would overthrow British rule on the island. Bashur had learned long before that in the business of earning a living with a tramp steamer, one could not ask too many questions or accept any answers without vigilance and care.

The *Thorn* never left his thoughts. Each night before going to sleep, he pored over the photograph of the ship. He even made what was undeniably a rough calculation of its dimensions and cargo capacity based solely on the snapshot, in which the smiling couple added a touch of intrigue and nostalgia that kept him awake for hours: Who was this Jaime Tirado, this Mirror Breaker, about whom Maqroll harbored so many suspicions? The answer would not be long in coming.

From Limassol he traveled to La Rochelle. His agent there had sent a telegram asking him to come to the port as soon as possible, and Abdul left for France with a shipment of zinc in the hold and the premonition, almost the certainty, that something involving the *Thorn* was developing. He was right. A contract to carry cargo to Guayaquil was waiting for him in the harbor of ancient Aquitaine. The shipment consisted of twenty huge crates of textile machinery that filled the hold of the *Princess Bukhara* to capacity. In La Rochelle he bought a navigational chart of the Ecuadoran coast and another, more detailed map of the mouth of the Mira River. During the crossing he spent his time studying the two maps with the captain, a man we have not yet introduced to the reader—an inexcusable oversight on our part, since he had long been Abdul's invaluable right hand. His loyalty and ability to get along with people were indispensable for handling crews assembled according to the availability of seamen in port.

Vincas Blekaitis was a native of Vilna. He had the pale-gray eyes so common among Baltic peoples, from whom he had also inherited his Herculean size and the unhurried movements that concealed millennial astuteness and stormy mood swings. He had worked with Abdul for many years, whenever the Lebanese had a ship. Vincas felt unreserved loyalty and a somewhat childish admiration for his employer, even though he was much older than Abdul, whose name he could never pronounce correctly. He called him Jabdul, which often provoked the rest of the crew to laughter. On occasion, Maqroll jokingly called him Jabdul as well, and Bashur would smile in amusement.

They anchored in Guayaquil after a crossing plagued by difficulties. In the Caribbean they were caught in a storm that made the sides of the *Princess Bukhara* tremble as if they were paper. The cargo shifted in the holds and had to be reloaded in Panama City. Another delay, in Colón, was caused by a fleet of American warships passing through the canal on their way to maneuvers in the Pacific. A warm, sticky, persistent rain frayed their nerves and undermined their spirits. Vincas said he was sure that frogs would hatch in his ears. This, apparently, was the only humorous remark anyone had ever heard him make. The final straw was in Guayaquil, where they learned that the crane operators in the port were on strike, and they had to wait ten days for the derricks to operate again. It was the time of year when the Guayas River overflows its banks, producing a sinister plague of massive insects, similar to crickets but rounder, and slower, which escape the flood and invade the city, entering houses and hotels through the tiniest cracks and even paralyzing traffic. Cars skid on the greenish, foul-smelling crust created when automobiles run over the armies of insects that fill the streets. At a temperature of almost 110 degrees, the experience takes on Dantesque proportions. Ships' crews are obliged to remain on board, which increases their short tempers and surliness.

The *Princess Bukhara* was ready to sail after three days of unloading. Vincas told Bashur it would be a good idea to explain to the crew that they were heading for the mouth of the Mira River and would have to spend several days there. After the restrictions on their movements in Panama City and then in Guayaquil, they were feeling belligerent. Many of the sailors were from the Baltic and found the tropics almost intolerable. Bashur decided to offer the crew a special bonus as compensation for the hardship of being restricted to the ship again, when it anchored along the coast of Ecuador. Vincas managed to calm their anger, and the promise of a bonus had its intended effect.

They reached Manglares Cape, at the mouth of the Mira, on a sunny morning, the first they had seen after weeks of gray skies and constant rain. There was the *Thorn,* with its sleek lines and the aristocratic, dignified air conferred by age. The *Princess Bukhara* anchored alongside the elegant freighter, which seemed abandoned, although the deck and bridge indicated a certain amount of maintenance. Not a soul could be seen on board. Abdul decided to take the launch and have a closer look at the ship. When he was just a few meters away, an obese black, obviously still half asleep, appeared at the deck rail and in a gruff tone demanded what they wanted. Bashur explained that he had heard the ship was for sale and wanted to get in touch with the owner. The man made no reply, turned abruptly, and went into the cabin, where the radio was probably located. He emerged a short while later, and in the same ill-tempered voice said that the ship was not for sale, that the owner lived upriver and had no desire to talk to anybody. Bashur did not accept defeat despite the man's clearly aggressive unresponsiveness, and he asked if Señor Jaime Tirado, known as the Mirror Breaker, was still the owner. The watchman changed immediately. Fearful and suspicious, he asked Bashur if he happened to know Tirado. Abdul replied that they had mutual friends who had told him about the *Thorn*. Once again the man disappeared, returning much later to say that Don Jaime would come that afternoon to talk to him. Abdul went back to the ship to wait for Lena's friend. Vincas, who had followed Bashur's conversation with the guard on the *Thorn* from the deck of the *Princess Bukhara,* said, "Blacks from the Pacific coast are like that: unfriendly, sullen, but terrifying when they're angry. Just the opposite of Caribbean blacks." Abdul was aware of this and nodded his head in agreement.

The wait seemed interminable. There was not a cloud in the sky, but because of the humidity, the sun had formed an opaline mist above the calm waters, creating an atmosphere of Celtic legend in the middle of the equatorial zone. The silence was unreal and oppressive. Each noise on the ship reverberated in this setting with an almost irreverent sound. The *Thorn* seemed suspended in air. Its graceful silhouette, repeated in the serene estuary, evoked posters from the 1920s depicting packet boats of the great shipping lines lying at anchor in exotic Asian or Antillean ports. Abdul did not weary of admiring the design of the vessel, which awakened nostalgia in him for a time he knew only through the reminiscences of his elders. There, in front of him, was the ship of his dreams. (He had not been able to linger over the previous object of his desire, and the *Nebil* had not been framed in this hypnotic illusion of timeless tranquillity.) The light began to fade, and all around him a pale orange color slowly deepened into an operatic red that vanished all at once, driven away by the sudden fall of the great tropical night.

As the first stars appeared in a purple-gray sky, the purr of an engine approaching from the far end of the delta was heard in the distance. A breeze stirred, rippling the surface of the water and shattering the reflection of the *Thorn* into a constantly shifting puzzle. At the point where the river narrowed between mangrove trees and rachitic, threadbare palms, a boat came into view, traveling at high speed. It was an expensive launch made of fine woods, with gleaming, perfectly designed bronze fittings, better suited to Monaco or Porto Ercole than this forsaken, somnolent tropical landscape. It stopped at the foot of the *Princess Bukhara*'s ladder. At the wheel was Lena's friend, wearing a pale-pink shirt with shell buttons, impeccably cut linen trousers with the creases required at any country club in Alexandria or Beirut, and a genuine jipijapa hat, the kind that is woven under water at night by Indian women and is worth a fortune. Beside him stood a barefoot black giant dressed in white; with a nickel-plated grappling hook on a fine cherrywood pole, he caught the rope that served as a handrail and helped his skipper onto the ladder, which he climbed with a quick, athletic step. When he reached the top, Abdul was waiting for him, observing each of his gestures.

He remembered all of the Gaviero's premonitions and analyses as he greeted his visitor. Slightly taller than average, he had the occasionally brusque agility of a man who has played sports for most of his life. But the initial impression of health vanished at the sight of his face; the features clearly exemplified what is called "the end of a line"—the last specimen of over a century of intermarriage among a very few families, alliances whose primary purpose was to preserve vast land holdings and the names that distinguished them, with no admixture of outsiders or recent arrivals regardless of their wealth. He had a slightly drooping, noticeably prognathous jaw; as a consequence, his mouth, with its thick, sensual lips, was always partly opened; his nose was prominent but straight and firm beneath a narrow forehead, where protuberant bones filled the meager space between heavy eyebrows; sparse, faded hair barely covered the baldness he made no attempt to hide. But the chlorotic Hapsburg face suddenly took on a feline intensity because of mobile, inquisitive eyes that always seemed to see the most hidden thoughts of any interlocutor. His large hands, pale as a cadaver's, moved with assurance, creating the impression of animal strength at deceptive rest.

"They said you were looking for me. Is that so? I assume you're Abdul Bashur," he said as he offered his hand, extending his arm as much as possible as if keeping the other man at a distance.

"Yes, I am," replied Bashur. "And you must be Señor Jaime

Tirado. Come aboard, please. Let's go to my cabin. We can talk more comfortably there." Abdul led Tirado to a small office that communicated with his cabin. Vincas observed the scene from a distance.

Despite the Gaviero's assessment, Bashur never thought he would meet so perfect an example of what in these countries is called a "rich kid" regardless of the man's age. Every gesture, every inflection of his voice, revealed that he was a person to be taken seriously. Beneath his good manners, his slow, deep voice, his perpetual smile, it was easy to detect an air of criminality, undoubtedly acquired after his education in expensive Swiss boarding schools and his athletic successes in the country clubs of various cities on the Continent. He had lost any accent that could have identified him with a particular Latin American country. As they sat down at a small table of polished mahogany, Bashur thought: "This man has killed more than once. He's one of those who have categorically passed over to the other side, as Maqroll would say." And then all the age-old alarms went off inside this son of the desert, and with them came the slight intoxication that danger brings, the headiness, so like erotic pleasure, that drove his ancestors to seek death in battle with Charles Martel in the sweet lands of France. And an equally inherent serenity possessed him, as if invoked in the name of the Prophet. Death was not a consideration. It simply did not exist. This was his frame of mind as he prepared to listen to his visitor.

"Tell me something, if the question is not indiscreet: Did you name this ship?" Tirado's unexpected question concealed so much insolent mockery, intended to humiliate the other man, that for a moment Abdul did not answer.

"Yes," he replied at last. "My partner and I gave it the name; it brought us luck in a business venture I think you would have found interesting."

"You don't say," said Tirado. "May I know what it was?"

"It's a complicated story, and not very orthodox. I prefer to leave you guessing." Bashur sensed that the battle had begun.

"You said you were sent by mutual friends. May I know who they are?" asked Tirado, changing his tone.

"Of course—the Vacaresco twins. My partner and I made their acquaintance not long ago in Southampton."

"Have they sunk so low?" interjected Tirado in another attempt to provoke Bashur.

"It was Lena, to be precise, who told me about you and the

Thorn and the trip you made here from Panama," Bashur continued, taking no apparent notice of the other man's remark. "I happened to see a photograph she had, the qualities of the ship
appealed to me, and she was kind enough to give me the picture.
I had to make a run to Guayaquil and thought I would take
advantage of the opportunity to see the ship and its owner for
myself."

Bashur removed the photo of the couple on the *Thorn* from
his wallet and handed it to Tirado, who took it without looking
at it as he revealed the other side of his character by concluding:

"Well, you've seen the ship, and as for me, I think you've done
everything that can be done in that regard. I understand you
already know that I'm called the Mirror Breaker. A strange nickname, don't you agree? The one who destroys his own image and
that of others, the one who shatters the other world, the one we
know nothing about. It doesn't offend me. I could almost say I've
gone out of my way to cultivate it and, perhaps, to deserve it. I'll
tell you later how it began. It's a foolish story, but in a sense, those
who gave me the name were right on target. As for the *Thorn*, I
want to tell you at the outset that I'm not interested in selling it,
but I would be interested in trading it. That's different. I'd give it
to you not for money but for something else. I don't know if you
understand me."

"No, the fact is I don't understand. I'd like you to explain,"
replied Abdul, who had understood perfectly. He reached for the
photograph that Tirado had not even glanced at.

"You were so interested in the ship. How strange. I can't picture you as a collector of old tramp steamers. This ship that we're
on, for example, this couldn't be part of the collection," said the
Mirror Breaker, clearly intending to continue his search for
Abdul's weak spots. As calmly as a sheikh negotiating the passage
of an Aramco pipeline through his lands, Bashur replied:

"No, I don't collect old ships. In my family we build ships and
carry cargo, on a modest scale, of course. The *Princess Bukhara,*
despite the name that amuses you so much, serves my needs perfectly. But a ship like the *Thorn* appeals to me more for my personal
use and the pleasure of reconditioning it. So. You've mentioned
trading. That interests me. You know that for four thousand years my
people have been doing just that, with a certain degree of success.
Don't you agree?"

"I do," answered the Mirror Breaker, letting his lower lip hang
in what was meant to be a pleasant smile. "But remember that

each trade you people make today puts those four thousand years to the test. All right. Let's get to the point. I suggest you come back with me, have supper at my house, and I'll let you know there my conditions for possibly letting go of this jewel. One doesn't feel inspired in the middle of a wasteland. We'll be more comfortable at my place."

This was when Abdul Bashur used the card he had hidden in his sleeve to play at the right moment.

"I'd be happy to go with you. To tell you the truth, I much prefer negotiating with the Mirror Breaker than with Jaime Tirado. It's more familiar territory. Forgive me for not offering you a drink, but I'm a Muslim and don't use alcohol. We can leave whenever you like. I'm ready." He stood, the other man followed suit, and with a smile not quite as natural as the one he had worn on his arrival, he said:

"I can't believe you imposed your dry laws on the Vacaresco sisters. They drink like cossacks. And if you prefer to deal with the Mirror Breaker, that's up to you: whatever makes you feel more comfortable. As for territory we have in common, I could tell you a few things that might make you change your mind, but in any case I'll call and raise you, as they say in poker."

Abdul made absolutely no comment. He stood aside to allow Tirado to precede him out the door, and followed him to the ladder.

"Give me a moment to leave some instructions. I'll be right with you," he said, and walked back to the bridge to speak to Vincas. The Mirror Breaker climbed down to his launch and, with an indifferent attitude, sat down to wait.

Abdul briefly described the conversation to Vincas and told him to be on the alert, to arm the most reliable men with the three Israeli rifles and the Walther 99 pistols they had on board, and to put a twenty-four-hour watch on both the *Thorn* and the route Tirado's launch had taken.

"I don't think that ship is worth risking your skin for. That guy's one of the worst I've seen in all my years at sea," Vincas said with a worried air.

"It's not the ship anymore," Abdul replied. "It's something else. I never could swallow insults like these without having some kind of reaction, and the *Thorn* probably won't agree with me either. It's just as well."

Bashur climbed down the ladder and saw Tirado talking quietly to the black man. There was something in their gestures, a secretive intimacy that had nothing to do with either Abdul or the *Thorn* but with their own relationship, and a curious suspicion passed through his mind. "That too," he thought. "Our man is definitely more complicated than he looks in the photograph."

The night had settled in, with its immense equatorial skies and the constellations that seem within reach. The full moon illuminated the landscape with a milky brilliance of unusual intensity. The trip in the launch took about two hours. The area of mangroves that marked the beginning of the route produced an indefinable desolation in the spirit. The silence, scarcely broken by the splash of water against submerged trunks or the purr of the engine, and the monotony of that dwarf vegetation with its metallic leaves, gave the atmosphere a taste of death and ashes. They pressed upriver. Great trees appeared, with gaudy flowers of a phosphorescent orange color, and flocks of parrots returned to their nests with shrill calls that were answered by other birds from the thickness of the forest. The landscape took on a festive animation that helped erase the memory of the mangrove swamps. The vegetation grew denser, and in certain places branches from both banks intertwined over the water and hid the sky. Bashur and Tirado exchanged a few trivial remarks about the landscape and the weather. Each was saving himself for what might happen later on.

Suddenly the launch turned sharply toward shore and entered a narrow channel hidden by dense growth that made it almost invisible to anyone who did not know exactly where the entrance was located. Half an hour later they reached a concrete landing fitted with the most modern equipment. They left the launch and walked across the dock, which was enclosed by a nickel-plated railing that shone in the moonlight. Abdul was reminded of great waterfront villas in Istanbul and Alexandria, Ostia or Jean-les-Pins. The Mirror Breaker led the way along a path that passed through a luxuriant grove of flowering orange trees. The sound of their footsteps on gravel created an impression of sumptuous prosperity. They reached the end of the grove, and there stood a one-story Bauhaus structure, its broad glass and aluminum surfaces illuminated all at once by spotlights concealed in the garden.

A woman with pronounced Indian, almost Asian features came toward them at the slow pace of an obsequious servant. She was dressed in meticulously selected men's clothes: Italian jeans, a white shirt buttoned to the neck, and a tie in a Polynesian print, knotted with affected carelessness. Her bare feet displayed toenails painted pale blue. She greeted them with a respectful nod and waited for instructions. The young, elastic body in the glare of the spotlights was like a mannequin in the window of an expensive shop. Tirado gestured to her, and she walked into the house while they followed in silence, entering a reception area that was actually a terrace, with a pool in the center where one could see the perpetual movement of phosphorescent fish that had surely been brought in from the Amazon. They walked down a corridor hung with paintings in the style of Rothko and Pollock. Bashur was not surprised by any of it. With his first glimpse of the launch, he had known what Tirado's residence would be like. And he no longer had any doubts regarding the source of the fortune that allowed such luxury in so primitive a place.

They sat down in comfortable rattan armchairs upholstered in linen with a subdued pastel pattern. The woman asked what they would like to drink. Abdul asked for iced tea. The owner gave an ironic smile and asked for a frozen margarita. Abdul let Tirado's smile pass without comment and praised both the house and the good taste of its furnishings. He remarked in passing that maintaining this kind of residence in the tropics must be extremely difficult.

"It's no problem if you have a well-trained staff and someone to oversee them with a firm hand," explained the Mirror Breaker. "That's taken care of by a butler I brought from Porto Alegre; his German grandparents passed on to him the iron discipline of their people. I chose the style of the house more for reasons of comfort than taste. Imagine what it must be like to live in this hell in a Tudor house like the one my parents have in the capital. Well, if you have no objection, we can talk about our ship. I don't believe you came out here to chat about the virtues of Mies van der Rohe's architecture."

The woman brought in the drinks, silently placed them on the table between the chairs, and left again without making a sound. "I'll explain my idea to you very simply. Your arrival has been providential. Just yesterday I received a radio message from Panama City. A ship was supposed to sail here to pick up a fragile cargo that must be delivered by a certain date, but it couldn't leave port because of an engine failure that will take several weeks to repair. It occurred to me that if you took care of transporting the cargo, I would consider your fee the down payment on the *Thorn*. These are the only terms under which I'd be willing to sell. And with two or three more trips, you could finish paying for it. What do you think?"

Deep inside, Abdul felt a kind of relief. This was the trap that had been laid for him. It came as no surprise: With the Mirror Breaker, something of the kind was to be expected. But what attracted him in this affair was precisely the danger. It had been clarified and defined, and it sent a chill down his spine. As he had told Vincas when he left, it was no longer a question of the *Thorn*. And so he decided to follow his opponent's game and see where it led.

"In the first place," said Bashur, "I need to know more about the ship. Can it sail under its own power, or would it have to be towed? And of course, I'd like to know what the fragile cargo is and where I'd have to take it. When these two points are cleared up, I'll be prepared to give you an answer."

"As for the first question," replied Tirado, relishing the last drops of his margarita with a certain lingering gluttony that seemed more crass than childish to Bashur, "the *Thorn* would have to be towed to Panama City, where it can be repaired and made seaworthy. The engine has not been used for several years, and I'm afraid it's worthless. Converting it to a ship for your personal use—an idea, if you'll pardon my saying so, that seems a little peculiar to me—could be done in New England or Istanbul, but you know more about that than I do. As for the second point, I'd like to wait until morning before I answer. I expect to have certain indispensable information by then. For the present, I invite you to be my guest at supper. They're preparing the meal now, and we could certainly use it. Your room is ready. If you'd like to shower and freshen up, please feel free to do so. I told them to lay out clean clothes for you in case you want to change. Don't worry; they're your size, not mine. Obviously."

The chill still traveling along his spine told Bashur that he was now in the eye of the storm. He excused himself and followed the girl dressed as a man, who had appeared as if by magic. The room had unexpected amenities worthy of a great luxury hotel. The shower, which he made very hot, gave him a much-needed sense of well-being. He shaved with a new electric razor that he found in the bathroom cabinet. Then he tried on the clothes brought by the woman with the Annamese cheekbones. Everything fit perfectly. The fresh poplin shirt, the linen trousers and underwear, were very similar to what he had been wearing. He slipped his feet into a pair of soft esparto sandals and returned to the terrace. The Mirror Breaker, holding a second frozen margarita, was waiting for him. They went to the table, where they

were served a series of Japanese dishes prepared in the most traditional, impeccable manner. The sushi in particular was of a variety
and freshness unimaginable in that place. Abdul remarked on this
to his host, who only smiled with a satisfaction that began to drift
into cunning.

In order to change the subject, Bashur said, "Now I'd like to
know the origin of your unsettling nickname. I bring it up only
because of your earlier promise, and I think it would be a perfect
complement to our enjoyment of this magnificent meal. I don't
know if you're in the mood to humor me."

"Remember," replied Tirado, without changing his expression,
"I told you the reason for the name was fairly obvious. It happened a long time ago. I was training with my team for the polo
championship in Palm Beach, and the play was becoming rather
violent. The handle of my mallet suddenly slipped as I was hitting
the ball, and it crashed through the picture window in the dining
room of the Polo Club and shattered a large Venetian mirror that
some coffee magnate had left them in his will. My father paid for
the mirror without a protest. But there's more. The following
year we were playing against a really outstanding Chilean team. I
hit another fatal drive that went foul and broke one of the side-
view mirrors on the enormous presidential Packard, known
throughout the city because there wasn't another automobile like
it at the time. The president himself, who was watching the
match and had been best man at my father's wedding, named me
the Mirror Breaker. Before he went into politics, he had been an
outstanding golfer and a prominent clubman. From then on
everyone called me by the presidential nickname. It's never really
bothered me. Now that my life has taken a direction so radically
different from the one it followed all those years ago, the name
goes very well with a certain reputation I've earned for getting
what I want regardless of laws, authorities, or other people's
interests and lives. Well. Now that I've had the pleasure of satisfying your curiosity, I suggest we go to sleep before the mist gets to
us. It's a fog that comes in just before dawn and makes people
talk nonsense."

The Mirror Breaker said good night to Abdul and disappeared
into the grove of orange trees, where Bashur assumed his room
must be located, separate from the house and safe from any surprises. His deduction proved false, however, because he heard the
launch start upriver.

In bed but, understandably enough, unable to sleep, Bashur

began thinking about how to escape the ambush his host had set for him, which he, attracted by the lure of the unknown in the world of crime, had walked into voluntarily. He spent many hours developing a stratagem for getting out alive. He had no doubts regarding his opponent's character. When Tirado abandoned the class into which he had been born, he gave free rein to the morbidly sadistic instincts that his forebears had hidden behind a barrier of good manners and skillfully administered greed.

The Mirror Breaker certainly intended to get rid of him in the event he did not accept his proposition. Bashur carefully prepared the plan that would save his life, and when he had examined all the details point by point, he began to doze, resigned, like a good Muslim, to whatever the higher powers might decree. He was half asleep when the launch returned. Tirado's footsteps on the gravel path were the last thing he heard. He concluded they were heading not toward the house but to the place where Tirado's room was probably located.

A timid knock on the door woke him.

"Come in," he said in the thick voice of someone not yet fully awake. The attractive Indian woman who dressed like a man came in with the clothes he had taken off the day before, placed them on the bureau, and said without looking at him:

"The master is waiting to have breakfast with you on the terrace. Would you like tea or coffee?"

Abdul asked for tea, and toast with marmalade. The woman left, not making a sound. As he soaped his body under the shower, and then as he was shaving, he realized she had a certain androgynous quality that deflected the initial interest awakened by her looks. He recalled the intimate whispering between the Mirror Breaker and the black man on the launch, and the connections he made seemed to confirm his suspicions that the owner of the *Thorn* had more than one deviation in his sexual behavior. Before he left the room, Abdul reviewed the plan he had devised during the night. Everything was in place, and also in the hands of Allah. When he reached the terrace, the Mirror Breaker was pouring a large cup of steaming, aromatic coffee. He said good morning and made a courteous gesture toward the seat Bashur had occupied at supper.

"Did you sleep well?" he asked as he tasted the coffee with the relish of an addict.

"Very well," replied Bashur. "And you? I have the impression you didn't go straight to bed."

"That's true. I had to do a little work for you," Tirado replied, a perverse glint in his eyes.

This observation elicited no response from Abdul, who began to pour his tea: an authentic Lapsang Souchong, strong and smoky the way he liked it.

"Well," Tirado began, putting his hands on the table. "I believe the time has come to talk in concrete terms and hear what you think of my offer."

Abdul moved his hands in a gesture meant to stop the other man, who sat looking at him, somewhat disconcerted.

"Before we go any further, I'd like to say something. I thought about this for a long time last night, and I want to tell you my decision. To begin with, I've lost all interest in the *Thorn*. As things are now, my partner and I are making enough money with the *Princess Bukhara*. I never planned to acquire a ship like yours except for pleasure, for my own personal use, but if I did buy it I'd have to put the vessel to work in order to maintain it. And so I'm really not interested in hearing your terms for letting me have the *Thorn*. I'd rather not know. Obviously, I won't say anything to anyone. This is where I'd like to leave matters. Having said that, I think we should go our own ways as if nothing had happened, as if we had never met. It's best for both of us."

The Mirror Breaker stared at him for a moment that seemed like a century to Abdul, and then, in a voice that tried for an equanimity he did not achieve, he said:

"I don't believe this is your final word. If it is, then I must confess I was sadly mistaken about you. I've known compatriots of yours, and they had the stomach to face the unknown. Well. If this is your final decision, then answer this question: Did you really think, even for a moment, that I was naive enough to believe that a man who has sailed the seas and surely seen countless ways of breaking the law doesn't know what business I'm in and, knowing that, will never say anything about it for the rest of his life? My God, Bashur, you and I, as the Brazilians say, are too old to swallow that toad. Care for more tea?" he asked, reaching for the teapot. Bashur nodded and realized at the same time that Tirado had moved his foot to press something on the floor. The Mirror Breaker served the tea and lit a cigarette, inhaling deeply.

Moments later footsteps were heard on the path that led to the dock. Two athletic blacks emerged from the orange grove and headed for the terrace. Abdul assumed they were coming from the place where his host slept. Like the man who had been on the launch, they belonged to the race of Sudanese who lived along the equatorial Pacific coast and whose ferocity was legendary. When the two hired killers were just a few steps away, the characteristic thud of a vessel pulling alongside the cement landing sounded in the distance. At a gesture from Tirado, the men made a half turn and raced back toward the dock. Bashur and Tirado were silent for a moment, trying to hear what was being said on the landing, then Tirado stood abruptly and ran in the direction of the voices. Abdul followed close behind, assuming that an ambush had been planned for him at the table. When he reached the landing, the Mirror Breaker and his bodyguards were holding their hands in the air and staring at the launch of the *Princess Bukhara,* where two gigantic Polish sailors, signed on in Gdynia, aimed their rifles at them, while Vincas held his pistol to the head of the guard on the *Thorn,* who now looked at his employer with frantic, tearful eyes. The Lithuanian signaled Bashur to board. Abdul did not obey immediately but turned to Tirado and said in a low voice:

"You people say that God moves in mysterious ways. We think the ways of Allah are even more inscrutable. Thank you for your hospitality, and I hope we never meet again. Although you may not believe it, I don't want to know anything about your business. I'm really not interested."

He jumped onto the deck, and the launch turned at full speed, heading down the channel through a dense overhang of vegetation that barely left room for a boat to pass. With that Slavic impassivity in which everything is to be feared and nothing can be read, the Poles continued aiming at the dock. As they passed alongside Tirado's luxurious launch, the sailors fired two volleys at the flotation line, sinking her in a few seconds. A short while later, there was the sound of a body hitting water. It was the guard from the *Thorn.* One of the sailors had untied his hands and kicked him overboard. The launch, piloted by Vincas, reached the Mira and, maintaining its speed, traveled toward the mouth of the river in a dizzying zigzag intended to elude any shots that might be fired from shore. Bashur asked the captain how he had managed to arrive in so opportune a manner. Vincas replied that he would explain everything on the ship, which they had to reach as quickly as possible because there still might be some trouble in store.

The launch continued downriver as fast as the outboard motor would allow, until they came out into the estuary. As they passed the *Thorn,* Abdul stared at it. "Another ship slips through my fingers," he thought. "What a strange curse pursues me. Or perhaps destiny insists on saving me from some deadly thing that lies hidden in these dinosaurs from another time." Vincas too stared at the old ship, his eyes wide with panic. Abdul could not understand his expression, which could also be seen on the faces of the two Poles as they looked at the venerable relic and its motionless reflection in the waters of the estuary. When they reached the *Princess Bukhara,* the engines were running and it was ready to sail. Their small boat, with all its passengers, was hurriedly raised, and by the time it was level with the deck and its occupants were on board, the freighter was already heading for the sea. Bashur was puzzled at the speed with which everything took place. Vincas quickly led him by the arm to the stern, where they stood watching the *Thorn.* Abdul still did not understand, and became absorbed in looking at another of the many ships that had filled his attacks of insomnia. A sudden thundering explosion shook the bay, and the *Thorn,* enveloped in infernal flames and black smoke reaching toward the sky, began listing gently to port. When the hull caved in, its algae- and seaweed-covered ribs were exposed. There was a heartrending indecency in the accelerated death of this noble museum piece. They watched it disappear in a whirlpool of water dirtied by rust and oil and pieces of charred wood spinning sadly in a vertiginous rush. This was all that was left of the *Thorn.* The stain spread like a final symbol of misfortune and decay.

Vincas led Bashur to the bridge. Abdul was thunderstruck. The captain ordered the helmsman out of the cabin, then locked the door and took over the controls. His story did not take long to tell. Events had occurred in a rapid, nightmarish sequence but had followed an extremely straightforward logic. When Abdul left with the Mirror Breaker, Vincas felt uneasy, plagued by forebodings that arose, for the most part, from the disagreeable impression made on him by Tirado. They already knew that the guard on the *Thorn* was in radio communication with his employer's residence. Late that night, Vincas resolved to visit the *Thorn,* accompanied by the two giants from Gdynia, who were armed with high-powered automatic rifles, while he carried a Walther 99. They climbed on board, making no explanations, and the guard did not dare to offer any resistance. The unfortunate man's face betrayed a consternation so great he could barely stammer a few disconnected words. He was trembling like a leaf and asked them to leave the ship immediately. He was more terrified of the Mirror Breaker's reprisals than of their weapons. Vincas had him locked in an empty cabin next to the radio room and left one of the sailors guarding the door. Then he had a look at the transmitter, and when he put on the earphones, he heard a conversation between the Mirror Breaker and a place that he referred to as Post Two. They were obviously avoiding the use of real names. The communication lasted some fifteen minutes and was followed immediately by another, with what was called Post Three. A phrase repeated by Tirado in both conversations made Vincas realize the mortal danger that threatened Abdul: "I have the owner of the ship here with me. It doesn't matter whether he's willing or not. Either way he'll have to be killed, either now or later, after he does what we need him to do. He's seen too much, and besides, he's no tame dove." Vincas was ready to move without delay. He had learned from the radio conversations that Tirado had several tons of coca leaf waiting to be transported to a Colombian port on the Pacific coast, close to the Panamanian border. From there the shipment would be moved inland by those whom he referred to as "the factory." If Abdul accepted the deal, he would be killed after delivering the coca leaf. If not, he would be eliminated that morning and his ship taken by force. The *Thorn* was to be blown up the next day: They suspected that the authorities had located the radio signal. The charges were in place, and Tirado would activate the explosives from the shore by remote control. The "posts" were, in fact, coca plantations owned equally by the Mirror Breaker and the proprietors of "the factory." Tirado received a share of profits from the final sale of the drugs. Vincas ordered the guard to sail downriver with them and lead them to the house where Bashur was being held. They would leave immediately and wait until dawn to try to rescue Abdul. The black man was still trembling, large tears rolling down his heavy cheeks and wetting his shirt. "He's going to kill me," he repeated between sobs. "That man's going to kill me. You don't know him. Oh, God, I'll never get out of this one!" He barely heard Vincas say they would let him escape before they reached the house. They sailed into the mangrove swamps. The guard guided them into the channel, where they turned off the motor and rowed until Tirado's house came into view. They waited for dawn, hiding in the thick growth along the bank. When they heard voices coming from the orange grove, they headed for the dock. Their boat thudded against the cement edge, and two blacks came running toward them, but the rifles aimed by the Poles brought them to a sudden stop. Then Tirado arrived, followed by Bashur. Abdul knew the rest. The guard had refused to go ashore in the mangrove swamps. "Mother of God, where can I go?" he lamented. "You don't know the Mirror Breaker. I won't last a day." This was why they had been obliged to throw him overboard after they rescued Bashur. If Abdul regretted the loss of the *Thorn,* he ought to know that the ship had no engines and had been totally dismantled. It had been kept there only to allow communication among the various bases in the operation set up by Tirado and his partners. Since the signal had been located, the destruction of the ship was inevitable. The guard was to die with the *Thorn;* it was not worth it to the Mirror Breaker to save him.

When Vincas finished his story, Abdul ordered a course set for Panama City. In a few brief words he expressed his gratitude to the captain and praised the speed with which he had acted. Quite simply, he had saved his life. Vincas translated for the sailors from Gdynia, who smiled with satisfaction and expressed their pleasure in a dialect that only Vincas could understand, and only partially. Of course he told them nothing about the Mirror Breaker's business. Despite their unquestionable loyalty, their tongues might have been loosened during one of the endless drinking bouts with which they celebrated their arrival in any port.

They anchored at Panama City and waited to pass through the canal. That afternoon, a police launch carrying two inspectors and four agents armed with submachine guns drew alongside. The officals came on board and asked to speak to Bashur, who calmly answered their questions about the ship that had exploded in the Mira River estuary. Bashur's responses dealt concretely with his interest in acquiring the ship and his finding it impossible to talk to the presumptive owner: The guard on board had refused to put Bashur in touch with him. They had waited until the following day, when, as they were leaving, the *Thorn* exploded and was enveloped in flames. That was all he knew. His interrogation by the inspectors went no further. They did not seem very interested in knowing more than Abdul told them. It was a routine, pro forma investigation, which made clear how far the tentacles of the Mirror Breaker could reach.

The *Princess Bukhara* sailed through the canal and headed for Fort-de-France in Martinique, where it would take on cargo for Le Havre. Maqroll was waiting for them in the French port. He came on board with a singular individual whom he introduced as the painter Alejandro Obregón, his dear friend and companion on his travels through Southeast Asia and the Pacific coast of Canada—adventures that have certainly been mentioned elsewhere. They dispatched three bottles of the splendid rum from the Trois Riviéres islands, which Abdul had bought in Martinique for the pleasure of guests, while he told his story and the tale of his providential rescue thanks to a conversation overheard on the radio and the diligence of Vincas Blekaitis. When the story was over, Maqroll remarked:

"My premonitions regarding the virtues of the Mirror Breaker turned out to be all too true. I didn't think he was that complex, but the photograph of him and Lena didn't permit much more in the way of predictions. I would have liked to meet him. Those playboys gone wrong are perfect personifications of evil. The absolute evil that consumed Gilles de Rais and Erzsébet Báthory."

Obregón objected, shaking his head.

"Don't believe it. Those guys aren't so bad. I know a few who fit the pattern of the Mirror Breaker, and they're nothing to worry about. They don't have the grandeur of the historical figures you've just mentioned. There's always some poor devil concealed in the most remote corner of their souls. I think pure evil is an abstraction, a mental creation that never appears in real life."

The rest of the last bottle from Trois Riviéres was consumed while Maqroll and Obregón told Bashur and Vincas of their travels through Malaysia, which were far from exemplary.

IV

It is time now to describe the event that completely changed the course of Abdul Bashur's life, an event about which we learn very little directly from him. In his correspondence with Fatima, he mentions it only in passing and adds no commentary. I learned the relevant details from the Gaviero, either in conversation with him or through his letters, although the details in these were certainly rather sparse, as if Maqroll were trying to respect a tacit desire on the part of his friend. I am referring to the tragic death of Ilona Grabowska in Panama City under circumstances that are still somewhat unclear. Following this disaster, Maqroll sailed with Bashur to Vancouver. A few months later I met the Gaviero, and he told me about the tragedy in which he had been not only a witness but, in a sense, a protagonist as well. All of these details, together with certain events that preceded them, were described by the Gaviero in a book that is now making its way through the world and is, for the most part, dedicated to Ilona, the Triestine friend of the two comrades. And therefore I will only summarize briefly what occurred in Panama City. Ilona and Maqroll had set up a profitable business there: a house of assignation staffed by women who pretended to be flight attendants on well-known airlines that flew to Panama City. Although Bashur was experiencing a run of bad luck at the time, he found a way to send a few pounds to Maqroll, who had reached the end of his rope in Panama. This happened before the Gaviero's chance encounter with Ilona, whose ingenious idea it was to establish a brothel with bogus stewardesses. Most of the earnings from this original and productive venture were sent to Bashur. With these substantial sums from his two friends, he bought a tanker that had been reconditioned to transport chemical products and named it *Nymph of Trieste* in honor of Ilona, which she did not find very amusing, since it seemed to reflect an Oriental fondness for bombast. Maqroll and Ilona tired of life in Villa Rosa—the name of the brothel—and of managing the women who came there regularly with their ill-assorted, always problematic clients. They decided to leave Panama City and meet Bashur's ship: He was en route to Vancouver and had told them when he would go through the canal. They did not inform him of their plans; they had wanted to surprise him. A few days before their departure, one of the women who came frequently to Villa Rosa began to display a strange attachment to Ilona, an interest that was not erotic, at least on the surface. A native of Chaco, named Larissa, she lived on a ship that had been abandoned at an Avenida Balboa jetty. She arranged to meet Ilona there one afternoon; her purpose was to beg her not to leave. No one ever found out exactly what happened, but the boat blew up in an explosion caused by a leak from the butane gas tank that fed Larissa's small stove. The two women were burned almost beyond recognition, and Maqroll went to Cristóbal to meet Bashur, who arrived the next day on the *Nymph of Trieste*. This is the portion of the story that has already been told.

Predictably enough, the meeting between the two friends was heartrending, especially in the case of Bashur, for whom the calamity had unforeseen consequences. The Gaviero boarded the ship, took his friend by the arm, and led him to his cabin, saying they had to speak in private. Bashur guessed that something had happened to Ilona, and his face took on the gray rigidity of a person who expects a blow but does not know where it will come from. When they were in Abdul's cabin, Maqroll briefly told him about the tragedy. Bashur was utterly crushed and, in a toneless voice, asked the Gaviero to leave him for a while. Maqroll went out to talk to the captain—Vincas Blekaitis, Abdul's faithful officer, who still could not pronounce his name correctly.

"What happened to Jabdul? Bad news? Didn't Ilona come with you?" he asked as he accompanied the Gaviero to the cabin that had been reserved for him.

"Ilona's dead, Vincas," Maqroll said in an opaque voice.

"Good God! And you left him alone?" the captain exclaimed in alarm.

"Don't worry," explained the Gaviero. "He asked me to. Bashur isn't the kind who would try to escape by the door you have in mind. It will do him good to be alone for a few hours and get used to living with the emptiness that lies ahead. The effects will come later, and I think they'll be deadly, but not in that way."

"All right. You know him better than I do. It's terrible to think of the pain he must be suffering now. He was so happy about seeing his friend and showing her the ship he named for her. But how did it happen? Did somebody kill her?" Vincas's grief was overwhelming.

Maqroll told him what had happened, and the poor Lithuanian could barely follow the absurd but fatal sequence of events. When the Gaviero was in his cabin, he spent a long time pondering the dreadful fate that seemed to mark those who shared any part of his life. Ilona's death was a crushing disaster for Abdul. His relationship to her, brotherly on the surface, yet strongly erotic, had created a connection much more solid than the nomadic Lebanese imagined. For Ilona, Abdul was the younger brother she had never had, and guiding his life gave her a secret satisfaction, a combination of sensual complicity and subtle domination wielded with an essentially feminine skill. On the other hand, her relationship with Maqroll meant perpetual challenge and continual surprise. She had never succeeded in holding, even for an instant, this man to whom she was obviously attracted yet whose enigma was too great for the tight, efficient web of her sorceress's premonitory intelligence. With Maqroll everything was always unresolved, nothing was ever brought to completion. The loose ends continually intrigued her and piqued her curiosity about him. This was why her behavior toward the Gaviero was invariably seasoned with an ironic yet affectionate humor that always allowed her an escape. With Abdul, on the other hand, everything was formalized in an order whose simple outlines, although not excluding adventure and danger, stayed within channels that did not elude her affectionate intelligence. The fact that the twisted figure of jealousy had never separated the trio was easily understood by those who knew the nuances in their relationship. Ilona's death left a void that did not estrange the two friends, but it did deprive them of an intermediary who had eased and lightened the handling of serious situations whose gravity eventually dissolved in the healthy common sense and unwavering devotion to life of their mutual friend and lover.

The voyage to Vancouver was tinged with the turbid dullness produced by the death of someone we have loved without reservation, someone who formed part of the most solid substance of our existence. Maqroll felt obliged from the start to make it clear to Abdul that the tragedy had been marked by inevitability. Larissa had kept her weapons concealed until the last moment, and Ilona rushed headlong into the ambush without allowing Maqroll an opportunity to intervene. Bashur insisted on giving a morbidly erotic explanation for what Larissa had done. The Gaviero repeated over and over again that in these matters Ilona had always been absolutely clear. On other occasions, when she had been involved in a passing adventure of that kind, she had discussed it openly. Making love to another woman was, for Ilona, a kind of game with no consequences, an exercise for the senses in which her sentiments never took part. What happened with Larissa had more to do with misunderstood compassion and an obscure sense of responsibility, which Ilona had taken on gratuitously and Larissa had used with the dark cynicism typical of a madness that has been well defined by psychiatry. Maqroll insisted that when she let the gas escape, lit the match, and caused the explosion, Larissa was avenging, in the person of Ilona, the bitter humiliations that had shaped her life of perpetual servitude and sordid dependency. The facts could not be clarified any further, and the Panama City police had not been especially interested in doing so, but the explanation of Larissa's secret motives were probably very close to the Gaviero's interpretation.

As time passed, Abdul Bashur, without Ilona's loving but subtle vigilance, tended more and more to follow the Gaviero, adopting his senseless wandering and his propensity for accepting fate without calculating the extent of its hidden designs. Traveling this road, and moved by the immemorial atavism of his nomadic blood, Abdul descended to the same dark chasms visited by Maqroll—perhaps even lower, as if he had lost a restraint, a lifeline that kept him back from his predilection for disaster. At times this has led me to think that his meeting with the Mirror Breaker occurred after Ilona's death. It is difficult to believe she would not have intervened in an adventure of this kind, which put the life of her lover at risk. But if we abide by the dates on the correspondence, that supposition must be discounted, and we would have to conclude that Maqroll's influence had begun to exercise its control even before Ilona's death, which is not a very credible assumption either.

V

In any case, by the time they reached Vancouver, Bashur had thrown all ballast overboard and, without giving it a second thought, accepted Maqroll's suggestion to sell the *Nymph of Trieste* and use the money to buy a freighter, the *Hellas,* that they would convert to the transport of pilgrims to Mecca. Abdul sold his ship, then they booked passage on a venerable Turkish freighter and sailed to Piraeus, where the *Hellas* was berthed. The diesel engine, a D-11 Scania Saab manufactured in Sweden in 1920, needed a complete overhaul. The freighter was modified in Piraeus while the engine was being repaired, and they registered the vessel in Cyprus.

The two friends, as mentioned in the story about the adventures of Ilona and Maqroll in Panama City, were already familiar with transporting pilgrims to Mecca. It is a fairly lucrative enterprise, but the problems and dangers of dealing with the passengers are easy to imagine. Abdul and Maqroll worked together for several years in this new phase of their Middle Eastern ventures. Although little worth the telling occurred during this period, one episode does illustrate the changes in Bashur's character. On their third or fourth voyage to the holy places of Islam, they encountered a company of pilgrims who almost put an end not only to their business but to their lives.

They had taken on a group of families from a small Muslim community in Jablanica, on the Croatian coast. They were survivors from the days of the Ottoman occupation, and for generations they had resisted with unyielding ferocity every effort by the Croatian authorities to eradicate them. The first incident was quelled in a timely way by Maqroll and did not burn out of control. The Gaviero had recently signed on a bos'n he had known for years, a man of rather extreme and susceptible temperament named Yosip, who had been born in Iraq to a Georgian family and whose affection for Maqroll had already been proved on several occasions. He set off the first dispute. The bos'n was responsible for settling the families in the hold, which had been turned into communal sleeping quarters. Yosip could barely understand their difficult dialect, and fighting broke out over a place he had assigned to one family but that another insisted on occupying. Yosip was attempting to settle the argument when the opposing sides suddenly joined forces and turned on him, intending to kill him. Just then the Gaviero came down to oversee the placement of the passengers. Knowing the fiercely antagonistic nature of the Croats, he always carried a .38 revolver in the pocket of his seaman's jacket. When he saw the situation, he fired two shots in the air and, aiming the gun at the belligerents, warned them to behave themselves, as he signaled Yosip to leave. The head of the community, an imposing old man with a long, graying beard and the eyes of a visionary, emerged from the rear of the hold and came forward to calm his followers. Then he spoke to Maqroll in Turkish, explaining that Yosip represented a kind of religious dissidence that was especially offensive to them. It would be wiser, therefore, to avoid as much as possible any further contact between the bos'n and the community. Maqroll agreed in principle to the imam's request, and matters apparently returned to normal. In fact, many years later, I was to meet Yosip when he was managing a cheap motel on La Brea Boulevard in Los Angeles and had taken in Maqroll, who was dangerously ill with a severe attack of malaria. This was when Yosip told me the story, his fervent gratitude to the Gaviero still intact.

The voyage seemed to continue with no further incident, but a sullen animosity was fermenting among the passengers, not only on account of Yosip but because they began to detect in Abdul Bashur a certain latitude in the strict observance of their religion's precepts. They knew he was a Muslim, and had been judging his behavior since the beginning of the trip. In communities like these, which have endured official ostracism in their own country, intransigence and dogmatism are emphasized for obvious reasons of religious survival in a hostile environment. Maqroll recommended that until they reached Mecca, Yosip, Abdul, and Vincas should always be armed. This may be an appropriate time to clarify Abdul's religious beliefs and practices. He was a Muslim at one with the avatars of Islam, and he belonged to a family that made religion an integral part of their daily routine, but even as a boy Abdul displayed the attitude of a marginal believer—an observant Muslim who concealed deep inside something that resembled a spirit of inquiry and the rational analysis of laws imposed by the Koran. This is not the attitude recommended for authentic, devout believers in any religion. His mother, a woman of great sweetness who felt an absorbing love for her son, attempted to correct this tendency but had to abandon her efforts when he reached adolescence. His constant travels, above all on the continent of Europe, did not alter the way Bashur lived his convictions, but they did intensify his reservations and perplexities. All fanaticism was extremely disturbing to him, especially when he realized that it constituted the authentic nucleus of Islamic belief: Its perpetual intransigence condemned the slightest deviation or indifference in the practice of Koranic precepts. The easygoing, conciliatory nature that had distinguished him since childhood shielded him on his journeys through the lands of the Prophet, where he always avoided any friction with his coreligionists. Bashur, in fact, came into more frequent conflict with his European acquaintances, who treated him like a Westernized Levantine; his wounded sensibilities invariably reacted to such crude incomprehension. One of the reasons for his solid friendship with the Gaviero was surely the innate, spontaneous respect for Abdul's beliefs that he showed from the start. Maqroll himself often berated any Westerner who saw Bashur drinking with other companions and thought this authorized offensive remarks about Islamic law. On these occasions Bashur maintained a silence that was both angry and contrite, while Maqroll chastised the imprudent man in a way he would not soon forget. Abdul had grown tired of repeating that the Book did not absolutely forbid the use of alcohol. What it did condemn without reservation was drunkenness, a great sin against the mind, which was an inestimable gift from Allah.

"Don't worry, Abdul," the Gaviero would console his friend. "These people understand nothing about Islam, and the worst of it is that their arrogant ignorance has not changed since the Crusades. They always pay for it dearly in the end, but they can't understand the warning and persist in their wrongheadedness. It's hopeless. They'll never change."

"They're not all like that," Bashur would say. "I know many

Spaniards and Portuguese who are much more open and sensible than other Europeans."

"Don't be so sure," the Gaviero would insist. "Remember the Inquisition."

"I understand there was more than one convert among the inquisitors. The fanaticism of my brothers frightens me more than the *rumi* zealots."

These words faithfully represent Bashur's own response to the centuries-old conflict between two civilizations that have held a dialogue of the deaf for more than a millennium. We have lingered over this aspect of Bashur's personality because it was on the pilgrimage with the Croatian Muslims that his attitude toward the religious problem was made manifestly clear.

When the *Hellas* left the Adriatic, a woman wearing somewhat Europeanized clothes—a flowered ankle-length dress—began coming on deck every morning. Bashur noticed her from the first day she appeared. Almost as tall as he was, slender and graceful, with small, firm breasts, she had an erect, withdrawn bearing that suited her perfect beauty. Her face was long and pale; its finely delineated features tended to follow the oval of her face, and her large, dark eyes, with the elusive, astonished glance of a frightened gazelle, were exceptionally attractive. The wind blew her dress tight against her body, revealing barely curving hips and prominent hipbones beneath the cloth. The woman was always alone and would remain on deck for two long hours, staring at the horizon, which awakened Bashur's curiosity and Vincas's uneasiness. From time to time she would run her hand through her abundant, deep-black hair in a gesture that barely expressed impatience. On the third day that Abdul walked by her on some pretext or other, he heard her speak in the Cairo dialect. She asked him the name of the islands they had passed a while ago and that were disappearing now over the horizon.

"Othonoi and Erikousa. You should visit them one day. They're a prelude to the fascination of Hellas," Bashur replied, with the evident intention of continuing the conversation.

The woman apparently possessed a more extensive and refined education than the rest of her companions. After a few conventional remarks, she explained that she was traveling to join her husband. Her parents had married her to an older brother of the imam leading the pilgrimage to Mecca. A highly respected merchant, he had been confined for many years to a wheelchair because of a stroke that had left him partially paralyzed. She had gone to Jablanica to visit her nieces, the daughters of the imam, and now she was returning home. As a single woman, she had lived in Egypt with some distant relatives of her mother and worked in a perfume shop in Cairo. Her parents died in a train wreck, on their way to settle in Zagreb. The imam was made the girl's guardian, and when she returned from Egypt he married her to his brother, who was already an invalid.

Bashur did not detect the slightest tone of complaint or self-pity in this recounting of her life. She related the facts with simple directness, as if they had happened to someone else. In part to repay her confidences, and very much in order to continue their talk, Abdul gave her a brief summary of his life. Then they moved on to reminiscences of Cairo, a place Abdul knew very well, and Alexandria, where he had lived as an adolescent, working with one of his uncles. In fact, it was in Port Said that he first met his associate and old friend, and he pointed to Maqroll, who was lying in a deck chair, completely absorbed in Gustave Schlumberger's book on Nicephoros Phocas. Bashur sensed a slight reticence in the woman's eyes and asked her straight out what she thought of the Gaviero. With natural spontaneity, she replied that the man made her apprehensive in a way she could not define. Perhaps, she said, because it was impossible to place him in a specific occupation or nationality. Bashur made no comment and began to talk of the trip they were now making and the ship's ports of call. The woman took her leave a short while later, but first she turned to him and said, "My name is Jalina. I already know that yours is Abdul and not Jabdul, as the captain says. By the way, why don't you correct him when he does that?"

"Because it amuses me," answered Abdul, smiling at her self-assurance, so unexpected in a Muslim woman. "And the Gaviero does it too when he wants to make fun of me."

"I could never do that," she said as she walked to the steps that led down to the hold. Her words suggested something that Bashur interpreted as a tacit promise of future intimacy.

They continued seeing each other every day, and their relationship became increasingly fluid and personal. Abdul realized that the woman appealed to him in a very particular way. More than attraction, this was an excitement generated by the lithe, slender body and the smooth matte pallor of her skin, which reminded him of the oft-cited Koranic verses describing the houris in paradise. He knew it was an unacceptable cliché, but he also knew that such clichés can be embodied and acquire a tangible presence. Because they are so obvious, they attain an obsessive, overwhelming fascination. Maqroll and Vincas both watched as their friend started down this dangerous path. The Gaviero, faithful to his principle of always allowing things to happen regardless of consequences, would not intervene under any circumstances. But Vincas, more ingenuous and less cautious, said to Bashur:

"For God's sake, Jabdul, the Muslims are already antagonistic enough. You know what you're risking if you take that woman to bed when she's married to the imam's brother. They'll cut off all our heads."

"Don't worry, Captain. I'll be careful. Nothing will happen. You know about the attraction of forbidden fruit. Besides, she's more civilized than the hoodlums she's traveling with," replied Abdul. Even though he was not really so certain there would be no repercussions, he had already resolved to take Jalina to his cabin, for he was tormented by her disquieting sensual appeal.

The initiative, however, did not come from him, and this heightened his desire. One night he was awakened from a deep sleep by a light knocking. When he opened the door, in came Jalina, wrapped in a large shawl that covered her from head to toe, as if she were a Phoenician priestess in a trance. Without saying a word, they embraced and fell onto his bunk. Abdul slept naked, and when Jalina let the shawl drop she offered her own total nakedness with the delirious frenzy of a woman possessed. In feverish episodes that followed one another in a seemingly endless vertigo, Bashur confirmed his premonitions regarding the temperament of this woman, whose caresses left him exhausted.

Their encounters were repeated every night, but she did not appear again on deck, perhaps in a vain attempt to hide her relationship with the owner of the *Hellas*. Vincas's fears were soon realized. Abdul began to notice bruises on Jalina's body, signs that she was being punished for her behavior. She attributed no importance to them and pretended she had fallen off her bunk while she was asleep. Abdul chose to believe the excuse. But one night when he opened the door, instead of Jalina the imam himself came in. The old man's attitude was not violent. Rather, he gave the impression of being uncomfortable at the sight of Bashur's nakedness and could not speak clearly. Bashur wrapped himself in a sheet and asked him to sit down. The man remained standing and stared at him. Bashur asked the reason for his visit, and the imam replied in a voice that contained a profound reprimand:

"You know very well the punishment imposed in the Book on adulterous couples. That is all I need to tell you. When we reach Mecca, that woman will be judged according to the law of the Prophet. As for you, we can do nothing here. One day your offense will be punished as prescribed. I warn you: Suspend all contact immediately with my brother's wife. If until now I have succeeded in restraining my people, who clamor to erase the shame that has fallen upon us, I cannot guarantee that I will be able to do so in the future. This is all I have to say, other than to proclaim you, with all the authority of my position as mullah, a villain unworthy of the infinite clemency of Allah the Merciful."

The next day Bashur told Maqroll about the imam's words and his plans for retribution. The Gaviero was thoughtful for a moment, as if he suspected the gravity of this announcement, and then he said:

"Ah, Jabdul! How sorry I am to have to admit that Vincas was right! On the other hand, I haven't exactly preached by example in this area, and there's nothing I can say. In any case, for as long as we're on the ship, the imam cannot impose his barbaric justice on that poor woman. We're under British protection. Don't forget that the *Hellas* is registered in Limassol. The old man knows English law would consider any attack on Jalina as a serious crime. He himself admits it when he says the sentence will be carried out when they reach Mecca. We've known each other a long time, and I know very well you'll look for a way to stay in touch with her and try to protect her. That will only inflame those savages. If they attack us, there's no question they'll finish us off in a matter of minutes. The only solution is for you to take her off the ship when we get to Port Said the day after tomorrow. We'll go on to Jidda, leave the pilgrims there, and come back for you. We have to see what papers the lady is carrying."

"She has a Yugoslav passport," explained Abdul, "but she lived in Egypt for several years, and the police must have a record of her name. I don't think there'd be any trouble if we got off in Port Said to wait a few days for the *Hellas*. But that isn't the real problem," Abdul continued in a disconsolate tone. "If they let us stay in Port Said, what really disturbs me is that I'd be taking on responsibility for this wild woman for who knows how long. You know it's just a passing affair. I've already told you how enterprising the lady is in bed and what a delirious experience it is to be with her. But there's a whole chasm between that and spending the rest of my life with a wild-haired Bacchante."

"That's been taken into account. In Port Said we'll give her enough money to travel wherever she wants to go. She doesn't look to me like a person who'd just accept being helpless. If she worked in Cairo and Alexandria, she'll get along anywhere. One thing's certain, and she knows it: If she gets off at Jidda with the rest of them, she'll be stoned to death before she ever sees Mecca. You have to find someone who will take an interest in her, and then leave her to him as a kind of inheritance. It's what I did with the incense widow in Kuala Lumpur, who ended up in the arms of Alejandro Obregón." Abdul responded to the Gaviero's final remark by shaking his head in a gesture more eloquent than any words and then saying:

"But what will those lunatics do when they see us getting off at Port Said?" It was evident he had not fully grasped his partner's plan.

"All right," the Gaviero replied. "You get off at night, very discreetly. Yosip will go with you. He's reliable, and he has Iraqi papers, so that's no problem. He'll say he's in port to deliver some documents to our agent. The important thing right now is for you to talk to your Dulcinea. I'm sure she'll do even the impossible to see you."

Jalina, in fact, came to Abdul's cabin at dawn, her face battered, her eyebrow cut and bleeding profusely, her back covered with the marks of a merciless whipping. Bashur tried to treat her wounds with what he could find in his medicine chest and gave her a strong analgesic to ease the pain, which must have been unbearable, although she did not complain and refused to say who had beaten her. Jalina listened to Bashur's suggestion that they disembark in Port Said, and agreed to everything. She confirmed that her passport documented her having lived and worked in Egypt. She let him know that she wanted to make love in spite of the beating, and Abdul complied, not wanting to oppose her just then. Before Jalina went back to the hold, everything had been arranged: On the following night, at a quarter to twelve, she would be waiting at the foot of the launch that would take them ashore. Bashur explained clearly which boat it was.

In the morning, Abdul told Maqroll and Vincas about Jalina's visit and her acceptance of the escape plan. There was still the problem of the pilgrims' reaction when they realized what had happened. The three men agreed to distribute weapons to the most trustworthy members of the crew.

That night they docked in Port Said and radioed a message to the office of the harbormaster: Two passengers whose papers were in order would be coming ashore, to wait there until the *Hellas,* which was carrying pilgrims to Jidda, the port of Mecca, returned for them. The authorities consented. Jalina came to the launch at the time specified by Bashur. She had been beaten again and could barely walk. Yosip and the sailor who would take them to the docks arrived at almost the same time. The hold was quiet. The Gaviero and Vincas, eager to know how things had gone in port, stayed on deck to wait for the launch. Time passed, but no one came back. Finally, when it was almost morning, the launch returned carrying only the sailor, who signaled for help in raising the boat. When he was on deck, the man told them what had happened without waiting for questions from his superiors. Abdul and Jalina had gone through immigration with no problem. An officer asked why the woman was in that condition, and they said she had lost her footing on the stairs down to the hold and had fallen almost four meters. She would be examined at the hospital in Port Said. When Yosip was ready to go back, an official asked for his papers, and he said he had not brought them, since he had no plans to come ashore. He was asked his full name, and other personal information, and told to wait. The same official soon returned with two armed guards and said to Yosip:

"You were in the French Foreign Legion, and there are military charges against you in France. You're under arrest." The guards handcuffed him and took him into the offices. When the seaman tried to intervene on behalf of the bos'n, he was told not to interfere and to get back to his ship immediately unless he wanted to be arrested too. He had heard Abdul and Jalina say something to Yosip, who must have passed them on the other side of the glass partition separating the immigration area from the other offices.

Yosip's presence on the ship was indispensable for facing down the Croats in the event of a disturbance belowdecks. The crew felt loyalty, respect, and admiration for him because of his checkered history in all the ports of the Mediterranean. Maqroll and Vincas went to their cabins to try to sleep, after deciding that in the morning they would communicate with the man who acted as their customs agent and ask him to do whatever he could to secure Yosip's release. At ten o'clock, they finally managed to reach him in Port Said; his voice sounded heavy with exhaustion. He put Abdul on the phone, who brought them up-to-date. It seems that Yosip had deserted from the Foreign Legion and the

French authorities had sent an extradition request to Egypt, where they thought he had taken refuge. Yosip claimed that the charge had been settled more than ten years before. If the Egyptian authorities would question the French about the case, everything would be cleared up right away. His passport, which Vincas had sent to shore that morning, showed that he had entered and left France, Algeria, and Tunis several times with no difficulty. The records in Port Said were simply not current. But it happened to be Saturday, and the French consulate would not open until Monday. Abdul recommended that they get under way as soon as possible, for obvious reasons. He also said that the sick person who had come ashore with them was now being treated at the English hospital and would be in condition to leave in a few days. It was urgent that they send ashore all the other papers that had to do with Yosip, which Vincas kept with the rest of the ship's documents.

As soon as the launch returned, they set sail for Jidda. That same night, the imam suddenly appeared on the bridge, with the solemn bearing of one who carries the wrath of Allah in his hands. He threatened to file a complaint with the Saudi authorities, charging that a female passenger had been kidnapped. They would all have to disembark at Jidda to answer for their crime. Maqroll replied, very calmly but just as categorically as the mullah:

"That woman came to us seeking protection and medical help because of the beatings and whippings she had suffered. She refused to say who was responsible. This is a serious crime, committed under British jurisdiction and punishable, as you must know, by several years in prison. She left the ship voluntarily and informed the Egyptian authorities to that effect. They have communicated with the authorities in Jidda. Mr. Bashur went ashore at Port Said to attend to matters related to our commercial operation. He has testified to this before the harbor officials. Therefore, at the first sign of rebellion against Captain Blekaitis and his crew, we will request assistance from the closest British authorities, and we will not hesitate to put the pilgrims ashore at the first place we can anchor. And of course we will file a charge of attempted piracy against a ship of English registry. Any act of violence by your people against us will be met with weapons, under the authority granted to the ship's captain by international maritime law. I advise you to bear in mind what I have just said, to return belowdecks and meditate on the consequences of any violence."

The aged minister of the Prophet did not say a word. He turned and walked toward the hold with a stiff, exaggerated solemnity, so unnatural it was clear he was trying to save face before his people, who had come on deck to see for themselves what had happened to their imam. Hopefully he would persuade them to forget about Jalina and continue on to Jidda without creating a disturbance; the old man must have succeeded, because the Croats remained calm until they reached the port of Mecca. In Jidda they boarded a tug that had come to pick them up, since Vincas, as an understandable precaution, did not want to anchor at the docks. As the group was leaving, a giant with fierce eyes, his lips trembling in anger, approached Vincas and Maqroll, who were closely watching the departure of the pilgrims, and raged at them in Turkish:

"Dogs, sons of dogs! One day we'll meet, it doesn't matter where, and I'll drink your blood and spit on your corpses until my mouth runs dry. Remember my name: The fury of Tomic Jankevitch will hunt you down and kill you."

Maqroll replied in the same language:

"Don't worry, Tomic. When we have the pleasure of meeting you again, we will anticipate your good wishes and feed your body to the crows. If they want it. Which I doubt."

The man moved as if to attack the Gaviero, who put his hand in his jacket pocket. Someone behind the wild man pushed him lightly and said something in his ear. He went on his way, muttering curses against everyone on the ship. Vincas remarked with amusement:

"It seems the ardent Jalina has admirers among the holy pilgrims to Mecca. Jabdul should be told."

The Croats left, and the *Hellas* was about to raise anchor when the harbor police approached the ship in a launch, its Saudi flag fluttering proudly in the warm breeze from the desert. Through a loudspeaker the captain was ordered to stop and wait for the authorities. When they came on board, Vincas regarded them with traditional Nordic impassivity. Two uniformed officials were accompanied by four guards armed with submachine guns. The highest-ranking official asked the captain about a woman; according to the statement made by the imam when he came ashore, she had been a passenger on the ship and had been taken off against her will in Port Said. Vincas explained in English that she had disembarked voluntarily and had testified to that effect in the immigration offices in Port Said. It was easy to verify if they

radioed the Egyptian authorities. The woman had also been brutally beaten by her compatriots and was receiving medical attention in Egypt. The Saudi official asked to see the ship's documents, and Vincas immediately produced them for him. The two
functionaries examined them carefully, and somewhat desperately,
as if they did not understand English very well. The leader
returned the papers and without further comment gave his men
orders in Arabic to go back to the launch. He turned and
climbed rapidly down the ladder. Once he was in the boat, he
told the captain he could leave whenever he wished.

The return trip was made without incident. Everyone on the
ship was anxious to hear from Abdul and Yosip. When they
reached Port Said, they anchored at the entrance to the port, and
a short while later Abdul arrived in a launch, accompanied by
their customs agent. Maqroll and the captain greeted them
enthusiastically, and then Vincas asked about Yosip. With a broad
smile that made any further comment unnecessary, Abdul said:

"He's clear of the charge of desertion, but he has to remain on
Egyptian territory for a month. That's required by Egyptian law
when an extradition request from any foreign government is canceled. He is complying with this purely bureaucratic formality
with enormous pleasure, because it allows him to go on taking
care of Jalina, who is slowly recovering from the blows and beatings she received, with the consent of the imam, at the hands of a
giant who was courting her. She and Yosip have discovered that
they get along marvelously well. You can be sure that we'll soon
see them turning into an exemplary couple. Well, I must ask you
to excuse me. I'm going to my cabin; I'm collapsing with fatigue.
I haven't slept for two days. But first I'll give you some advice:
Don't discount the addresses that Malik has for you if you want
to enjoy yourselves in Port Said. I assure you they're worthwhile."
Malik, the agent, was a paunchy Egyptian with a placid, good-
natured face. He smiled through a large, hennaed mustache that
grew down over the corners of his mouth and gave him the
appearance of an operetta Turk.

Just as Abdul predicted, Yosip became Jalina's inseparable companion. He traveled the world with her, working at the most varied jobs. He gave up life at sea, in good part because his wife did
not want to sail with him. Vincas lost the best bos'n he ever had,
and Maqroll gained two friends, whom he saw on various occasions. The woman developed a fervent affection for the Gaviero
when she learned it had been his idea for her to go ashore in

Port Said. In this feeling of Jalina's for the Gaviero there was a good amount of compassion, which she always expressed in a single sentence:

"He's more alone than anyone, and more than anyone else he needs the people who love him."

In the sordid motel on La Brea Boulevard in Los Angeles, where the Gaviero found a mooring years later when he was devastated by fever, she would show the extent of her love for him. This was the subject of another story, which is already in the hands of those readers who are interested in the wanderings of Maqroll.

<h2 style="text-align:center">VI</h2>

The direction of Abdul's life would soon alter radically. Although Maqroll, Bashur himself, and, most of all, the members of Bashur's family mentioned the coincidence, a review of the letters and other writings belonging to what might be called the second stage in our friend's life makes it clear that Ilona's passing determined the change. After she died, and he gave free rein to certain mechanisms that Ilona had perceived as soon as they appeared and had the wise and mysterious ability to keep under control, Abdul allowed a rampant blind fatalism to lead him to the furthest extremes of negligence and indifference. This does not mean that his generous, inquisitive character changed. Bashur was still the same man, but he was traveling down paths and through environments entirely different from the ones he had frequented before. Things happened gradually. At first it was not easy to see the change, even though the luck that had followed him began to forsake him, until it vanished entirely on the horizon of his wanderings. The first serious symptom appeared when he lost the *Hellas,* an event that was mentioned at the beginning of this account. It is time to tell the whole story of what happened then.

After the episode of the Croatian pilgrims and the turbulent Jalina, the *Hellas* returned to Cyprus and made a few short runs in the Mediterranean. They were not especially profitable, but they did not require significant expenditures either. The crew was reduced to eight. Yosip's replacement was an Irish bos'n who had worked with Abdul years before on his family's ships. The man had an unimaginable capacity for storing whiskey in his body. But he also knew how to maintain friendly relations with his men and at the same time rigorously demand their best work. No one ever saw him drunk, and the only sign that he had reached a high tide in his consumption of Scotch was a constant, quiet singing of tunes in the dense language of Erin the Green. His name was John O'Fanon. The idea of transporting arms and explosives to Spain started with him.

In a tavern in Tunis, John met a young couple who said they were on their honeymoon. They were both Catalonians and spoke several languages fluently. She was dark and rather short, with expressive, constantly mobile features. He was one of those tall, lean, melancholic men who have the air of a seminarian, say very little, and always give the impression of just having suffered a great misfortune. From the start the couple showed great friendliness to the bos'n of the *Hellas* and spent a good part of the night listening to his stories about the sea and the anecdotes, some of them highly suggestive, about his life in various ports. O'Fanon was in no condition to suspect their sudden show of amiability or the close attention they paid to his torrent of talk filled with the ordinary incidents common to every seaman's life. Before going back to their hotel, the couple eagerly accepted John's invitation to visit the *Hellas* and have a drink with the owners, whose virtues he tirelessly praised. O'Fanon said nothing of this to Maqroll or Bashur, for by the next day he had completely forgotten his enthusiastic invitation. At about five in the afternoon, the Catalonians appeared at the foot of the gangway and asked for their friend O'Fanon. Maqroll was almost finished supervising the unloading of a cargo of cement from Genoa. Intrigued by the strange couple asking for the bos'n with such familiarity, he sent for O'Fanon, who recognized his friends from the previous night and recalled the invitation he had made in a Scotch-induced euphoria. He mumbled some excuse and went down the gangplank to greet his friends. Now that he was sober, and revived by the cutting mid-January wind that blew out of the Tunisian interior, John discovered surprising new traits in the couple. The man had lost much of his clerical air and looked around warily, especially in Maqroll's direction. The woman, her exuberant gamut of expressions seeming more like a nervous tic than anything else, also displayed a tense vigilance that O'Fanon had not noticed the night before. The Irishman introduced them to the Gaviero, who was already on his guard with the visitors because of the behavior he had noticed from the bridge. They toured the ship, looking at everything but not lingering over any of the details that the bos'n pointed out and explained to them.

When they came to the bridge, both owners were there, and the couple was introduced to Bashur. Abdul's sixth sense had already detected certain signs that he did not find reassuring. In a growing silence, when no one seemed to have anything left to say, Abdul finally asked the question that he had wanted to put to them for some time:

"Can we help you with anything else besides showing you a poor run-of-the-mill freighter? It doesn't seem a very interesting way to spend a honeymoon."

The melancholy Ampurdane (he had already said he was a native of La Bisbal) reacted immediately to Bashur's invitation and replied calmly:

"As a matter of fact, we would like to talk to both of you. We have a business proposition to make. Can we go somewhere private?"

Maqroll grasped Bashur's intention at once and invited them into the small office he shared with Abdul. It was located between the two cabins where they slept. O'Fanon observed all this with sky-blue eyes opened wide in astonishment, shook his head like a man who understands nothing, and left, saying he had something urgent to attend to.

Once they were sitting at the small worktable, the young honeymooners turned into something entirely different from what they had claimed to be. Although the couple were cautious about revealing their activities, the owners of the *Hellas* did learn that their visitors belonged to a Catalonian anarchist organization responsible for several attacks that had been highly publicized in the European press and had cost the lives of dozens of soldiers and civil guards. They wanted to hire the freighter to carry weapons and explosives to the port of La Escala on the Costa Brava. Maqroll would take the ship and deliver the merchandise, and Bashur, remaining with them and another couple, who were waiting down on the dock, would go to Bizerte until the operation was completed.

"That means you'd be holding me as a hostage," Abdul stipulated in a neutral voice that made no assessment of this detail.

"That's exactly what it means," the woman replied in the same tone. "You can't believe we're naive enough to leave a matter of this kind entirely in other people's hands. It means we'll be certain of two things: The cargo will be delivered, and you will be discreet. It seems to me that both you and our Lebanese friend have understood perfectly," she said, turning toward the Gaviero.

"It couldn't be clearer," he answered with a thin smile.

"Aren't you interested in knowing how much we're prepared to pay for this service?" the woman asked with a self-assurance that irritated Maqroll.

"Of course we're interested. But the way you've outlined the plan made me think you expected us to do the work for nothing," he replied, beginning to lose his self-control.

The man gestured with his hand to stop the dispute and mentioned the figure they were willing to pay. It was equivalent to what they had earned on the *Hellas* in the past six months by working hard seven days a week, a consideration that led both Bashur and Maqroll to accept the offer simultaneously.

Abdul left with them the next day, and the weapons and explosives were loaded on the ship under the supervision of Maqroll and Vincas, who watched everything with his expressionless gray eyes and made no comment. The cargo was concealed in large crates and described on the manifest as parts for an anchovy packing plant in La Escala. An account of what happened to Maqroll appeared at the beginning of this story, when I told about my meeting with Abdul's sister Fatima in the station at Rennes. I also described the luck that accompanied the Gaviero, thanks to the English and their complex arrangements on the disputed Rock of Gibraltar. Vincas had to take the *Hellas* back to Cyprus, where the shipping license issued to Abdul and Maqroll was revoked. A Syrian shipbuilder took advantage of the situation and acquired the *Hellas* for a pittance. Vincas went back to sea for the Bashur family. Abdul, without a job or a destination, began to roam the ports of the Middle East and the Adriatic. Maqroll left for Manaus and his journey up the Xurandó in search of illusory sawmills; this too has been described elsewhere.

I would need several pages to enumerate all the temporary occupations to which Bashur dedicated himself from then on. It is enough to mention the ones he refers to in his correspondence and those alluded to by Maqroll: He was a distributor of pornographic publications and photographs in Aleppo, a provisioner of ships' food stores in Famagusta, a contractor for naval painting in Pola, a croupier in Beirut, a tourist guide in Istanbul, a hustler who lured the ingenuous in a billiard room in Sfax, a supplier of adolescent female personnel to a brothel in Tangier, a boiler cleaner in Tripoli, a shill for a money changer in Port Said, a manager of a circus in Taranto, a pimp in Cherchell, a knife grinder and hashish dealer in Bastia. The list goes on, but this

sample gives a measure of the depths of misfortune and reckless-
ness reached by our friend, the same successful and enterprising
Lebanese shipowner I had met years before in Urandá. Despite
his graying, unkempt beard and the ruined clothes, stained by so
many different occupations, that he was wearing on the occasions
when I saw him during his descent into the ninth circle of
vagrancy, Bashur retained his courtly gestures and language, and
the charm made up of a laconic, skeptical humor, a constant,
uncomplaining defiance of his fate, and the moving loyalty to his
friends that was so characteristic of him. Yet what stands out during this stage of Abdul's existence is its concordant synchronicity
with the darkest, most abysmal experiences of his eternal friend,
Maqroll the Gaviero. One might almost think they had agreed
that each of them, on his own account, would travel that abject
road all the way to its final consequences and not lose his
haughty vision of a destiny chosen and drained to the last drop of
misfortune. And one would be mistaken in only this particular:
Maqroll, who had started out long before Bashur on this reckless
journey, lacked the familial ties and connections to his people
that Abdul insisted on preserving until the last day of his life.

The episode I am going to narrate in detail is eloquent testimony to how far Abdul was willing to go. Although it is not one
of his most criminal and dangerous adventures, it does faithfully
represent the profound depths he had fallen to. Some of the facts
appear in a letter to his sister Fatima, which was included in the
package she sent to me from Cairo, and others are found in two
long letters to Maqroll, who sent them to me much later from
Pollensa. At the time Maqroll received them, Bashur was being
treated for a strange disease at a charity hospital in Paramaribo.

But before I go into the details, it may be appropriate to return
for a moment to the obsession that pursued Bashur most of his
life, which we mentioned earlier: his longing to own the ideal
freighter that would meet the design, draft, and mechanical speci-
fications he had forged in his mind, the ship that had been within
his grasp on a few memorable occasions. The repeated disappointments, indicating a hidden irony in his destiny that always
kept him from achieving his illusory goal, became confused in his
thoughts with the death of Ilona, convincing him that with this
brutal sign Allah had announced other plans for him. Having
interpreted events in this way, Bashur forgot his obsession and
allowed the days to follow one another in whatever form the
Magnanimous and All-powerful ordained. As far as Abdul was

concerned, his odyssey through the lower depths was dictated not by curiosity or disenchantment but by a serene wish to conform to laws higher than his own poor will or inconstant desires. It is extremely important to keep this in mind in order to understand the state of mind of Maqroll's friend as he accepted trials that apparently befell him by chance, which is, in fact, a game only the gods are permitted to play.

Prowling from place to place in the Mediterranean, Bashur happened to land in Piraeus, where he fell into the good graces of a woman who owned a shabby tavern on the beach at Turko Limanon. To round out her budget, the lady rented out three rooms, located above her drinking establishment, for transient, *non sanctus* purposes. Her name was Vicky Skalidis, and she had a blind brother, who peddled miraculous medals. From time to time he took care of the tavern when his sister had to go shopping in the port. This individual, called Panos, was a model of vice and craftiness, and despite his blindness could control the dubious, heterogeneous patrons who frequented the shack that bore the unlikely name Empurios. It is doubtful that the gods of Hellas, even in their darkest avatars, would have agreed to live in Vicky Skalidis's tavern, least of all under the vigilance of old Panos, whose infernal temper would have frightened Zeus himself. Abdul arrived there after leaving his position as bookkeeper on a ship that hauled cement between Piraeus and Salonika. Moved by necessity, he had exaggerated his knowledge of mathematics. His accounts conformed less and less to Pythagorean laws, and finally, with a month's salary in his pocket, he was unceremoniously put ashore in Piraeus. He spent several days making the rounds of dilapidated hotels and miserable boardinghouses until he found himself on the beach at Turko Limanon, selling potions against impotence and erotic postcards, which he obtained at a sordid shop run by a man who had been a sailor on the *Princess Bukhara* of imperishable memory. This was how he came, one afternoon, to ask for a room at the Empurios. He spoke first to Panos, who for some obscure reason took a liking to Abdul. They held a long conversation that revealed the perilous lives of each and awakened in Panos a certain respect for the serene acceptance of adversity displayed by the other man. When Vicky returned that night, she found them engaged in an exchange of unedifying confidences. Vicky was a typical Greek woman of about sixty, who had put on weight as she aged, but her smooth olive skin and large green eyes gave her a youthful air that still attracted many admirers, none of them disinterested, unfortunately. She had been married twice, the second time to a Greek from Chicago—this was the origin of her anglicized name. When he died suddenly of apoplexy in a Wabash restaurant, she came into some money and decided to use her inheritance to open the Empurios. One day her brother Panos showed up; she thought he had disappeared years before. He protected her against her suitors but was also an irascible judge of his sister, who retained a healthy flirtatiousness, in no way innocent but judiciously dispensed. Panos introduced Bashur to her in such warm terms that Vicky thought they were old friends and therefore agreed to let him live in one of the rooms. Obviously, this was not how she normally operated her business, which was based on renting the rooms several times a day to couples who came from Piraeus to conceal their love affairs or erotic urges. Bashur told her he was perfectly happy to vacate the room whenever a client wanted it. Vicky soon discovered her mistake regarding the friendship between Bashur and Panos, but by then she was more interested in her guest than she could have imagined at first. Bashur had let his beard and mustache grow in. They were both an attractive salt and pepper, trimmed in the George V style that was popular at the time, which gave him an air of superficial respectability. In these circumstances, it was not long before Abdul was sharing Vicky's room at the back of the tavern and satisfying the autumnal amorous desires that had lain dormant in her life as a respectable widow. Panos at first reacted to the new situation with overly sensitive reservations that Abdul was able to allay— not totally, but at least enough to make their living under the same roof tolerable. Bashur cultivated his friendship with the blind man, thinking it might prove useful to him one day. Panos ran a vast school in the arts of roguery and the crafts of deceit, which sparked certain plans in Abdul's mind. They were imprecise but promised an interesting future, and he had learned to wait, to allow circumstances to mature in their own time. In the marginal, ambiguous world through which he now moved, haste was doomed and hurry was inadvisable.

From the moment he began to share his landlady's bed, Abdul Bashur roundly refused to take on any work in the tavern. Not, of course, out of shame or modesty, but in order to be free to carry out projects significantly more profitable than serving ouzo or opening beers for the rough patrons of the Empurios. When he was not obliged to look after the establishment, Panos left each morning for Piraeus to sell his miraculous medals in front of the Church of the Holy Trinity. That, at least, was his pretext for standing on a crowded street and engaging in other activities, about which Abdul harbored well-founded doubts. Gradually he learned that Panos was the head of a gang of young pickpockets, none of them older than fifteen. The blind man's other senses were unbelievably acute and permitted him to track passersby without arousing suspicion. He would give his pupils a prear-ranged signal that meant they should approach a potential victim. The sound of footsteps, the scents he could detect at a distance, and other, more subtle information, even their breathing, all allowed him to define pedestrians and infer the class, character, and origins of his clientele. When night fell, the boys religiously turned over the spoils of their pillaging, and Panos would send the objects to their destinations: several secondhand shops whose owners were friends of his.

Panos, of course, had told nothing of this to Abdul. But one day, when Bashur went to the port to mail some letters, he saw the blind man on the corner by the church. He was about to walk over and say hello when he heard him give a curious whis-tle. Two ragged boys instantly accosted a woman, begging for money, and followed her until she had turned the corner, then came back to the blind man and dropped something into the sack where he carried his holy medals. Abdul understood imme-diately and left without speaking to Panos. One afternoon a few days later, the two men were alone because Vicky was shopping, and Bashur broached the subject as if it were something they both knew and had already discussed. Panos smiled with brutal sarcasm, turned his face upward as if searching for an uncertain light, and said:

"Those little angels are an untapped gold mine. Right now I'm just keeping them in training for higher things. I'll think of something brilliant soon."

"To begin with," replied Abdul, "I don't think you're operating in the most profitable sector of the port. The places frequented by tourists should be exploited. And you have to start working them from the moment they walk off the boats that carry them from the islands, then along the streets where the bouzouki taverns are, and finally at the entrances to the luxury hotels."

"I thought of that too. But at this stage I can't do it alone, and some of the boys are not as skilled as others."

Abdul decided the time had come to propose the plan he had

been thinking about and refining for the past few days.

"The first thing is to make a rigorous and careful selection of the ones who are really ready for fine, delicate, and interesting work. The others should not be discouraged but should go on operating where they are now, independently. The action has to focus on objects of value: expensive watches, bracelets, necklaces, wallets with dollars, pounds, or marks. And that's all. Another thing to consider is the sale of what they bring in. Your friends in the old-clothes trade are robbing you. They keep the lion's share. That has to be looked into more carefully. The really valuable goods should be sold in Istanbul. Your pupils will be paid but can't ever be allowed to keep what they steal."

As Bashur explained his plan, the blind man kept turning his face toward him with an expression of incredulity that increased as the project was outlined. He had only one objection.

"Don't think it's easy to deceive those little animals or keep them in line. They're used to getting a good amount of the loot, and I don't think we'll be able to control them."

"I don't agree," argued Abdul. "At the start we explain very clearly to the ones we choose that this is an entirely new and different operation. They've been selected as the best, and they'll earn much more than they did before. Those are the conditions. Anyone who doesn't like it can go back with the others and work on his own. When they get their first money they'll see that we're serious, that it's worth it to work for us."

This conversation lasted for several hours and was dedicated to studying and refining every detail. Then each partner began to put his part of the plan into effect. Bashur communicated with friends of his in Istanbul who worked in collaboration with that city's underworld, and he went to the places in Piraeus where tourists tended to congregate and noted the times of day when they were most crowded. Panos, in the meantime, selected his most qualified pupils, made up a list of their names, and reviewed it case by case with Bashur. The two men interviewed each boy to determine his abilities. When everything was ready, Abdul revealed his ace in the hole: At each place where they would operate, they would set up a refreshment stand and sell an iced oat drink sprinkled with cinnamon, which he had first tasted in Cartagena de Indias. A friend of his, an affectionate woman who loved to dance the cumbé, had given him the recipe. The drink would be kept in a large pot. Bashur would serve the customers with a dipper. There would always be chunks of ice in the pot, the same pot into which the young thieves would quickly and discreetly drop their goods as soon as they had stolen them. If the police caught and searched the boys, they would find nothing. This is what they would do with jewelry, watches, bracelets, necklaces. They would drop the billfolds full of money behind the pot, and Bashur would pick them up immediately and hide them. Verifying the boys' loyalty was very simple: Panos had a distant cousin on the Piraeus police force, who would let him know about complaints filed by the victims, which should correspond almost exactly to what the boys had taken each day. The objects would be removed from the pot at home, and that would be that.

The location where Bashur and Panos began what they called "Operation Ice" was the embarcadero for ships carrying tourists to and from the Aegean islands. They planned to keep moving the center of their operations in order to exploit other areas rich in tourists and to avoid the police, who would be alerted by frequent complaints in a particular district. The profits from this first stage, on the docks, surpassed all their calculations. Then they started to work the area surrounding the bouzouki taverns, where they met with even greater success. But predictably enough, the boys began to realize that the pot of iced oat drink never returned the most expensive watches and precious jewelry they remembered tossing into it. Abdul and Panos did not mention these valuable objects. When asked, they would say they had no knowledge of such marvels, which in any case were difficult for the thief to identify in so swift an action. What the pot returned was exactly what they said the pot returned, and that was the end of the discussion. Besides, the boys were making ten times their previous earnings at the Church of the Holy Trinity, and it was unfair for them to complain now that they had more than they had ever dreamed possible. The boys, of course, did not accept the pill that the two men so cynically and emphatically wanted them to swallow. Some of the boldest and most rebellious even made rude allusions to the progenitors of their employers, who pretended they had not heard a thing.

Months later, the group moved to Athens. They had run out of suitable locations in Piraeus, where the last places they had worked were the entrances to the large hotels. The police became suspicious when complaints from tourists and their respective consulates began to pour in with unusual intensity. In Athens they went immediately to Plaka, the long street lined with taverns that never closed, and here Bashur and Panos reaped such

bountiful rewards that the blind man decided to retire and communicated his decision to his partner. Bashur, with the police at
his heels, made a sudden trip to Istanbul, where he had been
depositing his earnings when he visited the city to sell stolen
goods. He did not attempt to say goodbye to Vicky Skalidis, who
in any event already suspected that there was nothing innocent in
the activities of her lover and her brother, and anticipated that it
would all end either in prison or in Bashur's sudden departure.
Abdul, in a final gesture of gratitude to his protector, left a letter
praising her physical and moral qualities and promising to come
back one day and resume the idyll interrupted for reasons beyond
his control. He offered his most heartfelt thanks for the help she
had given him at the time of his greatest need, when he had lost
all hope of ever getting back on his feet. She put the letter in a
small trunk where she kept souvenirs of her love life, mementos
still fragrant with perfumes that awakened pleasurable memories
in the owner of the Empurios.

VII

This was how Bashur came back to the surface, leaving behind
the tortuous, ancient paths of Mediterranean criminality. The
money he had accumulated in Istanbul allowed him to comfortably reestablish his life in merchant shipping. But his long pilgrimage through the world of transgression, studded with
episodes not as easily confessed as the ones recorded here, had
wrought notable changes in his character and his view of life.
Buying another tramp steamer and then having to sell it at a loss,
as he had been forced to do with the *Princess Bukhara,* the *Nymph
of Trieste,* the *Hellas,* and so many other anonymous, forgotten
ships, was something he now found unthinkable.

It was Maqroll the Gaviero who testified with greatest accuracy to this change in his old friend and accomplice. They had
met on countless occasions during Bashur's dark years, which, as
we have said, corresponded to a period no less calamitous for the
Gaviero. When I had the opportunity to meet with him and
asked about Abdul, Maqroll would expound at length on the subject, analyzing in detail the changes and trials his friend was
undergoing. In his correspondence with his family, Bashur made
only a few veiled allusions to all this, except in the case of several
letters to Fatima, his favorite sister, in which he was more
explicit.

"In Abdul," Maqroll would say, "there was a kind of playful inclination to savor life and defy the snares laid by fortune, which made him an ideal companion at difficult moments and a perfect one for enjoying the good times. As far as he was concerned, nothing was impossible or prohibited, nothing was forbidden, and when life confronted him with its challenges he would adopt an attitude of open defiance, a position that has become less and less my own. When his luck changed and he turned up in Istanbul with some capital at his disposal, I could tell that he was maintaining a certain distance, a discreet but firm reserve in the face of what destiny proposed. His aggressiveness had turned into skepticism: He observed reality with the indifference of a man going to the gallows, his thoughts already fixed on the next life. Women, as you well know, were once his strongest temptation and greatest source of joy; they are now the object of curiosity and wonder, which almost always leaves them intrigued, even uncomfortable. Of course, he no longer talks about the ship of his dreams. He still alludes to the characteristics it should have, but he does so as if he were mentioning something impossible, something unimaginable that belongs to the world of the illusory and unattainable—a world that no longer holds any appeal for him, no longer moves him to initiate explorations and involvements he knows are futile. I don't mean to say he's become a man embittered by frustration. Abdul is still warm and devoted to his friends, but there is a kind of veil in his attitude, a kind of opaque screen separating him from the whirlwind that buffets other men, and he accepts it with the gratitude due any intervention by the gods."

An eloquent indication of the change in him is that when Bashur moved to Istanbul, he did not return to his old love and go to sea in a freighter, but settled instead for acquiring, in partnership with a distant cousin who lived in Uskudar, a ferry that served the two cities. The business, while not really prosperous, produced enough for its owners to lead reasonably comfortable lives. His beard was almost white and his shoulders were slightly rounded, but Abdul still had that air of a caliph traveling incognito which had always distinguished him and awakened the interest of everyone who met him.

He would spend long hours in the cafés along the Bosporus that were frequented by merchants and seamen. Between glasses of arrack with ice, which he drank with the circumspection prescribed by the Koran, and cups of steaming, aromatic coffee, he would review his life as a sailor and listen with amiable attention to the tales of his companions, always showing the lively interest the sea inspired in him. He had two or three women friends. From time to time he would have supper with one of them and spend the night with her in his apartment near Kariye. The women soon learned not to have any illusions regarding either the duration of the affair or, of course, Abdul's fidelity. Each knew exactly what to expect, but Bashur's appeal was still strong enough to attract them to his company and his bed.

VIII

Among the last papers that Maqroll sent to me from Pollensa, Mallorca—all of them related to his friend of so many years—I found twenty numbered pages, handwritten on the back of instructions for assembling and using a complicated wood saw manufactured in Finland. The first sheet has a crudely underlined title: *A Dialogue in Belém do Pará*. The writing is undoubtedly the Gaviero's; an old friend of his once characterized it as resembling Dracula's, and Maqroll himself repeated the description, which is as accurate as it is macabre. The dialogue takes place between two protagonists identified as M. and A. After reading a few lines I had no trouble recognizing Abdul and Maqroll but still could not determine the time of their meeting and the ensuing conversation so faithfully transcribed by the Gaviero. Since I have received no further communication from him, and no replies to the letters I have sent to Pollensa, it has been impossible for me to learn this directly from Maqroll, and I have had to be content with applying an analytical method to the text itself. In this way I have deduced the following: The conversation took place after Bashur's move to Istanbul and not long before his fatal trip to Lisbon and Madeira; evidently Maqroll had already experienced the dreadful trial of sailing up the Xurandó in search of illusory sawmills but had not yet encountered the arms smugglers in Puerto Plata. As for Bashur, it can be established that after his apparent retirement in Istanbul he made at least three trips: one to Cádiz to supervise caulking operations on one of his family's ships, a journey to which Fatima refers in one of her letters to Maqroll; another to San José, Costa Rica, to close a deal involving the purchase of coffee and to see Jon Iturri, the captain of the *Halcyon* and the lover of Abdul's sister Warda, who owned the ship; and the last journey of his life, the one to Madeira by way of Lisbon. The question remains: When did he pass through Belém de Pará and meet with Maqroll? I can only attempt a hypothesis that is reasonable though impossible to prove: After his visit to Costa Rica, Bashur went on to Belém to discuss one of the many projects Maqroll was always planning. Perhaps Abdul did not refer to it because nothing concrete resulted from the meeting and he had no reason to mention it in his correspondence. This is by no means the only blank space in the parallel lives of the two friends. It must also be remembered that long intervals separate Bashur's letters to his family, and as I believe I have already indicated, he omits many episodes or conceals quite a few details if he does say anything about them. One final possibility, which should not be entirely discounted, is that the meeting never took place, that in these notes Maqroll was attempting to summarize the essence of certain themes repeated in many of their conversations at different times in their lives. Knowing the Gaviero and his fondness for such games—they appear constantly, for example, in his Xurandó journal—this may be the most valid hypothesis, although it leaves several important questions unanswered.

Under these circumstances, it has seemed appropriate for me to transcribe the dialogue re-created, or created, by the Gaviero. Yet it is still unsettling to think that Maqroll chose to record this probable encounter, at this precise moment in their lives, and not any of the other countless occasions when the two friends were together. There are repeated coincidences of the kind in the life of Maqroll. They are not really coincidences but seem to be troubling premonitions that reveal his sure ability to pull at the precise thread in the blind tangle of the future. This talent—it is no exaggeration to call it visionary—becomes even more evident in the trembling strokes of his handwriting from beyond the grave. And so, whatever its origin or motive, let us see what the dialogue can tell us about these two singular beings whose troubled passage through life I have attempted to record.

A DIALOGUE IN BELÉM DE PARÁ

MAQROLL I wonder what you would do now that you've returned from the treacherous, disreputable places I thought you had sunk into forever. What you would do, I mean, if the ship you've dreamed of all your life suddenly appeared.

ABDUL Before I answer, let me clarify something that's extremely important to me. You, and other friends, and members of my family, all insist on talking about a descent when you refer to this recent phase of my life. I don't see it as a fall, and I never lived as if it were. For me the world where I spent incomparably full years is no lower or higher than any other I've lived in, and making that moral assessment means not knowing it and distorting its reality. During that period in my life I met people burdened with the same defects and mean-spiritedness, the same virtues and generous impulses, as all those who live in the supposed realm of law and order. Besides, in the underworld, in irregularity and misery, which all amounts to the same thing, generosity and solidarity are more fully expressed and are deeper, I would say, than in the world where prejudice, repression, and frustration are a rule of conduct. But you know all this as well as or better than I do. I don't need to go on like a conventional preacher. As for the ship I've always dreamed of, well, I can say yes, I would go to find it and try to buy it, because I feel it's something I owe myself. But if that doesn't happen and the ship never appears, it wouldn't matter. I've learned the habit of deriving solid reasons to continue living from unfulfilled dreams. Of course, Maqroll, you're a past master at this, and God knows I can't tell you anything about it. My archetypal tramp steamer is no less illusory than your sawmills on the Xurandó or your fisheries in Alaska.

MAQROLL You're right, of course. I think you and I always know ahead of time that the object we set out to find, with no thought to obstacles or fear of dangers, is entirely unreachable. It's what I once said about the caravan. Let's see if I remember: "A caravan doesn't symbolize or represent anything. Our mistake is to think it's going somewhere, leading somewhere. The caravan exhausts its meaning by merely moving from place to place. The animals in the caravan know this, but the camel drivers don't. It will always be this way."

ABDUL There's nothing for me to add. It can't be said better. So I don't know why we're even talking about it.

MAQROLL I was only trying to confirm something I was fairly certain of otherwise. Your partnership with Panos in Piraeus; your selling more or less adulterated food supplies to the ships docking in Famagusta and helping the roulette wheel to favor certain numbers in Beirut; your catching ingenuous tourists off guard in the Golden Horn and recruiting repaired virgins for the brothel in Tangier; your changing dollars or pounds for travelers drunk on phony arrack and exploiting two poor Sardinian women in the alleys of Cherchell—for all of this, and much more I won't mention, you don't feel the slightest trace of guilt, or even the thrill of having tasted forbidden fruit.

ABDUL In the first place, there's no such thing as forbidden fruit. You mention it simply as a rhetorical device. That leaves the act, plain and simple, uncategorized and unjudged, what was lived as if it were a pure, absolute fruit, eaten in the fullness of its flavor and the ripeness of its flesh, ready to be transformed in the equivocal process of memory until it is utterly forgotten. Something lived in this way cannot leave a trace of guilt or be subjected to the test of morality. That's clear, isn't it?

MAQROLL That's what I wanted to know, wanted to hear from the lips of my friend Jabdul, the man spoiled by Ilona, devoured by Jalina, initiated by Arlette into the arts of the bed.

ABDUL If not initiated, then certainly confirmed. Of course you can't know that Arlette died three years ago, and I just learned a few weeks ago that I'm her sole heir. One of these days I'll go to claim my inheritance. Come to think of it, it wouldn't be a bad idea to give you power of attorney so you could do it for me. That would have a certain poetic justice.

MAQROLL Spare me your lyrical justice, Abdul. I'd be happy to go, but I don't think there's much to claim. The last time I was in Marseilles, she was being swindled by a couple of ambiguous adolescents who both went to bed with her at the same time. With no appreciable benefit to her, I would think, but a good deal of profit for the two boys from La Canebière. But look at the humor of our coming to this Amazon hell and drinking mediocre rum and lukewarm beer just to talk about lunatic schemes and faded loves. It could only happen to us.

ABDUL One of the many things I've learned from you is to never renounce the past. "What happened happened," I heard you exclaim with delight one day when we met in Martinique, after I'd returned from the Mira River and my encounter with the Mirror Breaker.

MAQROLL Do you want to know something? I'll always regret not having gone with you that time. On the journey through this world, it isn't always easy to run into a representative of evil in its pure state—evil to the highest power, I would call it. I still insist he surrendered himself fully to that rare state. My friend Alejandro Obregón refused to attribute so much to the Mirror Breaker, but I think he was wrong.

ABDUL Yes, he was, there's no doubt about it. But I must tell you: Meeting someone like that, someone who represents absolute evil, has dark and harmful consequences. I'll try to explain: When I faced the Mirror Breaker, when I went to his lair and had supper with him—that entire night, and for the first time in my life, I felt a kind of animal fear, the terror of a trapped beast, which had less to do with death itself than with the possibility that death would come to me because of someone like him. As a Muslim I'm a fatalist, and from that fatalism I've derived a rule of conduct. But in the Mirror Breaker's mansion, deep inside me, fatalism was taking one path and the ambush set by Tirado threatened on another—an unprotected area of my being where an attack, at least until that moment, had always been unthinkable. It isn't easy to explain. It was as if my own death would suffer a savage violation. I'm sure you understand what I'm talking about.

MAQROLL Yes, I think I do, in fact. But first think for a minute about his name: the Mirror Breaker. A mirror—and this is something found in all the world's myths—a mirror must not be broken. A mirror reflects our other image, the one we'll never know, just as Tirado said; but a mirror is also the road to the unknown world that will forever be forbidden to us if we break the glass that conceals it. Perhaps the absolute sacrilege, the greatest challenge to the gods, the most senseless transgression a man can commit, is breaking a mirror. Well, as for dying at the hands of that individual, it's clear such a death would have been extremely serious. It's always a question of knowing which death is waiting for us. I don't mean the purely physical or painful aspect of the matter. Death, when it comes at hands like his, is not the death we were destined for, the death prepared over an entire lifetime from the moment we are born. Each of us is cultivating, selecting, watering, pruning, shaping our own death. When it comes, it can take many forms, but its origin, the moral and even aesthetic circumstances that ought to shape it, is what really matters and makes it not tolerable, which is very rare, but at least harmonious with certain secret, profound conditions, certain requirements that have been forged by our being during the time of its existence and outlined by transcendent, ineluctable powers. The death that comes from someone like the Mirror Breaker offends a certain order, a veiled harmony that we've attempted to impose on the course of our days. Such a death betrays and denies our very selves, and that is why we find it intolerable. More than fear,

what you felt was profound grief, an essential nausea at ending that way.

ABDUL Yes, I think you're right. While you were talking I was
reliving those hours, feeling what I felt then, and that's exactly
what it was: a fundamental revulsion at dying at those hands.
Externally I was calm, as if I were floating on indifference: It's
an old exercise learned thousands of years ago by my race of
desert lords. Internally I was in an agony of revulsion. There's
no other word. But don't tell me you've never felt the same
thing at some point in your life, during the time you were
undergoing trials so severe I often wonder how you endured
them.

MAQROLL Well, my dear Abdul, I remember experiencing something similar only once, which is why I'm sorry I wasn't on
the Mira with you. It was in Mindanao, at a miserable mooring near Balayan. After two days and nights of visiting bars
with the crew of an Irish fishing boat of unfortunate memory,
I found myself alone one night in a brothel outside town, in
the middle of a network of poisonous canals. I wanted to
sleep more than anything else. A girl—the only thing I
remember about her is how young she was, and her piercing,
childish voice—took me to a shabby little cubicle made of
mismatched planks, one of a row of rooms at the back of the
house. I fell into a deep sleep and didn't even touch her. Many
hours later I awoke with a start. My clothes, my papers, the
little money I had, and a watch that Flor Estévez had given to
me—it had all disappeared. There was a knock at the door,
and in came an ancient toothless woman who could have
been a hundred years old and who kept repeating in English,
"Hundred fifty dollar, sir, hundred fifty dollar," while her
rheumy eyes searched the room as if trying to see if anything
of mine had been overlooked. I asked to speak to the owner,
and she kept repeating her litany of "hundred fifty dollar." I
was in my underwear, without any clothes, in an abandoned
hovel I realized only then was a sinister den of thieves, with
no possibility of communicating with anyone I knew, in the
hands of the most violent, pitiless criminals in all of Asia and
perhaps the world. After a few minutes a man came in. He
was probably the manager; at least that's what I thought then.
He sat down at the foot of my bed, staring at me with the
eyes of a rat ready to attack. He was an obese dwarf, with a
flat, full-moon Asian face covered with pockmarks, and gold

teeth that gleamed in a smile filled with the worst omens. He wore a stained, garish-colored T-shirt and equally filthy Bermuda shorts buttoned below a dropsical belly that protruded like a shapeless tumor. Without saying a word, he put his hand behind him, at the level of his waistband, pulled out a short .32-caliber revolver, and aimed at my head. That was when the same terror and nausea you felt in the house of the Mirror Breaker rose in my throat. Death, my death, could not come to me by so vile a route. In his face I could see that this method of doing away with recalcitrant patrons who were brought to the shack by a complicitous cabdriver was normal routine for him. I felt uncontrollable, blind, raging fury at the thought of dying at his hands, and I attacked the dwarf, throwing the sheet around his neck and desperately pulling it tight. He managed to fire two shots before he died of strangulation, with rasping snorts that increased my revulsion until I almost vomited. One bullet grazed my cheek, causing a deep wound that bled heavily; the other was buried in the planks of the cabin. I still have the scar, as you can see. I ran out the back, and when I reached the canal, filled with stinking black water, I jumped into a canoe that was tied to a tree, paddled with my hands, and got away from the place. I came to a highway. A car passed from time to time. One driver responded to my signals. He picked me up and made no comment. It must have been a normal occurrence in that district. I asked him to take me to the docks. We drove up to the ship, and I climbed the ladder as quickly as I could. The bos'n was waiting on deck, looking at me in horror. I asked him to give a few dollars to the man in the car and went to the crew's quarters for the first-aid kit, to treat my wound. Only as I was telling my shipmates what had happened did I realize that there was absolutely no one in sight when I ran out of the shack. Someone said those places are usually abandoned: Nobody lives there, but at night two or three prostitutes serve as bait, and a couple of thugs wait for the victims brought by a cabdriver who is their accomplice. Then they rob and kill their unsuspecting prey. Well, that was the only time I almost received the death that didn't belong to me. The one whose direction and origin were not destined for me.

ABDUL There's a good deal to say about the subject. For example: The Mirror Breaker was a much more elaborate and refined villain than the Filipino dwarf, but it's certainly true that in the end, the nausea is the same.

MAQROLL The nausea, in fact, is identical. But it's worth remembering that the supposed refinement in Tirado can barely mask the same instinct for death—primary, elemental, stripped of everything that might suggest what people have agreed to call "humanity" but which fundamentally belongs to the aesthetic realm, to the *harmonia mundi* of the ancients.

ABDUL Since we've embarked on the difficult terrain of the art of dying, I've just thought of something that never occurred to me before: It's unlikely, almost impossible, for the sea to offer us a death different from the one that, as you say, has always belonged to us. Only at sea are we safe from the ignominious fate that threatened us, you in Mindanao and me in the pretentious villa on the Mira River.

MAQROLL That would be equivalent to thinking that the ocean possesses an essential dignity. Perhaps it's better to think so. The truth is I'm not so sure, but the idea is attractive and it does offer a precarious consolation, though ultimately it's no more than a consolation.

ABDUL I've suddenly realized that Ilona died at sea. I wonder if it was the death that was waiting for her, the one that had always been destined for her. What do you think?

MAQROLL First of all, she didn't die at sea. She died in a wreck up on the rocks of the jetty. Second, I firmly believe she found the death that was hers. We'll never know what Larissa meant to Ilona, but whatever it was, I can assure you it wasn't evil. It was something else, not the pure evil of the Mirror Breaker or the Filipino. The proof is that she went to the encounter with full knowledge of who was waiting for her.

ABDUL I hope you're right. After all, I wasn't there, and I don't know how things were deep inside her. I would have given anything to meet that woman.

MAQROLL You wouldn't have learned a thing. I can only tell you that she was misfortune itself.

EPILOGUE

The self-evident premonitory meaning of the dialogue here transcribed needs no comment. The very fact that the Gaviero recorded it so faithfully demonstrates that he was moved to document the meeting by his gift for clairvoyance. The chain of events that carried Abdul Bashur to his end occurred so quickly that one could say, in the words of the poet: "It took less time than I need for the telling."

Maqroll was in Lisbon on his way to La Coruña—an old companion in his Alaskan forays was waiting to meet with him and make final plans for a similar excursion in a small freighter adapted for transporting cattle—when he heard about an old tramp steamer on the island of Madeira. Built in Belfast early in the century, it had been put on the market by the executors of the estate of a wealthy Canarian shipowner who had died not long before. The ship was in very good condition. Maqroll could tell by the photographs that this was an authentic museum piece. He flew to Funchal to talk to the sellers and see the ship in person. It was, in effect, a unique example of its class, with all the original cabin, office, and bridge furnishings intact. It had a Krup-Mac diesel engine, made in Kiel, that could provide good service for several more decades. Without thinking twice, the Gaviero signed an option to buy, at very little cost. He returned to La Coruña, where he and his partner arranged all the details of their Alaskan undertaking, which would range down the Pacific coast to Vancouver. Then he went to Istanbul to talk to Bashur and show him the photographs he had taken of the freighter in Funchal. When he saw them, Abdul decided to see the ship for himself and, if he was convinced, to purchase it immediately, taking advantage of the option signed by his friend. His cousin was interested in buying his share of the Uskudar ferry, and he would use that money to pay for his ship. Maqroll and Bashur traveled together to Lisbon. From there, the Gaviero left for La Coruña to supervise the conversion of his freighter to cattle transport. Abdul took the plane to Funchal.

In the kind of coincidence that is very common in our encounters, I happened to be in Santiago de Compostela on one of my periodic visits to the Apostle, regarding whose protection I have convincing proofs. I learned that Maqroll was in La Coruña, and one morning I called him at the hotel where he usually stayed. We arranged to meet there two days later. The following afternoon, an urgent message from La Coruña was waiting for me, asking me to call right away. I telephoned the Gaviero immediately, and before I could ask what was wrong, he said in a blank voice that sounded terrifyingly near:

"Abdul died yesterday in Funchal. The plane crash-landed. The weather was bad. I don't know your plans, but I'd like you to come with me when I collect the remains and send them to his family."

The weather was still bad when we reached Funchal. The small Convair landed without too much difficulty, but it vibrated in the wind like a box of matches. The airport police had been informed of our arrival and were waiting for us when we left the plane. Abdul's body had been burned to ashes, they said, and they had placed it in a small wooden box. Did we want to see it? We both answered at the same time that it was not necessary. Our plane was flying back to Lisbon in two hours, and we had time to go to the city, but the Gaviero suggested visiting the site of the accident, at the beginning of the runway. They drove us there in a jeep. A shapeless pile of twisted metal and blackened remains of metal plates and fabric rose near the sea, still choppy because of the storm that had just passed. In the background, in a small cove, one could see the svelte outline of the tramp steamer, its hull black with a thin cadmium-red stripe along the upper edge. The bridge and cabin section gleamed white, as if they had been painted the day before. For a long while we stood looking at this apparition that seemed to us like an indecipherable message from the gods. On the way back to the jeep, we stopped again in front of the jumbled heap of burned metal. I heard Maqroll murmur in a barely audible voice:

"This was your own death, Jabdul, nurtured each and every day of your life."

I could not understand the meaning of his words at the time. But I was struck by his addressing the friend of his soul with the intimate *tú* he had never used when Abdul was alive.

That was when I remembered the photograph of the boy absorbed in contemplating, with large, squinting Bedouin eyes, a pile of smoking wreckage, the snow-covered mountains of Lebanon in the background. Months later I brought the photograph to the Gaviero, intending to give it to him. He responded, in the same blank voice I had heard on the telephone in Compostela:

"You'd better keep it. I can't hold on to anything. It all slips away between my fingers."

Triptych on Sea and Land

*T*hree episodes in the life of Maqroll the Gaviero are collected here. Each in its own way, and in its own time, disclosed regions of his soul he had not known before, revelations that marked him for the rest of his days. He did not often speak of them, and when he did he sought out cautious detours that would keep him from returning completely to the arduous passage they had represented at the moment he lived them. He alluded to these events with sibylline phrases; the most frequent was: "I've traveled at the edge of chasms compared to which death is a puppet show." Our friend was not willing to recall such matters, and it has been no easy task to learn, from his own lips or from those who were close to him, the exact nature of the corners he was forced to turn by destiny.

Appointment in Bergen

Günlük işlerdenmiş gïbï ölüm
(As if death were an ordinary matter)

Ilham Berk

*T*he fact that this had to happen in Brighton is something
that would have been taken as natural and predictable by
anyone who knows the popular Sussex resort. Brighton, where
Londoners repeatedly go down to the sea in the midst of a
gloomy collection of Victorian and Edwardian buildings that far
exceed the most feverish imagination; where even the most modest bar makes a point of serving us precisely the whiskey we did
not want, and women on the streets and along the wide, desolate
seawalk, pounded by an icy gray ocean, offer a long list of caresses
that at the moment of truth turn out to be a hurried, homeo-
pathic version of what an Anglican understands as pleasure: It was
in Brighton, then, the place where we know we do not belong as
soon as we arrive, that I was forced to spend three days confined
to bed in a miserable boardinghouse. Between bouts of diarrhea
and boredom, I was sure I would die there.

I had gone to Brighton to meet Sverre Jensen, my old friend
and partner in fishing ventures in Alaska and along the coast of
British Columbia. He, in turn, had made an appointment there
with a shipbuilder, retired now because of a serious heart disease,
who occasionally furnished us with the means to lease a fishing
boat for our work. From the moment I boarded the train in London, I knew that not all the sea urchins I had eaten in a Thai
restaurant near the Strand were as fresh as they should have been.

As an improbable antidote to the worst possibility, I had ordered a bottle of white Portuguese wine that turned out to be as questionable as the sea urchins. I felt the first spasms just before we reached Brighton. With a tremendous effort, I went to the house of our shipbuilder, but no one answered when I rang. The place seemed empty. All my joints ached, and my head had turned into a kind of bell struck in implacable rhythm by a hammer, leaving me breathless and almost blind. I took a taxi to the boarding-house Jensen had recommended. It was situated in a gloomy alley that had the not very encouraging name of Monkeyhead Lane. The landlady, an opulent Italian with the shadow of an incipient mustache, had me fill in the registration card and handed me the key to a room on the fourth floor of the building. The stairway was a via crucis that seemed endless. A short while later, she brought me a bitter tisane with iridescent glints of an oil I made no attempt to identify. The authority of the woman, to whom I had mentioned the poisonous effects of the London sea urchins, allowed no resistance, and I did my best to swallow the potion. The treatment lasted for three days, during which time the infernal remedy was my only nourishment. When I could stand and take a few steps, I was cured, but I felt like a nonagenarian struggling to enjoy his last few months of life.

I did not know anyone in Brighton. Years before, in one of those seizures that Ilona called *l'appel de mon sang slave,* we had gone to Brighton to spend a few weeks during the summer. I don't know what idea my lamented friend had formed of its wonders, but after two weeks of making love in a foul little room where the unbearable smell of English cooking hung in the air, we resolved to leave for Trieste and stay at the house of one of Ilona's cousins, who welcomed us as if we had come from the most forsaken spot on earth. When I told her about the pervasive smell in our room in Brighton, Ilona remarked:

"The Gaviero calls it English cooking, but that was the stink of Pictish cuisine, and I suspect their illustrious descendants have not made much progress since then."

That was my only memory, my only and utterly unpleasant experience, of the famous English resort.

When I went back to the house of the Welsh shipbuilder, whose sonorous name was Glanmor Conway, my entire body still felt as if it had received a merciless beating. This time the door was opened by a young woman who looked studious and shy, one of those typical English women with transparent skin and a rather languid air but possessing unlimited inner energy and a complete gamut of cunning stratagems to make their way in life. All this, I repeat, behind an expression of innocence that can deceive anyone not familiar with so fearful a species. I told her my name and said I had an appointment with Mr. Conway. The girl asked me in and led me to what must have been his study. She indicated a chair, invited me to sit down, and then occupied the chair behind the desk, which was clearly intended for Conway's exclusive use. I must have looked surprised at what seemed a strange impertinence, because Cathy—she had told me her name when I had given her mine—fixed her barely visible blue eyes on that distance where born liars always look and explained:

"Glanmor is an uncle twice removed of my mother, and when she died, he brought me here to live. I have no other relatives. My father died in the wreck of the *Lady Ann,* which you surely must remember."

I did recall something about the sinking of one of Conway's old tramp steamers when it hit a mine at the entrance to the port of Aarhus in Denmark. That was almost twenty years earlier, of course.

Then Cathy said that her instructions from Glanmor were that both Sverre Jensen and I should stay in the house and wait for his return. He had been obliged to leave for a few days to attend to some business in Bristol. I had known Conway for many years, and despite his legendary cordiality, this offer to take us into his home seemed somewhat unusual to me. But I decided to accept because my funds were almost depleted, and the statuesque Italian with the authoritarian mustache showed no signs of being a person with the patience to understand any delay in paying the rent. I asked Cathy if she had heard from my Norwegian friend, and she said she had not but that Glanmor had told her Jensen would arrive at about the same time I did. I replied that in any case I was happy to accept her uncle's invitation and would return soon with my gear. She smiled, and her expression, somewhere between decorous and crafty, made me vaguely uneasy. When I came back from the boardinghouse with my duffel bag on my shoulder, Cathy led me to an attic reached by steep stairs that left me short of breath. We walked into a spacious room with two beds, each one placed beneath a casement window, a large armoire from the time of William and Mary, and an accumulation of spyglasses, compasses, and unidentifiable nautical objects that interfered with every step. The bathroom was at the end of a narrow hallway that crossed the length of the attic. Cathy also showed me the room where she slept, which was next to the bath. She did this with no particular expression, like someone offering routine information. I could not immediately reconcile the niece's living at the top of the house and at the same time sitting in her uncle's desk chair to talk to strangers. I went back to my garret, arranged the three or four books that always travel with me, and put my bag and clothes into the large armoire, which groaned like a tired animal. Cathy disappeared without saying a word, and I did not hear her going down the stairs. Now I understood why no one had answered the door the first time I came to the house. She must have been in her room, where the front doorbell certainly could not be heard. Everything still seemed very strange to me, but knowing that nothing should surprise us when we deal with the English, I decided to lie down on the bed and rest for a while. The move had exhausted me: My recovery from food poisoning was obviously taking longer than I had expected.

I stayed in my room for the rest of the day. Cathy came up twice with tea and toast, the only thing I could eat without feeling nausea, although that was slowly beginning to disappear. This was when I learned many aspects of Glanmor Conway's life, not all of them edifying and some positively grim. Cathy had come to the house of her distant relative when she was not yet an adolescent. Conway used her as a servant for simple tasks under the supervision of an old Welsh domestic who barely spoke English. When Cathy reached puberty, he sent the old woman back to her remote village in the mountains of Radnor, took the girl into his bed, and at the same time burdened her with all the work in the house. Conway was then over seventy and profoundly suspicious. He never permitted Cathy to leave the house except to go to the grocery store at the corner, and he kept strict track of the time she spent on these errands. Apparently the old man had gradually reduced his physical contact with the girl and used her now only as a servant.

One night, two days after my arrival at the shipowner's house, Cathy came to my room with a sheet wrapped around her and slipped in beside me, covering me with caresses. We spent the night together, and the girl turned out to be more inexperienced than I had supposed, even though with each embrace she fell into a kind of trance in which it was very difficult to draw the line between simulation and sincerity. I knew perfectly well that this was a path that would only further complicate my situation, which was already precarious enough. When Sverre Jensen arrived, I felt a liberating relief. I told him everything that had happened, and he looked at me with the greatest astonishment. When I finished the story, he would only comment, in his proverbially laconic style:

"Something in this doesn't fit with what I know about Conway. We'll see what the explanation is when he gets back. What we need is for him to arrange the boat without too much delay, because the tuna season opens in just a few weeks. For now, Maqroll, I'd advise you to forget about this Cathy, who's much more dangerous than she looks."

Before continuing, I think I should tell you about my good friend Sverre Jensen, an old veteran of the North Pacific fishing grounds, a man with a heart whose nobility was matched only by the strict modesty with which he concealed it. We had met in the Kitimat jail, in British Columbia, after I had been accused of committing adultery with a young Indian woman married to a Polish lunatic, who had made the charge and threatened to kill me. Jensen was in prison because of his involvement in a tavern fight during which two Portuguese, whom nobody knew, had been stabbed to death. The knife that killed them belonged to Sverre, but he swore that when the fight broke out someone had pulled it from the sheath attached to his belt. For two months we shared a cell, suffering from the cold: Each dawn found us shivering and almost frozen. During our long confinement, we had an opportunity to talk about our lives, and there was such a curious coincidence of places and circumstances that we often asked each other in surprise how it was possible we had not met before. Sverre's innocence was finally proved through the indiscretion of a black from South Carolina, who became hopelessly drunk in a bar and described how he had killed two Portuguese who were in league with the devil and trafficked in blacks lured from Angola with promises of work in America. It was later discovered that the man was deranged and had committed the murders in a moment of frenzied insanity. I was released at almost the same time, after the offended Varsovian withdrew the charge. That was when Jensen and I began to travel together, at first as net haulers on a variety of fishing vessels, and then as owners of a two-masted fishing boat, which we were able to buy thanks to a modest inheritance that Sverre received at the death of his bachelor brother, who was a justice of the peace in Bergen. I supplied the rest of the purchase price with money I had saved during the time we were hauling nets, an economy imposed on me by Jensen, who knew my tendency to think rarely, if at all, about the future. This is not the time to give a full accounting of the years Sverre and I spent together, earning a dangerous livelihood as fishermen. I'll come back to it on another occasion.

Sverre had not changed at all despite the passage of time. He belonged to that race of Scandinavians who acquire in midlife the physical appearance that stays with them to the end of their days. His rough, burly body seemed to have been put together with pieces from other bodies of the same race, but all of a different size. His long, bony face showed the same lack of harmony but was saved by the smiling expression in his eyes and an air of kindness that could not be located in any one of his features. Ordinarily a man of few words, he was also capable of wild, fearful mood changes that instantly turned him into a devastating, unpredictable avalanche. Nothing physical unleashed these attacks of rage; rather, it was a certain sense of gratuitous injustice, the result of other people's stupidity. I once saw him smash a table with a blow of his fist, as if it were made of paper, when a tavern owner in Antwerp hit a waitress who had dropped a tray filled with mugs of beer. Five giants from the harbor police managed to subdue him after a fight that left three of them in need of hospitalization.

When I told Jensen how Conway's niece had welcomed me, my friend was not very convinced and, as I've said, warned me against the girl. Several days went by with no sign of the Welshman, and we decided to question Cathy regarding his whereabouts. Her answers were disturbingly vague, and Jensen proposed investigating the matter on his own. To further complicate matters, one night she tried to slip into Sverre's bed, employing the same bold tactics she had used with me. The Norwegian sent her packing. He already suspected her intentions. The days passed, and we were beginning to run out of money, when by a remarkable coincidence a piece of paper fell out of a Bible and into the hands of my friend, who, like a good Protestant, read the book from time to time. Written in pencil was an almost illegible address in Portsmouth and five digits that obviously corresponded to a telephone number in that city; we called from a pub we visited every day, and Glanmor Conway himself answered. We were not very surprised, since we already suspected that Cathy had fabricated the story about his being in Bristol. What we learned from Conway completed the picture of her outrageous lies, which I had believed, unforgivably. The house in Brighton was for sale, and Conway had asked his presumptive relative to assist the staff of the real estate agency that was showing the property. Glanmor had left word with Cathy that we should communicate with him immediately, since he had decided to liquidate his business and had already sold the ships still registered in his name. At no time had he given her instructions to lodge us in the house: Its use and management were obviously in the hands of the agency. He regretted the deception that had been foisted on us and warned us very seriously against Cathy's scheming; she had gone to work for the agency as soon as Conway left Brighton. Naturally, we had to leave the premises right away if we wanted to avoid problems with the real estate agents, who would interpret our presence there as flagrant trespassing on private property.

Before we went back to the house, we agreed that we would leave immediately without giving any explanation to Cathy. She watched us pack and did not ask a single question about our departure. As we walked down the stairs, she shouted from the attic:

"What a pair of imbeciles! You could have lived here as long as you wanted and not paid a cent! You didn't understand anything!" Cathy screamed with hysterical laughter as she made this last remark.

We returned to the Italian's boardinghouse. She agreed to let Sverre sleep on a sofa that was kept in the room I had previously occupied, and charge just a few shillings extra. Her only comment was:

"I don't think he'll fit. I've never seen such a big man."

Jensen turned to look at me, as if wondering whether all the women who crossed our paths now had suddenly gone crazy. I shrugged and suggested we review our finances. I was afraid we did not have enough money between us to live for very long. The situation was very tight. If we ate once a day and gave up the sinister Scotch served in the Brighton pubs, we could get by for two weeks at most. Since this has been my general circumstance for as long as I can remember, I was not particularly worried. But Jensen, a methodical, austere Norwegian, felt a panic he could not disguise.

"What are we going to do now, Maqroll? Conway would have leased the boat to us and advanced us some money. I was counting on that, and now I must confess I can't think of anything else to do." His voice sounded thick in his throat and conveyed a disheartened melancholy that could not have been more inopportune.

"To begin with," I said, injecting my words with an enthusiasm that was not very convincing, "we have to leave this awful city. It has brought us nothing but misfortune. The Victorian buildings, and the no less ominous architecture of the illustrious heir, attract bad luck. Do you know why? One of the many reasons is that they face the sea, and that is an insult the gods do not pardon. All the bleached-out, avid faces of people who walk the streets of Brighton like zombies, trying to forget their London ennui, tell us we are in the land of the dead. Don't you see that everything here is a lie, which is why all of this is true? There's nothing here but death; it hovers over the great domes of colored glass, the wrought iron trying to recapture times that are gone forever, the flock of human sheep who don't know why they've come here. Let's use our money to get out; it doesn't matter where we go, as long as we leave."

Sverre had long been accustomed to my phobias and denunciations, and he agreed that we should leave immediately. And in fact, the next day we boarded a freighter bound for Saint-Malo; we were allowed to hang our hammocks in a cabin next to the engine room, surrounded by hellish noise and a smell of diesel that took away the appetite. But as for me, I felt I was in paradise, knowing we had escaped the sinister nightmare of that refuge for a middle class that is actually starving to death while it attempts to preserve its fictitious dignity. The channel crossing took two days and nights because we had to make a stop in Cherbourg to unload some merchandise or other. I've gone to sea on every imaginable kind of ship, but I've never sailed on a hulk as ugly as the *Pamela Lansing,* a name that only served to increase the grotesque calamity of its appearance. The captain, an Irishman who looked as if he'd had a last-minute reprieve from the gallows, told us the ship had been used to transport troops to Gallipoli during the First World War. That being said, there was nothing more to say.

We went ashore in Saint-Malo, our ears still ringing with the infernal racket made by the engines and the metal hull plates of the *Pamela Lansing.* But during those two days and nights, the dark omens shadowing the destiny of my good friend Sverre were revealed to me. I will try to explain how I reached this conclusion, although he offered no explicit information that would justify my harboring so grim a certainty. Ever since we had met in Brighton, I had sensed a certain weariness beneath his warm cordiality, a kind of detachment from the issues and concerns that had once absorbed all his measured enthusiasm. Yet the cause was clearly not physical: He was as full of health and energy as ever. It came instead from some corner of his soul, which emitted a toxic substance that was gradually distancing him from the things of this world. I knew that his religious convictions were limited to the routine observance of a few precepts of his Protestant faith, and therefore I did not attribute Sverre's condition to a crisis of belief. On several occasions I tried as discreetly as I could to broach the subject, but Jensen indefatigably avoided any confidences. His wife had died many years earlier, following a prolonged bout with cancer that had made her suffer cruelly, although she never complained. Sverre stayed at her side with an affecting devotion and love. They had no children, and he returned to his prolonged fishing expeditions and never thought of remarrying. I had met the women in certain ports with whom he maintained a relationship, if not amorous then certainly tinged with a good-natured affability that was as lighthearted as his phlegmatic Scandinavian character would allow. It was typical of his eccentric sense of humor that he called each woman by a name that was not her own. I remember, for example, a Florence he insisted on calling Rosalie, claiming she had been born in Grenoble when in fact she was from Seattle and did not speak a word of French. Matters became complicated when a more radical disparity appeared: There was a black woman from Martinique who pampered him, enjoyed being with him, and celebrated his arrival with a thousand demonstrations of her affection, and whom he insisted on calling Yukio-san, which supposed two intolerable absurdities, since the use of *san* in her case was not permissible.

Another constant in my friend's character was what might be called his covenant with God. He was not a man of regular or deep religious habits, but whenever the Supreme Being was called upon in his presence, either in the course of some dangerous ship's maneuver or during a task made difficult for any reason, Sverre would make an emphatic gesture with his hand, as if he were setting aside something close by and very delicate, and each time he would say the same words: "Let's leave him out of it for now. He has enough problems to worry about." I was struck by how seriously he spoke, with no desire to amuse, let alone preach, in the tone he would have used to say, "Reduce speed on the left engine" or "You don't need to force the winch so much. Can't you see it's overheating?" What I always found remarkable was that no one, as far as I remember, ever dared to answer Sverre when he placed God outside ordinary tasks, or to respond with the most elementary theological argument that might have occurred to the many sailors who were the sons of ministers, which is quite common in the places we frequented when we were fishermen.

I could mention many other curious personality traits in my companion of so many years, but there will be an opportunity, I hope, to describe a few of them in the course of this story. For now, I will only add that he was one of the most personally fastidious men I've ever known, and despite his seaman's labor, he kept his clothes in impeccable condition. They were simple and unaffected, yet had a distinctive touch of elegance. When we made a port call and had to replace certain items in our wardrobe, it was astonishing to watch him in the stores that specialized in sailors' clothing as he carefully chose a shirt or pair of trousers from the many brought by the sales clerk. The result of this long process of selection was an article whose color and cut were perfect but never pretentious. When he had arrived in Brighton, the first thing that puzzled me was his appearance: without being careless, it revealed a certain diminution in the vigilance to which Sverre normally subjected himself, which was so notable that at expansive moments I would affectionately call him *Beau de la Régence*.

At first I paid no particular attention to the matter, but during our trip to the Breton coast it became clear that this indifference went along with certain reflections, articulated at the most unexpected times and filled with a vague distance, a steady retreat from the things of the world, which began to concern me. I clearly remember one of those conversations—it may have been the first—that set off an inner alarm. We were talking about our fishing expeditions in the Alexander Archipelago and the pittance we had earned after suffering countless deprivations and burning out the diesel engine in our struggles against the ice.

"We'll go back," I said as a kind of consolation, "at a luckier time. There's good fishing in that area, and we've known it for a long time."

"I don't think I'll ever go back, not to the Alexanders or any other place where I'd have to go through what we went through then," Sverre replied with a firmness that awakened my curiosity.

"Well, either the Alexanders or somewhere else that's not so harsh. Where you don't kill yourself with work and then barely make enough to cover expenses," I added.

"There's no need to kill yourself that way. That's not what I'm talking about. Dying is a pact we make with ourselves. The important thing is to know when and how to carry it out, and to be sure it's not a return trip." Sverre spoke with serenity, almost with indifference. But it was clear we were no longer talking about our fishing ventures and that the conversation had taken another direction.

"That's interesting," I remarked, "because I made my pact a long time ago, but I don't think it can be talked about. When these things are said aloud, they begin to smell like melodrama."

"You're right, but I still believe there's a moment when it's an obligation, a question of loyalty, to inform the people we care about that it's time for us to drop out of the game."

"I certainly agree with that, Sverre. It's not so much saying goodbye as letting them know they can no longer count on us. But I don't know why we're talking about this," I said emphatically, trying to discover how far my friend intended to go.

Sverre was thoughtful for a moment, and then he looked at me again with slate-blue eyes that had just lost all their transparency. He clearly wanted to say more with this glance than his words expressed.

"If there's anyone in the world I should talk to about this, it's you," was all he would tell me. "Let's forget it for now, but I want you to understand that you're the only person who'll know how and when I decide to leave this world of shit and its equally foul inhabitants." Without saying another word, he dedicated himself to the consuming task of filling his pipe and looking out at the Breton coast, which he had always found singularly attractive.

It was not the first time I had heard Sverre judge other people so categorically. He was not a man given to mistrust, but neither did he make improvised friendships or have impulsive enthusiasms. "We humans are not the best thing on earth," he said to me one day when we had to sacrifice a magnificent Labrador retriever that had taken sick on board. The words were etched in my mind as a warning and a symptom. But anyone concluding that the Norwegian was an embittered, rancorous soul would be totally mistaken. He was indulgent, and his patience had more than generous limits, but our species, as such, simply held no interest for him, and whatever kind feelings he had were purely the child of his reason, never of a spontaneous humanitarian impulse. In reality, it is not easy to sound a person with these kinds of beliefs, and only long, close dealings with him allowed me to reconcile such contradictory extremes.

When we came ashore in Saint-Malo, it was evident we did not have enough money to live there. We spent a few days looking for work, a task made even more difficult because we lacked the famous *permis de séjour* without which earning a salary in France is unthinkable. Sverre was the first to devise a way around the authorities and obtain the francs we needed to go on waiting for a providential solution. He went to the docks and began unloading a Norwegian ship as if he were one of the crew, and after that he worked the night shift as a replacement for stevedores who failed to show up because of illness or some other reason. A part of his salary, of course, went into the pockets of a foreman who looked the other way. We had taken a room in a pension on the Rue de la Soif, in the midst of the din from bars, taverns, and the fights that broke out all night long, with shouts and curses in every language on earth. Jensen slept during the day while I discreetly made the rounds of cheap cafés and restaurants, searching for a familiar face. What I never suspected was that the solution, at least a temporary one, was right beside us. Next to the pension was a cabaret that advertised the inevitable striptease dancers and a happy hour that lasted from four in the afternoon until eight at night. I don't know what possessed me one afternoon to go into this fairly sordid place, audaciously named The Floating Paradise. I went up to the bar to order a beer and found myself face-to-face with Lev Mason. We hadn't seen each other for years, not since a memorable night in Tangier when, with the help of a fierce fake cognac, we planned a white slave trade between the Caribbean coasts and the brothels of Morocco and Tunis. The next day the immigration authorities invited Lev, rather forcefully, to leave the port, which he was obliged to do immediately without even having time to inform me of his departure. I later learned he was wanted in at least three different countries for crimes that ranged from smuggling arms to falsifying commercial documents in order to avoid paying taxes. Lev was a Belgian national, the son of Jewish parents who had lived in Antwerp since the beginning of the century. Of the many incidents in his tumultuous life, the only one he refused to talk about in detail was his participation in the struggles of the

Jabotinsky neo-Zionists in Palestine. But I know the entire story, and I can assure you it surpasses the most intricate fiction you can imagine. Mason spoke of Jabotinsky as if he were a personal friend. He undoubtedly knew him but not, of course, with the intimacy he boasted of on the rare occasions I heard him recount his experiences as a terrorist in Haifa and other eastern Mediterranean ports. Narrating the subsequent paths taken by Lev Mason would fill a volume with many pages—a catalogue of the most daring stratagems for circumventing the law and waylaying the imprudent on all five continents and the seas that surround them. We met at various times in the course of those years but never undertook any venture together. Lev had a special penchant for carrying out his extraordinary schemes with dynamite and high-power weapons, which has never been my way. There is, in certain people, a kind of will to death, a senseless defiance that leaves no way out and verges on self-destruction. It is certainly true that more than once in my wanderings I have been in danger of perishing, but I have felt no hurry to fall into the nothingness that is, in any case, waiting for me around some corner. I would simply prefer to leave it at that corner instead of constantly provoking it into making an early appearance. A generous spirit, a kind of animal, extravagant goodheartedness, is frequent in men like Lev, and like many of them, he too eventually looked for a peaceful, ordinary harbor in which to end his days. The true heroes of despair and fury appear once every hundred years. They are the ones who achieve a kind of mythic greatness and occupy an exceptional, tragic place in history, becoming permanent archetypes of an inflamed heroism from which there is no escape.

I had previously seen Lev in Martinique, selling electrical appliances in the shop of a paralyzed Hindu, who moved around the store in a wheelchair, growling instructions and complaints in Farsi, which fell on the Herculean shoulders of the old neo-Zionist militant without ever troubling him. Then I happened to meet him in a wretched place with the gleaming, silvery name of La Plata, a hamlet that lay dying on the banks of a great river that emptied into the sea of the Antilles. It consisted of a handful of miserable hovels and a sinister army barracks, where I came very close to breathing my last. Lev arrived on one of the side-wheel boats that still plied the river from the interior down to the flourishing port, which took in all the wealth of the Andean massif. His martial bearing and great, firm mercenary's strides had been reduced to a heap of bones eaten away by fever and hunger. All he had left, in the depths of his green, almost phosphorescent eyes, was that lethal glint, that incandescence found in men who return from sowing death all around them—an intimacy with death that marks them forever. He was working in the galley as a dishwasher, and at night he tended the improvised bar on deck, pouring undrinkable rum and an anise-flavored aguardiente that corroded one's brain. I told him I was negotiating a deal to carry some dubious merchandise on muleback up to the cordillera, and he was very explicit in his warnings:

"Don't get mixed up in that. I have a good idea what it is, and it's not for you. I know what I'm talking about."

If I had listened to him, I would not have gone through an ordeal that planted fear in my belly forever after.

And now, in Saint-Malo, right next door to the miserable room I shared with the good Sverre, there was Lev Mason standing behind a bar lit by garish neon lights, surrounded by an incongruous procession of bottles, glasses, and full-color photographs of naked women in poses that were meant to be sensual but achieved only a soporific mindlessness.

"But, Maqroll, what the hell are you doing here? You must have just come ashore. I have a good single malt Scotch for special customers. We'll drink one right now to celebrate our meeting."

To my surprise, the whiskey was first rate and worth lingering over as we told each other of our travels, following no particular order or plan. He could not believe that for the past few weeks I had been right next door with a Norwegian friend. I told him about our frustrated efforts in Brighton to reestablish ourselves.

"Brighton?" he said in surprise. "That's the last place on earth I would have imagined you treading the asphalt."

From his early days in the synagogue, he had retained the often florid, high-sounding language his people preserve in memory of the land to which Jehovah led them. By the second whiskey, I had told him I was at the end of my rope and had no prospects for finding work. He immediately offered me money, which I refused. I wanted to find out first about his situation and what he was up to. He explained very briefly. He was living with the owner of the bar, a Jew from Nice whose husband had been killed fighting in the international brigades on the Aragón front. In his youth, Lev had been a friend of the husband. Their political beliefs had driven a wedge between them, but he had not lost his warm affection for his old friend. His widow had gotten along very well and saved enough to buy The Floating Paradise with all its fixtures, including the insuperable name. Lev had come there by one of those coincidences that is not coincidence at all but part of the vast, intricate network of itineraries imposed on us since the beginning of time. Then he told me how the place operated: The striptease, certainly improvised and elementary, was a pretext for drawing in sailors who were passing through the venerable Breton port—the cradle of fearful pirates, at times in the service of His Most Christian Majesty, at times in the service of their own purses, and always with no scruples. In The Floating Paradise, the crews of freighters that came, for the most part, from England and Holland had an opportunity to spend some time, have a few drinks, and go to bed with a more than willing woman, who was, of course, obliged to leave a portion of her money in the cabaret till.

At this point a smiling, opulent woman came into the room, wearing her sixty years with truly impressive elegance and authority. Her heavy eyelids and generous chin could not conceal an infallible instinct for judging situations and people, the inheritance of several millennia of diaspora. Lev introduced us, and there was an immediate, undeniable current of sympathy between us. She was called Denise, but something made me think that was not the name given to her at birth. She sat on a stool next to mine and asked Lev to give her whatever I was drinking.

"Well," she said, staring at me with a curiosity that would have seemed childish if she were not so imposing a matron, "at last I have the good luck to meet the legendary Gaviero, the man I've heard so many stories about."

"Lev exaggerates," I protested cautiously. "Compared to his life, mine has been fairly calm and proper."

"If I knew only what Lev had told me, perhaps I would agree. But I've heard about you through other channels, and I think your life and his are comparable if we eliminate the dynamite and the Uzis that made him crazy for so many years."

She evidently had her own information about me, but at that moment I was in no frame of mind to find out more regarding her sources. I preferred to concentrate on the present, which was uncertain enough, at least in my case. I mentioned Sverre Jensen again, and spoke in passing of his work on the docks.

"He ought to give that up right away. It's very dangerous," said Denise in a tone that left no room for doubt. "We'll see what we can do for him. For now, you can tend bar with Lev at night. The work is becoming a little hard for him to handle on his own. We'll take care of your Norwegian friend later. Don't worry about the rent for your room. I own the house, and you must know already what the rooms are used for."

There certainly was a notable coming and going of couples at night, but I had not connected it to the nightclub next door. I also recalled that the porter—an old man in his nineties with a white walrus mustache, who always used an Alpine shepherd's staff that trembled constantly and made it seem as if he were about to fall down at any moment—had referred to the building owner on two occasions, speaking of her as someone who did not tolerate lateness or excuses in paying the weekly rent. When I mentioned him to Denise, she answered with the greatest naturalness: "Yes, he's my father. He's almost a hundred years old, but he doesn't want to stay home and take it easy. He likes tending to the clientele and having conversations all the time about any subject. It keeps him alert."

I thought about the surprise in store for Sverre when he woke to go to work. Denise herself went to tell her father that when the guest in number three came down, he should tell him we were waiting for him in the bar next door, and under no circumstances should he leave without seeing us first. A new bottle of malt whiskey replaced the one we had emptied, and the three of us went on trying to place pieces in the complex puzzle of an irremediable past.

Jensen came in around eight, with his huge, brawny body and his bony, ill-shaped Viking face, which still showed traces of the sleep he could not shake off. By then I was behind the bar and beginning to serve the early patrons, with Lev beside me whispering the location of the glasses and bottles I needed for each order. It was obvious that some of the stock was meant for special customers, and I learned this immediately. Denise, still on her stool, her back to us, was checking the arrival of the first women, who greeted her with a slight inclination of the head and went to sit at their usual tables. Sverre looked at me but showed no surprise. On the contrary, it was as if he were witnessing something he had foreseen and was now watching materialize in the normal course of events. I introduced him to the owners and briefly told him about my long-standing friendship with Lev.

"Before I go down to the docks, I'd really like to have a drink with you." He had just had a whiff of the whiskey in my glass, and it met with his unreserved approval.

"You're not going down to any docks, my friend," said Denise. "I invite you to stay here and finish this bottle of malt whiskey that has been waiting for the two of you for many months now."

Sverre did not know how to respond and looked at her, taken aback by so much authority in so new an acquaintance.

"And who'll pay for the room if I don't work? Unless Maqroll is going to earn as much behind that bar as I do on the docks. But I don't believe in those kinds of miracles." Sverre found himself lost in a confusion that threatened his impassivity.

I signaled to him that we'd talk later and that for now he should obey our friend, who came to my aid, putting the matter definitively to rest.

"Look, Jensen. You don't know what you risk by working on the docks this way. The union here is no tea party, and early one morning they'll find you floating in the bay, with a hook through your heart."

Sverre accepted her words with a resignation that puzzled me. He drank his Scotch with slow relish and poured another without even looking at us again. We said nothing for a long time, and Denise went to tell something to a couple of girls who had just settled down at a table near the entrance. Lev glanced occasionally at Sverre from the corner of his eye and then regarded me with an expression that indicated a certain sympathy for my friend's silence. Jensen finally looked up at us as if he were waking from a deep sleep and said in a dull but firm voice:

"I've seen this coming for a long time. Now I know: It's the end of our fishing expeditions in the North Pacific, the end of the sea, the end of our perpetual struggle against the elements, which always win in the end. And do you know something? For a long time I've also known that I never liked the work. The ocean is a monotonous, intractable, cruel enemy, and we never should have had anything to do with it. Maqroll understands this, and from time to time he returns to land even though it's just a different slavery, with other demons. At bottom it's all the same, I know that now, but at least he's found a way not to be crushed by the monstrous tedium that always turns its back on us, for which we are no more than contemptible, intrusive specks of dust. I'll stay here for now. Then we'll see. But I'll never go back to sea, do you hear, Maqroll? Never. Thank you, Lev, and thanks to Denise too. You haven't opened my eyes exactly, they were already open, but you have lit up the stage and let me see clearly. Cheers."

He drained the glass of whiskey he had just poured. His face showed no tension or uneasiness. He was deep in that serenity to which his forebears turned after their ferocious incursions on the Continent. He gave the impression of having appropriated an order of things from which he would never emerge. In his eyes an occasional spark indicated the awful power of the forces that were taking their rightful places in his soul after years of rankling, unrelieved rebellion.

Sverre, of course, did not return to the docks. He spent a good part of the days sitting on the edge of the walls that surround the old city, looking at the ocean and watching the tide come in every afternoon as if it were a novel operation on which his destiny depended. I did not bother to tell him that at the tip of a small peninsula, on a promontory that by the end of the day was separated from the mainland as if it were an island, Chateaubriand, a writer who has been one of my most constant companions, lay buried. It would mean nothing to him, and all the Viscount's doubts and perplexities, tempestuous convictions and passions, would have left him indifferent.

At night, he would join us at The Floating Paradise and slowly drink one glass of rum after the other. The malt whiskey had soon given out, and we had changed to rum so as not to put a burden on the small profits earned at the club. Lev took a great interest in Sverre and kept watch over his reactions with a mixture of affection and uneasiness. They became good friends but barely spoke to each other. I continued to help behind the bar, washing the glasses and keeping a supply of ice as well as the other ingredients needed to mix the infrequent cocktails that patrons would occasionally ask for. Whenever I protested that I had to make some decision regarding the immediate future, Lev and Denise in unison would tell me to forget about that, to let the days go by and not put pressure on destiny.

"Don't worry about the room, please," explained Denise. "If I ever need it I'll just ask you for the key and put it to use while you two wait down here. Everything will come in its time; there's no rush."

I don't know if she was aware of how much truth her words contained. One night, a few weeks after he left the docks, Jensen said imperturbably:

"I have enough money to buy a passage to Bergen. I'm going to take the first freighter headed in that direction. I'll stay at the

Seamen's Shelter in Bergen, and I'll be in touch with you from there." He continued drinking his rum with meticulous slowness, his gaze lost in the mirrors that repeated the ill-assorted collection of bottles in every color.

He made this announcement with so much conviction that none of us dared make any comment. Denise walked away, shaking her head to indicate that it was hopeless, and went to sit at a table with two slender black girls recently arrived from equatorial Africa. Lev and I cleaned the glasses with automatic gestures and were silent for a long time. When Sverre said good night and went up to the room, Lev remarked in a quiet voice:

"Our friend is running on empty. I mean, he's out of reasons to continue swimming against the current, which is what you and I persist in doing, the devil knows how or why. I've blown up the earth in the four corners of the world, and I've shot a good deal of lead into anonymous bodies that I really did not care about. I know when the fuel gives out and you begin to live as if you were floating over the abyss. You and I just keep going on as if nothing had happened. For others it means the end of the line."

There was nothing to say; his words were an accurate summary of our situation and Jensen's.

A few days later a freighter on its way from the Cantabrian coast to Bergen before crossing the Atlantic to Montreal, came into port. Sverre took his leave of Lev and Denise with firm, silent handshakes. At the door he turned to look at them and said with a huge smile and an expansive wave of his hand:

"Thank you, thank you for everything. I won't forget you."

I accompanied him to the ship. At the foot of the gangplank he looked at me as if seeing me for the first time and gave me a warm embrace. He muttered a few incomprehensible words, walked on board with slow, almost majestic steps, and did not turn around. I saw him disappear down one of the passageways on the bridge, his seaman's bag on his shoulder.

I lived in Saint-Malo for two months, helping Lev and having long conversations with Denise, whose proven wisdom occasionally left me perplexed. One night I went out to buy a few bottles of gin at a small supermarket that stayed open all night. A fight broke out among some sailors in the cabaret, and when I walked in, the police had already taken away the most belligerent. Vincas Blekaitis was leaning against the bar, using a handkerchief to stanch the blood flowing from a cut on his left cheekbone. I went over to try to help him, and all he could think of to say was:

"You missed a good one this time, Gaviero. I couldn't control my men, and three of them are sure to spend some time in jail. Two were seriously hurt. And what the hell are you doing here?"

Vincas, of course, had been the captain on various freighters owned by Abdul Bashur and me. He was a Lithuanian, with an experience at sea the likes of which I have rarely known. I explained my situation and introduced him to Denise and Lev, who were observing the scene, intrigued. Denise took Vincas to a small office behind the bar, where she treated and bandaged his wound. He came back and drank down several glasses of vodka, one after the other. Vincas was captain on a freighter that traded along the coast from Lisbon to Hamburg. It was owned by some Portuguese shipbuilders who had hired Vincas two years earlier and were apparently very satisfied with his services.

Blekaitis invited me on board the ship, where he offered me a job with duties that were not very specific. I was happy to accept, and I went back to say goodbye to my friends.

"Since you'll pass here every time you sail up to Hamburg, we'll see you often. I won't press you to stay because I know there's no point. Take care of yourself, and come back soon." Denise's words were accompanied by resounding kisses on my cheeks, while her eyes filled with tears. Lev threw his arm around my shoulder and walked with me to the door. He took his leave with a quiet "*Shalom ve lehitraot*" and went back inside, not saying another word.

The years I spent working with Blekaitis immediately preceded my settling in Pollensa as watchman at some abandoned shipyards on the outskirts of the port. During my first few weeks with Vincas, I could not get the thought of Sverre Jensen out of my mind. My friendship with him had a peculiar characteristic: its direct and exclusive connection to our life at sea. Very close, always cordial, it was based on a mutual understanding of our often opposite ways of understanding life and our relationships to other people. On land our conversation would gradually dry up, but this did not affect our friendship. It was as if we set off in opposite directions when we were away from the sea, but our affection remained intact and reappeared the moment we were sailing together again. During the long periods we spent on land, Jensen would take refuge in some port in his country, and I would resume my customary wanderings, looking for a way to satisfy the nomadic restlessness that has marked my days for as long as I can remember.

Jensen's final words in Saint-Malo left a desolate, bitter taste in my mouth, an ominous premonition. My fears were soon confirmed. Less than six months later, our ship stopped in Saint-Malo for repairs to the engine that would extend its life a little longer. The first thing I did when I came ashore was to go to The Floating Paradise. After Denise's maternal embraces, Lev handed me an envelope: It was addressed to me and had Norwegian stamps postmarked in Bergen. His gray, inexpressive face boded nothing good. I put the letter in my jacket pocket, and Lev said in a muted voice:

"You'd better read it now. Go into the office—you won't be disturbed there."

I closed the door of the small cubicle they called their office. Sverre's letter was written in English, the language we spoke to each other. I recognized the simple, severe handwriting he had learned in school and never changed. The letter's direct, almost telegraphic style concealed the piercing grief of a final farewell. This is what it said:

My dear Maqroll:

I've decided to take my life. I wouldn't explain the reasons for this decision, which I don't think can be of interest to anyone, if it weren't for you, whom I have always considered my best and—why not accept it?—my only friend. I've been thinking about suicide for many years. Even in my adolescence I daydreamed about the idea. It's evident that my life at sea, the only one I could imagine, has come to an end. We've talked about this on countless occasions. You have the capacity to adapt, for a time at least, to life on land, even though in the end you always find your way back to the coast and board the first ship that will take you. I've never had that ability. On land I have too much time, I'm overwhelmed by a boredom that eventually paralyzes me. But this isn't really the main reason for my suicide. Even if I had another chance to go to sea, I know that for a long time I've been storing up something I can only define as a weariness with being alive, with having to choose between one thing and another, with listening to people around me talk about things that basically don't interest them, that they really know nothing about. The foolishness of our fellow humans knows no bounds, my dear Gaviero. If it didn't sound absurd, I'd say I'm leaving because I can't stand the noise the living make. You're the only one who understands what I'm saying. We've never talked about our friendship. One of the reasons is that from our first voyage together (do you remember the fishing expedition off Tierra del Fuego, its disastrous end in the port of Aysén, the Englishman you had to kill—you shot him three times—because he was going to take everything and leave us stranded there with just the clothes on our backs?), I think we've known how to communicate without needing words. It's obvious that the things that really concern us and determine our destiny are not to be talked about. And words won't help me now to say goodbye. A provisional goodbye, because as long as you live I know you'll think sometimes about old Sverre and the dangers, the problems, the failures, and the brief successes we shared on almost all the seas of the world. Do you know when I realized that my vague flirtation with suicide was taking concrete, definitive form? One night in Vancouver, in Cass Montague's tavern, after we broke all the glass in the bar and I don't know how many chairs, and had chased everyone out of the place, we sat facing each other while Cass tore at the few hairs he had left and could not understand what had happened. You looked at me, and with a seriousness I know very well and that you keep for very rare occasions and people, you said: "Jensen, if we were consistent, considering what we feel deep inside about all this, about life, we'd have to put a bullet in our brains right now. But we won't. Tomorrow we'll go back to the ship and hunt for tuna, but in the end it won't do us any good, because that isn't where these things are settled." Then you were silent until the police came and locked us up for four days. The lawyers took everything we had earned on the last fishing trip. I wasn't as drunk as you, and those words remained etched in my brain until today, when I've decided to make them mine, and go.

It would be foolish to put any responsibility on your shoulders. If I'm telling you this it's because, long before you said what you did in Vancouver, I had made the decision, deep inside me, not to endure past a certain limit—vague, perhaps, with regard to the proper time but totally reasoned and definitive. I

*also want to tell you that the person who finally clarified for me
the few reasons that were still not apparent, that lay hidden in
some corner of my soul, crouched and ready to spring to the surface, was your friend Lev. He and I never spoke about this, but
I'm aware that from the first moment we saw each other, Lev
knew I was traveling this road. His wife, Denise, knew as well.
I repeat, and you know it better than anyone: These things are
not talked about.*

*Well, Maqroll of all the demons, enough speeches. I'm going,
and I'm grateful to life for allowing our paths to cross. That's all.
Keep wandering the world. I know you'll choose another way
out. Whatever it may be, I'll be waiting on the other side so you
can tell me about your departure. It's the only thing I'm curious
about in this world that I'm leaving with no regrets but also
with no hope of finding anything on the other shore. Goodbye,
Gaviero, or see you soon—who knows? That doesn't matter
either.*

Sverre

I read the letter several times and was still holding it when I
went back to Lev and Denise.

"He killed himself, didn't he?" said Lev with a certainty that
bewildered me.

"How do you know?" I asked, handing him the letter, which
he passed on to Denise without reading it.

"As soon as he walked through that door, I knew he would."

"He says that in the letter. You should read it too."

"I will, in a moment. Do you know something? I envy Jensen.
I'll never follow his example; I've never thought of doing that, no
matter how awful the trials I've gone through. But I envy him.
There's something clean and simple in his action, and I admire
that."

Denise gave the letter to Lev, who read it, nodding his head
frequently in agreement with Sverre's words. He returned it to
me and made no comment. I drank the vodka that Denise
poured for me, and then I said goodbye.

I was at the door when Lev called to me.

"Maqroll!"

I turned to hear what he had to say.

"No, it's nothing," said Lev. "Go on tossing from place to place like a ship without a pilot. It's another way of doing what Jensen did."

"Yes, it is the same," I said, and walked into the nocturnal labyrinth of Saint-Malo's narrow streets, heading for the port, where the ship was waiting to leave at dawn.

A True History of the Encounters and Complicities of Maqroll the Gaviero and the Painter Alejandro Obregón

To the memory of Micho, Michín, and
Orifiel, and for Miruz and Mishka, who
accompany and protect us with their
remote, masterful wisdom

*We brought with us only time to live between
the lightning and the wind.*

Eugenio Montejo

Non, non, pas aquérir. Voyager pour t'ap-
pauvrir. Voilà ce dont tu as besoin.

Henri Michaux

I was in Madrid, enjoying a fino sherry at the bar of the Hotel
Wellington, an establishment I have always liked. I used to
stay there in better days so as to be close to Retiro Park, whose
agreeable fin de siècle tranquillity has a soothing, evocative effect
on me. I was absorbed in searching out, at the edge of things, that
golden light of a Madrid afternoon, which seems to leave every-

thing suspended in midair, verifying once again that I was in the place that had been the frontier of Al-Andalus.

Suddenly an iron arm seized me from behind, and I was immobilized, unable to speak. The brush of a large Franz Josef mustache against the back of my neck revealed the identity of my attacker. "What the hell are you doing here?" he said as he released me, and I turned to confirm my suspicions. It was Alejandro Obregón. "Damn! I had no idea you were in Madrid," he protested, sitting beside me and ordering a fino as well. His slate-blue eyes scrutinized me with the curiosity typical of our friends who are painters as they try to detect in others the passage of time. We had not seen one another for five or six years. Alejandro, powerful and intense, was trying as discreetly as possible, during the first moments of our meeting, to break the trammels of his shyness, an effort that was one of the most affecting and constant signs of our long friendship. It is important to know that behind several layers of libertinism, which convinced no one, Obregón concealed one of the most gentle-mannered men I have ever known.

A short while later several of Alejandro's friends came in, among them the bullfighter Pepe Dominguín. Our conversation became general and turned inevitably to the topic of the day: the death of a young bullfighter, at the height of his glory, who had been gored in a town in Andalusia. Alejandro and his wife were flying to Colombia at midnight. Carmen and I had just arrived and were preparing our second trip to Galicia to visit the Apostle. At the edge of the desultory, fairly vapid talk—only natural among people who have just met—Alejandro and I tried to catch up on each other's lives in the old, always renewed stream of common memories, experiences, and affections that have united us for so many years, but it was impossible. The subject of bullfights continued to dominate with overwhelming insistence. Suddenly, with a word he let fall during a brief silence, I realized he wanted to tell me something that had no connection to this conversation. The certainty grew more and more intense. At last we both stood, almost at the same time, asked the others to excuse us, and moved to another table. With no preamble, Obregón said:

"Life is so strange. For the past few weeks I've been wanting to talk to you, but I never dreamed it would happen so soon. I have to tell you something you'll find very interesting. This kind of thing happens only to us. Listen carefully; it's a long story, and every detail is important. This will bowl you over: Almost a year ago, I met a friend of yours in Cartagena—an unforgettable individual. You've written things about him that once seemed strange to me, but now I think they don't go far enough. You've guessed who it is, haven't you? I was with Maqroll the Gaviero."

I must confess that of all the possible chance combinations about which I often speculate, this meeting had never occurred to me. But now that Obregón was telling me it had, their encounter suddenly seemed absolutely logical and predictable, and I was only surprised it had taken so long. In an instant I could see clearly all the characteristics the two men shared, as well as the profound differences that separated them. I told him all this very quickly, while he scrutinized me, like a smiling inquisitor, with those blue eyes that turned violet and distant when they regarded something closely. We still had a few hours at our disposal, and with a dearth of courtesy we forgot our companions at the other table, and our wives observing us with amusement and curiosity, and became totally submerged in the story of an encounter that, in a certain sense, completed the spiral design of our lives. Relating the episode in Obregón's words would mean becoming lost in intricate sandbanks of outrageous exclamations, indecipherable stammerings, and asides that ended in Homeric laughter. Although I run the risk that the tale may lose much of its color and flavor, I have resigned myself to transcribing it in a form the reader can follow.

Very late one night, Obregón drove some guests to the hotel where they were staying in Cartagena. It was frankly naive to think about a cab: The husband had made so many toasts with Tres Esquinas rum that he could no longer fend for himself, and the wife, a half-Hindu, half-Irish Panamanian, had begun a series of rather salacious confessions regarding her past as a chorus girl in Bremen. Alejandro put them in his Land-Rover with the patience only serious drinkers can show to those who are not, and left them, passably sober, in the lobby of their hotel. As he drove back along a dimly lit street with an unsavory reputation because of its proximity to the red-light district, he saw two men attacking a third, who had a noticeable limp and was defending himself with the weariness of someone who is at a distinct disadvantage. Alejandro stopped the jeep and turned the headlights full on the three men. He climbed down, prepared to rescue the man from his attackers, but when they saw him charging with all the force of a bull trapped inside the gestures and features of an official of imperial Vienna, they fled into the darkness of the nearby alleyways. Obregón helped the man into his car and, without knowing why, spoke to him in French, asking where he wanted to go. The man answered in the same language, explaining that he was the bos'n on a tanker anchored at the docks and that as he was leaving a miserable brothel, the two thugs had followed him, offering to change his dollars at a suspiciously high rate.

"But I don't know," he said, "why we're talking in French. I've spoken Spanish for so long that I think of it as my own language." Then he suggested finding a bar and having a drink together. Obregón said that nothing was open and invited him to his house, where they could wait for daylight since it was too late to think about sleeping. The other man was happy to accept and introduced himself with a quick, strange smile that seemed out of place.

"My name is Maqroll, Maqroll the Gaviero."

Obregón stared at him, suspecting a joke, but the man continued to smile.

"Well, I know who you are," replied Alejandro. "I know your name. An old friend of mine has narrated some episodes of your life in books that have not met with much success but which I enjoy."

Obregón introduced himself in turn. When he said he was a painter, the other man shrugged with resigned acceptance, as if to say, "That's all I needed." With some difficulty, Maqroll climbed the steep stairs leading to the main floor of the large house located on Calle de la Factoría. "I'm still suffering the effects of a spider bite that almost put my leg out of commission. It had closed, but now, after my trying to fight off those two, I think it's opened again."

With the first glass of rum the conversation began to flow between these two old veterans of life's adventures and narrow escapes, and the ancient craft of human tenderness.

Alejandro could not remember the exact ground over which the thread of confidences unwound, but he did recall clearly that Maqroll suddenly began to tell him about the cats of Istanbul. Sharing his guest's interest and being a longtime believer in the secret knowledge possessed by these felines, Obregón listened with the attention that alcohol awakens in those who know how to negotiate with it and determine its status.

"The cats of Istanbul," explained the Gaviero, "possess absolute wisdom. They exercise complete control over the life of the city, but they are so prudent and secretive that the inhabitants are still not aware of the fact. The phenomenon must date from the time of Constantinople and the Eastern Empire. I'll tell you why: I've made a careful study of the routes taken by the cats. They start out at the port and, with no deviation, always follow what were once the outer limits of the imperial palace. These no longer exist, at least visibly, because the Turks built houses and opened streets in what had been the sacred precincts of those anointed by the Theotokos. The cats, however, instinctively know these perimeters, and every night they walk them, going in and out of the structures raised by infidels. Then they proceed to the end of the Golden Horn and rest for a while in the ruins of the palace of the Blaquernas. At dawn, they return to the port to check on the ships that have come in and to verify the departure of those that are leaving the docks. Now, the unsettling thing is that if you bring in a cat from another country and set it loose in the port of Istanbul, that same night the newcomer unhesitatingly follows the ritual path. This means that cats all over the world retain in their prodigious memories the plans of the noble capital of the Comnenos and the Paleologos. I have not told this to anyone, because the imbecility of people is immeasurable and there are secrets that should not be disclosed. But my familiarity with the cats of Istanbul goes even further. Whenever I land there, some old feline friends are waiting for me, and from the moment I come ashore until I walk up the gangplank to leave, they follow me everywhere. Two of them respond to the names I have given them: Orifiel and Miruz. It would take too long to enumerate all the hidden corners these two friends have revealed to me, but each is intimately related to the history of Byzantium. I can tell you some of them: the place where Andronicus Comnenus was tortured; where the last emperor, Constantine XI Palaeologus, fell dead; the house in which Empress Zoe was possessed by a Saxon who had been ordered to put out her eyes; the site where the monks of the Holy Trinity defined the doctrine that cannot be named and cut out one another's tongues so the secret would never be revealed; where Constantine Copronymus spent a night of penance for having harbored impure desires for his mother's body; where German mercenaries took the secret vow that bound them to their gods; the mooring of the first Venetian trireme that brought the algid plague. And I could list many other places that shelter the hidden soul of the city and were shown to me by my two feline companions."

Obregón understood as no one else could the Gaviero's interest in cats, and he in turn told Maqroll about some of the prodigies he had witnessed in Cartagena, involving the cats who occasionally visited his studio. Among them, the Roman cat who became frantic the day the painter began a sketch on canvas of an angel turning his back to the viewer, and the cat who jumped and somersaulted in a very strange way whenever he heard the name of the archbishop and viceroy Caballero y Góngora. When morning came, the friendship between the two recent acquaintances had become as close as if they had known each other for years. Maqroll prepared the kind of coffee a sailor drinks before a difficult watch, and they sipped it slowly, not saying very much. Walking down the stairs was even more onerous for the Gaviero than the ascent. They said goodbye at the door. Maqroll refused Alejandro's offer to drive him to the port.

"You'll be hearing from me," he said as he left. "Before the ship sails I'll come by so we can talk some more," and he limped away to find a cab. The painter became absorbed in pondering the things that happen to people when they know how to be loyal to the arduous weaving of a true friendship.

I interrupted my friend at this point to tell him that the most recent news I had about our comrade was not very reassuring. He had gone on some senseless adventure up the Xurandó and had become involved in problems with the army, a conflict from which he was saved through the providential intervention of a Middle Eastern embassy and the positive feelings he had awakened in a member of military intelligence, who agreed to drop the case. But there were still more surprises waiting for me that afternoon in the Wellington bar. Obregón folded his arms across his chest, a characteristic gesture when he was about to reveal something that concerned him deeply, and said:

"No, that isn't the end of the story. We just sailed together on a mad trip between Curaçao and Cartagena."

At my expression of astonishment, he agreed to tell me about the episode in all its details. There was still time before we had to leave for Barajas Airport. Our wives had gone up to our rooms to inspect the purchases they had made in Madrid. Pepe Dominguín and his group had discreetly disappeared. We remained loyal to the fino; it began to fill us with that knowing warmth in which everything glides to a rhythm from the Omayyad caliphate.

Before his ship left Cartagena, the Gaviero came to Obregón's house to say goodbye. A complicity had been created between them, the complicity of those whom life has subjected to uncommon trials and who know, better than most, the hidden springs that move the uncertain mechanism which the naive call chance. They drank a couple of bottles of the colorless rum that Obregón liked to compare, in my opinion somewhat carelessly, to vodka, and returned to the subject of the cats of Istanbul. Alejandro countered with his story of the pelicans who lost their way. Maqroll let the matter pass, aware he was dealing with someone to whom such a thing might well have happened, and told two equally improbable tales regarding seagulls. When they parted, they promised to keep each other informed about their wanderings. Several months went by, and Alejandro had already catalogued his encounter with the Gaviero along with other extraordinary events of his past, when he happened to run into him, again by chance, in Curaçao. He was looking for a restaurant where lunch would consist of something other than the eternal Chinese menu that was horrifyingly and fraudulently monotonous. He had been told about a place that specialized in Indonesian cooking, and when he walked in, there was the Gaviero, trying to improve an unconvincing old-fashioned with improbable additions. They said hello as if they had seen each other the day before, and decided to venture onto the reefs of a somewhat improvised Malaysian cuisine. They ate fewer than half the dishes served to them, and turned to bourbon and ginger ale so they would not proceed blindly along the venerable path of intoxication. This was when Maqroll the Gaviero made the tempting offer that almost changed forever my friend's destiny as a painter.

"Come with me on the *Lisselotte Elsberger*," he said. "We're returning to Cartagena by way of Aruba. I promise you'll enjoy yourself. The captain, a Prussian from Kiel, was a submarine commander during the First World War and lost a leg at the battle of Skagerrak. He has an endless repertoire of sea stories and a few from land, none of them particularly edifying. If you have to go back to Cartagena, there's no reason not to travel with us."

Obregón did not hesitate for an instant, and after stopping at his hotel to pick up his clothes and two boxes of Dutch paints that he had bought in Curaçao, he went down to the docks with the Gaviero. The *Lisselotte Elsberger* was anchored there, in urgent need of a painting. They boarded but did not see the captain, because he was taking an apparently interminable siesta. There was an empty bunk in the Gaviero's cabin, and Alejandro stowed his gear. They went back on deck and began walking from one end to the other, trying to ignore the stink of gasoline that polluted the air.

"When we weigh anchor, the wind makes it more tolerable," commented Maqroll, not insisting too much. Obregón said that the smell of paints and solvents had been with him for most of his life. Gasoline was not too different. At nightfall, the captain appeared on deck. He was a giant, two meters tall, who managed his artificial leg with great skill and spoke all the languages of the world with a slight German accent. He had the equine, clean-shaven face of an officer of the kaiser, and an indulgent, weary smile that gave him an ecclesiastical air. His hard-won astuteness was concentrated in his eyes, where innumerable experiences, transgressions, compromises, things forgotten, and things remembered were carefully stored. His eyes were a vague coffee color and moved restlessly under wild, bushy brows and long, almost feminine lashes. Never resting on a fixed point, they seemed to examine people and objects with constant, feverish interest. His name was Karl von Choltitz, and he said he was a distant cousin of the Nazi general who claimed to have saved Paris at the last moment from being blown up. After a few polite phrases, the captain asked Obregón to excuse Maqroll. They were preparing to weigh anchor. The ship was carrying a heavy cargo that reached above the flotation line, and the operation demanded a great deal of care. Obregón stayed on deck, watching the sun set over Curaçao and wondering why he had ever accepted such a stupid invitation. But his old instinct for not interfering with the indecipherable decrees of fate allowed him to contemplate the incursion of night as it started to fade the motley festival of colors that ranged from blood red to the most delicate orange. He was reminded of the landscapes on the tins of Huntley Palmers biscuits that he had known as a boy in pre-Nazi Berlin. The voyage began without incident. The ship glided, slow and somnolent, through the waters of a calm sea. The sound of a bell brought him back to reality, and he saw Maqroll beckoning to him from the bridge to come and have supper in the captain's quarters.

Nothing could have been more bereft of personal, intimate details than Captain von Choltitz's cabin. No family photographs, no view of his native city, nothing that would bring back memories of the past. Two old maps of the Caribbean and a signal chart were the only objects on the walls. This produced a singular disquiet in Obregón; it was like an external emptiness that reflected another bottomless, internal void in a soul that had turned the past into a blank slate. But what most attracted his attention was the sight of a large Viennese silver bowl on the small serving table, surrounded by matching trays of silver that held appealing canapés of black bread and the most exquisite salmon, herring, caviar, smoked trout, tuna, and sea urchin. The captain indicated the seats where his guests were to sit and then began a ceremony that increased Alejandro's astonishment. He uncorked a bottle of prestigious French champagne and began to pour it into the bowl, while with his other hand he poured in a bottle of German lager beer and then a second, emptying it and the champagne bottle at the same time. He then handed round crystal cups with handles in the shape of heraldic wings and invited them to drink with the courteous gesture of a Junker. Maqroll signaled to his friend that this ritual was customary and should not surprise him. And so began a long night of memories and anecdotes to which each of them contributed the best of his repertoire. The bowl was regularly refilled by the captain, who showed no sign of weariness, let alone intoxication. They went to bed at first light. At about eleven in the morning the ceremony was resumed, and it lasted until dusk and began again late that night, after they had attended to certain necessary duties. Not one of the three, obviously, gave any sign of inebriation.

Four consecutive days of this treatment visibly confirmed the previously latent affinities and similarities between Obregón and the Gaviero, and revived for von Choltitz the better days of his career at sea. The captain, in the euphoria brought on by long sessions of nostalgia and drink, invited Obregón to travel with them during the period of a two-year contract in the Mediterranean, transporting fuel between Algeria and Corsica. Alejandro spent the whole night toying with the idea. They reached Aruba, where the *Lisselotte Elsberger* spent a day loading on airplane fuel bound for Cartagena. The three men, united by the atmosphere of evocations and rigorous testing of their resistance to the deadly cocktail, did not even bother to go ashore. When they dropped anchor at the Mamonal docks in Cartagena, Alejandro, in a moment of lucidity and aspirin, managed courteously to decline von Choltitz's offer. As Obregón stammered complex excuses, the Gaviero gently nodded his head, approving his friend's decision. He had learned to admire his painting, feeling curiously close to it because it revealed the profoundest depths of his own spirit. He accompanied Obregón to his house, where they made their farewells after dispatching a bottle of island rum purchased in

Curaçao. "When I told him I had known you for many years," Alejandro said as he finished his story, "he asked me to give you his best if I saw you and tell you he would send you some papers in which he describes certain episodes in his life as a miner in the cordillera, which you don't know much about. He also said he could never understand your interest in his wanderings, which he finds obscure, routine, and extremely ordinary. That's what he said."

At this point Alejandro's wife came to the table to say that if they did not leave immediately they would miss the plane. Obregón sat for a moment, absorbed, staring into that indeterminate, desolate distance where he took refuge when life assailed him with demands he found unacceptable but to which he acceded with the wisdom of a medieval rabbi, an inheritance from his Catalonian forebears. We said goodbye with our usual warm embrace.

As might be expected, Alejandro's revelation of his encounter with Maqroll the Gaviero was to have consequences that would be felt before long. Two individuals with such sharply defined and uncommon natures cannot cross paths without leaving behind a train of planets in disorder. Months after our meeting in the Wellington bar, a thick envelope postmarked in Manila was delivered to my house. It contained a detailed but capriciously ordered account of the Gaviero's life as a prospector, and a long letter in which he brought me up-to-date regarding his current whereabouts and the usual misfortunes of his nomadic, unpredictable life. He spoke of Alejandro in two long passages. I cannot resist the temptation of transcribing them here. They complement and significantly enrich the story of this friendship in which, as always when it comes to Maqroll, I play the rather thankless role of simple intermediary. The first fragment reads as follows:

* * *

And so I decided to spend some time in Kuala Lumpur. I stayed in the house of a woman who made funeral incense and perfumes for religious ceremonies. She awakened immediate curiosity in me. I had been put in touch with her by a motorman from Singapore, with whom I maintained an amicable relationship that developed on two very different planes. We would drink palm wine with absinthe at a clandestine bar on the outskirts of the city, frequented by English and Scandinavian

*tourists looking for exotic sensations. I don't know if their
curiosity was satisfied, but I am certain that our desire to have
relations with white women was amply met. Long, continual
contact with Asian women tends to cause a kind of surfeit that
leads to coldness. On the other hand, Malacca Jack—that was
his name—would pick me up when he was driving his streetcar,
invite me to sit beside him, and chat while he followed his daily
route. He was an indefatigable conversationalist, he knew the
deepest secrets of the city and its inhabitants, and the trolley ride
became an extremely diverting and instructive experience. When
I told him I was going to Kuala Lumpur for an improbable
trade in teakwood that had been proposed by a dubious, elusive
Portuguese with the even more suspect name of Fernando Fer-
reira de Loanda, Malacca Jack recommended that I visit Khalitan and mention his name. She too turned out to be an endless
source of information about the life and miracles of her compatriots, a secretive people if ever there was one, with dangerous con-
volutions in their character that one must know thoroughly
before having any dealings with them. As you might expect, we
ended up in bed, where she always used a Malaysian dialect
and could not articulate a single word in any of the other languages she spoke with relative fluency. One day, when she
returned from the sumptuous funeral of a multimillionaire who
was the capo of a gang involved in smuggling archaeological
treasures, she told me that through the smoke from the incense
used in interminable propitiatory rites, she had seen the face of a
white man with blue eyes and a heavy mustache that grew into
the reddish sideburns of an artilleryman. He appeared and disappeared in the heavy funeral smoke, shouting the wildest, most
brutal curses in English and in some language that resembled
Spanish but also sounded like French. "I thought he said your
name," said Khalitan, who was both intrigued and mocking,
"but when I approached him he ran away, leaping as if he were
being exorcised." I immediately asked her to take me to the
funeral site so I could search the area for the individual in question. Something told me I knew him very well. Those blue eyes,
that Franz Josef mustache and sideburns, the exclamations in
English and Catalan—a language my friend could not identify
but which she described with some accuracy—could belong to
only one person. At first Khalitan refused to accede to my
request. The idea seemed absurd: The ceremony had ended several hours before, and the district was an area with large, preten-*

tious estates, empty parks, and no commercial life. I insisted, managed to convince her, and we set out; the place was just as she described: desolate avenues lined with great trees offering perpetual, humid shade, endless fences surrounding semiwild gardens, and behind them the most unexpected structures in the most inappropriate styles, ranging from antebellum mansions from the southern United States, to Tudor houses with slanting roofs waiting for a snowfall that was inconceivable in the oven heat of the tropics, to California Spanish, Hollywood Moorish, and Art Deco buildings stained by rain and the resins dripping from the lush vegetation. We went up and down several identical streets in Khalitan's rickety cart, while she tried to accelerate the gait of the patient, skeptical burro that pulled the wagon with an exasperating lack of conviction. "Only the mad Gaviero could think up something like this," she scolded me. "We won't find your friend around here—we won't find a living soul. I'd like to know what you're going to say to the first police patrol that pulls us over."

Not five minutes after Khalitan's fatal premonition, an old Ford painted the green and gold colors of the police stopped us. But instead of asking questions, the officers opened the door, and, like a jack-in-the-box, out sprang a madman, his face streaked with the red and blue clay used in Kuala Lumpur by those attending a funeral ceremony, who bellowed, "Cullons, nano, you shit-eating Maqroll! Are you going to leave me in the clutches of these yellow men who stink of rotten fish?" Just as I feared, it was Alejandro Obregón, left behind when he was supposed to change planes. The reason for the mishap depicts him perfectly: He had been trying to seduce a Bengali nurse who was stoically waiting in the airport bar for the arrival of an Air India plane. Obregón climbed into the cart. I introduced him to my friend and mentioned how she earned her living. "Perfect!" Alejandro remarked. "Nothing could be better or more appropriate. I'd like you to burn those essences for me; they produce marvelous colors." I had already told Khalitan about Obregón, how we had met in Cartagena, and about our trip on the Lisselotte Elsberger. *Still, she observed him with a look of astonishment on her face. Alejandro, with the dandy's gallantry he displayed from time to time, attempted an even more outlandish explanation. "My dear girl," he said to her, "when I saw the funeral procession go past the Air France offices, where I was trying to arrange my passage, I couldn't help following it and leaving everything else for later. The shades of priests' vestments and the red, green, and orange hues of your incense simply dazzled me. Anything in those colors cannot take place without obliging us to follow the procession to its final consequences. I painted my face with clay offered to me by a girl who was walking at the foot of the widow, and I joined the mourners, repeating the gestures I saw them making all around me. From time to time a man in a toad mask painted with saffron and sky-blue spots came up to me and had me drink a kind of syrup that tasted of cinnamon and sandalwood. It made me phenomenally drunk, but I think we were all in the same state. Since Maqroll had sent me a postcard from this city, I decided to invoke him in every language I know. When the funeral was over, I fell asleep under an enormous mango tree that almost hides the entrance to the dead man's house. That's where the police picked me up. What a bunch they are! They have the really dangerous cruelty of a mild-mannered reptile. Well, as you can see, it all worked out, and here I am." This explanation, as I said, rather than reassuring my friend, left her even more disconcerted. In the meantime, we had returned home, and with an absolutely spontaneous hospitality that permitted no reply, Khalitan offered Obregón a room off the back passageway, which extended precariously over a canal of still water where canoes carrying flowers and fruits in unbelievable colors passed by from time to time. With comparable spontaneity, Obregón moved into the room after we picked up his luggage at the Air France office in the airport.*

Alejandro's life in Kuala Lumpur was filled with the most varied episodes, but he spent most of his time painting. He had set up an improvised easel in the passageway and framed his canvases himself, using semiprecious woods that Khalitan bought in the market. I'd like to say something about Alejandro's painting. You know very well that I'm hardly an expert in these matters, but I feel so close to the world created in his pictures that I don't think I'd be out of line if I did express an opinion, given the interest you've shown in the contradictory life of this nomad.

Obregón's painting relates to another world, completely different from the one we live in. It portrays a reality that he creates out of unimaginable places in his soul. It is angelic painting, but these are angels from the sixth day of creation. I always carry with me a small oil sketch on cardboard that he painted one starry, humid night in Aruba. It shows a chair viewed from an

unexpected angle. But the chair itself has nothing to do with
what we normally call a chair. It is, I repeat, a chair from
another world. In that sense I call it angelic painting. The pictures he completed in Kuala Lumpur—they all sank in the
Gulf of Aden when the freighter they were on hit a mine that
had escaped from some naval base or other—fascinated me for a
long time. I often dream about them. They had all the elements,
from tropical to exquisite, from baroque to decadent, that make
the landscape of Kuala Lumpur unrepeatable. Yet not a stroke in
the paintings copied reality. Obregón had simply recorded in his
memory certain essences, colors, and volumes, and transposed
them to his particular, unique world, where they took on a new
life. Khalitan became enthralled when she watched him paint,
and then she would say to me in a low voice: "I think he's
praying." One night I discovered her burning funeral incense all
around his paintings. I woke Alejandro and took him to see
what she was doing. He did not even seem surprised. He
thought it the most natural thing in the world. "She'll burn
down the house, with us inside it," I whispered in his ear.
"Great!" he replied. "That would be magnificent!" I prudently
led him back to his room. In his eyes—the eyes of a cat from
the Ensanche in Barcelona—there was a gleam that made my
hair stand on end. We almost met our death on a funeral pyre.
There is another aspect of Alejandro's painting that I find
extraordinarily intriguing, and you, who knew him so well and
attended his first show, can surely tell me if it was already present in his early paintings: When Obregón paints people, they
too have a kind of dangerous innocence, a sensuality that ante-
dates sensuality—again it's angelic, but with refined, heretical
modifications—and it gives us the impression that we've made
unauthorized entry into a forbidden world. I saw some of his
self-portraits on the night we first met, and this was my first
indication that he was someone out of the ordinary, a visionary
marked by unknown gods eaten away by plague. On those canvases was the man who was talking to me, the man who had
saved me from thugs, but at the same time, looking out at me
from the painting was a being entirely unlike the original, a
being who had something to say and was certainly about to say
it when he was fixed on the canvas, but who had come back and
taken refuge in a silence that saved mortals like us from something unspeakable. Well, I'm becoming tangled in a description
of something that you know much better than I and which I'm

sure you can speak about with a great deal more certainty.

Several months went by. The teak venture was still up in the air, because my presumptive Portuguese associate preferred to establish a soap factory in Brazil, leaving me with the desperate feeling that I had missed out on the deal of a lifetime. I'm so familiar with this experience that I use the appropriate antidotes immediately and continue on my way. I decided to go to Cyprus; I've already told you about the ordeals and undertakings that were waiting for me there. By this time Khalitan and Alejandro had established a relationship that certainly did not disturb me, for it allowed me to leave without guilt, happy to know that our friend would learn about a world in which the esoteric was skillfully joined to a spontaneous, somehow propitiatory eroticism.

* * *

The second fragment that mentions Obregón appears at the end of Maqroll the Gaviero's long letter; it is shorter than the first and erupts without warning in the middle of other incidents that apparently have nothing to do with this subject. It reads:

* * *

I came into Vancouver on a Canadian coast guard cutter that had miraculously rescued us minutes after the damned ship, under the command of a captain and a boatswain who surely had a pact with the devil to make our lives miserable, sank with its cargo of stinking hides. With no papers and no money, the first thing I thought of was to take refuge in the Seamen's Shelter, a charitable institution that provides the basic necessities to sailors in circumstances like mine until they are back on their feet. Since you're familiar with my situation as far as papers and documents are concerned, and know how precarious these have been when I have managed to obtain them in ways better left unsaid, you can understand my position in British Columbia, where the winter promised to be the coldest in fifty years. At the shelter they gave me warm clothing that they found in a closet where they stored the gear of sailors who had died there. That's what I was wearing when I took to the streets, not really knowing what to do. Because I'm not registered in any of this world's merchant marine files, and no consulate knows anything about

*me, you can appreciate my eagerness to find some way out before
the end of the thirty days granted by the immigration authorities
when I came ashore.*

*A week went by, and each day saw my prospects growing
dimmer. Suddenly I decided to go to the Colombian consulate
and send an SOS to my friend Alejandro Obregón. Why did I
think of him and not any of my other friends, few in number
but loyal and true, scattered throughout the world? "Because
that's how things are, damn it," Alejandro explained when I
asked him the question. At the consulate they sent my call for
help to Cartagena, where the response was that Obregón had
gone to San Francisco for a show of his paintings and was staying at the Francis Drake Hotel. As far as our friend was concerned, it hardly seemed logical that he would have chosen a
place with that name. They allowed me to call him from the
consulate, and I briefly explained my situation. His only
response was: "Shit! I'll come up there. Don't disappear on me.
Let me talk to the consul." I passed the receiver to the official,
who, as he listened to Obregón, looked at me with curiosity and
suspicion. When he finished speaking he took some bills from
the drawer of his prehistoric desk and handed them to me, saying, "The Maestro asked me to give you this to tide you over
until he arrives; I think he'll be here next Saturday." I
expressed my gratitude, in this case absolutely sincere and even
heartfelt, and the only response he could think of was: "Not at
all, Señor, think nothing of it. When dealing with a man like
Maestro Obregón, one can deny him nothing, no matter how
strange it may seem." I turned and left, trying to digest, without
its affecting my serenity, the dark reservations contained in his
words. Life has taught me how to perform this rite in an almost
reflexive, impersonal way. Besides, my appearance could not
inspire confidence. I had not yet visited a barber, and it was
obvious even at a distance that the dead man wore a much
larger size than I do.*

*Alejandro arrived as promised. He burst on the scene with
the exuberant warmth that was one of the constant signs of his
character, tempered, as always, by his inbred decency and his
inflexible desire to respect the privacy of others. He also brought
with him a passport from a small Caribbean republic, adorned
with a photograph that had some of my features hidden behind
a whaler's whiskers. "You'll have to let your beard grow,
Gaviero. It's just as well you have a good head start," he said,*

roaring with laughter as we drank a weak, perfumed Canadian
whiskey that we tried to make tolerable by mixing it with ginger
ale. He told me how matters had concluded in Kuala Lumpur.
"I was not too sorry to leave all that. My relationship with your
friend had turned into a kind of violet-colored Mass surrounded
by all the perfumes of Buddhist orthodoxy. Well, I don't know if
the damn thing was Buddhism. Whatever. But I took a nonstop
flight to Rome, and when I opened my suitcase it smelled just
like the deceased at the funeral that brought us together."

   We changed the subject. I asked him what he was painting
now. What he told me is impossible to forget, but it was so full
of interjections that when I omit them, I have the impression
I'm betraying our friend. This is what Obregón said, in more or
less these words:

   "Look, Gaviero, the thing about painting is very simple—
but also very complicated. It comes down to this: You always
have to tell the truth. Just like in life, in a painting there's only
room for truth. That's where the picture gambles on immortality.
Lying means falsifying life—in other words, dying. Is that clear?
Good. Now comes the problem of colors. You have to be sure
every minute that you, the painter, are the one who manages
them, the one who controls them. The one who creates them, to
make a long story short. But they celebrate on their own too.
When they get together and become a new color, it gives them
an unimaginable pleasure. But always—don't forget that—
always with you directing: with the brush or the palette knife in
your hand, without trembling, without stammering, with the certainty that you're the lord and master in that kingdom. Tell the
rainbow to go to hell. Never pay attention to it, or the painting
is wrecked, it sinks into a sea of drivel. Look, with the rainbow
and all that, you have to do what I did many years ago with a
flock of pelicans flying very low in formation. I think I may
have told you about it. I was on the beach when I saw them
coming. I took a stick and drew an enormous arrow in the sand,
pointing in the opposite direction from the one they were taking.
When they saw the arrow they became flustered; they kept circling over me and broke formation, and when they finally re-
formed they flew off in the direction of the arrow I had drawn in
the sand; in other words, in the other direction. It's the same
with painting: You must mark the destination of the colors and
composition, the direction the elements in the picture should
take. I know, it's easy to say, but that's how it has to be. Look,

Gaviero, it's exactly the same with every damn thing that hap-
pens to you in life. What you don't control always turns against
you. What happens is that people don't understand this. Well,
people, you know, people aren't worth very much. Nothing
bothers me more than people. A poet from my country, who
would have been a good friend of yours and an ideal companion
in breaking open bottles of the densest alcohol in the most unbe-
lievable taverns, used to say: 'Ah, all those ignorant people
always expressing their opinions!' But that's another story. Let's
get back to painting. So we agree, then, that what I paint, every-
thing I've ever painted in my life, even the simplest drawing, is
all truth and nothing but the truth. And the only thing that
interests me is that those who see the painting know this imme-
diately. Now, the important thing is to learn how to look, to get
to know how to look, look at everything: objects, people, the sky,
the mountains, the sea and all its creatures. Everything we look
at always hides something, keeps it in shadow. That's what you
have to get to, what you have to illuminate, discover, decipher.
Nothing can remain hidden. I know, it's a lot to ask. But it
can't be helped. The sea, for example: You've sailed it so much
and you know it so well. The sea is the most important thing in
the world. You have to know how to look at it, follow its mood
changes, listen to it, smell it. Do you know why? It's something
very simple that people all think they know but I don't think
they really understand: Life was born there, we came from there,
and part of us will always be submerged there among the algae,
in the darkness of the deeps. Now I'm almost ready to begin an
old dream that's been pursuing me for years: painting the wind.
Yes; don't look like that. Painting the wind, but not the one
that blows through the trees or moves the waves or flutters the
skirts of girls. No, I want to paint the wind that comes in one
window and goes out the other, just like that. The wind that
leaves no trace, that's so similar to us, to our work in life, that
has no name and slips through our hands without our knowing
how. The wind that you, because you are a lookout, have so
often watched as it comes toward the sails and then changes
direction and never arrives. That's the one I'm going to paint.
No one has done it yet. I'll do it. You'll see. It's a question of
knowing how to catch it at the precise moment when there's no
possible doubt about its passing. I know, to do that you have to
know how to look, I've already said that: look at the hidden
side of things. It's the same with the wind, and what I really

know how to do is look, look until you're not yourself anymore. What the hell! I've gotten lost again, but I think you understand me, Maqroll, because if you don't understand me we're fucked." I replied that I did understand him, and although it all seemed very clear to me, that way of looking at life supposed a severity, an asceticism, a vigilance, that were very difficult to sustain all the time. *"It can't be helped, Gaviero, it can't be helped; that's how it is."*

We were in a bar whose owner, a Greek with heavy eyebrows and an ill-tempered appearance, had insisted on serving us a vile ouzo that we refused in favor of Canadian whiskey on the rocks. The man regarded us with haughty suspicion, which naturally made us laugh, since the place was not very commendable and the business being transacted at the other tables, among people of the most diverse nationalities, looked anything but honest. "We really are innocents," said Obregón, "innocents in the Russian sense of the word, which means vigilant servants of the truth. And that's the most dubious state there is for people. That's why we're suspect here." The owner looked away and pretended, with feigned seriousness, to be involved in the glasses he was washing. We spent two more days visiting establishments in the port no better than the one I've described. Obregón went back to San Francisco and never let me thank him. With a categorical movement of his hand, he canceled out all my efforts in that direction. I went to the airport with him, and we said goodbye with a warm embrace. At that moment his eyes were steel gray; the blue had disappeared. I interpreted this as an indication of strictly controlled tenderness. The following day I sailed south in a freighter that was going down to Valdivia. A breakdown in the radar forced us to stop at the port of Los Angeles. . . .

* * *

This is the Gaviero's story of his encounters with Alejandro Obregón, the painter.

It all took place a long time ago. Today the lives of the three of us have changed completely. I have heard nothing of Maqroll the Gaviero for many years; there are many versions of his death, none of them confirmed. Since this has happened before, those of us who are his friends still make inquiries about him. Alejandro Obregón died in his house in Cartagena, the house of a retired pirate, which smells of paint and solvents and whose terrace offers a view of an unbelievable ocean that makes us think we are about to see galleons. I, in Mexico, attempt to leave some mark in the memory of my friends by narrating the trials and tribulations of the Gaviero. I don't believe I will achieve very much along this road, but no other seems open to me.

Yet a rumor has been circulating for quite some time. I did not look into it very closely, perhaps for fear I would finally confront one of those surprises to which Maqroll has accustomed us and which empty into the void. But now, suddenly, as I was narrating these encounters between the Gaviero and Obregón, the story I had put aside began to gnaw at my mind, and I looked for the manuscript of another dear comrade who completes the quartet of friends—I am speaking of Gabriel García Márquez—in which he writes a portion of the tale that says it was Obregón who found the body of the Gaviero in the swamp where he lost his way with Flor Estévez and both of them apparently died of thirst and hunger as they searched for a route out of the marshes. This is what Gabo tells us:

"Many years ago, a friend asked Alejandro Obregón to help him look for the body of the skipper of his boat; the man had drowned at twilight while they were fishing for twenty-pound shad in the Great Swamp. They spent the whole night searching that immense paradise of faded water, exploring its most unexpected turnings with hunters' lanterns, following the course of objects on the surface, which usually lead to the deep pools where the drowned go to sleep. Suddenly Obregón saw him: He was submerged to the crown of his head, almost sitting in the water, and the only thing floating on the surface were the errant grasses of his hair. 'He looked like a medusa,' Obregón told me. He seized the sheaf of hair with both hands, and with the uncommon strength of a painter of bulls and tempests, he pulled the drowned man out of the water, open-eyed, enormous, dripping the mud of anemones and manta rays, and tossed him like a dead shad into the bottom of the boat. . . ."

In Gabriel's delicious and expert prose, something was suggested, was trying to surface among the details that in no way agreed with the alleged death of the Gaviero in the marshes of the Great Swamp: fishing for shad, the fact that the dead man was not the owner of the craft, and the allusion to a boat, a word that might perhaps be used for the flat-keeled vessel in which Maqroll became lost but is not the correct term, and that is inconceivable in Gabo's writing.

These facts helped to subvert, or to invalidate, the not unreasonable conclusion that the drowned man was Maqroll.

But in the prose poem that appears in *Caravansary*, I mention a customs launch that discovers the barge with the two bodies; this is the same launch alluded to in the version I had heard of the death of the Gaviero. Since Gabo not only is the very great writer we all know but also is proud, and with reason, of being a good journalist, we must assume that he verified the information at the time. The first thing I did, obviously, was to question Obregón about my doubts. He only smiled in an amused, distracted way and changed the subject. I am afraid he felt that the stories his friends told about him were not charming tales but an abusive distortion of his private life.

This is the state of affairs and, as usual when dealing with the Gaviero, the truth slips between our fingers like a fish wriggling out of our grasp. But no one can disabuse us of the idea that if the corpse rescued from the marshes by Obregón was really Maqroll, his companion and accomplice in Cartagena, Curaçao, Kuala Lumpur, and Vancouver, then the story closes with an elegant precision that is rare in our lives. Knowing the two protagonists as I do, this ending fits so beautifully with their characters and the contrary design of their days on earth that I cannot help mentioning it here, of course without endorsing it as true, but not emphatically denying it either. Artists and adventurers tend to plan their end so it can never be clearly deciphered by others. It is a privilege that has been theirs since the days of Orpheus the thaumaturge and the ingenious Ulysses or Odysseus.

Jamil

Sinon l'enfance, qu'y avait-il alors qu'il
n'y a plus?

St.-John Perse

*T*here is an episode in the life of Maqroll the Gaviero
that has almost nothing in common with others I have
narrated in recent years, yet it represented an essential change
in his disordered wandering. Late in life, it brought him to a
kind of serene acceptance of the arduous path of his destiny
and led him to follow, to its ultimate consequences, his doctrine
of embracing without reservation the high secrets of the
unnamable. Not that his existence, after the experience I am
about to relate, was free of turmoil or events of the most
diverse nature and origin, but the spirit with which Maqroll
confronted them was no longer tinged with challenge—the
tenacious, hopeless defiance that had once characterized his
wandering through the world.

Taken by itself, this may seem normal to readers, an every-
day occurrence in any person's ordinary routine. But if they
are familiar with Maqroll's past, they will realize immediately
that an event we may regard as commonplace and conventional was, for the Gaviero, an entirely extraordinary and
unfamiliar experience that revealed to him a virgin corner of
his emotional life.

I could have told the tale directly in the guise of the omni-
scient, omnipresent narrator. I chose instead to transcribe the

words Maqroll used when he recounted his experience, which I wrote down immediately after hearing them. They contain all the unspoken grief this event cost him, as well as all its revelatory moments of unshadowed joy. This is how I came to hear the story:

I visit Cartagena de Indias whenever I have the chance, for my memory of the city is so charged with nostalgia, so full of moments that have indelibly marked the rest of my life, that I cannot resist wandering the magical labyrinth of its narrow streets and gazing with rapture upon the slow dance of the Antillean sea from the watchtowers of its proud, austere fortified walls. When my dear friend the painter Alejandro Obregón was still with us, I would visit him at his house on Calle de la Factoría, where, with the help of a bottle of Scotch whiskey that he kept for his friends, we would undertake the long pilgrimage to our common past, which would merge with memories of childhood, his German and mine Belgian.

On one of these visits to the Heroic City, I knocked at Alejandro's door just as one of the interminable, devastating rainstorms that assail the city in October suddenly broke overhead. Alejandro himself opened the door, smiling and wearing the expression of a child who has just received an unexpected gift.

"Damn! I'm glad to see you! It's just the excuse I need to stop painting and celebrate the surprise with a drink."

We went into his studio and sat on the familiar leather armchairs covered with blotches of paint in every imaginable color, testimony to his struggle with the very stuff of his paintings. Recently completed canvases hung on the walls: An oneiric magic flowed from angels with the bodies of young girls, dazzling adolescents who emerged, among mauve shadows, from a gamut of greens that ranged from the tender shade of budding leaves to the dark tones of the impenetrable jungle, all of this surrounded by an explosion of intense blues and reds that turned into luminous orange. It was Obregón's new world, a new period in his painting, which was strangely connected to what I was writing at the time. I expressed my enthusiasm, and he replied with a characteristic gleam in his steel-blue eyes indicating extreme pleasure:

"I knew you'd like it. Those angels come to me now in dreams, and I paint them so they can't escape me. What doesn't return to us in dreams won't accompany us in the next life."

I was accustomed to my friend's emphatic assertions, and it was best not to explore them too deeply because then he became embroiled in even more muddled pronouncements.

The rain served as our pretext for finishing the bottle of Dewar's that Alejandro had put in front of me on a table covered with brushes and empty tubes of paint. As I've said, we talked of our now distant youth and of friends whose memory evoked areas of our shared past. In the midst of this whirlpool of reminiscences, Alejandro suddenly asked:

"Where are you heading now?"

I told him I was going to Spain on vacation.

"That's good," he commented, "because I have a job for you. It has to do with our friend Maqroll. I'm going to show you something that will disturb you as much as it disturbed me."

He went to another table, also covered with brushes and tubes of paint, where in one corner he kept a folder containing all kinds of papers. He returned with an envelope and handed it to me in silence.

The stamps were Spanish, and it was postmarked Pollensa, in Mallorca. Inside was a letter written in the unmistakable Transylvanian scrawl that immediately identified the Gaviero. It consisted of a few lines on stationery with a letterhead that read: "Saint Jaume Parish Church. Mossén Ferrán Alaró, Rector." This is what it said:

Alex:

Abusing the hospitality of my good friend the parish priest, I am writing these lines that go out to you like the proverbial bottle tossed into the sea. This time life has managed to strike a blow to my very core. I can't comment on these things in a letter. I'm feeling fairly discouraged and lost. None of the paths that once alleviated my disquietude appeals to me now. If you could come here, which I imagine is highly unlikely, it would be a great relief to tell you about it, and to enjoy your company. The same applies to our friend who spends his time writing down my wanderings and recording my misfortunes. I know he often visits Spain because of his devotion to Al-Andalus, the Omayyad caliphate, and the kingdom of Mallorca, all subjects he likes to bore us to tears with. If you see him, show him this letter. That's all for now, my dear painter of pubescent and per-

*turbing angels. No one but the two of you can understand what
lies behind these lines.*

With a warm embrace from your friend,

Maqroll the Gaviero

Knowing *him as well as I did, it was clear to me that the letter contained a barely disguised call for help. Maqroll was not a
man given to complaining. Instead, he would occasionally let
loose with two or three curses in Turkish or French and recover a
relative calm. But this was a different matter.*

*Although Mallorca was not part of my vacation plans in
Spain, I resolved to visit my friend in Pollensa and told Alejandro so. He said with satisfaction:*

*"That's good. Now I can rest easy. I know things will go bet-
ter for him after a good talk. And you're the best person to do
that. I know: I've spent so many years telling you my misfortunes."*

*A slight blush appeared on Obregón's weather-beaten face. At
bottom he was very modest, and to tell the truth, I did not
remember hearing confessions of that kind from him. At least
not openly. I had realized some time earlier that many of his
hermetic, labyrinthine remarks probably concealed emotional
events. Perhaps the affection and patience I felt when I heard
them traveled along secret channels and brought him a certain
forbearance. True friendship rests on such hidden but effective
avenues of communication.*

*The rain stopped a short while later, and we said goodbye
with the same close, silent embrace with which we always separated, as if we would never see each other again. Our last
farewell, which occurred not long ago, I keep in my memory
with an affliction that does not recede.*

*My wife and I reached Mallorca in mid-autumn, but the
hordes of tourists still paraded their Teutonic affluence through
the streets of Palma and then stripped it off, to the horror of the
island's prudent countryside, on any beach they could find. Carmen had called Mossén Ferrán from Barcelona, and he met us
at the airport. Large and ungainly, certainly past sixty, he welcomed us with a kind of peasant courtesy and addressed my
wife in Catalan, making an effort not to include too much Mallorcan. From then on, our conversation followed these linguistic*

*principles; I participated in Spanish but understood what they
were saying, thanks to the coaching I had received during more
that a quarter century of marriage to a Catalonian. I was especially struck by the priest's expressive face: his dark, heavy
brows and thin-lipped mouth, which always wore the spontaneous, lightly ironic smile of someone who has lived long
enough to give importance only to the essential and put everything else aside, except for the suffering of others. His dark,
alert eyes, always attentive to the person he was addressing, testified to the Saracen substratum in the island's natives. The
amiable priest's warm bass voice gave a somewhat theatrical
emphasis to everything he said. He insisted on carrying my
wife's suitcase, and as we walked to the taxi that was waiting
to take us to Pollensa, he said in a pleased voice: "Our friend
is waiting for you and is very happy about your visit. He
asked me to apologize for his not coming to meet you, but his
aversion to airports has become more acute here because of the
invasion of tourists."*

*The taxi was an ancient car in a condition that caused me
the gravest reservations regarding its ability to travel as far as
Pollensa. When he saw the doubt on my face, Mossén Ferrán
quickly reassured me:*

*"Don't worry. This taxi, just as you see it, drives all around
the island every week and has never broken down. The man
responsible for this miracle is the driver, my nephew Roger, who
preferred Seat automobiles to marriage. Well, God knows what
He's doing. It's gone very well for Roger, and for me too: I'm
the owner of this antiquity."*

*The young driver, who was putting our luggage in the trunk,
smiled in amusement and greeted us with a nod that was both
friendly and distracted. He had his uncle's eyebrows and the
same olive skin, but his black, tightly curled hair was an even
clearer indication that the armies of the caliphs had occupied the
island. He too had a bass voice, though it was not as deep as his
uncle's and had a more emphatic tone.*

*Mossén Ferrán occupied the seat next to his nephew, and we
sat in the back. We were silent as we crossed the city, still occupied by tourists, who took over the streets and made it difficult
for cars to pass. When we reached the countryside, I was once
again struck by the luminosity of the Mallorcan night. It com-
municates a kind of inner order to me that I always long for and
rarely achieve. There is something Homeric in the distant phos-*

phorescent glow of worlds peaceably traveling through the deep Mediterranean night.

I attempted to direct the priest to the subject of the Gaviero. I wanted to hear his opinion of the melancholy reflected in Maqroll's letter, which I mentioned to him.

"It's better if he tells you everything himself," he replied, in a tone both cordial and peremptory. "As I said to your wife when we spoke on the phone, it's not a question of the Gaviero's health, much less any economic difficulty. You both know that the man never has a cent in his pocket. What they pay him for looking after those abandoned shipyards and the machinery corroded by rust and saltpeter is just enough for him to live with an austerity I suspect has been a constant in his life. Something has changed deep inside his soul, even though he still accepts the capricious decrees of fate and is destined to wander perpetually. He is here for now, apparently resolved to stay for an indefinite period of time, but in the wonderful conversations we have several times a week, he never loses an opportunity to mention, with evident longing, distant ports or illusory enterprises in the most remote corners of the world. There's no lady involved," he added, turning toward my wife with a complicitous smile. "But I shouldn't say anything else, because I want Maqroll himself to tell you about the ordeal he suffered and how it undermined his spirit, leaving him with a sense of hopelessness and defeat that I suspect he has not experienced before."

We spoke of other things. I asked the erudite cleric about his library on the history of the kingdom of Mallorca. With a satisfaction he made no attempt to hide, he told me it was the most complete private collection on the subject and began to explain his curious theory, according to which the entire history of Western Christendom either originates on Mallorca or manifests itself on the island at critical moments. "Certain key events that shaped modern Europe have occurred here," he declared. The idea, stated in this way, presented quite a few points that were problematic or difficult to prove, and I found myself tempted to discuss some of them with Mossén Ferrán. But the priest of Sant Jaume parish church proceeded to mention my stories that have the Gaviero as the central protagonist, and my poems in which Maqroll speaks of his nomadic life. In his opinion, I still had a good deal to learn about our friend's character, and he criticized, not without a certain caution, my having passed so quickly over Maqroll's ideas regarding historical events, which,

he said, the Gaviero knew better than I had indicated in my
books. I attempted to dispute this, saying I had always avoided
developing historical theories that would deform the spirit of my
narratives, let alone my poems. His only reply was that if I had
done so, it would have given me the opportunity to clarify an
aspect of Maqroll's personality that he tends to hide from the
curious gaze of others.

"The Gaviero," he said, "is a born anarchist who pretends
not to know that about himself, or to ignore it. His vision of the
human journey on earth is even more ascetic and bitter than the
one he reveals in his ordinary dealings with people. The other
day I heard him say something that astounded me: 'The disappearance of our species would be a distinct relief for the universe.
Soon after its extinction, its ominous history would be totally
forgotten. There are insects better able to leave more permanent
and less fatal traces of their passage than those left behind by
the human race.' Naturally, I tried to counter with theological
and historical arguments, and he would only reply, with the
peculiar emphatic tone of a man commanding on the bridge,
which he uses to cut off any discussion: 'You, my dear Mossén
Ferrán, wear the armor of a faith and a religious tradition that
protect you against all doubt. I did too, in my youth, but mine
crumbled away like dried-out bark. There at the top of the highest mast, in the crow's nest where the lookout questions the
horizon, all mystery vanishes in the flight of curlews and gulls
and the crack of the sail in the wind, and nothing is left standing in us. Believe me.' And now you can understand," the priest
continued, "that he did not give me much chance to continue the
conversation along those lines. What I find admirable is that in
the midst of so much wreckage, emotional and otherwise, he still
preserves his strong, unsentimental goodness. That is another of
the enigmas in our friend."

I was struck by how well Mossén Ferrán knew Maqroll, and
I thought, not without a certain envy, of the animated, endless
talk that had forged a friendship sustained by common interests
in historical matters and by the simple but always disquieting
and revealing events of our daily lives.

A long silence fell after the priest had spoken. Mossén Ferrán
began to nod drowsily, lulled by the motion of the car. Half an
hour later we drove into Pollensa.

The lights of the city were reflected in the calm water of the
bay. The yachts anchored at the Nautical Club rocked lazily,

their mooring lines moaning with a faint, sleepy sound.

We stopped at the modest hotel where Mossén Ferrán had reserved us a room that overlooked the beach. The owner, Doña Mercé, was a cousin of his, a pleasant woman of few words who dressed in perpetual widow's mourning, worn like a special distinction that highlighted her dignity. She had prepared a supper for us, which we welcomed enthusiastically, for we were hungry after our trip. While the final details for serving the meal were being attended to, I decided to see Maqroll, and Roger drove me to the abandoned shipyards where the Gaviero worked as a watchman.

Absolute darkness reigned in the partially ruined buildings. The dry dock exposed the stumps of its old concrete structure, and the elements had collapsed the wooden frame. A shed made of sheets of zinc, black with rust, had probably housed the offices. The driver tapped lightly on the horn. On the second floor, at a window partially obscured by cardboard that replaced glass panes broken long ago, the light of a lantern shone on us for a moment.

"I'll be right down." It was the unmistakable voice of the Gaviero, with its lilting yet impeccably articulated Mediterranean accent. In spite of or, perhaps, because of this, he was often thought to be from the French Midi. Through the gaps between the sheets of zinc, we watched the lantern descend a stairway that creaked in an alarming way. Maqroll lit the wire-enclosed bulb over the front entrance. It shed a full, brutally harsh light on the Gaviero's face.

I could not disguise the effect this had on me. It was not that the years had suddenly aged him. Rather, I thought he had suffered another attack of the fevers that devastated him without mercy. He noticed my reaction and, with a pale, unconvincing smile, tried to discount it. He told the driver he could go, thanked him for bringing me, and invited me inside the ramshackle building. Roger said he preferred to wait, because those were Mossén Ferrán's instructions, and supper would be ready in about half an hour. The Gaviero shrugged as a sign of assent, and we began to climb stairs that threatened to collapse with each step we took. We came to the first landing and went into what once must have been an office and now served as the caretaker's living quarters.

Maqroll had converted a large leather sofa into his bed by means of two worn sheets and a pillow covered with stains of uncertain origin. The Gaviero placed the lantern on an unsteady table full of books and lit a kerosene lamp that hung from a hook in the middle of the room. On what had been a desk were a few cups, two glasses, several tin canisters that probably contained ground coffee, sugar, and other foodstuffs, and, in the center, a small alcohol burner. On the walls hung the plans of ships of the most varied kinds and sizes, from large two-stack freighters to three-masted sailboats, and diagrams of diesel motors and sketches of hulls and riggings, all of them so deteriorated that they looked as if they would fall to the floor at any moment. Yet the atmosphere corresponded perfectly to the life and customs of Maqroll, and knowing the vile holes where he had spent long years of his life, I suspected it might even seem warm and welcoming to him. I had met with him in miserable dens in Amazonia and El Chaco, in horrifying garrets in Amsterdam and Vancouver, in the foul hovels of poverty-stricken districts built over swamps in Guayaquil and Buenaventura. By comparison, the shipyards in Pollensa seemed a comfortable refuge for him, with the companionable presence of his favorite books about illustrious lives and forgotten wars. He cleared away a pile of nautical engineering magazines, which must have been lying there for years, from a chair that tilted because it had a lost a wheel from one of its legs, and invited me to sit down. Knowing him as I do, I realized it was not advisable to begin to talk right away about the reason for our visit. We spoke instead of Alejandro Obregón, and then I said something about the letter he had received. Maqroll did not react and asked instead what Alex was painting now. We discussed the various periods in the work of our mutual friend and remarked on his having abandoned aquatic life, mojarra fish, and condors for a paradisiacal world of angels with female bodies.

"One day he'll abandon these disquieting creatures too," said Maqroll. "Do you know what Alex's problem is? It's very simple but has no solution: He dreams of painting life one day; not the daily, mindless human routine but life, real life, the one that finds an answer only in the absolute silence of death. That goal will always elude him, yet a man like Obregón will never admit defeat. He'll die in the attempt, but he won't retreat. You know it's true. Life attacks us like a blind beast. It swallows up time, the years of our life, it passes like a typhoon and leaves nothing behind. Not even memory, because memory is made of the same swift, ungraspable substance out of which illusions emerge and

then disappear. And how can anyone paint something like that?"

His voice vibrated slightly in the lower registers of each sentence. Something told me it was the moment to broach the subject at hand.

"Well," I said, "it's been such a long while since we've seen each other that I thought this vacation was a good opportunity to come and talk over some things that were left unresolved after our last meeting. Besides, I must confess that what you told Obregón about your state of mind disturbed me, and so here we are. We have plenty of time. You know my weakness for Mallorca and the old roots that join me to this country. And the truth is that Mossén Ferrán did not tell us anything. I think he's a fine man and a good friend to you, and he gave me the impression that he wanted you to be the one to tell us what happened. I can't imagine what it might be. I thought I was past being surprised where you were concerned."

"That's what I thought too," replied the Gaviero, his gaze fixed on a vague distance, "and I was terribly wrong. At the edge of death there'll be surprises waiting for us that we never even suspected. But where's your wife? Didn't she come to Pollensa?"

The question, asked so suddenly, as if he were waking from a bad dream, indicated that he would not tell me anything that night. For some reason I could not fathom at the time, he seemed to need a woman's presence to do it. The Gaviero confirmed what I had suspected.

"I would prefer your wife to be with us when I tell this story. Only women can decipher the depths of a child's soul. That's what this is about, and we men, in this as in so many other things that have to do with the emotions, are as clumsy as wagon drivers. Tomorrow Doña Mercé, who's also a friend of mine, will cook a wonderful Mallorcan soup for us, and some fish, which she prepares with real genius. We'll sit on the terrace that overlooks the sea, and we'll say what needs to be said. I'll come on my own. Don't send Mossén Ferrán's taxi for me. I like walking along the bay. The sea has always been an infallible adviser in my life. You know that."

I was bewildered by his allusion to a child's soul and a woman's ability to sound it. I turned it over and over in my mind but could not guess in what labyrinth our friend had lost his way. All that was clear was his having suffered the kind of

trial he had not known before. This was revealed by the vulner-
ability and longing in his eyes, and a certain silent anxiety he
did his best to conceal. His eyes, like those of a dervish at rest,
had sunk into their sockets as if trying to disappear. Shadows
crossed his forehead without ever settling into a definite expression, and his lips attempted to clamp shut as though they were
rejecting an undeserved, turbulent grief.

We spoke awhile longer about unimportant generalities, and
then he walked to the car with me and said goodbye with words
that brought back the Maqroll I had always known:

"I knew you would come. You couldn't just ignore another of
my stories. But this one will take you to places you never imagined. Thank you very much for having answered my call. Please
give your wife my most affectionate regards." He closed the car
door with a languid gesture and returned to the ruined building.
I waited until the light at the window of his refuge had gone
out, and left, less disturbed and more intrigued than before.

That night, when I told my wife about my conversation with
the Gaviero, she would only utter a sibylline prophecy that
would later be confirmed with an accuracy I've been accustomed
to for many years:

"The worst is over for him. Now he's trying to find his usual
path again. I have a feeling he's suffered one of those ordeals
that men aren't made for, because they lack certain resources that
women have."

Maqroll came to the hotel at about one the next day. Doña
Mercé welcomed him affectionately and listened to his instructions for the kind of meal only she knew how to prepare. We
heard the conversation from our room, and it showed how fluently Maqroll now spoke Mallorcan. When we went down, we
found him sitting at a somewhat isolated table at the far end of
the terrace. He was slowly sipping a white wine that he poured
from a Mallorcan ceramic pitcher decorated in an intense yellow.
By the light of day, the marks of hopelessness were more evident
on his face, battered by every climate and lashed by storms on
all the seas he had sailed from the time he was a boy. His voice
was still breaking in its rough passage through the lower registers, a sign, for as long as I've known him, that he was weather-
ing a squall.

He greeted my wife with a slight bow over her hand and
invited us to sit facing a beach that had not yet been invaded,
fortunately, by the army of tourists. In the distance, the marina

at the yacht club still sheltered vessels of every size and prove-nance.

"This wine," said the Gaviero, "is from a small vineyard owned by Mossén Ferrán's family. It's a little sharp and rough, but it soon takes on the taste of sun-drenched earth, which gives it an unexpected nobility. Don't hesitate to drink it. I think it's as good as some of the Catalonian whites you've known since you were a girl." Maqroll always enjoyed referring to my wife's country. On this occasion, I felt he was doing it to establish a certain complicity that he found indispensable.

The virtues of the wine praised by Maqroll did not seem as evident to me as our friend had proclaimed, but we continued drinking it while we waited for our meal and ate delicious fried sardines sent to our table by the owner as a preview of the mar-vels to come from her kitchen.

We spoke of our trip and our plans to visit Cádiz again. The Gaviero meandered through a long discourse on Alejandro's painting, then began to praise Obregón's rare qualities as a part-ner in adventures, not all of them confessable. He was clearly trying to gain time until the conversation took on the tone of familiarity required for what he wanted to say. His uneasiness was apparent from the first, as was his desire to gain my wife's attention and sympathy for the story he would tell. Doña Mercé herself served the steaming clay bowls of Mallorcan soup. As she moved about, she did not take her eyes off Maqroll. She was obviously interested in knowing how he would manage on this occasion, with people who knew nothing of his recent ordeal.

Mossén Ferrán arrived at the same time as the dessert. The priest sang the praises of the egg custard Doña Mercé was serv-ing us, and sat down next to the Gaviero. This seemed to be the long-awaited signal for Maqroll to begin his story. A light breeze blew across the bay. The Gaviero ran his hands through his coarse graying hair, as if preparing to confront an arduous but inevitable difficulty. After asking Doña Mercé for another pitcher of wine and ordering coffee for all of us, he began to speak.

A little over a year ago, I received a letter from Port-Vendres. Even before I opened it, the place it had been mailed from was enough to awaken a discomfort in me that was easy to explain. To my misfortune, I had landed there many years before. I was working as a supernumerary hand on a Turkish freighter I had boarded in Salonika, carrying false papers that indicated I was a Belgian citizen. At first the captain did not pay much attention to my documents, but when the bos'n examined them more closely, he realized the deception and ordered me to leave the ship at the first port we come to. I managed to persuade him not to put me ashore in Tripoli, our next port of call, where I would not have stayed alive for more than a few hours. It's a very long story, and I'll tell you about it some other time if you think it's worth hearing. Then we went to Genoa, but the harbor officials refused to let me disembark. It seems that certain police files there were still current, although I thought they had lapsed. Well, my life hasn't been easy, and you're well aware of my fatal tendency to interpret the law in my own way. In any event, the next stop was Port-Vendres, where the ship was to pick up a group of French émigrés going to try their luck in Tunis. In those days, Port-Vendres was the necessary point of departure for the wave of immigrants who, since the beginning of the century, had sought their fortune in lands less punished by wars and economic crises, yet not too far from their native country. By promising to leave for Algeria within ten days, I convinced the authorities in Port-Vendres to let me disembark. I signed a document that had the weight of a legal oath, and they gave me permission to come ashore.

Port-Vendres did not always have the air of a modest, quiet summer resort that it wears, not very convincingly, today. Back then it was a ramshackle little town whose life revolved entirely around the passage of immigrants to North Africa. One almost had the impression that the whole city belonged to the famous Compagnie de Navigation Paquet, which practically had a monopoly on the transportation of the dense, transient multitude whose misery and longing to be on their way gave the port a permanent, dramatic feeling of disaster. As for me, what really bordered on lunacy was my idea of finding some permanent work that would free me from the promise I had signed for the police, in a town where everybody was prepared to depart and not give a thought to what they were leaving behind. All the businesses were on the verge of failing, or were for sale at desperate prices. You know I've gone through terrible periods of sickness and hunger, most of them in climates as appealing as Alaska, Tierra de Fuego, Amazonia, the barrens of the cordillera, or the mangrove swamps of Louisiana, just to mention a few of the infernos where fate, for want of a better word, has taken me. It may be difficult for you to believe, but Port-Vendres was where I had the deepest sense that I had come to the end of the line. When I spent the last of the few francs the Turks had given me when they sent me on my way, I tried to leave for Tunis or Algiers, as I had promised. But in one of those hellish inconsistencies in French bureaucracy—they always remind me of the fearful Colbert, whom Madame de Sévigné called "le Nord," and his empire of red tape, which still prevails in France with unimaginable tenacity—I learned I could not travel to North Africa because I wasn't a French citizen and did not have an authorization from the colonial government, whose bureaucratic hysteria, by the way, was practically psychotic. I'll never forget the little pockmarked functionary, with the face of an anemic rat, who passed sentence on me, leaving his sepulchral bad breath floating in the air: "You will never travel there. After all the formalities are completed, there is a seal that I must stamp on the papers. I never will, because we don't want people like you. We are French, we have fought a war, and we have a right to those countries. People like you who come from nowhere can go back to your nowhere, which is where you belong." He slammed down his window with so much rage that I was reminded of the guillotine and the *tricoteuses* of the Jacobin Terror.

For a few days I worked as a waiter in a café. When it closed, I was hired as a replacement on the night shift at a machine shop that repaired cranes for the Compagnie Paquet. After a week, the union had me fired. I no longer remember all the other ways I tried to earn a living, but one day I found myself sleeping in a corner of the stairway that leads to Obelisk Square. I had eaten nothing since the previous day, even though I had gone so far as to beg at the tables in the few cafés in the port that were still in business. With no clear purpose in mind, I went to the docks and began to wander around the installations where the immigrants were processed before boarding their ships. I was on the verge of passing out, and I leaned against a large window with white-washed panes. In the lower corner the paint had been scraped away and a sign put up that advertised for an assistant cleaner in the first-aid room located at the far end of the sheds that served as waiting rooms. I went to the hose hanging from one of the cranes and worked the pump. I drank some water, and with my stomach full of liquid, which temporarily alleviated my dizziness, I walked to the building indicated on the sign.

I rang the bell discreetly, and the woman who opened the door reminded me again of the matrons of the guillotine. She had no teeth, and it was extremely difficult to understand what she said. I finally resorted to gestures to describe the announce-ment in the window, and she let me in while she muttered vague curses and protests. The witch led me to a small consulting room. Behind a screen that had once been white was the unforget-table—at least for me—Maître Pascot, as he had everyone call him. I've never known anyone who could deceive so absolutely with his appearance. Corpulent and rosy, he had a perpetual, benevolent smile that extended over his beardless face until it reached pale-blue eyes whose gratuitous vivacity constituted the first warning sign for anyone who observed him carefully. Dr. Pascot had usurped all the gestures and physical traits of what is called a *grand patron* in the French medical world. In reality he was a crafty villain capable of wearing away the most patient and tenacious of his subordinates.

The job in question, which I clutched at as if it were a life-saver, consisted of scrupulously cleaning a first-aid room that was supported by some charitable organization to help immigrants who required medical attention. The flood of families waiting to board the ships poured in twenty-four hours a day. They came from every corner of France, but naturally most were from the south. The patients at Maître Pascot's dispensary were women about to give birth; men wounded in the endless fighting to keep one's place in the constant lines that formed at every window; children suffering from whooping cough, smallpox, or advanced dehydration; drunks in an acute state of alcohol poisoning; victims of incurable diseases who wanted to die in the illusory paradise on the far shore of the Mediterranean. The room, as Dr. Pascot repeated with unobjectionable emphasis, had to be kept absolutely clean and hygienic. The patients came in continually, day and night. I would have no days off, since I was the only one responsible for this drudgery worthy of a horse turning a millstone. I had to eat my meals there in the room, between patients. The salary, naturally, was a pittance, but it was enough to buy three frugal, rapid meals a day and an occasional article of used clothing in the secondhand stores that abounded around the docks. The day I began working, I mentioned to Pascot that I had not eaten in forty-eight hours. The man put his hand into the pocket of his tunic and gave me two francs, saying: "Go to the café just past this door and come back in half an hour. This is the first and last time I'll do this for you. You'll pay me back next weekend when you receive your wages. I represent a charitable institution, but I am not that institution. They are two very different things. Do you understand?"

I had understood him very well, and the days that followed made me see even more clearly. I will spare you the details of my life in that emergency room in Port-Vendres and the swindles used by Pascot to cheat his victims. His first words to the sick were: "My services here are entirely free, but you must pay for the medicines I prescribe. I'll sell them to you myself, and they'll be cheaper than at the pharmacy."

More than once I saw enraged immigrants about to attack this sinister Tartuffe, but they were always stopped by his serene smiling eyes and the laborer's strength visible beneath his immaculate physician's tunic. Others withdrew in tears, evidently lacking the money to buy the medicines he prescribed.

When I asked where and when I would sleep, he replied, with an angelic expression: "There are one or two births every day. They usually take a few hours. I don't need you then, and you can spend that time sleeping. Ask for Mr. Grancier in the lost-luggage office. Tell him I sent you, and he'll show you a quiet corner where you can sleep to your heart's content."

Grancier, a perfect replica of his superior, did not offer this service free of charge but rented out the wretched cot where he himself slept behind the pile of suitcases and bundles. I would collapse there in exhaustion, surrounded by the clamorous noise of the immigrants, who were subject to an entirely comprehensible hysteria, until, with a light kick in the ribs, Grancier would wake me and announce that I was wanted in the consulting room. A laconic man with the face of an executioner, he attended to inquiries regarding mislaid baggage with a shrug and a shake of the head while, with little conviction, he looked over the mountain of luggage. It was easy enough to deduce that the villain was a faithful supplier to the old-clothes dealers around the docks.

Well, that was my life for four infernal months, a time when I learned in my own flesh, as if I were still in need of another lesson, the limits of sordid cruelty and unfathomable misery that a man can endure without resorting to crime or suicide. I managed to escape through a miracle of the gods. One night a Danish captain came to the emergency room because he had dislocated his shoulder during some operation in the machine room. Pascot ordered me to hold the patient while he tried to turn the joint in its socket. In the midst of spasms of pain, the captain stared at me. Once he was bandaged and the sedatives the doctor had given him began to take effect, the Dane spoke to me in a barely audible voice. "Maqroll. Maqroll the Gaviero. What the hell are you doing here? Don't you recognize me? I'm Olrik, Nils Olrik, the captain of the *Skive*." His face had been so contorted by pain when he came in that I had not known him. We were old friends. I had worked for him on several occasions. I've already told that story.

* * *

Of course I remembered perfectly the episodes in the nomadic life of the Gaviero in which Olrik had participated. Maqroll continued speaking.

* * *

I told him about my situation and my lack of papers, which kept me a slave to Pascot, a cunning, lying scoundrel. He asked if I had signed a contract or any paper that bound me to the doctor. I said no, and without further preamble he told me to leave with him. The ship would sail in a few hours. I didn't need to worry about papers. He was taking me on as a member of the crew. He knew how to do that. He said this in German, of course, in order not to alert the doctor and to forestall any stratagems he might think of. We walked out arm in arm, to the astonished gaze of Pascot, who could only scratch his large bald head and repeat like a fool: *"Pas possible, pas possible."*

Olrik entered my name on the rolls as having signed on in Hamburg two months earlier, and indicated that because of illness, I had been obliged to travel overland to meet the ship in Port-Vendres. When I ate my first meal on board, I had to hold back tears of rage and relief. We sailed at dawn for Corsica, carrying a cargo of wheat and barley.

I wanted to tell you my first experience in Port-Vendres in some detail, first so that you could understand the sick feeling the postmark produced in me, and then because there is a certain irony in this place of adversity giving rise to one of the fullest, most enlightening experiences of my life. When I opened the envelope, a quiet voice told me nothing good could ever come out of Port-Vendres. That voice was utterly mistaken, even though the text of the letter was disturbing. I brought it with me to read to you.

* * *

The Gaviero took a wrinkled envelope out of the pocket of his seaman's shirt. He unfolded a sheet of paper, handwritten on both sides, and read us the following letter (I subsequently had the opportunity to copy the text):

* * *

Señor Gaviero:

Although I don't know you personally, I have heard about you. Some years ago I lived with your friend Abdul Bashur, at two different times, between his voyages to Mediterranean ports. I'm from Alcazarseguer, and as a child I went to live in Algiers with my family. I learned Arabic dancing there, and my profession has taken me halfway around the world. I met Abdul in Tunis. He was sailing on a ship that you and he owned together. I don't remember the name. We lived together in Bizerte for about a year. I became pregnant and had to stop dancing. Abdul always said that if anything ever happened to him, I could go to you for help. Abdul used to visit us from time to time. After he died in Funchal, I had to go back to dancing, but it wasn't the same anymore. Jamil, my son, needed my care, and I didn't want to subject him to the constant traveling my work entails. I found a job at a store selling tourist souvenirs and spent two years there, until the store closed. I've had a series of different jobs since then. Now, thanks to a woman I know who has worked in Germany for two years, I have the chance for a job in a factory in Bremen. She's from Port-Vendres, and I've come here with Jamil to get ready for the trip to Bremen. My idea is to save enough money to go to Lebanon. Warda, Abdul's sister, has asked Jamil and me to live with her. She has been very loyal and kind to me. We've never met, but we write to each other often. I urgently need the advice of someone I can trust about this whole situation, which is very difficult to explain in a letter. Warda gave me your address, and I'm asking you to do me an immense favor and come here to tell me what I should do, because I can't take Jamil with me. My working papers in Germany require me to go alone. All of this is very confusing, and the only thing I can think of is to ask for your help. Abdul had a very high opinion of you and always said you were the only person he trusted without reservation. I have no one else to turn to. My parents are dead, and I have no brothers or sisters or any other family. And I don't want to burden Warda and her brothers and sisters with the responsibility of caring for Jamil while I'm in Germany. I'll explain my reasons when you're here. I'm sorry for the trouble and inconvenience this may cause you. I'm making the request only on the basis of your friendship with Abdul. I hope to see you soon, and send you my fond regards.

Lina Vicente

P.S. If you decide to come, you can reach me at this address: Ancien Café Mogador, 44 Quai Pierre Forgas. Port-Vendres, Pyrénées Orientales.

Lina

* * *

The letter revealed a woman with a strong, mature character, gained at the cost of great suffering. I was struck by the dignity, good sense, and respect in the tone of her words, because these are not the most common virtues in people who have led lives like hers in that part of the world. And so I decided to meet with Lina. I checked the itineraries of freighters that might be making a port call at Port-Vendres or someplace nearby and obtained permission to sail on one that would dock in Palma two weeks later. I sent Lina a telegram informing her of my arrival and left for the Mallorcan capital. I don't have to tell you that after Lina's call for help, the image of Bashur and the memory of all our travels together were constantly in my mind. The past became an obsession as I sailed from Palma to Port-Vendres. I searched my memory and recalled certain allusions made by Abdul to his relationship with this woman and the child he'd had with her, but my recollections were vague, and I couldn't remember the words he used when he spoke about her. My friend's emotional life consisted of a series of episodes that were often stormy and always ended in a dramatic break. The one exception, of course, was Ilona. I've talked about this on several occasions. After the tragic death of our mutual friend, accomplice, fairy godmother, and lover, Bashur broke with his past and followed unexpected, tortuous paths. I've described those too. It was during this period that he met Lina Vicente and fathered Jamil.

In the narrow cabin that I shared with a monk who had left his order and an Armenian silversmith running from some crime he had committed in Sicily, I tried to reconstruct my encounters with Bashur during that time, and I could not recall any image of the woman who now sought my help. I tried to imagine her features, give her a body and gestures to match the qualities suggested by her letter, but I could only assemble a confusing puzzle that told me nothing. I reached Port-Vendres early in the morning and went immediately to the Ancien Café Mogador. The Port-Vendres I remembered had completely disappeared. All that remained were the installations of the Compagnie de Navigation Paquet, with a weathered sign as a memorial to times of vanished prosperity. The city displayed a tranquillity that was entirely new to me. The facades of the hotels and cafés had a welcoming, peaceful urbanity just right for attracting tourists. It was October, and the flood of visitors from the north had dissipated. The café mentioned by Lina had a small terrace on the avenue that ran along the bay. Across from it one could see the docks, which were almost empty. I went in and was greeted by a waiter who had the look of a Catalonian, which was then definitively confirmed by his accent. I asked for Lina, and a broad smile lightened his somber expression. He went to a room at the back of the café, and a few minutes later Lina came out. As so often occurs on occasions like these, her appearance was entirely different from the mental image I had created. She was tall, with a firm, elastic step and rather wide shoulders, and something in her bearing suddenly made me think of Ilona. But any resemblance ended there. Lina's angular face and slightly curved nose, which gave her the air of a falcon, and a prominent chin that seemed to repeat in reverse the line of her nose, reminded me of faces sometimes seen in the Basque country or in certain regions of the Balkans. Her slightly protruding eyes were a dark green that an effect of the light turned pale, and they had the steady, scrutinizing intelligence that tends to distinguish Levantines. There was something of an ascetic in her glance, or a priestess of a forgotten rite, which confirmed the character traits revealed by her letter. She smiled with some hesitation, and one could see in her a tension, a disquiet, which surely had its origins in her uncertainty regarding the future. I tried to estimate her age, but it was impossible. She conveyed a sense of mobility, a perpetually active and vigilant inner strength, which could as easily indicate youth as a maturity that comes with the blows of an adverse fate. She might have been thirty or fifty. Later, when I learned her age, I was astounded: She had just turned twenty-five. As she came toward me, moving among the tables and chairs on the terrace with feline lightness, I understood the attraction a woman like her held for Abdul. She had all the qualities that could make my friend lose his senses and throw himself into the kind of involvement whose ending I knew by heart. Her greeting was affectionate, and she sat down at my side, not taking her eyes off me and smiling with an expression both surprised and gratified. "I knew you would come. I never doubted it. Abdul told me so much about you, I feel as if I've known you for a long time. Before I tell you my reasons for asking you here, I'll take care of getting you settled. Come with me."

Her Spanish was correct and fluent but had a marked Arabic accent. I followed her past the tables on the terrace; inside the café, we passed a small bar. The kitchen was behind it; at the far end, a spiral staircase led to a kind of flat roof where several bedrooms were located, as well as a laundry area, adjoining a common bathroom. Lina insisted on carrying the seaman's bag that held my belongings and a few books. We entered one of the rooms. It contained an army cot and a small wooden bureau. We left my things there, and Lina handed me the key, saying I could come in or go out at any time of the day or night. The café opened at seven and closed at one in the morning. If I came in later, I could open the front door, at the back of the terrace, with my room key. I was struck by her gestures and words, which revealed a clear, unwavering judgment. I thought that such firmness could not have been easy for a man with Bashur's character to accept in daily life. Later, when I became familiar with her extraordinarily sweet and appealing smile, I understood all the charm of this unusual combination. We went down to the terrace, and Lina explained that she had to take care of certain duties in the kitchen and wait on the patrons who were beginning to come into the café. We would see each other at lunch, after twelve o'clock.

I left to see the city and places where I remembered spending times of the most awful poverty. As I said, none of it remained. It had all been refurbished, and it breathed an ambience of amiable comfort, of modest but stable prosperity. Many of the visitors circulating through the cafés and along the docks spoke Catalan. They evidently came from Figueras, Gerona, the entire Costa Brava, to enjoy French food and wine in a familiar atmosphere not far from home. There was nothing left of the long sheds that housed the immigrants ready to set sail for Morocco and Algiers. Only the weathered, almost abandoned building with the Compagnie Paquet sign was still standing, but its air of peaceable innocence brought no memories to mind. In those days, it must have been hidden by other iron and glass structures, which had now disappeared. I felt a kind of disillusionment, a bitter protest at this dissolution in time of a past I still found painful to recall: not a corner, not a brick, could still bear witness to my days of utter destitution, which would now join so many others lost in the labyrinths of memory. A splendid sun reverberated on the white facades of houses and buildings arranged in an amphitheater around a small bay of calm, transparent water. So much well-being pained me, making me feel distant from, almost rejected by, an Eden not meant for me.

I returned to the café at the time Lina had specified and took a seat on the terrace. A short while later she appeared, holding the hand of a boy whose surprised, smiling eyes looked at me with an expression very similar to his mother's. He came over to my table and greeted me in hesitant Arabic. What amazed me from the start was the similarity between his gestures and those of Bashur. The same disharmony between the movement of his hands and the words he spoke, the same turn of the head toward a distant, indeterminate space before looking back at his companion to answer questions. His eyes and the lower part of his face were

Abdul's, but without the squint that had given his father an air of indefinable mystery. I could not help recalling the photograph of a boy standing beside the burned wreckage of a plane, the one you showed me when we went to Funchal to collect Abdul's remains. A pang of sorrow and irremediable nostalgia almost took my breath away. I tried to hide my feelings and asked Jamil something, I don't remember what. He didn't answer but placed his hand on my arm and smiled as if to say he knew everything and understood everything. We spoke the well-worn trivialities used on such occasions. It was evident that Lina wanted Jamil and me to become acquainted before she told her story. In a short while she told Jamil to go up to the roof and play while we talked. The boy obeyed immediately and said goodbye to me with a smile and the scrutinizing glance of someone who wants to know hidden aspects of his interlocutor's personality.

Lina's story was one common to women who have lived with a man, had his child, and then made their own way in life. She and Abdul met in Bizerte, during the time he and I owned a freighter that was confiscated in Barcelona for carrying smuggled weapons for the anarchists. When Bashur learned that Lina was expecting a baby, he sent money regularly to help support her and to pay for the clinic when she gave birth. Her father was Algerian and her mother Spanish. From the time she was a girl she had shown an outstanding gift for dancing, and her mother had her take classes with a belly dancer who was a distant relative of hers and lived in retirement in a corner of the casbah. Her parents died in a bus crash when they were traveling to Constantine, where her father had obtained a job at the petroleum installations. She was thirteen when she was orphaned, and her dancing teacher took her in, along with the few belongings left by her parents. The woman cared for her until the girl began dancing at parties and gatherings in the neighborhood; she soon achieved recognition as a talented professional and joined a dance company that toured North Africa and the Middle East. She had taken her mother's family name when she learned that her parents were not married. Hers was the life of all the women who dance in the ports of the Mediterranean. She possessed the millenarian wisdom of a dance that is really a ritual developed within strict patterns set down in the remote past of the children of the desert. Lina met Bashur during one of her performances in Bizerte. His love for belly dancing was proverbial; I too, by the way, am a confessed and convicted addict of the art.

At that time I was involved in other occupations, to give some kind of name to my travels to Kuala Lumpur and the peninsula and nearby islands that now form the Malayan Federation, where I happened to meet, in circumstances I've already described, our beloved Alejandro Obregón, thanks to whom we are all together now. This was why I knew very little about the relationship between Abdul and Lina. Two or three vague allusions in his letters were all I heard of this story. Bashur continued to visit Lina when he was in Bizerte, but then, when he entered that phase in his life when everything became confused, he saw her again only in very brief encounters. You've already written about our friend's passage through the shadows of a marginal world. Lina learned of Bashur's death in the plane crash at Funchal shortly after it happened. By then she had stopped dancing and taken a series of jobs, first in Algiers, then in Oran, and finally in Marseilles, where she met the friend who was asking her now to work in Germany. As she had said in her letter, Lina was in touch with Abdul's family, especially Warda, who worked for the Lebanese Red Crescent.

The reason for not wanting to send Jamil to live with his aunt had its origin in her desire that he grow up in the shade of his father's memory—not, however, the Abdul remembered by his relatives but the one she had known. Since I was his oldest and closest friend, before she left for Germany, where she intended to earn enough money to make her relatively independent of the Bashur family, she wanted me to take charge of the boy and keep him with me for the time she would be away. Lina was afraid that without intending to, Abdul's family might create a distance between her and Jamil by turning him into one more of the numerous grandchildren of the old shipbuilder Ahmed Bashur, whose prestige in the region's merchant marine was still intact so many years after his death. I thought this misgiving was typical of her personality, but at the same time it reminded me of the mixture of reserve and warm affection that Abdul insisted on maintaining with his people.

"It's clear," Lina added, "that the only course left open to me is to turn to you for help, even though it will cause you a good number of difficulties, but I was sure you would respond to my request. I know you through Abdul, and he told me so much about your life together that, as I said, I feel as if I've known you for years. Now I just need to hear what you think of all this."

I replied that my decision had been made from the moment I received her letter. She could count on me without hesitation or reservation. But I did say that having a child like Jamil live with me was the last thing I could ever have imagined. After a life like mine—no family ties or commitments of any kind, always on the verge of disaster and wandering the most remote corners of the world, never caring about what might happen tomorrow or worrying about what I was leaving behind, moving from failure to failure, owning nothing but the clothes on my back—after all this, it was difficult to picture myself caring for a child who would depend on me for everything. Still, I said, something told me that for Jamil I might be a temporary substitute for his father, whom I loved dearly and whose absence I did not think I would ever be cured of. Lina nodded but said nothing, as if she had known beforehand that things would happen this way. Then, with no allusion to what we had just said, she presented an immediate problem.

According to Jamil's papers, he was a Tunisian, and his traveling to Mallorca created certain difficulties, since the residence permit issued to him in France had expired several months before. Lina had a different kind of permit, valid for a much longer time, because she had been born during the French mandate. We had to think of how I could take Jamil back to Spain with me. This would require a few days, and in that time the boy would get to know me, making the separation from his mother less painful. We continued to explore various solutions until it was time for lunch. The terrace began to fill with patrons, and Lina had to go to the kitchen to supervise the service. She said I would eat with Jamil. Lina went to work, and a short while later her son came to the table. He sat across from me in silence and looked at me with his large eyes. Their earlier expression of surprise had changed into one of uneasy questioning, but always with the smile he had inherited from his mother. When it was time for dessert, I asked him what he wanted, and he said very directly, this time in Spanish: "An ice. But not here, because they're not very good. I'll take you to a place that has the best ones." I found the naturalness of his answer appealing. We walked down the avenue along the port and went into a café, where the tables were beginning to empty. The waiter came over and greeted Jamil like an old friend. He looked at us, waiting for our order, and Jamil, after thinking a moment, said: "I want one scoop of lemon and one of coconut." He spoke French with a strong Arabic accent. The waiter turned to me, and I asked for coffee. "Don't you want an ice? They're really delicious," Jamil proposed with a certain disenchantment in his voice. "At this time of day I prefer coffee," I answered, fascinated by Jamil's assurance, so like Bashur's when he was in his best humor.

Now I think I must make a digression so that you can understand my relationship with Jamil more clearly. It isn't easy to explain what I felt when we met in the Ancien Café Mogador and he looked at me with that surprised expression, full of intensity, very childlike and at the same time tinged by a maturity without disillusionment or bitterness. This wasn't a child in front of me. At least not the conventional image of a child pictured by adults when we have little experience in that area. What I can tell you is this: From that moment on I felt a warm solidarity, a total, unreserved sympathy toward him. It surprised me at the time. It was something I had never known, and I thought I had experienced all the nuances of relationships in the difficult trajectory of my innumerable displacements and misfortunes. It was as if, in the most hidden part of my being, a door had suddenly opened onto a vast, unexplored territory filled with the most disconcerting marvels. I can't explain it any better than that, and I'm afraid I'm falling into sentimentality.

* * *

"I don't think so," commented my wife. "It's perfectly clear to me." She said this with enormous conviction, and Maqroll's relief at hearing her words was obvious.

"That's good," he said with a faint smile, and he returned to his story with greater naturalness and more tranquillity. It was clear that until now, it had been difficult for him to speak of certain aspects of his experience with Jamil.

* * *

When we were sitting in the café and Jamil, with great circumspection, tasted first a spoonful of lemon and then one of coconut, I felt as if I had been with him since the moment he was born. He was part of my life. And even though his being Abdul's son and my knowing I would take the place of his father were factors that undoubtedly helped to awaken those feelings in me, it was also true that the boy, as a person in his own right, possessed overwhelming grace and charm. For a moment I even thought I was deceiving myself, that because I never had anything to do with children, I took as extraordinary something that for others must be normal and ordinary.

But certain remarks we exchanged while Jamil was finishing his dessert confirmed my initial impression.

"You live on Mallorca, don't you?" he asked while he scraped the last of the ice from his dish.

"Yes," I answered, "in Pollensa. A very pretty port. But the place where I live is abandoned and in ruins." I thought it better to let him know about the deteriorated condition of my lair. Jamil shrugged, as if to say: "What difference does it make? That's fine." When he finished eating, he sat looking at the dish in an attitude of severe condemnation and then remarked in a sibylline tone: "It's always gone sooner than I expect. That's how things are. That's what my mama says."

Once again I had the impression that I was hearing Bashur, that Abdul was sitting beside me. Jamil's remark so echoed his father, and he said it so spontaneously, that for a moment I felt as if I were taking part in a supernatural invocation.

When we returned to the Ancien Café Mogador, Lina was waiting for us, leaning against the jamb of the door that led to the kitchen. From the expression on her face, I knew she had already perceived with absolute clarity my fondness for Jamil and my fascination with him.

"It never occurred to me that Jamil would force you to eat ices. That's where you went, isn't it?" she said in a lighthearted way. She had lost the tense uncertainty I had observed earlier.

"He didn't want any. He had coffee," Jamil replied impassively.

Lina looked at me for my reaction.

"Don't worry," I said. "I see that I'll be eating an ice next time, and that I'll enjoy it."

That afternoon I went to the docks to find out if there was a ship sailing for Mallorca. In fact one was, and the captain, whose name was listed on the arrival announcement, turned out to be someone I had known for many years. I thought I might work out an arrangement with him so that Jamil could travel with no difficulties. Two days later the freighter came into port, but at the offices of the shipping company that chartered it, I was told that the captain had been replaced at the last moment for reasons of health. Jamil had come with me to make the inquiries. We spent the entire day together, and the previous night he had slept in my bed, demanding to hear every detail of a tuna-fishing expedition in Alaska that almost cost me my life when Sverre Jensen and I lost the boat we had bought in Vancouver after many sacrifices.

We passed a good part of the day on the docks, and Jamil

bombarded me with questions: "Why do ships float? How can those tiny propellers move ships that are so big and made of iron? Who's higher, the chief machinist or the bos'n? Why is it so easy for ships to change flags when people can't change their countries?" and many similar questions, which seemed easy enough to answer, though when I tried I found myself stumbling into hopeless obstacles; and more questions followed, all of them equally perplexing. We walked back on the avenue along the port, and Jamil insisted on having an ice at the café, where he was treated like an old and valued customer. That afternoon, while Jamil ate two scoops of vanilla, we watched the activity in the port. There was slow, modest traffic, in no way comparable, of course, to Amsterdam or Hamburg, which had been the subjects of long conversations with Jamil. We saw a coast guard cutter towing in a small boat with hauled sails, whose only crew seemed to be a man at the helm watching the maneuver with a disconsolate air and occasionally moving the wheel in order to follow the vessel of the harbor police. Jamil asked what had happened, and before I could answer, the waiter, who was standing next to our table and observing the operation, explained:

"They're smugglers from the Costa Brava. Poor men, there's no hope for them. They still haven't learned that these days it's too risky to work their trade. They're always caught."

"Gaviero," said Jamil, who still couldn't pronounce my name very well (the combination of *q* and *r* was too hard for him). "What's a smuggler?"

"They're people who take goods from one country to another and don't pay the customs duties charged for foreign products. The coast guard stops them and arrests them."

"But are the men in the coast guard bad? Do they kill the smugglers if they try to escape?" asked Jamil.

The waiter answered quickly. "No, Jamil. They're not bad, and they don't kill them. That was long ago, when people were wilder and there was more smuggling. Since we're so close to the border, this happens all the time. They're held here for twenty-four hours, their goods are confiscated, and they're sent back to Spain."

"Poor things," said the boy. "I wouldn't do anything to them."

The waiter's reaction was clearly sympathetic to Jamil's words. That was when I thought of a plan that might solve our immigration difficulties. I decided to tell the waiter about our problem, and when I had finished, I said that in my opinion the easiest thing would be to take Jamil to Spain by land. But we needed the help of someone in Port-Vendres who would not arouse suspicion at the border checkpoint. The waiter, with no hesitation, told me in a low voice:

"You already know the person you need. Pierre Vidal, a Catalonian from Roussillon, works at the Ancien Café Mogador. Talk to him. Trust me."

Jamil finished his ice, and we set out for home. As we walked, he stared at me as if trying to decipher my plan. He already knew that his future was at stake. I tried to explain the situation to him as simply as I could:

"For you to come with me to Pollensa, we first have to go to Spain and take a boat from Barcelona. But since the police here don't accept your passport the way it is now and would ask a lot of questions, we'll do it an easier way."

"Yes," Jamil remarked with a touch of pride, "like the smugglers. But suppose they stop us?"

"They won't. Nothing will happen. You trust Maqroll, don't you?" I asked him directly to see his reaction.

Jamil's reply was one of the boy's famous answers, which Mossén Ferrán and I have conscientiously collected:

"Yes, I do trust the Gaviero," he said. "The ones I don't trust are those men in the coast guard with their launches, their reflector lights, and their guns. They scare me."

My answer was, of necessity, somewhat haphazard:

"It's just a question of not running into them. We'll travel overland. It's not as risky."

Jamil turned to look at me with a mischievous, contented expression. The overland route opened new possibilities for adventure that he found very appealing. But since he knew I was a sailor, I don't think he had much confidence in my ability to travel on solid ground. Once again a confused tangle of memories filled my mind. I felt as if Abdul Bashur himself, with his delighted circumlocutions in response to my plans for challenging the monotonous routine of destiny, were walking beside me.

Lina was waiting for us at the Ancien Café Mogador. We sat down to eat, and when the meal was finished Jamil began to blink, overcome by sleepiness. The night before, we had chatted until it was very late. Lina took him to his room and came back almost immediately. She had guessed that something was brewing with regard to our trip to Pollensa. I told her of my conversation with the waiter at the other café and my plan to cross the border by land. When I had finished, she expressed her approval of the project and then went to find Vidal.

"This is Pierre Vidal," she said when she brought the man back to the table. He looked at me attentively. "And this is Maqroll the Gaviero, as you know. Well, he'll tell you what this is about."

I explained the general outline of my plan. He showed the greatest interest in helping us. His somber expression disappeared, and he smiled with satisfaction at being able to contribute his knowledge and experience to our success.

"Don't even think about trying it by sea," he said. "They're very strict, especially at Spanish ports. You're right: The only way is overland, crossing the border at Le Perthus. You ought to do it in a car with plates from Perpignan or any city close to Spain. Then they almost never ask for papers. They don't on the Spanish side either. You drive to Figueras and take the train to Barcelona. You already know about the trip from Barcelona to Palma. They don't ask for documents on the ferry."

It all sounded suspiciously simple; he must have noticed my reaction, because he insisted:

"Yes, sir. That's how it is now. You must have been here many years ago, and that's why you even thought of taking a ship. These days it's very simple. You just tell me when you plan to leave, and I'll make the arrangements with a cousin of mine who goes to Junquera several times a week; he owns a restaurant there, and one of his nephews manages it for him. Everything will be in the family. Just let me know ahead of time—two days or so. It'll be fine. Don't worry."

I felt tremendously relieved, and my reservations vanished. We continued talking, and I told him of my experience many years before in Port-Vendres. He expressed his compassion with an even broader smile and said he had been an adolescent back then. He remembered the flood of immigrants like a painful, gloomy nightmare that had saddened his youth. He left to wait on a table occupied by a family of Dutch tourists who were signaling to him and beginning to protest.

Having cleared the way for our trip to Spain, I had only to arrange with Lina how and when we would leave. Taking advantage of the fact that Jamil was still sleeping, Lina expressed her feelings very directly, making no attempt to hide them.

"I want you to know," she said, "that I'm very confident about going to Germany and leaving Jamil with you. I can see that the two of you get along wonderfully. He talks about you all the time and feels an affection for you that I think is returned. Things are so strange: The most unlikely decision was the best one. If I told people who know you that I was going to leave Jamil in your care, they'd tell me I'm crazy. Someone like you—no permanent home anywhere, a man whose life is unsettled and filled with sudden, drastic changes, a man who lives at the edge of lawbreaking and prison—you don't seem the ideal person to take care of a boy who isn't even five years old. But I trusted my intuition and remembered all the stories Bashur used to tell me about you, and I thought there was no one better to take care of my son. And now I know I was right. I think you two should leave first. I have some things to take care of, and I need to arrange the details of our trip to Germany with my friend. We'll go by train, of course, but we have to find the fastest and cheapest way to Bremen. You can't imagine how hard it is for me to leave my son, yet I know it's the best thing for both of us, and I'll try to hide what I'm feeling. But children always know, and it won't do any good. Well, we'll see."

I told her I could leave at any time. I was reassured that she knew Jamil was in good hands and would be cared for with great affection.

Lina went up to Jamil's room, and I remained on the terrace, thinking about the new situation that destiny had presented to me, one that never would have entered my wildest schemes. Vidal approached the table and, seeing my state of mind, tried to raise my spirits.

"Jamil is a wonderful boy," he said. "It'll do you good to have him with you and be able to watch this new life that's awakening. I have two grandchildren. For my wife and me, they're like bathing in water that renews feelings we thought had died long ago. It's very intense, and very energizing. Everything will be fine. You'll see. I can almost say I envy you."

He returned to his duties, and each time he passed my table, he winked as a sign of complicity. Lina's words, and then Vidal's, filled my thoughts. I was becoming aware of aspects of my decision that I had ignored until now. I realized that Jamil was connected to my life, a life I had considered resolved and stable in my Pollensa refuge. It was strange: The change, rather than weighing on me like an unexpected responsibility, infused me with a kind of enthusiasm I had stopped feeling for anything many years before. It was evident that Jamil would give himself

unhesitatingly to whatever I might propose. His joyful participation in our relationship, especially when I described the details of
our future life in Pollensa, seemed like a magnificent gift from the
gods. I thought of my life spent careening from port to port, from
corner to increasingly wild and remote corner of the world, passing
through indescribable hells and being roughened by experiences I
often think must have been lived by different individuals and not by
just one man, whose survival I cannot explain—all this, in short, to
end up as a counterfeit uncle to Abdul Bashur's son, a boy whose
life and destiny would depend completely on every one of my gestures and words. There was something insane about the situation,
but I thought it best not to scrutinize it too closely. One must not
provoke the powers that move the strings but do not come down to
consult with us. It's possible, I told myself, that this belongs to the
order I have dreamed and hoped for so often and that so often
slipped out of my hands. Had it been offered to me now in the person of this child, who was saying to me: "This is the great test they
have sent you. I will be at your side to assure you that at least once
everything happens as it should and not as it usually does: the work
of an ominous fate that pursues you"?

Just then Jamil appeared. He sat beside me and began to watch
the harbor traffic. As if he had guessed my thoughts, he suddenly
asked with an inquisitive look:

"Is it like this in Pollensa?"

We had spoken of Pollensa and our trip, but not in detail. I
hadn't known how we would leave Port-Vendres, and I didn't
want him to take as conclusive things that were still tentative.
Now everything had become clear and definite, and it was time
to talk about our future. I was aware that Jamil took everything I
told him as literal, incontrovertible truth. I know now that this is
common to all children, and with a little introspective effort I
could have discovered it by recalling my own childhood. But I
also know that from the time I was a boy working in the crow's
nest on fishing boats, I had been obliged to attend to what each
day rained down on me in a torrent of dangers and sudden
alarms. I did not have time to return to my childhood, and it had
been lost in the daily vertigo of an implacable present.

I replied that the Mallorcan port was on a larger bay than the
one in Port-Vendres and that the landscape was very different.
The light was more intense, and it was everywhere; the water was
more transparent and calmer; the city, smaller than Port-Vendres,

extended over a plain with low hills in the distance. There were no Templar fortresses like the ones in Port-Vendres, which chilled the spirit on gray, rainy days. In Pollensa they spoke the Mallorcan dialect, very similar to Catalan, which he had surely heard in the south of France. Pollensa was quieter, and there were fewer ships than in Port-Vendres. There were many pleasure yachts, some of them large and luxurious. We would live in abandoned shipyards where they had once cleaned the ships and repaired the hulls and all the metal fittings when long use at sea made that necessary. From a window in our room we could watch the arrival and departure of the ships, most of them recreational, which made the view of the bay so lively.

Then I told him how we would cross the border into Spain at Le Perthus. "And if the guards catch us, what will they do?" he exclaimed.

"In the first place," I said, "they won't catch us. People go through without a lot of red tape and don't always have to show their papers. But if that does happen, they'll just send us back to France and that'll be the end of it." I had to lie a little. What might be waiting for me in the event we were stopped was somewhat more complicated.

"Then they're good police," said Jamil, as if trying to reassure me that there was no reason to feel the uneasiness his first question might have provoked.

"The police, Jamil, are not there to be good or bad but to be police." I waited for the boy to reply, but he only gave me a look of commiseration that said: "There's no hope for you. Sometimes you don't understand anything."

Then he bombarded me with questions regarding the trip, with a wild excitement that he communicated to me. I thought it was extraordinary; after all that has happened in my life, to find myself feeling that feverish enthusiasm about something that should have meant no more than a simple, unimportant routine. The reason lay in Jamil, in my discovery of Jamil and his bottomless desire to embrace everything, know everything, see everything. I'm afraid I'm boring you terribly with this insistence on the novelty of my experience, when it is probably very familiar to you. Surely you must find it ridiculous to meet up with someone for whom a relationship with a baby less than five years old becomes a revelatory experience.

*   *   *

*"No. That's not true," said my wife. "You're not boring us.
Every encounter we have with a child discloses an astonishing
world. Whatever psychologists may say, there are no rules or
principles that can predict the surprises this experience holds in
store. But I wasn't thinking about that. I must confess, Maqroll,
that I've been wanting to ask you something for a while and
haven't dared to."*

*"I know, Señora. Don't worry. Jamil is fine and living where
he ought to live, with his mother and Abdul's family. I'm the
one who isn't fine. But I have an old addiction to accepting destiny, and I know what I need to do."*

*Mossén Ferrán placed one of his large laborer's hands over the
Gaviero's hand as it lay on the table. The gesture was more eloquent than the words he would not or could not say. Maqroll
looked away from us for a moment and then returned to his
story.*

* * *

On the following day, the friend who was going to work with
Lina in Germany came to visit her. Lina insisted that I be present
during their conversation and meet the woman she called, with a
certain touch of irony, "my protector." In many ways she was the
exact opposite of Lina. Blond and plump, she had a perpetually
distracted gaze, fixed on something that was never there but
which she searched for continually. Asunta Espósito had a curious
background: Her father was Savoyard and her mother was from
Roussillon. She breathed an air of absolute honesty and obstinate persistence in pursuing her goals, concealing both qualities
behind the constant smile of a store-window mannequin and the
air of someone who really isn't in the place where you find her.
She clearly felt an admiration and affection for Lina that made
her seem younger than Jamil's mother, although, as I subsequently
learned, she was actually several years older. I had the immediate
impression that the good Asunta would never have returned to
Bremen if it were not for Lina's company, which guaranteed her
an emotional stability that made exile tolerable. When she spoke
she stumbled slightly over the *s* sound, which she pronounced by
pushing her tongue more than usual against her palate.

"I thought you'd be younger," she said abruptly before she sat
down beside me. "No, that's not what I mean, but Lina told me
about your travels and your wandering as if you loved adventure,
and you don't look anything like that kind of person. You remind

me more of a monk who travels the world searching for his lost monastery."

Lina tried to excuse her friend's remarks. "Asunta crashes around as if she were blind, always seeing things that aren't there and people whom she invents."

I replied that, on the contrary, it was possible that Asunta was not so far off the track, that it was not the first time I had heard the comparison, although searching for the monastery seemed like a revelation. We all laughed at the same time, and then Asunta asked me what I thought of Jamil. I didn't want to go into great detail; instead, I tried to reassure them that I would be very careful with the boy. I was certain this was what most concerned both women, Asunta more than Lina, who by this time was better acquainted with me. I explained that Jamil was like a nephew and that I found him much brighter and more intelligent than his age would lead one to suppose. Asunta blushed for no apparent reason and looked at Lina as if approving her decision to call on me: She had obviously harbored some doubts. We talked of Germany and the Germans, and of Bremen's sinister climate. At this point Jamil appeared and wanted to go with me to the port to watch the arrival of an Italian warship, which had been announced on the blackboard outside the harbormaster's office. I said goodbye to the women, and as we were leaving, Lina remarked, with the naturalness of a person speaking of something that had been decided a long time ago:

"Vidal has to be told this evening that you're leaving. Everything will be ready in two days."

I looked at her with a certain surprise, and she, ignoring my reaction, began to talk to Asunta about the documents she had to pick up at some office. Jamil said nothing, but as we walked to the port, his silence indicated clearly the impression his mother's words had made on him.

That night we spoke to Vidal and arranged our departure two days later. His cousin would come by for us before noon. Lina spent the time buying new clothing she said Jamil would need in Pollensa, and preparing the clothes the boy already had. Mossén Ferrán had discreetly placed some French money in my pocket as I was boarding the ship in Palma: The amount I had taken with me would clearly not be enough. I offered to go shopping with Lina and pay for the purchases, but she rejected the idea and would not allow me to insist.

On the day of our departure, Vidal's cousin, Ramón, came for us at about ten in the morning. His features resembled Pierre's, but he was heavier and had an air of athletic youthfulness; in this respect he was entirely unlike his cousin, who had a sickly, feverish quality that was unsettling. Lina came down with Jamil, who was carrying a small suitcase that had seen better days but gave the boy the dignity of an experienced traveler. Lina held him for a long while, doing her best to hide her sorrow. Jamil, intrigued by his imminent adventure, did not show much emotion at the time. Vidal watched us with interest, and when his cousin's small Renault van pulled away, he put one arm around Lina's shoulders and with the other repeatedly waved goodbye in an affectionate gesture. Both sides of the van displayed the same rather crude, brightly colored painting of a dish of prawns and the words "Can Miquel. The Best in Fish and Seafood. La Junquera."

We sat beside the driver. I was in the middle and Jamil by the window, because he did not want to miss a single detail when we crossed the frontier. Jamil hugged his little suitcase as if it were a precious object. He agreed to Ramón's suggestion that he put it in the back of the vehicle, but the boy would turn around to look at it from time to time, as if afraid it might not be there. Our driver was calm, almost indifferent, and this fascinated Jamil. As he drove onto the highway to Spain, and I read aloud the sign that pointed to it, Jamil turned to look at him and asked the question he'd had in mind for some time:

"If the guards arrest us, will they take your car?"

Before answering, Ramón waited a moment, raising and lowering his heavy eyebrows in a way that made us laugh. Finally, he replied in emphatic Catalan, as if he had been asked an inconceivably absurd question: "For God's sake, boy! Nobody's going to arrest us. What an idea! The guards are reading the newspaper and having their second cup of coffee, the one they always enjoy most. They won't even look at us. You'll see—they'll wave as if they were brushing away a fly, and that's all they'll do."

Jamil did not seem very convinced, but he asked what the small forts were that appeared at regular intervals along the hills as if guarding the highway. We explained that they had been built in the old days, when the two countries were at war. It was evident that he wished they were still in use and represented a current danger. A short while later he was sound asleep, leaning against my arm. I moved him so that his head was on my chest. He breathed with an innocent serenity that I found touching. His long eyelashes fluttered from time to time. He surely was dreaming about police and smugglers. Again I felt a warmth flooding my chest, a dense, almost painful tenderness. Jamil, the son of the best friend life had ever offered me, was asleep, confident of the affection he had awakened in me from the moment we met. In his gestures, in every aspect of his relationship to me, the boy displayed a kind of energy, a surprising power that unleashed a torrent of sensations I had never known. I must have experienced them in childhood and then been careful to hide them deep inside. Life had impinged very early, and I had been obliged to swallow a good amount of bitterness administered by adults with the indifferent brutality of what is called "the struggle to survive." Again it's something I can't explain, but as I held Jamil's curly head in my arms, I felt a live current emanating from him, a kind of messenger who led me through the forsaken disorder of my life to a newly created world, a fortunate beginning over again that wiped out past errors and troubles and returned me to a state of willing enthusiasm that was close to intoxication. Well, it's more complicated than that, and simpler. Señora, certainly you understand me.

* * *

My wife nodded and smiled but said nothing. Mossén Ferrán shook his head, visibly moved, showing his long familiarity with these discourses of the Gaviero. As for me, I remembered something Abdul Bashur had told me at the time I met him, which helped me to establish a lasting friendship with Maqroll.

"The Gaviero," he said, "is like those crustaceans that have a shell hard as a rock to protect their delicate flesh. He hides that inner, sensitive area so carefully, it's easy to think he doesn't have one. Then come the surprises, and in his case they can be revelations."

* * *

As we approached the French border station Jamil awoke, as if he had guessed that the moment he had waited for so eagerly had arrived. A French guard, his helmet pushed back from his forehead, was reading the paper with a sleepy, good-natured air. He turned to look at us, noted the vehicle, and waved us on while he returned to his reading with an almost insulting lack of concern. Jamil, in an immediate, uncontrollable reaction, pointed his finger as if he were shooting at the guard and shouted in Arabic:

"We won, bang bang bang!"

I tried to put my hand over his mouth, but it was too late. The guard did not even look up from his paper. Ramón's rebuke was severe:

"*Cullons!* This is a fine place for the boy to talk Arabic! Is he *boig* or what?"

Jamil looked at us mischievously and shrugged with a feigned indifference. We drove over the border into Spain. At the checkpoint the guards were chatting peaceably and smoking what must have been their tenth cigarette of the day. They waved a friendly greeting at Ramón, who put his foot on the accelerator and waved back, his hand out the window. Jamil looked at me and remarked:

"We won't kill them, because they're Ramón's friends. Did you see them wave?"

We reached La Junquera, and Ramón dropped us at the station for buses going to Figueras. He said goodbye with the cordiality of an old friend, and running his hand through Jamil's hair, he said to him affectionately:

"While you're here, save your Arabic for when you're alone with the Gaviero. It can make trouble for you in this country."

Jamil observed him with interest and nodded as if to let him know he accepted the advice without understanding it very well.

We went to a café to wait for our bus. Jamil withdrew into a silence that made me think he had not realized until then that he was away from his mother. He was on the point of tears, but with some difficulty he managed to hold them back. Finally, he decided to speak:

"My mother told me never to forget Arabic. She said my father spoke it and all the Bashurs speak it, and what'll I do now if they don't let me speak it here? And Mama, who will Mama talk Arabic to in Germany?" Large tears ran down his cheeks.

"You and I will speak Arabic whenever you want. People who live near borders are always very cautious and don't want to be taken for foreigners. Your mama will talk with her friends at work: Many of them are Palestinian or Syrian. When she comes for you in Pollensa, which will be very soon, you'll see that the two of you will speak Arabic the way you always did."

Jamil grew a little calmer, but there was a vague uneasiness in his eyes when he looked at me, as if he had never seen me before. We finished our café au lait and boarded the bus, which left immediately. We reached Figueras in the afternoon, and I took Jamil to have shellfish and rice at a tavern that Ramón had recommended. I was surprised at the boy's ability to shell the prawns, and I asked him where he had learned a skill that seems to belong exclusively to people from the coast. He said his mother had worked at a seafood restaurant in Perpignan and had taught him to peel the shellfish and prawns that she secretly brought back for him. When it was time to take the train, we went directly to the station. The Barcelona express was two hours late. I thought it would be more prudent not to walk the streets of Figueras without a fixed destination. The waiting room at the station was almost empty. We sat on a long bench of spartan discomfort, and Jamil began to ask me again about Mallorca and Pollensa. With a patience I did not know I had, I answered every question, trying not to build up his illusions regarding the attractions of the place or to insist too much on the precariousness of our lodgings. When the train pulled into the station, Jamil took me by the hand and said:

"Let's go, Gaviero, that's our train. I want to get to Pollensa soon."

He pronounced it "Pollentsa," and from then on there was no way to correct him. We boarded the train, and I told him we still had to take the ferry from Barcelona to Mallorca. He grew drowsy again and fell asleep in my arms. I must have been holding him very awkwardly, because a woman sitting across from us gave me an understanding smile. We reached Barcelona as night was falling. Jamil awoke shortly before the train pulled into Francia Station. We took a bus to the port. The ferry was leaving at eight. We bought our tickets and went to our small cabin. Jamil did not want to go back to sleep, and he took me up to the deck to see the ferry's departure. As the time approached, he was in ecstasies as he watched the arrival and departure of vessels in the port and followed closely the maneuvers of several large passenger ships and a few freighters setting sail for various parts of the world. His fascination with the sea was obvious, and it moved me deeply. He scrutinized everything and stored up all the details of the harbor traffic, along with the information he asked me for with insatiable curiosity. I could not help imagining how Bashur would have reacted to his son's interest in the things of the sea. I finally convinced Jamil to have supper with me, and then we went to our cabin to sleep. His desire to watch the ferry come into Palma woke him periodically. When we touched the dock, he opened his eyes with frustration at not having witnessed the mooring operation.

Mossén Ferrán was waiting for us in Palma. I remember his
first words:

"*Qué nen mes maco.* He looks like a hereditary prince traveling
incognito."

* * *

"*That was the impression I had,*" *Mossén Ferrán said to my
wife.* "*I remember as if it were yesterday. Jamil is a unique child.
These are grandfatherly reactions, born before you even realize
it.*" *My wife smiled, amused at the enthusiasm of the priest and
historian.*

*Night was beginning to fall, and the sunset, almost excessive
in its display of delirious oranges and violets, imposed a ceremonial silence on us. When this orgy of color faded into a purplish
red, slowly invaded by grays that recalled the landscapes of El
Greco, Maqroll was the first to speak:*

"*I'm afraid this has gone on too long. You must be worn
out.*"

"*Not at all,*" *said my wife.* "*I'm dying to know what happened to Jamil and what his life was like in Pollensa. If it's all
right with Doña Mercé, I'd like to propose staying here until
you finish your story.*"

*Mossén Ferrán and I agreed. The priest left the table to talk
to the owner and returned a short while later to tell us that
Doña Mercé said it was fine, that we should take our time and
she would soon bring something to eat. In the meantime, she
had given the priest a magnificent pitcher of sangría for us, with
sliced peaches and strawberries from her garden, which Mossén
Ferrán praised enthusiastically.*

*Maqroll sat staring at the horizon, where the great Mediter-
ranean night was beginning to settle. At that moment I sensed
the melancholy working inside him, the pit of uncertainty and
sorrow in which he surely had been submerged since his childhood. Buried and forgotten, his contact with Jamil had awakened those days, bringing back memories of a paradise he had
considered lost. It was clear that telling his story helped to
assuage his grief.*

"*Well,*" *he said,* "*I've asked myself if all my years at sea, all
my tumultuous, absurd incursions on land, did not contribute in
a significant way to the marginalization, or should I say the
amputation, of an experience that was revealed to me with
Jamil.*" *He turned to me.* "*You remember in the diary I kept on*

the Xurandó River, when I was looking for those damned
sawmills that vanished into nightmare, I mention the moments
in life when we think that the corner we've never turned, the
woman we've never seen again, the road we left in order to follow another, the book we never finished, all merge to form
another life, parallel to our own, which in a certain sense belongs
to us too? Well, a good part of the life I left behind came back
all at once when Jamil was with me, and the parallel current
merged for an instant with my real life. Then, when it returned
to its own channel, I was left battered and without a direction.
You can understand this better than anyone."

It was typical of the Gaviero to launch into disquisitions like
these before continuing his tales. He was moved by a need to
impose an inner order on the turbulent matter of his days, the
ungovernable chaos that his wanderings and sufferings kept at a
perpetual boil. I remember on one occasion, when I went to rescue him from an unconfessable enterprise at the mouth of the
Mississippi, in Grand Isle, I heard him say, after an orgiastic
night of bourbon and mulatto women in a miserable port whose
name I have forgotten:

"The only order we can trust, the only one that's certain and
definitive, is the order of death. I know that everybody knows
this, but the trick lies in continuing to live and trying not to
have a close relationship with death. When she beckons, you
have to turn your back on her. Not out of fear, of course, but
with the certainty that it's not us she's interested in but our poor
bones, the flesh she feeds to her legions. Still, her order is waiting
for us, the only valid order. Don't forget it, don't ever forget it."
And he seized my arm and shook it in blind despair. I remembered the episode that night in Pollensa, under the sky of the
Hellenes and the Omayyad princes, the sky that witnesses the
slow riding of the condottiere Giudoriccio da Fogliano through
the municipal palace at Siena.

Maqroll returned to his story.

*   *   *

What I had most feared produced the greatest pleasure in Jamil:
the disorder and poverty of my refuge in the shipyards. I thought
they would disconcert him, but for the boy they were a source of
endless diversion. We arrived after a long ride in our priest's taxi.
Mossén Ferrán could not find enough words to praise the viva-
cious spirit and lively gestures of our guest, and he accompanied

us to the shipyards. When he said goodbye, he looked at me for a moment as if fearing Jamil's reaction to the ruined place. The boy dashed up the rickety stairs to my room, threw the bag with his belongings on my bed, and ran to open the window so that he could look at the sea. The expanse of water reflecting the phosphorescence of the night sky cast a kind of hypnotic spell on Jamil. In the meantime, I arranged a provisional bed for him out of boards and two trunks filled with papers, the same kind I had once prepared on the occasion of a visit from my old traveling companion through Central Asia. When the bed was ready, I tried to convince Jamil to leave his observation post and go to sleep after our tiring journey. At last he did, but not without asking, when he was already tucked between the sheets:

"What are we going to do tomorrow?"

At first I did not know how to answer so menacing and concrete a question. My work at the shipyards consists of looking after the place and keeping the townspeople from completely dismantling what remains of the installations. I usually spend the interminable hours of leisure reading books, most of them lent to me by Mossén Ferrán, and reconstructing my memory of a past that I review as if it had been lived by someone else, someone I occasionally feel to be alien to the person I am now. Jamil kept his eyes on my face, waiting for an answer that eluded me. Finally, for some reason, it occurred to me to say:

"Tomorrow we'll go fishing."

"Where?"

"Here, on the dock across from the shipyards," I ventured with a certain caution.

"Are there a lot of fish there?"

"Well," I replied, a little surer of the road I had invented, "we'll see tomorrow. I've never gone fishing there, but you can see the fish from the end of the dock."

"We'll see tomorrow. If there really were any fish, you would've caught them by now."

"The fish are there. I've seen them. They're always there. Now it's time for us to go to sleep," I replied with precarious authority.

We slept very late. Jamil helped prepare the café au lait and toast with generous amounts of marmalade, his favorite breakfast, according to Lina. I had my usual tea and slices of black bread, and Jamil regarded me with undisguised reproach: The repugnance he felt for tea in no way agreed with the tastes of his desert forebears. We left for the village to find fishing rods. Mossén Ferrán provided us with everything we needed, and we returned to the dock. The loose boards at the end of the pier were our seat, and we settled down to wait for a highly uncertain outcome. My handling of the fishing rod could not have been very convincing, because after a while Jamil exclaimed as he laughed at my clumsiness:

"But, Gaviero, you don't even know how to fish. What did you do on those ships when you were a boy?"

"I never had time to fish when I was a boy on the ships. I had to climb to the top of the tallest mast and tell the crew what was on the horizon. Each person has his job on a ship, and there's not much time for fishing. When you fish in the ocean, you use nets, and it's very hard work."

Then I began a long explanation of how that was done, and I told him I had owned a fishing boat with a Norwegian seaman who had been my friend many years ago. Jamil looked at me with astonishment and skepticism, and then a fish began to pull at his hook. I helped him reel in the line while he held the rod with both hands. His eyes were shining with pleasure, and he gave cries of joy in Arabic. The fish weighed almost three kilos. I couldn't tell him what kind it was, which did not add much to his opinion of me as a fisherman. To console me, Jamil said very seriously:

"You'll have better luck this afternoon, Maqroll. Now let's take this fish to Mossén Ferrán, so he can cook it for our supper."

I explained that first of all, I wasn't sure the fish was edible, and second, Mossén Ferrán was a very busy person and we couldn't just impose on him like that. Jamil insisted, and finally we went to our friend's house.

* * *

"My cook," said the priest, "could not prepare the beast because it wasn't an edible species. Jamil was so disappointed that we had to wipe away the tears that rolled down his cheeks as he watched the cook throw the prize of his first fishing expedition into the garbage can."

Maqroll was withdrawn and absent again, and we were silent for a time. Then he went on with his story.

* * *

Fishing from the dock became our principal activity. Other fish swam past us, which were edible, and you should have seen the pride in Jamil's eyes at the table when one that he had caught was the main dish at Mossén Ferrán's house.

Then we tried our luck in a small boat, one of the two still left at the shipyards, which I managed to repair. I put in a mast and a sail, and we set out to explore the bay in search of places where the fishing was good. I taught the boy how to control the line that held the sail, which he did with utter delight, and my credit in his eyes rose enough for him to forget my failures as a fisherman. Our days went by in a peaceable rhythm, filled with our exploits as navigators and fishermen in the bay of Pollensa. There's no point in telling you how often I thought of the storms I had faced during my years of fishing in Alaska, the times I almost sank in an icy sea whose wrath is the terror of sailors.

When we received a letter from Lina in Germany, I would read it to Jamil, who listened with the attention and seriousness of an adult. He often asked me to repeat certain paragraphs in which she told about incidents at work or described her life in Bremen. Lina was obviously concealing the difficulties and sorrows she surely experienced in one of the gloomiest and most inclement cities I know. Jamil always wanted to answer his mother's letter immediately. "So she doesn't have to wait too long to hear our news," he would say, as if excusing his request. He talked to me frequently about his mother and told me anecdotes of their life together in the various countries where they had lived.

His image of Abdul had been constructed from Lina's constant allusions to Bashur and from the fantasies he himself had woven around his father's life at sea. One day I proposed describing Abdul as faithfully as I could, and Jamil listened with vivid interest and an occasional sprinkling of skepticism. I tried to be as straightforward as possible and at the same time pass over episodes the boy would have found difficult to understand. I told him about his father's obsession with owning the ideal freighter, whose proportions, design, and technical details he knew by heart, and how he had never been granted his dream. I especially insisted on his qualities as a loyal friend who was always ready to share whatever dangers and punishments fate might bring. As the days passed, I realized that Jamil had combined the details of my description with the fantasies he had created, which seemed as real to him as anything I had told him. It couldn't be helped, and I chose to leave matters as they were. Bashur, I thought, would have celebrated Jamil's inventions. It seemed admirable to me that Lina had not interfered with them either. Life would soon show Jamil the true image of his father, kept with devotion by his friends and family in the most far-flung corners of the world.

This was how a new life began for me. Every hour of the day and night was inhabited by this child who held my hand as he discovered the world and, at the same time, taught me something I thought I had always known. It was, in a sense, like returning to an arcane conversation with oracles. Each day increased my aston-ishment at the innate certainty with which Jamil established mas-tery over his discoveries. My refuge was becoming filled with the most unexpected objects; once chosen and saved by Jamil, they acquired an evocative, magical quality. Seashells of every shape and size, bottles and pieces of wood washed up on the beach by the tide, skeletons of birds and fish discovered in cavities in the rocks, bits of string and scraps of sail, unrecognizable metal objects, and even letters nailed onto weathered boards. Each object helped Jamil construct a history that conferred undeniable presence and value upon them. At night, in the light of the Cole-man lamp that illuminated our room, the boy went over his trea-sures and told me their stories, enriching the tale each time with surprising variations. One night he showed me a piece of purple rope and explained:

"With this rope they hung a pirate who killed everybody on an island and then took it for himself. He even killed the chil-dren. When warships came and captured him, he was hung from the highest mast on the flagship. Do you know what his name was? The Furious Leopard."

I ventured to ask where he had learned so many details and what he knew about pirates and flagships. He replied that on sev-eral occasions he had heard me talk about pirates and an island called Cecilie with Mossén Ferrán. "Sicily," I corrected him. This was how I realized that in his own way, Jamil had absorbed my conversations with Mossén Ferrán regarding the Almogávares incursions and had also looked through various books on the subject that our friend had lent me and whose pictures surely inspired the boy in creating his histories.

None of the objects rescued from the sea by Jamil could be moved. When, in a distracted moment, I attempted to do so, I was severely reprimanded. Jamil's reasons left me somewhat bemused:

"If you move them they won't know where they are. You

take them away from their friends and send them to live with strangers."

As time passed, I was no longer puzzled by the secret laws governing the world of childhood. I sometimes even found myself enthusiastically obeying them. My complicity became complete—just as it had been with his father—and soon we did not need to explain the reasons for our actions, which were always undertaken jointly in a world known only to us. I often had to make a mental effort to remember that he was a child of four and not an adult close to forty, which was Abdul's age when we first met in Cairo. The parallelism was accentuated because of certain of Jamil's gestures, which, as I said before, resembled his father's. A way of raising his arm and keeping it there as he began to say something he wanted to emphasize; the movements of his hands, so out of harmony with his words that it seemed as if someone hidden inside him were ordering those gestures for reasons of his own; finally, the habit of leaving certain phrases unfinished, creating a momentary silence between us. The days passed in undisturbed tranquillity, and Jamil acquired a healthier, more robust appearance than when I first saw him in Port-Vendres.

One day we received a letter from Lina in which her usual optimism and acceptance took on a more taciturn, dispirited tone. She was working at a chemical factory in the outskirts of Bremen and shared a small room in a sordid working-class neighborhood on the other side of the city with the blond Asunta and two Portuguese women. Her rent was higher than she had estimated, and there were frequent deductions from her salary for union dues and insurance premiums. In addition, she was doing piecework, and her fatigue and the frequent colds she suffered because of Bremen's climate kept her from earning as much as she had expected. She was determined to save an amount that would allow her to go to Lebanon and not be a burden on the Bashurs, especially Warda, who lived with an austerity dictated by her desire to contribute all she could to the charitable work in which she was involved. To accomplish her goal, Lina would have to stay in Germany for at least a year. As for Jamil, she confessed she was not worried about him because he was with me and Mossén Ferrán, whom she did not know but to whom she was very grateful for the warm welcome he had given her son. Of course she missed Jamil terribly and was sometimes tormented by the desire to give it all up and be with him again. She asked me to tell her more about him in my letters—the progress he was making, his games—and reminded me to mention her every day so that she could be as close to him as possible. This letter was sent to Mossén Ferrán's address, as were all the others, but the priest's name was on the envelope, not mine. I said nothing to Jamil about this news, which I was sure would have made him very sad. Lina did not have to insist on the need to keep the boy's image and memory of his mother alive. I talked about her constantly, and he too brought her into the conversation at every opportunity.

Shortly before Christmas, we sent Lina a photograph of her son on the docks where we fished. Taking the picture was nothing short of an odyssey. I had never used a camera and neither had Mossén Ferrán. Fortunately, we found a photographer who took pictures of tourists on the beach, and he handled the project. When I saw the snapshot, I could not help thinking of the one of Abdul as a boy standing beside the wreckage of the plane that had been shot down in Lebanon by French artillery. The same eyes, astonished and sad, the same wild, curly hair. I kept a copy of Jamil's picture. Things must have changed a great deal in me; remember I didn't want to have the photograph of Abdul that you once offered me because, as I told you then, things slip through my fingers. Now I think that having the boy's picture is a way of having his father's too.

* * *

The Gaviero took the photograph out of the pocket of his seaman's jacket and handed it to us. We looked at the picture. There was nothing to say. At that moment all words were superfluous. We returned the snapshot, and as he put it away a vague shadow—resigned but also affectionately nostalgic— passed over his face. Mossén Ferrán, with his deep, operatic bass voice, broke the silence:

"When we learned that his mother had to prolong her stay in Germany, I proposed to the Gaviero that we register the boy in a school the parish runs with the help of some well-to-do people in Pollensa. Our friend was not very convinced of how useful a step that would be. I detected a certain fear that Jamil might be the victim of aggressiveness on the part of the other children, who would see him as a stranger and, even worse, one who looked like an Arab. I insisted, however, and Maqroll reluctantly agreed, asking me not to present the decision to the boy as definitive but rather as a test. We did, and Jamil accepted the

*idea at once, although he constantly turned to look at Maqroll
as we explained our plan, and finally asked what the Gaviero
would do while he was attending school. Maqroll stammered
some confused explanation, but Jamil was not very convinced.
At first things went along smoothly."*

* * *

But one day Jamil refused to go to school. "I'm going fishing
with you," he said categorically. I could not, or would not, con-
tradict him, and we sailed to the middle of the bay. The boat had
an orlop deck where Jamil kept his fishing tackle and several of
the magical objects that, according to him, helped keep away
pirates and attract the big fish we would catch one day. As our
lines trailed in the transparent water crossed by fish that paid little
attention to our hooks, Jamil told me about his experience at
school. He did not want to go back because his classmates made
fun of his accent and picked on him and asked disagreeable questions: Was I his father or his grandfather? where did his mother
live? was I an Arab too? and others that were just as intrusive and
left him terribly confused. This was when I discovered that the
people of Pollensa had woven all kinds of legends around the
caretaker at the shipyards and the unexpected arrival of Jamil. The
tamest of their inventions was that I had been a convict who
escaped from a prison on the Continent, where I was serving a
sentence for white slavery and dark dealings with anarchists. But
the one that made me laugh most was another tale told to me by
Jamil, who of course expressed grave doubts regarding the truth
of the rumor, according to which I was the legitimate heir of the
king of Oman and was hiding in Mallorca because I had murdered my brother, who was my father's favorite. Naturally, I reassured Jamil and said they were lies, especially this last one,
although I did notice that he would have liked it to be at least
partially true, because it fit into his fantasies about pirates and
buried treasures. There was no way to convince him to return to
school, but at the same time he also put greater effort into learning to read with my help, a task for which I had no qualifications
other than my newly acquired patience. His time in school had
left him with the awareness that he was a foreigner and was
afflicted by some mysterious irregularity in his social status. Both
things made a painful mark that he did not like to talk about
directly but often alluded to, asking even more frequently about
his father and his father's family. He became more interested in

the precise details of the stories I told him about our travels, and I had to exercise a good deal of caution in order to hide the countless occasions when Abdul and I lived on the margins of the law. If this was impossible, I blurred the facts so that we would not seem out-and-out criminals. The years would soon show him the irreparable relativity of laws and how abusively men applied them. Through my stories, the image of Abdul Bashur became more vivid in Jamil's mind, and the boy's personality visibly acquired a sharper, more individual outline.

* * *

"I can testify to that," said Mossén Ferrán. "What the Gaviero did was to create a miniature Maqroll. The boy walked the streets of Pollensa and the beaches along the bay with an out-law, know-it-all air that attracted the attention even of stolid Nordic tourists, who, when he passed by, awoke from the uncon-scious state they keep themselves in when they're in the sun."

* * *

My impression, on the other hand, was that because of my efforts, Jamil would be master of his own personality when he joined his family in Lebanon. Although the calculations that adults make regarding children are usually mistaken, I don't believe it was true in Jamil's case. Living with him as he discov-ered the world, seeing at close range the secret, irresistible energy that all children have, which allows them to gain their place among adults, gradually made me change my idea of human beings. I had always been convinced that there was little to hope for from our fellow humans, who surely constitute the most harmful and superfluous species on earth. I still think so, each day with greater certainty, but instead of the tormenting anger and bitterness they once produced in me, I now feel something I would call indulgent tenderness. I believe that when they were children, the road they were meant to take was very different from the one they chose as adults. This has allowed me to accept my fate, to stay in Pollensa, marginalized and tranquil, and not attempt the new undertakings that once made my life a madden-ing sequence of misfortunes. No more sawmills, no more travel-ing up the Xurandó River with a drunken captain and a cunning Indian. Nothing would make me live again the experience of a brothel staffed by counterfeit stewardesses, not in Panama City, not anywhere. I would never again bury myself alive in the abandoned mines of the cordillera, searching for gold that slipped through my fingers. It isn't easy to establish a nexus between the revelations of life with Jamil and the disappearance of my nomadic madness. But the truth is that I've come to an unhesitating acceptance of everything, through the example of this boy entering the dark human labyrinth that leads to a small heap of gray ashes. We have agreed to call this life, simplifying things, as always, in a lamentable way. I don't know what will happen to Jamil, but I do know that for a long year his presence had a redeeming quality for me, and if it hasn't turned me into a different man, it has at least allowed me to become a resigned spectator of our battle with the darkness: its only dignity lies in knowing how to preserve the child we once were.

＊　＊　＊

"I believe you've always been one but didn't know it. Now you do," said Mossén Ferrán. "The child still in you could understand and love Jamil, and that has saved you."

Maqroll had become lost again in one of his absent states and did not respond to the priest's comments. Night had fallen without our realizing it. Mossén Ferrán invited us to his house, where, he said, a light supper was waiting, and the Gaviero would have the opportunity to continue his story. We were happy to accept and said goodbye to Doña Mercé, who refused to accept payment for our meal. In words of old-fashioned gentility, she let us know her invitation was meant to honor the Gaviero and his friends.

As we walked along the streets of Pollensa, barely illuminated by the streetlights but bathed in the milky brilliance of a full moon, I had the impression that the priest not only was inviting us to hear the end of the story of Jamil and the Gaviero but also hoped to show us his library. He knew of my fondness for subjects such as the history of Mallorca, and he surely counted on surprising me with more than one treasure. We reached the small church that in successive restorations had lost all traces of its original style, which I assumed to be late Romanesque. The rectory, as it is called there, was attached to the church, and could in no way be distinguished from any of the houses of indeterminate age that formed the residential district of the port. We went to Mossén Ferrán's study, a spacious room whose walls were completely lined with books, except for a small space containing a stone niche with a beautiful marble crucifix that most certainly had been carved in the Philippines in the seventeenth century. A silent, elderly housekeeper of marked Morisco appearance carried in a silver tray that held a generous bottle of wine and four glasses decorated with painted designs in various colors. Mossén Ferrán asked me to peruse the shelves of his library. And in fact, authentic treasures were housed there, almost all of them concerning the history of the kingdom of Mallorca. Among the many amazing finds were the 1562 edition in Catalan of the Crónica *of Ramón Muntaner, an even older edition of the* Llibre dels feits *concerning King Jaime I, and, of course, the inevitable complete works of the great French Byzantine scholar of the last century, Gustave Schlumberger. To tell the truth, this provoked the greatest envy in me of all the treasures that had been accumulated by Maqroll's clerical friend during his peaceful life as a scholar and shepherd of souls, two activities that may be antithetical but are equally rich in opportunities for exploring the chasms of the heart and the labyrinths of memory. I expressed my astonishment at the richness of his collection, and our host could not restrain a broad smile of satisfaction. The Gaviero had joined me in my inspection of the shelves. I knew from his comments that many of the books were familiar to him and that reading had filled the long empty hours of his position as caretaker at the abandoned shipyards. We went back to our armchairs, and Mossén Ferrán took delight in his knowledge of one of the most decisive and obscure periods in the history of the Mediterranean. His original ideas, born of solid erudition, revealed a hidden facet in the man who presented himself as a modest parish priest from a Mallorcan port. When Mossén Ferrán finished his learned disquisitions, the Gaviero made a gesture as if to indicate that now it was his turn to speak.*

Maqroll began in a dull, opaque voice.

✳ ✳ ✳

Here in this library I've been able to forget much of what is forgettable in my life, and learn and remember things that have helped me fill my solitude, which I am certainly not complaining about. I don't know how many times my friend and I, in the shelter of his admirable collection, have become entangled in the outrages of the Angevins in Mallorca, the unexpected details in the life of Roger de Lauria, the many reasonable doubts concerning the deeds of Don Jaume the Conqueror. Then, when Jamil was with us, he often fell asleep on one of these armchairs because he refused to stay alone in my room, and I had to carry him home well past midnight."

* * *

Mossén Ferrán smiled again as he tasted the wine with evident pleasure. Although it has never been my favorite, I must admit that this time it displayed more than notable qualities. I looked at Maqroll. I knew he was accustomed to harder, more vehement drinks, and he responded with an approving gesture while he raised his glass in a toast to my wife and returned without preamble to his story.

* * *

Six months had gone by since our arrival, and Jamil was a full participant in our life, which followed, without our planning it, a more or less unchanging routine: first breakfast and a dip in the ocean to drive away sleep; then a lesson in reading and writing according to a system devised by my faithful but inexpert knowledge and understanding, followed by fishing in the sailboat or walking to town to make necessary purchases and stop at the post office; then we returned home, to attempt some changes in the taboo objects collected by Jamil for secret, invocatory purposes, and prepare lunch, in which Jamil insisted on taking part by setting the table and sampling my frugal, monotonous recipes; I read aloud from the adventures of Tirant lo Blanc, or a chapter of *Don Quixote*, a book that produced indescribable pleasure in the boy, then back to the sailboat to teach him the rudiments of navigation. He had already learned to control the rudder with a great effort of his small arms, and he enjoyed this immensely. At difficult moments I would help him, but this did not stop Jamil from feeling he was an important part of the operation. At night, we either visited Mossén Ferrán or came back to my room to prepare supper and return to our reading. Jamil was not particularly fond of conversation. He could remain silent for long periods, which he undoubtedly devoted to weaving his imaginings and fantasies, all related to the sea and fed by the books I read to him and by my stories, which, as I've said, always omitted the episodes it was better he not know about for a while. The months passed, and although he asked about his mother and waited eagerly for her letters, the boy was moving farther away from his former environment and adjusting with absolute familiarity to our life in

Pollensa. Despite his long silences, he was always in good humor, and his tone was joking and playful when he responded to my observations and stories, and in this too he reminded me of his father. Like Abdul, he preserved intact a disposition open to knowing everything and trying everything with joyous plenitude. His answers or comments often made me laugh as I hadn't laughed for a long time.

But one day Jamil awoke with a dispirited look on his face. He complained that he was tired and had pains in his legs. I touched his forehead and knew he was burning with fever. I threw on my clothes and ran to Mossén Ferrán to find a doctor. In my case, illness usually overtook me in the most inhospitable places, and for cures I've had recourse to potions prescribed by people who did not even suspect the existence of medicine. I hadn't needed a doctor in Pollensa and did not know one to call on. Mossén Ferrán took me to an acquaintance of his, a retired physician who had not practiced his profession for many years. The three of us returned to the shipyards, and after a lengthy examination, the doctor diagnosed a malignant fever. The term seemed somewhat imprecise to Mossén Ferrán and me and left us more concerned than before. By now Jamil was delirious, calling for his mother in Arabic and mumbling incoherent phrases. The doctor signaled to us to walk out with him, and at the entrance to the shed he said it was advisable to take the boy to the clinic in Pollensa for laboratory tests that would establish the cause of the fever. There was a danger of meningitis, with consequences we were all aware of. Mossén Ferrán was known at the clinic because occasionally he was called there to administer last rites to dying patients. Saying goodbye to the doctor, we went to find the nephew who had driven us to Pollensa in the taxi. We took Jamil to the clinic and waited for the test results. I was overcome by uncontrollable anguish. Mossén Ferrán tried with no success to reassure me, and as the hours passed, my panic increased. I've never felt anything like it. It's true that the loss of dear friends, and women I loved, have been devastating ordeals. But hidden in a corner of my being there was always an unscathed area that gave me the strength to go on. Now it was as if an internal mechanism had broken down, and I could no longer reason or conquer the terror that overwhelmed me. When the director of the clinic and his assistant, a woman with graying hair and a pleasant smile, came toward us after spending a fair amount of time in Jamil's room, I felt impelled to call on some supernatural forces, some propitiatory gods, and plead with them to save the boy's life. Perhaps they heard me, because the news was encouraging. The crisis was over, and the meninges had not been affected. Jamil had a renal infection that was controllable, fortunately, in the early stages. The X-rays had shown a diverticulum in the renal passages, where urine accumulated and caused the infection and resultant fever. A month's treatment with antibiotics would take care of these symptoms. There was no question of operating now, but later, when the boy was ten or twelve years old, surgery was indicated. My face must have shown pitiable suffering, because the woman put her hand on my shoulder and comforted me in lilting Mallorcan. The good doctor was a grandmother and understood my panic, but I had no reason to be alarmed. Grandparents were understandably more vulnerable, she said, but in this case there was nothing to worry about. I couldn't explain my relationship to Jamil to her, and Mossén Ferrán did not attempt to correct the error either. I think we both felt more like the boy's grandparents than his temporary guardians.

We went into his room, and Jamil looked at us with his large eyes and a mischievous smile that filled me with joy.

"I'm okay now," he said. "The doctors said so. They were talking Mallorcan, but I can understand it. They'll give me some injections, and then we can go fishing."

He said this in Arabic and then turned to Mossén Ferrán and repeated it in Spanish, adding that he wanted to learn Mallorcan very well. My friend replied that there would be time for everything, but for now he had to take care of himself and get better. He left to attend to his parish duties, and I sat at the foot of Jamil's bed on a chair that creaked dangerously each time I moved, making him laugh uncontrollably. At nightfall, the same physician, the assistant to the director, came into the room, and when she saw me in animated conversation with the patient, she signaled that I should wait outside while she gave him his second injection of antibiotic. As I walked out, she told me it was better for the boy to be quiet and to sleep as much as possible. I could leave now. There was absolutely nothing to worry about. Tomorrow morning I'd surely see Jamil with no fever and well on his way to recovery. When I looked in to say goodbye, he was sleeping peacefully.

I came back to the clinic very early the next morning. I had spent a wretched night, and our room at the shipyards seemed unbearably desolate. Just as the doctor predicted, the fever had broken, and Jamil was still sleeping, with enviable serenity. I sat in a small waiting room on the ground floor, next to the entrance, and for several hours was beset by the images the hospital awakened in me, all of them related to the emergency room of the sinister Dr. Pascot. It was close to noon when a nurse came to tell me I could go up to see my grandson. I let the error pass: There was no point in trying to correct it. I found Jamil looking at a magazine from the time of the Second World War. I leaned down to kiss his forehead, and it was cool, with no trace of fever. "Planes aren't like this anymore," he said, intrigued, as he showed me a squadron of Stukas with swastikas painted on the fuselages. I explained that now turbines had replaced propellers. He immediately subjected me to a long interrogation regarding the difference between turbines and propellers. He was not very convinced by my explanations, least of all when I attempted to draw a diagram of a turbine, which left him totally skeptical of my aeronautical knowledge. When they brought his lunch, I went to a little café nearby to have something to eat. When I returned, the doctor was waiting in the lobby. She said I could take Jamil home that afternoon, following his injection. They would give me a prescription for certain medicines the boy was to take for two weeks longer; he should stay in bed for one week, or at least not go out or do anything that might tire him. At the time she had indicated, Jamil put on his clothes, and I picked him up to carry him to the shipyards. He did not like that at all and wanted to walk, but the doctor told him he mustn't. When I asked for the bill, I was told that Mossén Ferrán had already taken care of it.

*   *   *

"With what our friend earns at the shipyards," said the priest, attributing no importance to the matter, "he couldn't have paid for Jamil's first injection. I suspect his trip to Port-Vendres used up his meager savings."

Maqroll smiled, nodding indulgently, and went on with his story.

*   *   *

Jamil had a long convalescence, and I still felt uneasy at times. After a few days, no reason or authority could convince him he was not allowed to go fishing, and he became downhearted and gloomy. Once, he complained of pains at his waist and in his head. I consulted with the doctor, and she told me to ignore them: They were natural consequences of the crisis he had gone through. Mossén Ferrán came often to relieve me in my nursing duties and told Jamil stories from the Old Testament and the Gospels. Our young man seemed rather indifferent to these furtive lessons in sacred history.

* * *

*"My dear Maqroll, I must explain: It wasn't like that at all,"
said the priest. "I knew that Jamil's mother must have taught
him certain fundamental principles of Koranic law, and these,
more than any other doctrine, were the most appropriate to cultivate in the boy. For the moment, at least, it was better that
Jamil be a good Muslim than a lukewarm Christian. And so I
did not insist. But what did absorb his attention, in an almost
hypnotic way, were stories about the Crusades. The death of
Saint Louis, king of France, brought tears to his eyes, and he
responded with enthusiasm to the deeds of Saladin."*

*"But when I tried to tell him more episodes of the Cru-
sades," commented Maqroll, "Jamil would say: 'You don't tell
them as well as Mossén Ferrán. He makes it seem as if he had
been there.' I agreed, my storyteller's pride slightly wounded, but
at the same time I was happy to see the boy's interest in a
period that also appeals to me."*

*We were silent for a while. The evocation of Jamil by his two
protectors and friends had acquired so much intensity, we had
the impression that at any moment Abdul's son would appear
before us, encircled by a nimbus of the shimmering phosphorescence on the water in the bay. Maqroll finally spoke, his deep
voice occasionally touched by a kind of shudder of nostalgia and
sorrow.*

* * *

One morning at dawn I was watching Jamil as he slept, his peace-fulness a clear sign of recovery. Suddenly I became aware of something impossible to put into words. The idea that we would have to separate seemed inconceivable. No one had ever formed so deep and definitive a part of my life as this child, who made his way through the world with the gaze of his great, alert eyes and was endowed with grace and an almost miraculous intuition of life and its turnings. At the same time, another voice deep inside me asserted that Jamil's destiny lay with Lina and his father's family, and that soon, in obedience to a law older than the ephemeral passage of humans on earth, his mother would come for him. I thought with envy of the privilege the beautiful Warda Bashur would enjoy as she watched the growth and development of her nephew, similar in so many ways to her brother Abdul. For a brief moment the two voices were in conflict. Jamil would leave with Lina; that had been written since the beginning. I turned to my old custom of accepting the designs of the powers who speak from inscrutable darkness. The pain that had risen to my chest, immobilizing me at the foot of the child's bed, began to recede and slowly disappeared, leaving me in a state of melancholy resignation that I know so well I often think it is my natural condition. And I knew too that memory would return later to do its usual work of recalling a happiness not destined for me. It's something I've been familiar with for a long time.

One day the physician who was Mossén Ferrán's friend came to see Jamil. He said he could return to his normal life, and recommended that he follow a low-salt diet, drink a good deal of liquid, and stay in the sun as much as he could without burning. And so we resumed our former life, with its long days of fishing and exploring the rocks for treasures washed in by the sea, and its afternoons of reading either in our room or here in the library of our friend. Jamil could already write his name and decipher some of the headlines in the Palma newspaper that was delivered to the parish. I also tried to teach him the rudiments of Arabic, but we had no books to practice with. Several months passed in this way, and gradually, without our mentioning it, the certainty began to float in the air that Lina would soon be coming for Jamil. There was a less pessimistic tone in her letters, and on one occasion she asked me to write to Warda Bashur to tell her that before long Lina would have the money she needed to travel to Lebanon and live there in relative independence. Jamil received this news with a mixture of eagerness to see his mother and fear of leaving his current life and facing a new one in his father's country. I often found him staring at me as he let the fishing rod fall between his knees. The boy was clearly waiting for me to say something about an immediate future that troubled him. Finally, one day, he resolved to speak about it.

"You'll come to see us in Lebanon, won't you? It's not very far, and you used to go there a lot."

"Yes," I answered, somewhat taken aback by the abruptness of the question, "I know the way very well, because I traveled it so often with your father. Of course I'll come to see you, and your aunts and uncles; I'm very fond of them, especially your aunt Warda. She's someone I love very much."

"And can we go fishing there too?"

"Of course we can," I replied, trying not to show how much his words had affected me. "The bay is much larger and has many more ships and a good deal of maritime traffic, but close by there are places like this one, where we can fish with no problems. By then you'll know everything about being a sailor, I'm sure of that."

"You're the only person who can teach me those things, Maqroll. Nobody knows the sea better than you. I don't think my father knew as much as you do." He said this with the gravity of someone who wants to persuade himself that he is right.

"No, Jamil," I replied, feeling calmer, "you're wrong. Nobody knew as much about the sea and ships as your father. Abdul could estimate a vessel's tonnage from an enormous distance, and he was almost never wrong when he guessed where it had been built. He could even tell the brand of an engine from the sound it made. And do you know something? I'm certain you'll have those talents too."

The boy was thoughtful, and shadows of doubt and disquiet crossed his face. He couldn't imagine how he would acquire nautical skills without me. He had only a vague idea of Lebanon: He conceived of it as a mountainous country and thought his family lived inland, surrounded by snowy peaks. When I mentioned the Lebanese coast and talked to him about Tripoli—of course, I called it by its Arabic name, Tarabulus esh Sham—about Sidon and Acre, ports filled with history and famous for millennia among seamen, Jamil showed unexpected surprise, as if it were the first time he had heard of those places.

During the final months of his stay in Pollensa, Jamil seemed to carry his concern for me to extremes. He did not know how to express his affection, and he could not reconcile the desire to see his mother, and his curiosity about what lay ahead, with the attachment he felt for me and our life together. In a sense, he felt guilty about leaving me but did not know how to express it. This was the reason for his diligence and attentiveness regarding everything that had to do with me.

* * *

Through a large window in the priest's study, the night sky displayed the faint incandescence that lends an indefinable quality to nights in Mallorca. If it did not sound so pedantic, one might speak of Hellenic charm. A serenity suddenly shaken by tremors of foreboding, the signs of an overwhelming revelation that never comes, as if time, without really stopping, had changed the rhythm of its passage and granted us a moment of eternity. I said something to this effect, and we all looked out at the night while a light breeze carrying scents of iodine and undisturbed ocean depths came in through the partially opened window. I thought we all needed this restorative interval before continuing. It was clear that telling the story of Jamil had begun to take its painful toll on the Gaviero. As if she had intuited this, Mossén Ferrán's housekeeper came in with a splendid tray of pá amb tomáquet and a ham that promised to be memorable.

"My dear Mossén Ferrán," said Maqroll, "this marvel deserves a sauce more serious than the one we're drinking."

The priest motioned to the housekeeper, and she soon returned with a bottle that had no label, and ceramic goblets that looked medieval. Mossén Ferrán smiled contentedly; making no comment, he served us himself, pouring a dark, purplish wine with a bouquet of freshly plowed earth. I praised its magnificent rusticity, and he would only say:

"It's a wine from the modest vineyard I own at the foot of the Axartel Mountains. I keep it for my own use and the pleasure of those who can confront this hybrid with unprotesting palates."

Our host was right. Thanks to the bread and tomato, and the accompanying oil and delicious ham, this robust wine, which carried us back to the time of the kingdom of Mallorca, acquired a decorous character. We consumed the meal served in so opportune and amiable a manner, and comforted by the prestigious fruits of the Axartel vineyard, the Gaviero returned to his story.

*　*　*

Three months after Jamil's recovery, Lina sent a letter announcing her arrival. She said she had deposited a check for most of her earnings in a Beirut bank and would take a freighter directly from Bremen to Palma. The voyage would take two weeks, because they were scheduled to make several port calls along the way. At first Jamil's excitement was notable. But when I began to move some of my things to an empty loft at the far end of the building, and hung the hammock I always have with me so that Jamil could be alone with Lina in the room he and I had occupied, the boy displayed a morose disquiet that I did my best to alleviate. I was not entirely calm either, and the imminent departure of my companion of the past year was pushing me down into a piercing melancholy. Our conversations about the sea and ships and the great naval deeds of history became more frequent and more intense, as if Jamil wanted to store up the greatest quantity of memories that included my presence.

What the boy had learned was astonishing. I had to tell him all over again how you dock at night in Port Swettenham and how you travel by land from there to Kuala Lumpur; what the schedule of the tides was at Saint-Malo; what information a whaler has to give to the harbor officials at Bergen; the speed at which you maintain the engines in order to enter the bay of Wigtown and anchor across from Withorn when you visit Alastair Reid; the three words you must say to have the locks opened at Harelbeke; which birds sit for the longest time on the masts of a sailing ship or the aerials of a freighter; the name of the sailor who carried the lifeless body of Captain Cook back to the ship; the days and occasions when it is not advisable to say Mass at sea; the brand of diesel engine that gives the best service; the number of times you must sound the bell when a body is buried at sea; the weapons a captain is permitted to carry on board ship, and under what circumstances he can travel with his family; the measures that must be taken before opening the hatches of a burning hold; how safe navigation is on the Mississippi River; which three saints were sailors; the first ship to sink at the battle of Tsushima; which kings were also seamen; the signs carved on the mast of the *Marie Galante* and how they have been interpreted; who orders punishments on board, the captain or the bos'n; whether or not a left-handed machinist brings bad luck; how many knots a cabin boy in the Belgian merchant marine must know how to tie; what music can and cannot be played on board ship; what language is preferred in Tierra del Fuego; what Pollensa was called in the Middle Ages; whether Abdul Bashur was ever a sailor or only a builder and owner of tramp steamers; whether I ever captained a ship; the oldest flag at sea today; the length of the crossing in summer from Kamenskoye to Seward in Alaska; whether whales communicate in a language more complex than Arabic; who is richer, the owner of a freighter or the owner of a regular ferry. Naturally, the story requiring the greatest number of details was that of the passage around Cape Horn through an intricate labyrinth of islands, which fascinated Jamil. I had to repeat descriptions of Valparaiso, Amsterdam, Antwerp, Cartagena de Indias, and Portsmouth a thousand and one times. He never tired of hearing them, and too bad for me if I omitted something I had mentioned before, because the rebuke was immediate. During our last days together, his obsession with reconstructing voyages in complete detail made him wake in the middle of the night to ask me the draft of vessels that can dock at New Orleans or the documents needed to cross the Panama Canal. When I began my answer, he had already fallen back to sleep. It was as if he were dreaming fragments of my life and the life of his father. At breakfast the next day, the implacable questions continued.

When we received Lina's telegram from Barcelona announcing her imminent arrival, Jamil shut himself into absolute silence. A few days before we were to meet her in Palma, I had to go to town to buy bus tickets and reserve our seats. When I returned, a terrible surprise was waiting for me: All the objects that Jamil had collected with so much love had disappeared. I asked him where they were, and with a shrug of his shoulders he answered angrily:

"They're at the bottom of the ocean, at the end of the dock, where they should have stayed."

His father was in that answer, complete to the ancient reticence of the sons of the desert, who are zealous in hiding their deepest feelings and disposed to noisily externalize what scarcely touches them. I didn't know what to say, and my confusion sent him even deeper into silence. Two days later we left for Palma. When we arrived we went directly to the port. Lina was in the waiting room. She saw us and her eyes filled with tears. Jamil ran to embrace her, and she picked him up in her arms and held him to her chest, unable to say a word. I was so moved that a lump came to my throat. When she put Jamil down, I walked over to greet her. She gave me a warm embrace and at last could speak:

"How he's changed. He's not a baby anymore," she repeated several times in astonishment.

I carried Lina's two suitcases, and we reached the station just in time to catch the bus to Pollensa; Mossén Ferrán's taxi was not available. Lina looked tired, and her face bore the marks of her life in Bremen. She was thinner. It was easy to imagine the fascinating dancer she must have been years earlier. I mentioned this in passing, and she smiled with pleasure. During the trip, Jamil unleashed a constant torrent of dizzying descriptions of what he had done and learned and the things he knew about my life and travels. By the time we arrived in Pollensa, he had fallen asleep in

his mother's arms. Mossén Ferrán was waiting, and he accompanied us as far as the shipyards. Lina carried Jamil upstairs and settled him in his bed. We said good night, not really knowing what
else to say, because when Lina looked around our room, she was
again moved to tears. She kissed me on both cheeks and repeated
between sobs: "Thank you, thank you so much, you're an angel." I
don't think anyone has ever said that to me before. I went to my
loft, thinking that the angel was the child who slept with the
serenity of the elect.

The next morning Jamil came up to my loft and lay down
beside me in the hammock. He said his mother was still sleeping
and gave no signs of waking anytime soon. I asked if he was
happy, and he said yes, but there was a certain hesitation in his
words. He stared at me for a moment and said:

"I woke up very early, and I've been thinking that you'll be
very lonely when we go and will miss me very much, but I have
an idea: Why don't you marry my mama, and then we can all live
together, either here or in Lebanon."

Of course the idea was not Jamil's. I'm sure he heard someone
else say it, in Mossén Ferrán's house or at the Ancien Café
Mogador. I immediately discounted the idea that our friend the
priest had ever made any such remark, because he knows me very
well, and I know his prudence and discretion. In any case, I found
myself in a serious predicament. I thought it best to be absolutely
clear about why his proposal was impossible. I explained that first
of all, his mother had other plans, all of them based on living near
the Bashurs but doing everything she could not to be dependent
on them. Then I reminded him how often we had talked about
my travels on the five continents and sixteen seas, and my inability to stay very long in one place. Although I was living peacefully in Pollensa, there was no guarantee it would be permanent.
I'd soon return to my wandering, and that wasn't what Lina had
in mind for him or for herself, since she had already moved
around more than she wanted to. But I could promise him one
thing: I would go to Lebanon very soon to visit them. My ties to
Abdul's family were still close and affectionate. Beirut was at the
top of the list of my current plans. As I finished my explanation, I
saw two big tears run down Jamil's cheeks. I hugged him close,
and we were silent. When we heard sounds in the room where
Lina was sleeping, the boy climbed out of the hammock, gave me
a brief kiss on the forehead, and said with the serenity of an adult
resigned to his destiny:

"I know that nobody else can tell me the things you tell me. You're my best friend, and I don't think we'll see each other again."

No words can describe what happens to us inside at a time like that. It was Jamil's farewell. The one that had to take place between us without witnesses or last-minute goodbyes. I lay on my hammock, reviewing my life, and concluded that my pilgrimage through God's world had just come to an end. Whatever happened now lacked importance. It would be mere existing, I mean to say, something completely foreign to my destiny.

Lina came up with Jamil and looked at me, not saying a word. She understood everything as only a woman can understand, with her instinct and the high wisdom of the female heart. During the days she spent in Pollensa, I confirmed and enriched my earlier impression of her. She belonged to that almost extinct race of beings who take on, with complete independence and stoic simplicity, the obligations and sorrows that life brings, without complaining or trying to shift the burden to others. It would be foolish to deny it now: During this time the thought often passed through my mind that Lina might be one of those women, like Flor Estévez or Ilona Grabowska, who possessed all the traits and qualities for sharing what remained of my life with me. But somewhere it must be written in indelible letters: The "kingdom meant for me" would not be mine.

Yet another surprise was in store. Lina told me that the captain of the small Tunisian freighter that would take her from Palma to Beirut, with port calls in Alexandria and Cyprus, was Vincas Blekaitis, Abdul's old friend, and mine. I had lost track of him years before. She happened to run into him by sheerest coincidence when the ship that brought her from Bremen docked in La Rochelle. Vincas, who had known her in Bizerte, was very moved when he saw her and insisted she travel on his ship, since Palma was on his itinerary. She explained that she was in a hurry to see her son, but they arranged for her to board Vincas's ship in Palma and travel with him to Lebanon. And in fact, a few days later, we received word that Vincas had arrived in Palma. We drove there in Mossén Ferrán's taxi on the day they were scheduled to sail. From the starboard railing, where he was supervising the loading operation, Vincas waved to us with both arms. He ran down the gangplank, exclaiming in every language he knew. He picked up Jamil and looked at him in astonishment.

"Just see how Jabdul's son has grown!" The good Vincas never could pronounce our lamented Abdul's name. "He's a real cabin boy now. What did you learn from Maqroll? Let's hear, tell me."

"A lot of things," replied Jamil, intrigued by the Lithuanian's reddish beard.

"I don't doubt it," said the captain. "I learned a lot of things from him too. Let's go to the port and take care of your papers."

Night had fallen by the time we completed the process. When everything was ready, Vincas took us on board the ship, which would leave at midnight. Jamil stared in disbelief at every detail of the bridge when we showed him the instruments and levers, which he touched in wonder. Then we went down to the small cabin that Vincas had assigned to Lina and Jamil. The boy immediately climbed to the upper berth and decreed categorically:

"I'll sleep here and my mother down below. That's how it should be, right?" And he looked at me as if asking my approval.

I replied that it was exactly how it should be. Vincas signaled to me to go out with him while Lina and the boy arranged their things. We went up on deck, and Blekaitis praised both Lina and her son in the warmest terms. I told him briefly about what it was like to live with Jamil in Pollensa, and in the Lithuanian's pale eyes there appeared the deep, affectionate friendship that had been proved, abundantly and unforgettably, to both Abdul and me. I said I didn't want to keep the driver, who was my friend's nephew, until midnight, and that it was time for me to go. We went back to the cabin so that I could say goodbye to the passengers. Lina gave me a long, silent embrace, and Jamil, curled up on his bunk, burst into tears. I didn't want to prolong this, and I left without saying anything. Vincas walked with me to the car. He grasped my arm affectionately and mumbled something incomprehensible as he stared into my eyes. He walked quickly back to the ship, and I heard him say in his native language: "So many things, so many things." He waved goodbye but did not turn around to look at me. I climbed into the taxi, and we left immediately for Pollensa.

* * *

Once again silence fell in the priest's library. There was nothing to say. Any comment was useless and would surely have wounded the Gaviero.

After a moment, Maqroll poured us wine from the bottle that was emptied on this round, and said in a firm voice:

"This is all I had to tell you. I'm certain you know the relief it was to have you listen to me. As always, when Alejandro Obregón suggested this visit, he showed what the French used to call gentillesse de coeur."

Then, addressing himself especially to me, he remarked:

"I'm sure that you, who have told so many episodes from my life, never imagined you would hear a story like the one you've been kind enough to listen to now. I don't know if it was worth telling. Sometimes I think it's simply part of what a poet whom I admire a great deal once called 'ordinary examples of every human's fate.' I don't know. You'll have to decide that. I'm sorry to have taken a whole day of your visit to Pollensa, and tomorrow you're going back to Palma. We'll see each other again. We always say the same thing, and the gods always favor us."

He drained his glass and stood to say goodbye. He bent over my wife's hand and said with a faint smile:

"Good night, Señora, and my very special gratitude to you for having shown interest in this misguided lookout."

He shook hands with Mossén Ferrán and me, and walked to the door. We accompanied him to the street and watched him disappear into the moonless night when he rounded the small promontory behind which the shipyards were located. Then Mossén Ferrán walked with us to our hotel, and when he took his leave he said:

"Tomorrow morning I'll come to say goodbye. Don't worry. The worst is over for our friend. Jamil is now part of the memories that Maqroll says sustain him in the task of living each day. God bless you, and sleep well."

When we were in our room, I said something to my wife about how alone and forsaken the Gaviero was. Her reply was conclusive:

"But he himself once explained it very clearly. When he refused to accept the photograph of Abdul as a boy in front of the burned wreckage of a plane, he said he couldn't keep it because everything slipped through his fingers. People slip away from him in the same way: They're taken by death, or they're left behind while he goes on with his endless wandering. That's a phantom he's created. But he never dreamed that an experience like Jamil was lurking just around the corner. Now we'll see what he devises in order to escape from Pollensa."

There really wasn't much to dispute in her words. Jamil was undoubtedly the hidden snare waiting for our friend in the intricate labyrinth of his irremediable odyssey. As he so frequently said: "If it exists at all, the pity of the gods is indecipherable or comes to us when we breathe our last. There is no way to free ourselves from their arbitrary tutelage."